"Is that what I am to you? A deal?"

Yearning bled through her words, gave the lie to her defensive posture. Scott came up behind her to wrap her in his arms. "The best damn deal I've ever run across," he whispered into her ear. "And the only one I've ever truly cared whether I landed or not."

Gently, he twisted her around to face him, his fingers winnowing through her hair to cradle the back of her neck, their mouths so close he could feel her breath, coming in short, sweet bursts. "And if you can't trust your intuitions, trust mine. Because they've never been wrong."

Never in her life had she wanted to believe so badly. To let herself fall into the promise in those warm brown eyes. *If this is a dream,* Christina thought, *I don't want to wake up. Ever.*

But nobody knew better than her that wanting wasn't enough to change what was.

Dear Reader,

I adore Cinderella stories, don't you? Seriously, who doesn't (at least occasionally!) fantasize about a handsome prince (or reasonable facsimile thereof) sweeping her away to a life of ease and glamour and all the cute shoes she can cram in her closet. But when the fantasy arrives for Christina Hastings—in the form of telecommunications mogul Scott Fortune—her damaged heart warns her not to trust it. Or him. So Scott has his work cut out for him, convincing Christina that he's the one who's struck it rich.

Of course most of us buy our own cute shoes. And cars. And whatever else we need. But if our princes can't exactly hand over the credit card and say, "Go for it, honey," at least they've given us their hearts—which is worth more than a closet full of shoes, any day.

Enjoy!

Karen

FORTUNE'S CINDERELLA

BY
KAREN TEMPLETON

First published in Great Britain 2013
by Mills & Boon, an imprint of Harlequin (UK) Limited,
Eton House, 18-24 Paradise Road, Richmond, Surrey TW9 1SR

Special thanks and acknowledgement to Karen Templeton for her contribution to The Fortunes of Texas: Whirlwind Romance continuity.

ISBN: 978 0 263 90076 7
ebook ISBN: 978 1 472 00429 1

23-0113

Harlequin (UK)
recyclable produ
logging and man
regulations of th

Printed and bou
by Blackprint C

Since 1998, two-time RITA® Award winner and Waldenbooks bestselling author **Karen Templeton** has written more than thirty books for Mills & Boon. A transplanted Easterner, she now lives in New Mexico with two hideously spoiled cats and whichever of her five sons happens to be in residence.

To Marie Ferrarella,
Judy Duarte,
Nancy Robards Thompson,
Susan Crosby
and Allison Leigh,
who made my first attempt at
writing a continuity book so much fun.
And a lot less scary than I thought it would be.
We are now sisters.

Chapter One

Make it happen.

If Scott Fortune could attribute anything to his success—in life, in business—it was that simple mantra, doggedly applied to every challenge that dared him to fail. Too bad the weather on this blustery, end-of-December afternoon hadn't gotten that particular memo.

From underneath the expansive portico fronting the main entrance to La Casa Paloma, an exclusive resort where he, his parents and his siblings had stayed while in Red Rock, Texas, to attend his youngest sister Wendy's wedding to Marcos Mendoza, he glowered at the charcoal sky. But the heavens jeered at his insignificance, the icy rain jackhammering the battered winter lawn, the gravel drive where a pair of SUVs waited to ferry them to the regional airport ten miles away and the chartered jet that would take them home to Atlanta.

"You really have to go already?"

Scott turned, smiling in spite of himself at Wendy's newly wedded—and not-so-newly pregnant—glow. Behind her, through the open, intricately carved double wooden doors, assorted family members traipsed back and forth, while the groom and his two brothers, Javier and Miguel, carted luggage out to the cars. In a minute, he'd have to herd his other siblings. But now he opened his arms to let his baby sister walk into them—as much as she could, at least—thinking that Marcos Mendoza was the luckiest, and bravest, guy in the world, taking on the family's little princess.

"You know I've got to get back," he said into his much shorter sister's slippery brown hair. "As it was, I left several projects hanging to come here."

Snorting, Wendy disentangled herself. And gently smacked his arm, her all's-right-in-her-world grin a blatant affront to the dreary weather. "Well, excuse *me* for putting you out," she said, her warm brown eyes sparkling, her accent tilting more toward Texan by the second.

"And anyway—"

"I know, I know—Daddy's hot to get back for that New Year's Eve gala y'all are sponsoring." Her mouth pulled into a pout…for about a half second before she grinned again. Wasn't that long ago, however, that those pouts had been precursors to the hissy fits of a precocious, blatantly spoiled young woman who'd assumed being an heiress *was* her life's work. At their wits' end, a year ago his parents had packed off Miss Diva-in-Training to Red Rock for some serious grounding…as a waitress in Red, the Mendoza family's restaurant. Which Marcos managed.

Poor guy probably never knew what hit him.

And neither, in all likelihood, had Wendy, who was definitely not the same wild child she'd been then. Although the marriage had been far more to get their parents off her case than to please Wendy herself, whose penchant for doing things her way was legendary. And yet, there was more to that glow than hormones, Scott suspected. She seemed genuinely happy, and content, in a way that felt almost foreign to him.

"Why don't you come see us off?" he said, suddenly loath to leave her.

Palming her burgeoning belly underneath her too-tight sweater, she shook her head. "My doctor wants me to take it easy. And to be perfectly honest—" she grinned again "—having y'all around has worn me *out*—"

"…because when people pay a thousand bucks a plate," their father said as he strode through the door, his attention far more focused on his touch-screen phone than their mother, who trailed him like an agitated, delicate gray bird, "they expect the people who got them to part with their money to show up."

Spotting her youngest daughter, Virginia Alice Fortune dragged Wendy into her arms, a small pink box containing a sampling of Wendy's exquisite desserts swung from her French-manicured fingers.

"For heaven's sake," Scott heard his mother mutter, cupping her baby's head to her cashmere-covered bosom, "it's not as if we're going to serve them their salmon and buttered asparagus personally!"

Over the crush of her mother's embrace, Wendy's eyes popped, and Scott swallowed a sigh. Because God forbid their mother—who'd raised all six of them on her own, without a nanny in sight—should stand up to their father. Not that many people did. The impenetrable aura of his vast wealth notwithstanding, at six-foot-four, his full head of dark hair barely tinged with silver, John Michael Fortune's physical presence alone made most folks think long and hard about disagreeing with him.

Which made his mother's soft, "What's the harm in staying another day or two?" all the more stunning. And finally brought his father's confused gaze to hers.

"Because I promised the Harrises we'd be there," he said, his annoyance clear. "Which you know. And it's not as if we're never coming back." His eyes shifted to Wendy, who was soon to give him his first grandchild. "Baby's due in March, you said?"

"I did."

"Then we'll be here."

But as John Michael escorted their mother to the car, Scott caught Wendy swiping a tear from her cheek. What a weird bunch they were, he mused as Marcos bounded back up the porch steps to slip an arm around his wife's thickened waist, plant a quick kiss on her lips. For as long as Scott could remember, their father had rammed home to all six of them that you were either a success or a failure—there was no middle ground...and his mother, that nothing was more important than family. Dual mantras that defined everything they did. Everything they were.

And seemed to so often be in conflict with each other.

Suddenly restless, Scott returned to the lobby, an elegant blend of terra-cotta tiles and hand-plastered walls, wrought-iron fixtures and down-cushioned leather furniture, to see what was holding up the others. In a suit and tie, his older brother Mike paced the patterned carpet in front of the registration desk, his dark brows drawn as he barked orders at whoever was on the other end of his phone, while his younger brother Blake and their sister Emily were just entering the lobby from the restaurant, deep in conversation over something on Blake's iPad screen. Only their cousin, Victoria—close to Wendy in both age and temperament—

seemed to be "in the moment," scooting toward Scott in her high-heeled suede boots, her long, dark brown curls bouncing over her shoulders.

First through the door, Victoria threw her arms around Wendy, giving her a fierce hug, then, to Marcos, a stern, "And you'd better take good care of her or there will be hell to pay," before dashing across the flagstone porch and into the waiting, rented Escalade…but not before flashing a grin at Marcos's youngest brother, Miguel, as he hefted her bag into the back.

"Guys! Let's go!" Scott called to the others. "Mom and Dad are already in the car!"

Emily, her long blond hair uncharacteristically loose, picked up the pace. "Sorry!" she said breathlessly. "But Blake just came up with this killer campaign for Universal Mobile." Her green eyes sparkling with excitement, she glanced back at Mike, who, still on his phone, was making "Yeah, yeah, I'm coming" gestures in Scott's direction, then added, "As soon as Mike closes the deal and it becomes *Fortune* Mobile."

No sooner were they outside, though, than a Jeep with *Redmond Flight School* painted on the door pulled up behind Javier's somewhat battered Explorer and a tall, cowboy-booted guy in a flight jacket and a ball cap climbed out. On seeing Tanner Redmond, Scott smiled and extended his hand, his eyes level with the other man's. Apparently a long-time friend of the Red Rock Fortunes, as well as the Mendozas, Tanner had been at the wedding… and danced, as Scott now recalled, with his sister Jordana. Who, Scott also now realized, was nowhere to be seen.

"Glad I caught you," Tanner said, his own smile glinting in his olive-green eyes as he clasped Scott's hand. "Had to go out of town right after the wedding, but wanted to say goodbye before you all left. Although…" His mouth pulled tight, the former Air Force pilot peered up at the sky, shaking his head.

Scott blew out a breath, glancing inside for his missing sister before tucking his fists in his leather jacket's front pockets. "Don't say it."

Tanner grinned again, gouging deep creases in tanned cheeks. "Who's the pilot?"

"Guy named Jack Sullivan."

"Know him well. You're in excellent hands. Man does not do stupid. Besides, this is bound to clear. Eventually."

"Thanks," Scott said drily, earning him a low chuckle and a clap on the shoulder before Tanner walked away to talk to Blake and Emily, then lean into the Escalade to pay his respects to their mother. Still one sister short, Scott asked the mob at large, "Where's Jordana—anybody know?"

"Not going," came from the doorway where his middle sister stood in plain jeans and a cowl-necked tunic, her dark blond hair pulled into her customary don't-give-a-damn ponytail. Although a brilliant asset to FortuneSouth's research and development team, Jordana clearly had not inherited his other sisters' fashion sense. Or their confidence in non-business-related situations.

Standing by the car with Tanner, their father glanced over, then lifted his own bag into the back. "Nonsense," he said, her "rebellion" clearly not worth even considering. "Of course you're going."

Jordana's arms tightened across her ribs, as something Scott couldn't remember ever seeing before flashed in her deep brown eyes. Still, her voice shook slightly when she spoke.

"I t-told you, there is no way I'm flying in this weather. Especially in some dinky little puddle jumper."

"A Learjet is hardly dinky—"

"I'm sorry, Daddy," she said, her face reddening, "but I am not getting on that plane." Even though Jordana probably racked up more air miles than the rest of them for her work, flying had always scared the crap out of her. A quirk she'd kept hidden from their father, Scott wagered. Until now. "I'll get a commercial flight later. Promise."

Smiling, Tanner said something to John Michael that Scott couldn't hear, earning him a quick glower and an even quicker nod.

"We'll expect you back tomorrow, then," their father said, then ducked into the car. Scott gave Wendy a final hug, shook Marcos's hand, then climbed into the Escalade's front seat beside Javier. As they finally got under way, he waved to Jordana, standing under the portico, hugging herself and frowning. Tanner said something to her and pointed to the still-open door. Probably suggesting they go back inside, Scott guessed, where it was warm. And dry.

"How come you're not driving your own car?" he now asked Wendy's brother-in-law.

"Like I'd miss an opportunity to get behind the wheel of this beauty?" the black-haired man said with a grin, stroking the luxury car's leather-clad steering wheel with work-roughened fingers. "No way."

Scott sighed, letting his head drop back against the headrest. "I was beginning to wonder if we'd ever get out of there," he said in a low voice, even though, between the constant swishing of the windshield wipers and both his father and brother being deep in conversation on their phones, he doubted he'd be heard.

"I feel your pain," Javier said, tossing a bright smile in Scott's direction before once more focusing on the rain-drenched road. "With three brothers, I know what it's like trying to get that many people moving in the same direction at the same time…man," he said, angling his head slightly to look up at the clouds. "At least it isn't snow, right?"

"At least."

Behind Scott, his brother laughed. A calculated *We're all friends here, right?* laugh designed to put the other party at ease. A tactic Scott had mastered before his twenty-fifth birthday—

"You worried about your sister?"

The unexpected question sliced through Scott's thoughts. "What? Oh. No. Not at all. I—we—can tell, Wendy couldn't have done better than with your brother. I get the feeling he'll be very good for her."

Javier chuckled. "Think maybe it's the other way around, to be honest. Dude needed some serious shaking up. And Wendy was just the girl to do that. But I wasn't talking about her. I meant the one who stayed behind. Jordana, right?"

Scott frowned. "Worried? No. Jordana's a smart cookie."

"No doubt. But…maybe a little shy? At least, next to Wendy…"

A half smile tugged at Scott's mouth. "*Everybody's* shy compared with Wendy. But then, more than one Wendy in the family might have taken us all under. So, I hear you're a developer…?"

They fell into an easy conversation for the next few miles, everyone's chatter competing with the hammering of rain on the Escalade's roof, the windshield wipers' rhythmic groans. When the visibility worsened, however, Javier became far more intent on driving than talking, giving Scott a chance to check his own messages on his iPhone. Not that there were many this close to New Year's, but the business world never completely stopped, even for the holidays.

He heard his mother ask his father something, his father's curt, distracted reply. A relationship dynamic he'd always taken for granted…until witnessing Wendy and Marcos together.

As far as he could tell, the relationship his sister and new brother-in-law had seemed to be based on mutual regard and respect for each other's opinions and intelligence. God knew, he thought with a smile, his strong-willed sister was not easy to live with, but Marcos seemed to actually thrive on the challenge. The stimulation. And while Wendy would never be "tamed" by any stretch of the imagination, being with Marcos had obviously forced her to focus on something other than herself. And that could only be a good thing.

Which made Scott wonder—not for the first time, as it happened—what, exactly, had kept his parents married for more than thirty-five years. Loyalty? Habit? After all, it was no secret—at least to their children—that the relationship was strained. Strike that: it might be a secret to his father. Because as Virginia Alice's role as mother became more and more attenuated, Scott more and more often caught the haunted "Now what?" look in her eyes.

And yet, Scott had no doubt their bond was indissoluble, if for no other reason than appearances meant too much to both of them. Lousy reason to stay together, if you asked him. And why, in all likelihood, their older progeny sucked at personal relationships. Business savvy? The drive to succeed? Sure. Those, they all had in spades. But the ability to form a lasting attachment to another human being?

Not so much.

Scott exhaled, thinking of his own track record in that department. Granted, his lack of commitment was by choice. He enjoyed the company of women, certainly, but falling in love had never been on his agenda. Or in his nature, most likely.

Which was why seeing Wendy so...*blissful* was...unsettling. As though she hailed from a different gene pool altogether. Cripes, she was so young. So fearless, falling in love with the same reckless abandon as she did everything else—

His phone rang, rescuing him from pointless musings.

"Scott Fortune here—"

"Mr. Fortune, glad I caught you. It's Jack Sullivan. Your pilot?"

"Oh, yes... What can I do for you?"

He heard a dry, humorless laugh on the other end of the line. "Not a whole lot, I don't imagine. Afraid I've got some bad news—all this rain's flooded out the route I normally take to the airport." At Scott's muttered curse, the pilot said, "Oh, I'll be there, don't you worry. Just gonna take a bit longer than I'd figured."

"How much longer are we talking?"

"Hard to say. Might be a half hour or so, maybe a little more. But until this weather straightens out I'm not taking that bird up, anyway. So y'all just go on ahead and sit tight, have a cup of coffee, and hopefully this will have all blown over by the time I get there. Good news is, hundred miles east of here, it's completely clear!"

"Problem?" Mike asked quietly behind him. His brother's thinly veiled criticism made Scott bristle, as it always had. Not that he'd take the bait.

"Pilot's going to be late," he said mildly, slipping the phone back into his pocket. "Roads are flooded." At Mike's soft snort, he added, "Hard as this might be to believe, there are some things even *we* can't control."

As if on cue, they hit a squall that was like going through a car wash, making Javier slow the car to a crawl and Scott's mother suck in a worried breath.

"Man," Javier said. "I sure wouldn't want to fly in this

weather. I'm beginning to think your sister had the right idea, staying put."

Probably, but despite what he'd said to his brother, Scott was chafing, too, at their plans being derailed, at being in a situation over which he was powerless.

Because first, last and foremost, he was a Fortune, and Fortunes did not like being told "no."

Ever.

From behind the snack bar counter, Christina Hastings watched the well-heeled group trickle through the front door and across the tiled lobby of the chichi private airport and reminded herself of two things: one, that being envious was a waste of time and energy; and two, that being grateful for what you already had went a long way toward receiving more.

And besides, she had goals. Because a girl had to have goals, or she might as well shrivel up and die.

Sighing, she tossed her long braid over her shoulder, then checked the coffeepot to make sure it was still full, casting a baleful glance toward the two-story window running the full length of the lobby's back wall. It was dumb, letting the gloomy weather get to her. Dumber still that she'd agreed to come in on her day off, in case somebody had a sudden hankering for a premade Caesar salad with three bites of chicken or an overpriced bottle of water. By rights, she should be home, wrapped up in a throw on her sofa with her dog, Gumbo, smooshed up beside her, watching *Buffy* DVDs and enjoying the next-to-last day with her little fake Christmas tree before she took it down for another year.

Instead, she was amusing herself—although she used the term loosely—by watching the goings-on in front of her. Living in Red Rock—as opposed to under one—it had been impossible not to hear about the Fortune/Mendoza wedding at Red, the local family restaurant in town she'd only ever seen from the outside. Or that the small jet still in its hangar on the other side of the flight school building had been chartered to take the bride's family back to Atlanta. Not that it apparently mattered whether the men—all tall, all dark, all handsome, sheesh—were here, there or in Iceland, given their preoccupation with their spiffy, and probably five-minutes-old, electronic toys. As opposed to her ancient flip phone with half the numbers rubbed off. Made texting a mite tricky.

Not that she had anybody to text. She was just saying.

"Hey, there. What's good today?"

She smiled for the improbably red-headed flight attendant she'd seen once or twice before, dressed in a nondescript uniform of black pants and vest over a long-sleeved white shirt. "Same as always. Although the turkey sandwiches don't look half bad."

"Let me have one of those, then. And a Diet Coke."

"You flying out with this group?"

"Yep. The Atlanta branch of the Fortunes. Older guy's the father, the younger men his sons." As the flight attendant waited for her order, she nodded at the women now gathering in the posh lounge tucked underneath the second-floor offices on the other side of the lobby. "Not sure about the women, though. Although the little blonde looks exactly like the older one near to having a conniption, so I'm gonna guess she's a daughter." She pulled the tab on her soda. "Wonder what's got Mrs. Fortune so bent out of shape?"

She was, too. Elegant, reed-thin, the still-beautiful, silver-haired woman periodically pressed a tissue to her mouth, while the conservatively dressed blonde tried—with little success, it seemed to Christina—to comfort her distraught mama. A third woman—younger than the others, very pretty, oblivious to what was going on around her—flounced past them to plop down on one of the sofas. She leaned over to tug an e-reader out of her giant designer purse, her long, dark curls spilling over the shoulder of her cropped suede jacket, which matched her killer boots.

As the attendant droned on about the weather, Christina watched the Fortune brothers—one dressed like he was about to meet the president, another in a sportcoat and jeans, the third decked out in a wicked cool leather jacket and black pants—milling about, each in his own little world. Close in age, looked like. Lord, no wonder the older woman was distraught—she was awfully skinny to have pushed out that many kids that close together. A thought that evinced a brief pang Christina had no intention of indulging.

She handed the attendant her change; the redhead thanked her, then left to go talk with Mrs. Fortune. The brunette, apparently too fidgety to stay seated, got up to wander aimlessly into the lobby to look at a glassed-in display of model planes in the middle of the floor. A second later some guy in a cowboy hat strode past, carrying a stack of boxes…and winked at the brunette, obviously startling her into scurrying back into the lounge, where the oldest of the men and one of the younger ones had settled into opposite ends of the biggest sofa, yakking on their phones and ignoring the excited weatherman trying to get their attention on the big-screen TV.

Two more handsome young men ferried inordinate amounts of luggage into the building, piling it near the exit to the airfield. One lobbed a quick smile in Christina's direction before heading back outside. The highlight of her day, she thought morosely, only to mentally smack herself.

Overhead, thunder complained as the skies poured even

more rain across the glass wall, hard enough to nearly obliterate the small single-engine plane on the other side—

"Excuse me? Could I get an espresso, please?"

With a start, Christina jerked around, running into a pair of bronze-ish eyes. Ah. The One in the Leather Jacket. The *pissed* One in the Leather Jacket, apparently.

Christina shrugged, apologetic. Tried unsuccessfully to ignore the mouth. And the cheekbones. Holy moly. Not only did this family have, if the scuttlebutt was to be believed, more money than God, they had a gene pool to die for. "Sorry, all I've got is regular. Or decaf."

"You're not serious?"

Okay, the man was easily the best-looking guy she'd ever seen in her entire life—how she wasn't blinded, she did not know—but still. A pain in the butt is a pain in the butt.

This ain't Starbucks, Bucko, she wanted to say. But she didn't. Partly because she didn't have the energy, and partly because, along with his iPad, the guy was toting a silly little pink bakery box. Which for some reason tickled her no end.

"For what it's worth," she said, "which isn't much, I'll grant you, I've been after my boss to get an espresso machine ever since I started working here. He ignores me. So." Overhead, hail pummeled the steel roof, the sudden din making her jump. Outside it looked like God had dumped out His snowcone machine. When she turned back to Leather Jacket Dude, he was glaring at the deluge.

"It'll let up," she shouted over the barrage. Although why she felt compelled to reassure him, she had no idea. He turned the glare on her, and she sighed. "Regular or decaf?"

The man grimaced. And he hadn't even tasted the coffee

yet. Forget an espresso maker, Christina couldn't even get Jimmy to spring for a decent Colombian brew.

"Regular," he grumbled. "Black."

Christina opened her mouth, then shut it again, thinking *Just give the man his coffee, honey chile.* She poured it into a foam cup, smooshed a plastic lid on top, then set it on the black granite counter, wiping her hands on the seat of her jeans to keep from messing up her apron, which was a bear to get clean. "That'll be a dollar fifty. The flight attendant said you're all family?"

He barely glanced at her before reaching inside his jacket for his wallet, the slight move releasing a very pleasant scent. Probably not something he picked up at Walgreens. "Yes. We were here for my sister's wedding."

"Oh, that's nice. From Atlanta, right?"

He frowned slightly, like he couldn't figure out why on earth she was talking to him. Well, tough. Talking to people was what kept her from going insane, giving in to the loneliness that sometimes felt like it would suffocate her. Gumbo was a great dog, but his conversational skills were limited. "Yes," he said, looking up when the hail stopped, as abruptly as it had started.

"See?" Christina said. "Told ya. You watch, the sun'll be out before you know it."

For a moment their gazes touched, his a bit disconcerted as his cell phone rang. Almost like he heard the distinct *twannnnng* in Christina's midsection. Uh-oh. Distractedly he hunched it to his shoulder, mumbling, "Scott Fortune," as he handed her a twenty, then started to walk away.

Must be nice, she thought as the twanging died out, to be able to treat twenties like quarters. "Wait! You forgot your change—"

A deafening, blood-chilling roar drowned out her words,

raised the hairs on her arms. Scott turned, the startled look in his eyes tangling with hers a split second before the glass wall exploded and Hell rained down around them.

Chapter Two

The woman's scream pierced his brain, rudely dragging Scott back to consciousness. His heart pounding hard enough to hurt, he lay motionless, his eyes still closed, his ears still ringing, trying to regain his bearings…until she screamed again.

"For the love of all that's holy, *stop that.*"

After a beat or two of blessed silence, he heard, "I thought you were dead."

That raspy voice…ah. The waitress. "No. At least I don't think so—" The last word ended in a cough; yanking his jacket collar over his mouth and nose, Scott opened his eyes. Panic cramped his chest: through the occasional shaft of dust-clogged light eking through the rubble, he realized he'd come damn close to being buried alive. He fumbled for his phone, only to realize it had apparently fallen out of his pocket. Damn.

"Um, are you okay?" she said. "I mean, c-can you help me? I'm stuck."

Adrenaline spiked through him. "Hold on…" Debris clattered as Scott tried to heave himself upright, only getting as far as his knees when his right temple gave him hell. Flinching, he quickly brushed his fingers over the spot—no blood, thank God. "Where are you?"

"Close enough to think you were dead, obviously. I can see you, though. Kinda. Keep going, you'll find me."

"How long was I out?" he asked as he cautiously crept toward her.

"Not long. Couple minutes, maybe? You remember the tornado hitting?" she asked when he reached her, barely six feet away. Propped on her elbows, she lay back against what he assumed was the counter base, her legs imprisoned beneath a pile of rubble. Even through the haze he could see the grim set to her mouth.

"Yes," Scott said quietly, knowing he'd never forget the wind's brutal, relentless shrieking, like a million furious demons. "Guess I blacked out right after, though. Does it hurt?"

"I don't think…no. Not really. Not sure if that's a good thing or not. I can't move, but at least I don't feel like I'm being crushed. But something—" Grimacing, she strained to pull herself free; Scott's hand shot to her shoulder, stopping her.

"Stay still. Do you hear me?"

Not looking at him, she nodded. "Just…hurry."

"On it," he muttered as he snatched away the lighter stuff—wood lathing, plaster chunks, shards of glass. But despite having lifted weights for years, Scott was no match for the granite slab pinning her to the ground. He tried another angle, his back and shoulder muscles burning like a sonuvabitch, but no dice. Sitting back beside her, he punched out an exasperated breath. "Why the hell did they use granite for the counter?"

Her head fell back, her eyes shut. "And yet," she said through faint, rapid breaths, "no espresso maker. Go figure."

More dust sifted down beside them, the sound like scurrying ants. "Call me crazy, but this seems like an odd time to crack jokes."

"It's that or s-scream again. D-deal."

He groped for her hand in the dim light, found it; her fingers tightened around his, kicking his heart into overdrive. "Take some deep breaths before you hyperventilate. There, that's better," he said when she complied, then gently squeezed her hand. "You scared?"

A snort preceded, "Yeah, fear is kinda my go-to emotion when I think I might die."

"We're not going to die."

"Oh? Last I heard, death couldn't be bought off."

"What's that supposed to mean?"

Her eyes opened as she shifted, clearly trying to suppress a wince. And shivering. "S-sorry. Today hasn't gone exactly the way I thought it w-would…no, it's okay, I'm fine," she said when he let go to shrug off his jacket.

"I'm wearing a sweater. You're not. So no arguments. Can you sit up a little more?" Nodding, she did, at least enough for him to wrap the jacket around her shoulders, tug her smooth blond braid free.

"Thank you."

"Anytime." Elbowing aside the first stirrings of alarm, Scott glanced around. "This is…surreal."

"Yeah," she said. "Especially as I can't recall ever seeing a tornado around here before. Farther north and west, sure. But…" Her eyes lifted. "I think…I'm gonna pretend this is all a dream. And any minute I'll wake up and…it'll be over."

"Sounds like a plan." He inched a little closer. "I'm Scott, by the way."

"I know." Her eyes drifted closed again. "Heard you on your cell phone."

"Speaking of which, mine's gone AWOL. Do you have one?"

"Sure thing. In my purse."

"Which is where?"

She almost laughed. A sound that, under other circumstances, he would have found extremely appealing. "Around here somewhere. And you need to be quiet now."

Scott angled his head to see into her face. Her eyes were still shut. "You didn't tell me your name."

"Christina. Hastings. Now hush."

"What…what are you doing?"

"Praying. Trying to, anyway."

"You really think that'll help?"

"We'll never find out if you keep talking, will we?"

A damp draft swept through their little cave. "Is your head okay?"

"And that better not be you thinking I'm off my nut because I'm praying."

He did, but he wasn't about to say that. "Not at all. But if your head got hit, you might have a concussion. So you shouldn't close your eyes in case you fall asleep."

"Oh. No. Head's fine. Well, no worse than usual—"

A muffled sound from outside made Scott jump. Holy hell. How could he have forgotten—?

The initial shock sloughed off, he jolted to his knees again to claw at the wall of debris barely three feet away separating him from the others. "Blake! Mike!" He yanked at a chunk of drywall, sending plaster dust and small chunks of heaven knew what sifting down on them. "*Dad!* Can you hear me—?"

"For heaven's sake, stop!" Christina snapped behind him. "You want to bring whatever's left up there down on our heads?"

"No, but…*dammit!*" Terror erupting in his chest, he stared into the darkness quickly swallowing up what might as well have been a mountain. "Most of my family's out there. Somewhere."

"It'll be okay," she murmured, although he wasn't sure if the reassurance was aimed at him or she was trying to talk herself down off the ledge. Scott duckwalked back to where she lay, planting his butt on the floor beside her and listening to the unremitting drip, drip, drip of rain somewhere above them.

"You sure about that?"

A beat passed before she said, "Somebody's bound to know what happened, where we are. It might take a while, but…we'll be okay."

He could barely see her now, but that first image when he'd looked up from his phone earlier and actually *noticed* her was indelibly etched into his brain: the sass and intelligence in those enormous blue eyes, the barely repressed humor—at his expense, no doubt—behind her smile. "For somebody convinced a minute ago we were about to die, you seem amazingly calm now."

"I had my moment. It's over. Or I could be in shock. Hard to tell."

"Or maybe you did get beaned."

Her soft laugh melted something inside him. "Or maybe I did."

Crazy. Most women he knew would be in hysterics by now. And Christina's hair and skin had to be as caked with plaster dust as his, her eyes and mouth as gritty. Not to mention she couldn't have been more than five-two, five-three tops. And yet—

"You're tougher than you look."

"So I've been told."

More distorted sounds from the other side of the wall snagged his attention; he crawled over, shouting. "We're in here! Can anybody hear me? Javier! Is that you?"

"You're wasting your energy, you realize."

His head swung back to her. "I can't sit here and do *nothing.*"

"Looks like you don't have much of a choice."

"Doing nothing is not a choice."

"We're not doing nothing. We're waiting." She paused. "And trusting."

"Ah. That praying thing again, right?"

He sensed more than saw her shrug before she said, "Tell me about them. Your family."

"Why?"

"Maybe it'll keep us distracted."

Scott's gut contracted. "You *are* in pain."

"Let's just say I'll never complain about cramps again."

Honestly. "Do you always say whatever pops into your head?"

"Depends on the situation. This definitely qualifies. Besides..." She shifted slightly. "Either we're gonna die, in which case we'll never see each other again. Or we'll be rescued—which would definitely be my preference—and you'll go back to Atlanta, and we'll still never see each other again. Either way, I'm not too worried about making a good impression."

Except you are, Scott thought, startled, thinking if he had to be trapped in a pile of rubble with anybody, he could have done far worse than this smart-mouthed, cool-as-acucumber little bit of a thing with her soft, raspy voice and even softer blue eyes.

"So talk," she said. "How many of you are there, exactly...?"

He made her laugh.

And, bless him, forget. As much as she could, she supposed, given the situation. But considering their initial encounter, not to mention the frown lines he'd probably been working on since kindergarten, the last thing Christina had expected was for the man to have a sense of humor.

Not that she couldn't hear weightier threads lacing the stories about growing up with five siblings, despite Scott's obvious discretion at how he presented his family to a complete stranger. Even so, when, for instance, he told her some silly story about him and his older brother, Mike, setting up competing lemonade stands across the street from each other when they were kids, she could hear the frustration—and hurt—underlying his words. Mike couldn't let an opportunity pass to one-up his younger brother...and that their father had praised eleven-year-old Mike for his ingenuity at besting Scott, who'd only been in the third grade at the time.

She was also guessing that Scott had been busting his buns trying to win his father's approval ever since. Not that Scott would ever admit as much—certainly not to Christina, at least—but nobody knew better than she did what it was like to yearn for a parent's attention and respect.

His obvious loyalty—and genuine affection—was honorable. But good Lord, if half of what he'd said was true, this family took the concept of sibling rivalry to new heights, not only not discouraging competition but fostering it, pitting the kids against each other to make them stronger. More fierce. And yet, from what she could tell, they all loved each other, even if those bonds were mainly forged by their mutual interest in FortuneSouth's success.

It was enough to almost make her grateful she was an only child.

"So what do y'all do for fun?" she asked.

"Fun?"

It was almost totally dark by now. And cold. Cold enough that they leaned into each other for warmth. And comfort. The pain in her leg and foot had settled into a dull but constant ache. As had the fear, which was almost like a third person in the space.

"It's not a trick question, you know."

"More than you might think," Scott muttered, then parried, "What do *you* do for...fun?"

"I asked you first."

He blew out a heavy sigh, his breath warm in her hair. "Okay...we...go to a lot of charity events." His accent was pure Southern-privileged, his voice pure man, all low and rumbly. A delicious, and deadly, combination. "Dinners, that sort of thing."

"Sounds boring."

"Excruciatingly."

"For pity's sake—I said *fun,* Scott. Or do you need me to define the word?"

"How would you define it?"

"Well...fun is something that makes you feel good. Makes you happy. Makes you glad to simply be alive."

"Such as?"

She thought. "Goin' to the state fair and eating your weight in fried food. And cotton candy. Tossing burgers on the grill on a summer night, sittin' around and chewing the fat with friends. Driving to nowhere with the top down, stopping wherever you feel like it. Sittin' on the steps and watching fireflies. What?"

"Apparently your definition of *fun* doesn't include the word *exciting*."

"Does yours?"

"Good point."

"I said, it just has to make you feel good."

"So…is that your life? In a nutshell? Going to the fair and chowing down on burgers and watching fireflies?"

After a long moment, she said, "I said that's how I define fun. I didn't necessarily say that was my life. Not at the moment, anyway."

"That doesn't sound good."

"No, it's okay. I'm just…I'm kind of…focused on other things right now." When he got real quiet, she said, "What are you thinking about?"

"That I've never been to a state fair."

"Get out."

"It's true. But also…that I can't remember the last time I felt good about doing something that didn't involve improving the bottom line."

"And *that* is too sad for words."

"There's nothing wrong with making money, Christina. FortuneSouth provides jobs for thousands of people—"

"Oh, don't go getting defensive. I never said there was anything wrong with making money. But you have to admit there's something off about only getting your jollies from work."

Another pause. Then: "I don't *only* get my jollies from work."

"Lord, I can practically hear your brows waggling. And *that* doesn't count," she said when he laughed.

"It doesn't?"

"Not that it can't be fun—don't get me wrong. But it's so…trite."

Scott barked out a laugh. "Point to you."

"Thank you."

She felt him shift beside her. "You remind me a little of my youngest sister. Wendy."

"The one your parents sent out here because she was about to drive 'em up a wall?"

"The very one."

"Is Wendy your favorite?"

"Yes. But don't you dare tell her that. Or anyone else."

"Your secret's safe with me." Christina thought a moment, then said, "I'm very flattered, then."

Scott chuckled. "So tell me about *your* family."

Yeah, he would ask that. "Not a whole lot to tell. My father jumped ship when I was a toddler, never to be seen again, and my mother…we're not real close."

"I'm sorry."

"Yeah. Me, too."

"No brothers or sisters?"

"Nope. But I do have a dog…ohmigosh!"

"What?"

"I can't believe I forgot! *I have a dog.* And I have no idea if he's okay—"

Feeling her eyes burn, Christina pressed a hand to her mouth. Not being dead yet, she figured she was ahead of the game, but suddenly not having any idea how her baby was made her sick to her stomach.

"What's his name?" Scott said gently.

She lowered her hand. "G-gumbo. 'Cause when God made him he tossed whatever parts He had on hand into a bowl, and Gumbo was the result. Although he gets called Dumbo a lot, too," she said on a shaky little laugh. "Dog's dumber than a load of bricks, I swear. But he's mine, and I love him, and—"

The tears came whether she wanted them to or not. The shock came when Scott slipped his arm around her shoulders and pulled her head to his chest. Not saying anything, just holding her close.

So. Unfair.

Then her stomach rumbled. "How long do you suppose we've been here?"

"I have no idea. It's been dark for a while, though."

She listened. "Rain's stopped."

"Yep. In fact, there must be a full moon."

Christina blinked, noticed the silvery light here and there delineating the scene. "Oh, yeah." She sighed. "I'd kill for a burger and fries right now."

Another of those low chuckles preceded, "You and me both."

"While we have the light…there's a refrigerated case, if you can get to it, with food, such as it is. And water and stuff."

"Be right back."

He disappeared; for several minutes she heard scuffling, some cursing. Then a surprised, "I'll be damned. I found my phone. Although…crap. No service. But…hold on…"

A minute later he returned with a couple of sandwiches, two bottles of water and that little box. "The case was pretty banged up," he said, sitting beside her again. "But still cold. I have no idea what I got, though."

"Ask me if I care," she said, grabbing one of the sandwiches and ripping off the cellophane. "So what's in the box?"

"Heaven. Or so I'm told."

"Yeah?"

"Yep. After she started working at Red, Wendy discovered she had a talent for making desserts. So she gave all of us a sampling of some of her creations." He turned on his phone, the feeble light illuminating the contents of the box enough for Christina to see several kinds of cookies, some sort of bar thing and a Napoleon-like pastry. "Help yourself, I'm not big on sweets. But you'd better believe I wouldn't tell Wendy that."

The sandwich gone, Christina hesitated, then selected something that melted in her mouth. Butter and chocolate and caramel and maybe some kind of liqueur? It was the fanciest thing she'd ever tasted in her life, given that, for her, a "splurge" was buying real Oreos instead of the Walmart fakeouts. Which *she* wasn't about to tell *Scott.*

"That was amazing" was all she said, then closed the lid on the box.

"Please. I mean it. Take what you want."

Like she'd ever been able to do that in her entire life. "No, it's okay. I'm good."

Their meal done, they sat in silence for a little while, digesting what had happened to them—well, at least that's what Christina was doing—as well as their food. Outside, the wind had picked up enough to whistle through the jagged orifices left in the wake of the destruction. Close by, something periodically scraped against the wall on the far side of what used to be the snack bar.

Scott cleared his throat. "I think we need to keep talking—"

"Yeah, I think you're right. Absolutely." Then she yawned. "If I can stay awake. I think the adrenaline's gone."

"You comfortable?"

"I've been better. Been worse, too."

He pulled her close again. "Lay your head on my chest."

"I couldn't—"

"One, you already have. And two, I cannot tell you how little I'm in the mood for arguments right now. And I'm cold, too. So just do it, dammit."

All righty, then. Although, even before her cheek made

contact with his soft, soft sweater—and the hard, hard muscles underneath, Christina knew she was doomed.

Whether they made it out alive or not.

Scott couldn't remember the last time he'd held a woman close—one not related to him, that is—with no ulterior motive in mind. Or when doing so had provoked such mind-blowing feelings of…tenderness. Especially when, with a long sigh, Christina relaxed against him.

"Better?"

"Yes, actually." She lightly rubbed his chest. Probably not the best move. "What is this stuff? Cashmere?"

"Silk and lambswool. Wendy gave it to me for Christmas."

Her hand once more fisted near her chin, she said, "Gal's got good taste."

"That she does." Fingering her shoulder, he asked, "So tell me—who is Christina Hastings when she's not pawning off lousy coffee in an airport?"

A little laugh preceded, "You tasted it, then?"

"Unfortunately, yes. Well? What are your dreams?"

"Now why on earth would you be interested in my dreams?"

"Would you rather talk about sports? Politics?"

"God, no."

"Good. Because neither would I." He paused, then added, "I don't make small talk, Christina. Or ask questions I don't really want answers to. And we agreed we need to keep talking—"

"Okay, fine. Short term or long term?"

"Either. Both."

"Well, first, to finish getting my business degree. Although I've been working on that one for some time already. I didn't…I got sidetracked after I finished high school, so I didn't start college until I was twenty-one. And even then I've always had to work while going to school, so I've only been able to take a couple courses a semester. I'm definitely a tortoise and not a hare."

"Nothing wrong with that. But there's no one to help you out?"

"Not really, no. Although I'm hoping to finish up in the next year or so. And after that—*way* after that, most likely—I'd like to have my own business."

"Doing what?"

"You don't—"

"Christina. Captive audience. Go for it."

A moment passed before she said, "I've got a couple of ideas, although nothing's set in stone. But I'm good with animals, so I thought maybe a pet grooming shop. Or one of those spas where people could leave their pets for me to spoil while they go on vacation? Although that would mean owning someplace large enough to do that, so that's definitely on the 'someday' list…oh, it's silly, isn't it?"

"Now why would you say that?"

"Because…I don't know. My plans must seem like small potatoes to somebody like you."

"One, you are not allowed to sell yourself short. Two, all businesses start with a seed. An idea. Feed that idea with focus and determination and it will grow."

"And sufficient start-up capital," she said with a sigh.

"Somebody's done her homework. I'm impressed."

"Homework, I can do. Finding money lying around under rocks, not so much."

He smiled. "If the idea is good, the financing will fall into place."

"So would *you* finance my start-up?"

"Cheeky little thing, aren't you?"

"So would you?"

Scott chuckled. And got a sweet whiff of what was left of her perfume or hair stuff or whatever it was. "Show me a well-thought-out business plan and we'll talk."

"You're not just saying that because you're figuring we're gonna die here and then you'll be off the hook?"

"We're not going to die, Christina."

She snuggled closer, her arm banding his ribs as she whispered, "Do you know I've never told another living soul about this?"

"Not even your mother?"

"Especially not my mother." She paused. "Since she's shot down everything I've ever tried. Or ever wanted to do. Not exactly a big cheerleader."

"That's rough."

"Eh," she said on a shrug, "it taught me early on to be self-reliant. 'Course, that doesn't make an ideal mate, either. Prob'ly why I haven't been on a date in, oh…two years?"

Gal was definitely getting tired, Scott thought with a weary smile of his own. Inhibitions shattered and all that.

"Two years? Really?"

"Yep." She yawned. "Got tired of the stupid games. Of meeting a guy and thinking he's nice, only to find out he automatically expects something in return for taking me out to dinner. That he's not even remotely interested in getting to know me as a person. Sucked."

Bitterness, dulled and worn, veneered her words. And provoked him into defending his sex. "Not all men are like that."

"Then maybe I'm just lousy at picking 'em," she said, her accent getting heavier the sleepier she got. "But you know? I'm okay with being on my own. It's kinda nice, being able to make my own decisions about what's best for me without having to swing 'em past anybody else."

This last bit was accentuated with a sweeping arm gesture before she snuggled closer, rubbing her cheek against his chest. Damn.

"You're awfully young to be so cynical," he said into her dusty hair.

She shrugged, clearly unperturbed. "Better than havin' my head in the clouds."

She yawned again, one of those double yawns that signified that sleep couldn't be far behind. Yet despite her soft voice, her words were clear. "I'm a realist, Scott. I know who I am. Where I came from. Maybe not exactly where I'm going, but close enough. What's in my control and what's not. Like…if I never get married, maybe I'll…adopt someday." She hmmphed tiredly. "Never told anybody *that,* either."

And the longer she talked, the more her honesty seemed to wrap around his soul, nourishing something inside him he hadn't even known was hungry. "Were you always this wise? Or has experience made you this way?"

"Hell if I know," she said, and he laughed. "But I am a real firm believer in being true to yourself. In knowing who you are and what you want, and then doing your best to make those two things work together. Long as you understand the road between points A and Z might not always be a smooth one."

At that, Scott held her closer, resting his cheek in her hair, as if doing so would help him absorb some of whatever it was that had so firmly grounded her. "What if…you get so entrenched in Point A you can't even see Point Z? What if you're not even sure what Point Z is?"

He could sense her tilting back to look at him, even though he couldn't imagine what she'd see in the murky light. "Seems to me all you need to know is that where you are in your life? It's not working anymore. And then have the guts to do something about it. Because way too many people get so caught up in doing things the way they've always done them, living the lives they've always lived, that they don't even know they're unhappy. And that, to me, feels unbearably sad."

She molded herself to him once more, as though she belonged there. "I don't want to die with regrets, wondering why I didn't try to go after my dreams. And I have to say, if I did kick the bucket right now? Sure, I'd be pissed that I didn't get there, but at least I have the satisfaction of knowing I was on my way."

Scott's heart constricted as he fought the urge to tell her that she'd made him think more, *feel* more, in the past few hours than he probably had in ten years. If ever. That, suddenly and inexplicably, the thought of never seeing her again bothered him far more than the possibility of not making it out alive.

But he didn't dare say that.

Not in words, at least.

"Christina?" he whispered, waiting for her face to lift to his before cupping her cheek. "This is nuts, but I want—" He swallowed.

"Go for it, Bucko," she whispered, then softly laughed, low in her throat. "Not like anybody's gonna know but us."

Or at least that's what he thought she said over his pounding heart as he lowered his mouth to hers.

Chapter Three

"Holy hell! Found 'em—!"

"They okay—?"

"Think so, although the gal looks like she's stuck. Frank! Hernando! Get your butts over here, *now!*"

Jerked awake, Scott batted at the bright light searing his eyes…until it registered that was the *sun* shining in his face.

"Hey, buddy—how're you doing?"

Scott shook the last remnants of sleep and disbelief from his brain as Christina stirred in his arms, then let out a little cry. Although whether from relief, surprise or pain, Scott couldn't tell.

"I'm fine, but she's—"

"Yeah, we can see that," the rescuer said, his voice graveled with both age and what had undoubtedly been a very long night. "It's okay, sweetheart, we're gonna get you outta there in two shakes." Then, to Scott, "You did good, keeping her warm like that. Can you walk?"

"Yes. At least," he said as he tried to stretch out his cold, stiff muscles, "I could before I fell asleep—"

"Good," the rescuer said as three or four other people appeared, bustling around Christina, "'Cause I need you outta the way so the paramedics can do their thing—"

"But—"

"Go check on your family," Christina said, her voice rough, "they must be worried sick." When he still hesitated, she shut her eyes and commanded, *"Go."*

"I'll be back. I swear," he said, although he doubted she'd heard him.

Stooped over, he crawled through the tunnel the rescuers had made in the destruction, releasing a nauseous gasp when he emerged into what looked like the set from a disaster movie.

Momentarily paralyzed, Scott struggled to absorb the scene as dozens of rescuers, some in National Guard uniforms, swarmed around him—the odd wall, still inexplicably standing; the sunlight dancing across the glass-littered ground, glancing off twisted pieces of what Scott realized in horror was a small plane; rows of seats, the leather furniture from the lounge upended, mutilated, half-buried underneath what had been the second floor. And above it all, framing the destruction, the blue, cloudless sky, serene and still and contrite, as though denying the fury it had unleashed only hours before.

"Scott! Thank God!"

He wheeled around to see Blake and Mike striding toward him, dusty and muddy and scratched up, but otherwise okay, and his head snapped back to the present. Then his cousin, Victoria, her dark curls a tangled, filthy mess, appeared, squealing as she threw her arms around each one's neck in turn, all of them talking at once.

"—ceiling caved in so we couldn't get out—"

"—Javier's in bad shape, they've already taken him to the hospital, Miguel's with him—"

"—Dad's in an ambulance, something about chest pains—"

"—Mom's got a broken wrist—"

"—but they had to give her something to calm her down," Victoria put in, tears brimming in her eyes. "Because, that flight attendant? She…she didn't make it." Scott swore as Mike laid a hand on Scott's arm, the uncharacteristic gesture raising the hairs on the back of Scott's neck. "They haven't found Emily yet, either."

For a moment, he couldn't speak. Couldn't think. Couldn't, for the first time in his life, make a decision. Try to find his sister or go back for Christina? Honor a promise he'd only made a few minutes ago, or his duty to family?

Frowning, Scott glanced back over his shoulder, then sighed. Meeting his brothers' gazes, he asked, "Where was Em when the storm hit?"

"Over there, talking to Aunt Virginia," Victoria said, pointing to where the lounge had been, then shuddering. "But then, so was I, and I ended up way the heck over there." Her arms folded across her ribs, she nodded toward the other side of the building, then started to cry. "Oh, God—what if Em's…"

She burst into sobs as Blake wrapped one arm around her shoulders, a moment before a shout went up from about twenty feet away.

"We got her!"

Scott and the others picked their way through the wreckage as fast as they could, getting to Emily right as the rescuers pulled her free. Like the rest of them, she was dirty and debris-ravaged, but, other than a wonky ankle, she seemed none the worse for wear.

Physically, at least. Because Scott wondered what sort

of psychological toll the last fifteen, sixteen hours would have on all of them, none of whom had ever been through anything even remotely life-threatening before. Certainly he would never be the same, he thought as he made his way back to where he and Christina had spent that long, cold, miserable night, only to find that she, too, was already gone.

"Where?" he asked a state trooper on the scene.

"Same place they took everybody else. San Antonio Memorial." The trooper looked over at his brothers and cousin. "Y'all need a ride?"

"I…I don't know." Forking a hand through his hair, Scott scanned the surreal landscape. "The cars—"

"All totaled," the trooper said gently. "Except for that Escalade over there. Some dings and scrapes, but otherwise intact. Probably drives okay. Strange, how these things happen. I've seen entire blocks wiped out, except for one house left standing, untouched." Away from the mangled building by now, the officer nodded toward the SUV, which did indeed look virtually unscathed. "A rental, I'm guessing from the license plate."

Scott nodded, his throat constricting. Around them, lights flashed, radios squawked from assorted emergency vehicles. Out of the corner of his eye, he caught Mike climbing into one of the ambulances, its siren bloop-blooping as it started away. "Yeah. Ours," he finally got out as he took in the crushed Explorer lying on its side.

"Then you'll be wanting these," the trooper said, digging in his pocket and handing over the keys. "They were in the ignition, so I figured I'd better take 'em. Not that I expect anybody to come out here looking for trouble, but you never know."

Scott nodded his thanks, then said, "My brothers, they

said…" His stomach turned. "Javier Mendoza? Do you have any idea where he is?"

The grave, compassionate expression in the man's gray eyes said far more than Scott wanted to hear. "That must be the guy they got to first, lying right past the doorway. He's probably already at the hospital by now, they can tell you more when you get there." The man rested a hand on Scott's shoulder. "You okay, son? That bruise on the side of your head bothering you any—?"

"I'm fine. Or will be, soon enough. Thank you."

The trooper's radio crackled; with a wave he walked away, the same moment a reedy, but surprisingly strong, voice called out.

"Oh, Scotty—thank God you're all right!"

Forcing a smile for his mother, Scott made his way through the angled vehicles toward her, the warm sun again giving the lie to the wicked, bizarre weather from the day before. Wrapped in a silver Mylar blanket and propped up on a gurney, her arm strapped to her chest, his mother accepted his kiss, then asked, with anxious eyes, if they'd found Emily.

"Yes. A few minutes ago—"

"Is she…is she all right?"

"She's fine. Her ankle's a little messed up, but you know our Em—can't keep a good girl down—"

"And Jordana?"

Figuring whatever they'd given her, combined with the trauma, was playing tricks with their mother's head, Scott said quietly, "Jordana didn't come, remember? She stayed at the resort—"

"No, no—she called me on my cell about ten minutes before the tornado hit, said she'd changed her mind and was getting a ride to the airport with that Tanner person." She grasped Scott's wrist with her good hand, her eyes wide with fear. "Oh, God, Scott—if she was on the road—"

"I'm sure she's fine, Mom," Scott said evenly, even if his stomach didn't agree.

"All righty, Mrs. Fortune, we need to get going," the attendant said, adding, as another pair of EMTs wheeled Emily toward them, "Your daughter's going to ride with you, how's that?"

"Emily, sweetheart…!"

As the last ambulance finally pulled away with his mother and sister inside, Scott stood with his hands in his pants pockets, a light, chilly breeze ruffling his hair as he surveyed the decimated landscape—fences gone, trees uprooted or snapped in two, entire windbreaks felled like bowling pins. Oddly, the storm seemed to have inflicted far less damage to the flight school building behind him—it was still standing, at least—but Scott had overheard some of the rescuers saying that this tornado was only one of a series. That others—although not as devastating, thankfully—had also touched down in Red Rock itself, causing even more damage.

Blake came up beside him, one hand on his hip, the other cuffing the back of his neck. "Holy crap."

"That about sums it up."

"Think this is what's known as one of those life-altering events."

A lot more than you know, Scott mused, his thoughts drifting back to Christina—the heat of her hand gripping his, her trusting weight against his chest…the lingering buzz from that sweetly electric kiss. Still. Even in the clear light of day.

Crazy.

But damn if he didn't feel as though somebody'd flipped

a switch in his brain…a switch he hadn't even known had been in the "off" position.

He looked back over Blake's shoulder to see their cousin picking through the debris, wobbling on her high-heeled boots like a tipsy mountain goat. "What on earth is Victoria doing?"

"Looking for her luggage, she said. I suppose it's giving her something to focus on so she won't freak out." Blake met Scott's gaze. "She keeps talking about some dude in a cowboy hat pulling her out of the rubble then disappearing. Got any clue who she's talking about?"

"None," Scott said, thinking he had far more pressing things on his mind than Victoria's mystery cowboy in shining armor. Like the woman who, in one night, had twisted him far more inside out than a tornado ever could. Not knowing how badly she was hurt…

Pulling the rental's keys from his pocket, Scott called to his cousin. "Vicki! We need to get to the hospital."

She looked up, shielding her eyes from the sun. The wind caught in her hair, whipping it around her smudged face. "But…my things…"

"Now, Victoria," Scott said sharply, walking to the SUV, his brother and muttering cousin following suit.

"Sorry," she mumbled after she got into the back. "I'm just hungry. And exhausted. And…" She let out a muffled sob. "And when I think—"

"It's okay, honey," Scott said as they slowly pulled away, the car's shocks working overtime as they drove over the chewed up ground. "We've all had a rough time."

And yet, he mused as they reached the highway, where it became much smoother going except for the occasional jagged branch or chunk of somebody's shed, not once during their ordeal had Christina complained. Even though she had to have been in pain. And frightened out of her wits.

If anything happened to her…

He stepped on the gas.

Not surprisingly, the E.R. was borderline chaos, all the exam rooms filled, a pair of obviously harried nurses doing triage on the dozens of walking wounded flooding the waiting room.

"Scott! Over here!"

Emily was in a far corner, between a resigned-looking older man pressing a bloodstained towel to a gash in his head and a mother with worried eyes holding a sleeping toddler. His sister's foot, wrapped in an ice pack, was elevated on a pillow on the glass table in front of her. Blake scanned the crowd. "Wow. Did San Antonio get hit, too?"

Emily shook her head, her pinched brow the only clue she'd been through hell. "No, just Red Rock. This is overflow from the Medical Center. Look," she said, nodding toward the TV mounted high on the opposite wall, where a camera panned parts of the town, showing the damage. Considering what might have been, though, things could have been much worse.

For all of them.

He turned back to his sister. "Where's Mom and Dad?"

"In treatment rooms. Mike's been toggling between the two of them. I'd bug the desk for more information, except, one, I can't exactly move and, two, I'm afraid of that nurse. Yeah, that one, in the pink scrubs. Don't let the teddy bears fool you—she's fierce." The man with the bleeding head was called to see the doctor. With a heavy sigh, Victoria plopped into his vacated seat, laid her head on Emily's shoulder. She smiled for her cousin, then said, "Eventually

I'll get into the inner sanctum and find out what's going on, but…"

She glanced across the room, then whispered, "It's Javier I'm most worried about, if the look on Miguel's face is anything to go by."

Scott twisted around to see Javier's and Marcos's brother, who'd come from New York for the wedding, sitting in a chair on the other side of the room, his head in his hands.

"Go on, talk to him," Blake said. "I'll check on Mom and Dad."

Looking far more bedraggled than the rest of them, Miguel shakily stood at Scott's approach. A small, tight smile strained his mouth. "Your family—is everybody okay?"

"More or less. Miguel—for God's sake, sit, you look like you're about to keel over. How is he?"

"It's bad, man," Miguel said, sinking onto the seat, strangling his still wet ball cap in his hands. "Real bad." Terrified brown eyes lifted to Scott's. "He's…he's unconscious, they don't even know yet what needs fixing. His head, his legs…" The young man swallowed hard, obviously fighting for control.

"Damn…" Scott felt as though someone had put a stake through his chest. "You need me to make any calls—?"

"No, I already talked to Marcos. He'll get in touch with everybody else." He looked at Scott, obviously fighting tears. "I found him, right after the twister hit. I could tell he was in bad shape, but there wasn't a damn thing I could do—couldn't call 911 because the cell service was down, couldn't go get help because the roads were trashed. Best I could do was keep the worst of the rain off him, but…" Shaking his head, he looked away, a tear tracking down his filthy, stubbled cheek.

"Hey…" Scott laid his hand on the younger man's shoulder. "It's going to be okay. He made it through the night. That's got to count for something—"

"I can't stop thinking," Miguel went on, his left leg bouncing, clearly not hearing any voices except the nasty ones in his own head, "what if he didn't get help in time—?"

"And you're only going to make yourself crazy, worrying like that," Scott said, even though his own voices, making him worry and wonder about Christina, weren't doing him any favors, either. When he spotted Blake, he waved him over. "I need to go check on my folks, but Blake will stay with you until your family arrives. And listen," he added as he stood, "you know we'll help in any way we can. Whatever Javier needs, it's his. Got that?"

Miguel looked up, hope and terror fighting for purchase in red-rimmed eyes. "Thanks."

"No problem."

Despite Emily's warning, Scott had no choice but to confront the obviously frazzled nurse at the desk. "Yes?" she snapped, not looking at him.

"I'd like to see my parents. Virginia Alice and John Michael Fortune?"

"Rooms 1B and 1A," she said, jabbing a pen over her shoulder, "right on the other side of the door—"

"And you have another patient who came in by ambulance around the same time, Christina Hastings? Can you tell me which room she's in?"

"She a relative, too?"

"No, but—"

"Only family's allowed to see the patients, sorry."

"You're not serious?"

She frowned up at him. "Do I look like I'm in the mood to kid around?"

Frankly, Scott guessed that was a mood she was never in. "Then can you at least tell me her condition?"

"No."

Scott leaned over the counter, close enough to make the woman back up. "If it hadn't been for my family," he said in a low voice, "it's highly unlikely Miss Hastings would even need to be here right now. So if you don't mind—"

"Do you see all these people, Mr. Fortune? Do you also see how many more of them there are than us? Now, please, go see your parents and let us get on with what we're supposed to be doing. Which includes taking care of Miss Hastings."

When the woman turned her back on him to answer another staff member's question, Scott realized he'd lost that round. Which did not sit well. But, he thought as he strode toward the exam rooms, damned if he'd lose the next one.

He heard Mike's agitated voice before he entered their father's cubicle. Sitting with his ankle crossed over his other knee, his brother was on his phone, conducting business as though his Gucci suit wasn't filthy and ripped, his thousand-dollar loafers caked in mud. More than that, however, as though their father wasn't dozing in a hospital bed six feet away, hooked up to an army of machines and looking more vulnerable—more human—than Scott had ever seen him.

Tearing his eyes from his father, he said to Mike, "Somebody's gonna be all over your ass about that cell phone. If I were you I'd switch to text."

Behind him John Michael snorted. "Took you long enough."

Okay, strike the *vulnerable* part of that description.

"Been a little busy, Dad." Scott glanced at his brother, getting to his feet and walking out of the cubicle, presumably to continue his conversation without interference. "And Mike's been with you."

Their father grunted, his eyes drifting back closed. "True," he said, his breathing slightly labored. "I can always count on Mike."

And some things never change, Scott thought, although frankly he was too worn out—and this was neither the time nor the place—to take umbrage. "How are you feeling?"

"I've been better. But it's nothing a good night's sleep and some decent food won't cure."

"So the pain in your chest—?"

His eyes opened again. "Gone. For the most part. It's nothing, don't know why everybody's making such a fuss. They want to keep me overnight. Can you imagine?"

"I think that's called doing their job."

John Michael pulled a face. "Sticking it to my insurance company, if you ask me. I intend to fly back tomorrow, though. You'll make the arrangements, won't you? Might as well fly out from San Antonio. No sense returning to Red Rock."

Scott crossed his arms. "Don't you think you should wait to hear what the doctors have to say?"

"Flight's only two and a half hours. If need be, I'll hire a nurse to go with us. Which reminds me, how's your mother?"

That he should ask about her as an afterthought was no surprise. That it should irritate Scott so much now, when it never had before, was. "I'm about to go look in on her now. Victoria said she was pretty shaken up—"

"No surprise, there. Virginia always has been emotionally fragile."

"Dad. She just spent the night trapped in a tornado-demolished building. I think she's entitled to be a little shaken up."

His father gave him an unreadable look, then said, "Go on, tell Virginia I said to get some rest, but we're going to be on a plane tomorrow. We need to get home, dammit. And send Mike in, I need to talk to him…"

Moments later his mother greeted him with a slightly dreamy, "Oh, hello, dear," when Scott walked into her room. Leaning against the side of her bed, Scott took her good hand.

"How are you doing?"

"Better, now." She frowned at the cast on her wrist, as if not sure how it got there, then yawned. "Although whatever they gave me for the pain makes me very sleepy. And apparently—" she yawned again "—I also got a nasty bump on the back of my head. There goes next week's hairdressing appointment," she said on a sigh, then crinkled her pale forehead at Scott. "The doctor said your father and I are going to be moved upstairs, that we should stay overnight. As a precaution."

"I think that's very wise. Don't you?"

"I suppose," his mother said on another puff of air. "Although I'd rather be home. In my own bed." Virginia Alice grimaced down at the hospital gown. "Wearing my own things…oh, dear!" Her gaze shot to Scott's. "Our luggage! Whatever happened to it?"

"I don't know, to be honest. Could be in the next county, for all I know."

"I see." She thought a moment, then said, "Well, then, I suppose someone will have to pick up something for me to wear on the trip home. Since I certainly can't be seen in public in this!"

Scott smiled. "Not to worry, Victoria and I will take care of it."

Her eyes lifted to his. "Do you suppose they have size twos in San Antonio?"

"If not, I'm sure we can find a box of safety pins somewhere." When she pulled a face, Scott chuckled, then said, "And by the way, if Dad gets his way you'll be back in your own bed by tomorrow night."

Virginia smirked. "And since when has he ever not?" Then she sobered. "Any word from Jordana yet?"

"No." He squeezed his mother's hand. "Sorry."

She nodded, then pressed Scott's hand to her soft cheek. They'd gotten her cleaned up, but without makeup she looked even more frail. "Thank you for not spewing out some platitude, telling me not to worry. Worrying is what I do."

"No kidding," he said, and she softly laughed, then lowered their hands.

"You know why I do, don't you? Because your father doesn't. Or won't let himself, in any case. So I have to do his worrying as well as my own." She shrugged. "'Tis my cross to bear."

Smiling, Scott leaned over and kissed her forehead, getting a faint whiff of her familiar perfume, as though after using it for so long it was permanently embedded in her skin. "Get some rest, and I'll check in again later. As he turned to leave, however, Virginia called him back.

"Your father and I…I know how our relationship must seem to you kids at times—"

"Mom, this isn't the time—"

"I watched a woman d-die in front of me, Scotty. I thought *we* were going to die. That has a way of making you…think about things. About what matters. And what matters to me, right now, is that you and your brothers and sisters understand that, for all the…stuff your father pulls, I love him. And I know he loves me. Yes, there are times I want to smack the man senseless, for taking me for granted, for making me feel I come in a distant second to the business…"

She struggled to sit up straighter. "But I knew who he was when I agreed to marry him. Just like he knew I was a tenderhearted fool who jumped at the sight of her own shadow," she said with a smile. "I also see a side of him he refuses to show to you kids, for whatever reason. Yes, your father's the most stubborn human being on God's earth, but deep down, he's a good man who's always only wanted the best for his children. And don't you ever forget it."

Virginia sagged back against the pillows, her eyes fluttering. For a long moment Scott simply stood there, stunned, until her breathing slowed into a deep, easy rhythm—she was asleep.

Nurse Ratchet was still at her post at the nurse's station, sparing Scott the merest glance as she handed off a folder to another nurse.

"Your parents are being moved upstairs in about a half hour—"

"Not why I'm here."

She sighed. "Still can't tell you about Miss Hastings—hospital policy."

But before "Screw hospital policy" could leave Scott's lips, another nurse strode past, calling out, "Dr. Karofsky says to call County General, tell 'em we've got an orthopedic transfer."

"Name?" she barked to the other nurse as she snatched up the phone.

"Hastings. Christina."

Scott lunged across the counter to grab the phone out of her hand.

"Mr. Fortune! Don't make me call security, now—"

He waggled the phone. "I'd like to see you try," he said, and she huffed out a breath. "Why are you transferring her?" His gut twisted. "Is she…does she need some kind of special care?"

"No! She's—" Apparently realizing she'd stumbled right into his trap, the nurse sighed heavily. And held out her hand for the phone, which Scott relinquished. "She's fine. Broken foot, some bumps and scrapes, that's it. But she's uninsured. And we're a private hospital. Although we'll treat anybody who comes through that door, once they're stabilized we transfer them to a public facility. She'll be well taken care of there, I assure you—"

"She'll be taken care of right here," Scott said, yanking his wallet out of his pants pocket and throwing down his American Express card. "Consider her bills paid."

With a *Mama told me there'd be days like this* eyeroll, the nurse picked up the card, slammed it back onto the counter lip. "Then go settle it with Admitting. Right on the other side of those doors."

"Thank you." He snatched his card and stormed back to the E.R. lobby, barely stating his case to the gal behind the glass when he heard a shrieked, "Scott!" behind him. He spun around to see a breathless, disheveled Jordana rush across the lobby, an equally disheveled Tanner Redmond right on her heels, Jordana's luggage in his hands.

"Jordy! Thank God!" Scott said, all the air punched out of his lungs when Jordana threw herself into his arms, then launched immediately into a disjointed narrative about her changing her mind at the last minute and Tanner giving her a ride, except the car ended up in a ditch when he swerved to avoid flying debris, something about a shed, and the weather, that the National Guard guys who'd helped them pull the car out of the ditch had been at the airport and knew the family was here.

"Is everyone okay?" she now asked, shoving a hank of loose, stringy hair behind her ear. She was flushed and dirty and a mess and, strangely, the look suited her. An appraisal he'd keep to himself.

He quickly filled her in, then pushed out a breath. "Javier, though…"

She sucked in a breath. "He's not…?"

"He's alive, but unconscious. According to Miguel, it doesn't look good."

"Oh, Scotty, no…" Jordana's eyes filled with tears. "Is his family here yet?"

"On their way, I gather. And Mom's been worried sick about *you*."

"Oh, Lord, I can imagine. I'd better go see her…well—" Smiling, she turned to Tanner, her hand extended. "Thank you…so much. For everything."

Setting down the larger bag, Tanner frowned. "Um… you're welcome. You sure you don't need me to stick around?"

"No, really," she said, relieving him of her carry-on and grabbing the roller case's handle, jerking it up. "I'm fine. But thanks. Again."

A second later she and her luggage were gone. Scott turned to Tanner, standing with his hands in his pockets, his expression pensive but otherwise unreadable. "Thanks for looking out for my sister," Scott said. "Appreciate it."

Green eyes glanced off his. "No problem," Tanner muttered, then turned and stalked back out the door.

"Sir?" the woman behind the glass called. "I'm ready to finish up here if you are."

"Yes, of course," Scott said, returning to the window, hardly able to believe all his family obligations—for the moment, at least—were taken care of and he could finally attend to the one item on his never-ending checklist that didn't feel like an obligation at all.

In fact, what he felt as the admissions lady buzzed him

back inside the E.R., was something that felt an awful lot like…anticipation.

What a rush.

Chapter Four

Her foot splinted and Ace-bandaged within an inch of its life, Christina frowned at the nurse bustling around her. "What do you mean, you're getting me ready to go up to orthopedics? I thought I was being transferred?"

"Change of plans," she said with a bright grin.

"I don't understand, I can't afford…" She blinked back hot tears. It wasn't being poor that bothered her, it was having to tell people she was. "I know what the deal is, that y'all are only supposed to make sure I'm not bleeding to death or anything—"

"Your bill is being seen to," said the thin, pretty doctor with a Russian accent as she entered the tiny room. "So you can stay right here, all right? And you will be good as new in no time."

"Define *no time,*" Christina said, even as she tried to make sense of the first part of that message. Someone was paying her bill?

Hugging her clipboard to her flat chest, the doctor shrugged. "The breaks are not bad, so a few weeks, perhaps." When Christina groaned, Dr. Karofsky smiled. "And maybe you will be a good candidate for a walking cast. You should count your blessings," she said, her brown eyes softening. "The paramedics told me how they found you. We were worried, that your injuries would be much worse."

"I know, I'm very lucky—"

"Although you might not think so tomorrow. You still took quite the beating—you are probably going to be very sore…ah." At the sight of someone coming through the door, the doctor turned, smiling. "And here is your prince, I think." She jerked her head sideways to the nurse, and they both left, leaving Christina alone with Scott.

She flushed so hard and fast she felt like she was having heatstroke, as the memories came flooding back, about how he'd kept her talking, kept her from losing it, which naturally led to remembering The Kiss…which if she had a grain of sense she'd never think of again. Except there he was. Standing there. In the full light of day.

Yeah, good luck with that, babycakes.

"How are you—?"

"How's your family doing—?"

"They're all okay, for the most part," Scott said, yanking a metal chair around and straddling it backwards, the familiar, almost intimate position—like they were old buddies simply yakking in her kitchen—oddly unsettling. Especially since actually seeing him again only emphasized how waaaaay out of her league he was. And not only because he was a pretty boy, but his whole…bearing, the grace and ease with which he moved, how he managed to look almost regal even all messed up…

Then he smiled. A full-out, *You have no idea how glad I*

am to see you smile that started in his eyes and kept going. She half expected to hear angels sing.

"And you?" he said, still grinning like a fool, at which point it occurred to her she looked like something nasty the dog dragged in. Maybe the trauma had affected his eyesight.

"A couple of the bones in my left foot are broken," she finally got out, casually lifting a hand to tuck some of the hair that had worked out of the braid behind her ears, "and I'm banged up some. But otherwise, I guess I'm okay. Relatively."

"Do you need me to call anybody about looking in on Gumbo?"

Her heart knocked in her chest. "No…I mean, thanks, but I had one of the techs call my landlady, so it's all taken care of."

"Then he's okay?"

Christina nodded, momentarily unable to speak. "He's fine. Enid—she's my landlady—said a tree fell over, made a big mess in front of the office, some shingles got ripped off, but that was about it." Her brow puckered. "You remembered my dog's name?"

Now the smile went a little crooked. This was not going well. "You only mentioned it, oh, a dozen times or so. It stuck."

"Sorry, I guess I'm a little…attached."

"It's okay, I know the feeling."

"You have a dog, too?"

"Had. A horse. When I was a kid. His name was Blackie."

Christina snorted. "Original."

"Cut me some slack, I was only eight. And anyway he had some fancy-ass registered name I could never remember. Man, I loved that horse."

"You rode?"

"All of us took lessons, but I was the only one who stuck with it. When I left for college, though, Blackie went to live with a family with a little girl. I still miss him. Miss riding." A shadow seemed to flicker across his face before he smiled for Christina again, which made his eyes go all crinkly in the corners. God help her. "Gumbo's lucky to have you. How old is he?"

"Not real sure. He was still a pup, though, when he showed up out of nowhere one night, about five years ago. We were having this terrible storm, and suddenly through all the thunder and thrashing outside I realized there was a dog whining and scratching at my door…so I opened it and he ran right inside like he'd been waiting on me to let him in. Shook water all over me," she said with a little laugh, then sighed. "Funny thing, he happened into my life right when I needed…"

Realizing she was about to say *Someone to love me,* Christina jerked herself back to the here and now. "Is it true? That you're picking up my tab?"

His eyes latched on to hers and would not let go. "Yes."

"You didn't have to do that."

"Apparently I did, according to their rules."

"County General's okay—"

"I'm sure it is, but it's also damn inconvenient."

Christina frowned. "For who?"

"Me. Since it's hard enough to keep an eye on everybody without your being in another hospital."

Flushing again, she looked down at her lap. "Why do you think you have to keep an eye on me?"

When he hesitated, she lifted her eyes to his again, seeing in them a weird mix of confusion and determination. "I don't have to. I want to."

Apprehension pricked her skin. "Scott—"

"And you do not want to pull some pride number on me, okay? The only reason you were in that airport yesterday was because we were flying out of it."

"So you feel…responsible?" Her brow knotted again. "For something you couldn't possibly have foretold, let alone controlled?"

Their gazes locked again and she forgot to breathe. "For the tornado?" he said. "Of course not. For you?" His gaze softened. "Absolutely."

Oh, dear.

His cell phone buzzed in his pocket at the same time a tech appeared from behind the curtain with a wheelchair.

"All righty," the jovial guy said as Scott got to his feet, "time for your field trip upstairs."

"Then can I go home?"

"That, I couldn't tell you—"

"Javier's family is here," Scott said, "I need to go see them—"

Now settled in the wheelchair, Christina looked up. "Javier?"

Another shadow settled in Scott's eyes, this one far darker, and more ominous, than before. "The guy who drove some of us to the airport. My sister's brother-in-law, nicest guy you'd ever meet. He's…he's in critical condition."

"Oh, Scott…" Christina wrapped her hand around his. Words were useless, she knew. But sometimes it helped simply to know somebody cared. "I'm so sorry. Really."

Scott looked down at their joined hands, gave hers a gentle squeeze, then left.

"You part of the family, too?" the tech asked as he wheeled Christina out to the elevators.

"Not hardly. You might say fate…blew us in each other's path."

The tech chuckled. "You ask me, dude doesn't look like he's exactly unhappy about that."

So not what she wanted to hear.

Nearly as many Mendozas filled the waiting room as had been at the wedding, although obviously the mood was much more somber this time. Scott recognized Luis, Javier's father, and Javier's next youngest brother Rafe, an attorney who'd recently opened an office in Red Rock, as well as a slew of more distant relatives whose names he didn't remember. Wendy threaded her way over, shooting him a *Don't say it* look.

"Marcos is worried sick. There's no way I'm not going to be here with him. I saw the others—they went down to the cafeteria to get something to eat." Wendy glanced back over her shoulder at her father-in-law, who was sitting very still with his hands clamped to the armrests, listening to Rafe, before she led Scott a little further away. "The E.R. doctor said they've taken Javier into surgery."

"For…?"

"His legs. His head. To relieve the swelling. The doctor…he suggested the family contact their priest. Just in case." Her eyes filled. "The head wound…they're not giving any guarantees."

Muttering a curse, Scott patted Wendy's arm, then returned to the family. Javier's father stood and gave Scott a wan smile, although he looked ten years older and much grayer than he had barely a week before.

"We're very close friends with a top-notch neurologist in Atlanta," Scott said quietly. "He's the best in his field. I'm sure as a favor to the family he'd be more than willing to fly in for a consultation—"

"Thank you, son," Luis said, "but we wouldn't want to put you to any trouble—"

"It's no trouble, I assure you." He glanced at Wendy who'd come up beside him, her hand in her husband's, then back at Luis and his two other sons. "Besides, we're all family now, right?"

Smiling sadly, Luis touched Scott's arm. "You're very kind. But if you don't mind, I'd like to see what the doctors here say first."

"Of course."

At a staff member's suggestion, the family then headed off to the surgical unit's waiting room. A moment later the ambulatory Fortunes returned from the cafeteria, Emily hobbling along on crutches.

"Here," Blake said, handing Scott a white paper bag smelling of burgers and fries.

"Not hungry. But thanks."

"Take the damn food. And eat it. Or you're going to pass out. Speaking of which, we got a couple of hotel rooms nearby. The girls desperately want to get cleaned up, and honestly we're all about to collapse. Mom and Dad are both asleep, there's not much else we can do here. Mike and I had another couple of rental cars delivered so we don't have to travel in a pack—"

"You all go on ahead. I can't leave yet."

"Scott." At the sharp tone to Blake's voice, Scott frowned at his brother. "The world will manage without you long enough to catch a shower. And eat. And buy some clean clothes." He smirked. "Even you can deal with jeans and a T-shirt for a day."

Scott had to admit his brother was right—while everything was in limbo no one would miss him for an hour or so. So, burger and fries in hand, he forced himself to walk out of the E.R. doors and across the parking lot to the Escalade...where he wolfed down his food so fast he barely remembered eating it.

But instead of following the others to their hotel, or stopping to pick up clothes that didn't smell like a swamp, he drove back to the airport. Why, he wasn't sure. To convince himself it hadn't all been a bad dream? To come to terms with what had happened? Maybe.

But as he drove the fifteen miles or so along a gently rolling road that stretched out to forever, underneath a clear blue sky that stretched even farther than that, he realized what he had to come to terms with was whoever he was now. Because, for good or ill, he sure wasn't the same person he'd been a week ago.

Twenty-four hours ago.

He'd ignored *What-the-hell?* twinges, confusing and crazy, that had plagued him for the past few days—the bizarre whisperings that *this* was home. The more they'd persisted, the more firmly he'd shoved them into that dank, musty storeroom where he kept all the other *maybes* and *somedays* and *when the time is rights*.

Until a rogue tornado came along and ripped that storeroom all to hell and back, dumping all those *somedays* right smack in his face.

And with them, a pretty little gal whose raspy, wispy voice belied her steel core, whose determination to make her own somedays actually happen had shaken Scott far more than the storm.

Hell, up to that point he could have sworn he didn't even believe in love, let alone love at first sight. And yet...

And yet.

Feeling like a car commercial stunt driver as the SUV navigated the choppy terrain, Scott noticed Tanner's Jeep parked in front of the flight school building, then the man himself, walking the perimeter with his hands in his back pockets, scanning the damage. Which was more extensive than Scott had at first realized. In fact, in the almost surrealistic stillness the whole scene reminded him of a war zone photograph.

At Scott's approach, the other man offered him a nod and a grim smile befitting the bleak picture, the brim of his ball cap shadowing his eyes. "What're you doing here?" he asked mildly.

"Not sure. I think I simply needed…to see."

Tanner looked away. "I heard Sherri didn't make it."

"The flight attendant?" Tanner nodded. "Did you know her well?"

"Not really, no. I mean, we crossed paths maybe a couple times a month. Still. It's hard to take in, you know?"

"Yeah."

Tanner toed a small pile of crumbled, waterlogged masonry. Overhead a buzzard circled, hopeful and eerily graceful, like something out of a bad horror film. "How's your…family?"

"Doing okay. Dad's determined to leave tomorrow."

That got a short, dry laugh. "Yeah, your father struck me as the kind of man who wouldn't let a little thing like a tornado disrupt his plans. No wonder Jordana—" He stopped, shaking his head.

"What?"

"Nothing. By the way, I spotted some luggage in the ruins."

"You're kidding?"

"Nope. Figured you might want it. Couple of carry-ons, one larger bag. They're in my car. Would've brought it back to the hospital, but now you've saved me the trouble. Might be more," he said, leading Scott back to where he was parked, "but that's what I could get to." He helped Scott tote the bags back to the rental, then stuck out his hand to firmly shake Scott's.

"Y'all have a safe trip," he said, then strode back to his own vehicle, and Scott took a deep breath, a breath full of clean, sweet Texas country air, and simply…let go, giving in to something far more powerful than his own will.

Or even, he thought with a wry smile as he climbed back behind the wheel, his father's.

It always surprised Christina, on the rare occasions when she saw her mother, how disconnected they were. Like they weren't related at all. And frankly she wasn't even sure why she'd called Sandra, told her what had happened. She was even less sure why her mother'd come. Especially since Sandra had made it more than plain from the moment she walked into Christina's room that not only was her boss at the restaurant where she worked as a hostess, a job she'd held on to, according to her, "for security," even after her remarriage—not happy about her leaving early, but that she couldn't stay because she needed to get back to Houston ASAP. Probably to fix Helpless Harry—Sandra's husband, although not Christina's stepfather by any stretch of the imagination—his supper.

"But…I could use some help getting home," Christina said. "Since you're here and all."

"Oh." Sandra checked her watch. Something flashy. Christina was guessing Harry had Money. Taste, no. Money, yes. Then blue eyes rimmed with far too much eyeliner met Christina's. Her mother had been pretty, once upon a time, blond and cute and curvy. And she still was, on a good day, in the right light. Hospital fluorescents, however, were not kind to older women with penchants for fake tans and frosted lipstick. Her all-black outfit wasn't helping, either. "But…if I hadn't come, what would you have done?"

After Christina's father walked out—there'd been some talk of Christina's being a "surprise," that her father had only married Sandra out of guilt—Sandra hadn't exactly embraced single motherhood with grace and fortitude. Oh, she'd done her best, Christina never doubted that. Unfortunately, her "best" hadn't been very good.

"Never mind," Christina said, even though she had no earthly clue what to do. She didn't have cab fare, if she could even find a driver willing to haul her all the way to Red Rock. And her seventy-eight-year-old landlady didn't drive anymore. At least not that Christina knew about. She supposed she could call Jimmy, her boss, for a ride, but the very thought made her skin crawl. Recently divorced, Jimmy was a lonely man. A fact which he took great pains to impress upon Christina every chance he got.

"Oh, now, I'm sure you'll figure out something," her mother said. "You always do. Here," she said, upending a used Walmart bag onto the end of Christina's bed. Out tumbled a pair of blindingly purple Spandex capris and a badly pilled, black and silver sweater, along with a pair of underpants—at least three sizes too large—and a stretched-out camisole top. "I brought you some clothes, like you asked. But I didn't figure there was any point in bringing one of my bras—it would be way too big for you. Don't bother returning them, it's all stuff from the Goodwill pile, anyway."

Christina stared at the clothes, closer to tears now than when she'd thought she might die. Which at the moment seemed preferable to wearing these clothes. She never asked, or expected, anything from her mother, but just this once—since, you know, she *had* cheated death and all—would it have killed the woman to drop a few bucks for a pair of Hanes sweats or something? Some new underwear in Christina's size—?

"Oh, good—you're still here! They said at the nurses' station you were being discharged."

She looked up to see a grinning—and cleaned-up, she noticed—Scott, precariously hanging onto a potted plant, a ridiculously large stuffed hound dog, a box of candy and a helium-bloated "Get Well!" balloon in about a thousand eye-popping colors, bobbing up near the ceiling.

And her heart stuttered.

"And who is this?" her mother asked, her nostrils flaring like a bloodhound catching a scent.

"Mama, this is Scott Fortune. He…he and his family were also in the airport when the tornado hit. Scott, this is my mother, Sandra."

Somehow he shifted all the offerings into his left arm to shake her mother's hand. "Do you live in Red Rock?"

"Oh, good Lord, no. Not anymore. Been in Houston for several years now." Then her eyes narrowed. "Fortune? Related to the Red Rock Fortunes?"

"Distantly, yes." Scott set the plant on Christina's rolling food tray, handed her the dog. "I'm from the Atlanta branch of the family."

"I see," Sandra said, her voice frosting, and Christina's face warmed. Especially when her mother shot her an all-too-familiar look. "So your family will be returning to Atlanta, I suppose?"

"Tomorrow, if all goes well," he said, and Christina breathed a sigh of relief, that he was leaving, taking her inappropriate feelings with her. Because the last thing she needed was some rich dude who kissed like he invented it and brought her stuffed hound dogs. And dumb balloons.

"Well, honey," her mother said, "you take care of yourself," and vanished, leaving Christina wondering exactly who else she thought was going to.

Witnessing the obvious lack of affection between Christina and her mother, Scott realized he'd take his mother's obsessive worrying about her children any day. At least she *cared.*

But if her mother's aloofness—she hadn't even kissed her daughter goodbye, he realized—hurt Christina, she didn't let on. That is, until she gave Scott a bright smile that was so fake it made his chest ache. "What's this all about?"

"I couldn't decide what you'd like."

Blushing, she cuddled the stuffed dog to her hospital-gowned chest, her gaze fixed on the top of its head as she fingered the soft plush. "You know, you're not obligated to bring me presents just because…we, um, kissed."

The barest hint of melancholy in her voice turned him inside out. As though people didn't give her gifts very often. Or kissed her.

"Actually," Scott said as he eased himself onto the edge of her bed, "if I think a woman's worth kissing, I think she's worth at least flowers. Or a box of candy."

"Or a stuffed animal?"

"She has to be *really* special to warrant one of those."

Suddenly, she met his gaze, mischief tangoing with the wistfulness in her blue, blue eyes. A very strange, and oddly appealing, combination. "The kiss was that good?"

"*Amazing* is the word that comes to mind."

"Oh, stop," she said on a cute little giggle. Then she set the dog aside, patting it as if saying goodbye. "You're very sweet. But you didn't have to get me anything at all. Let alone half the gift shop. Also—" she sighed "—I have no idea how I'm gonna get all this stuff home."

"Then I guess I'll have to take you."

Her eyes shot to his. "I can't let you do that. You've got your family to think about—"

"All under control," he said, adding when she opened her mouth to protest, "Really. My parents are quite safe here for the night, and the others have hotel rooms. Strange as it might sound, nobody needs me."

Christina stared at her lap for what seemed like forever, then picked up the box of chocolates, slipping one finger underneath a seam in the cellophane and carefully peeling it away. "I wish I could say I don't, either. Need you, I mean." The box open, she carefully selected a piece of candy, popped it into her mouth, then held the box out to Scott, who declined. "Oh, right. You don't like sweets." She shrugged. "More for me, then."

Genuinely bewildered, Scott folded his arms. "I don't understand."

"About why I wish I didn't need you? I don't expect you to. So…I'm simply going to say thank you for the gifts—I'm crazy about chocolate, as you can probably tell—and for offering to take me home. Since I hadn't figured out how I was going to get there. Although…" Her forehead creased. "Fair warning—my place…it's nothing special."

"And why on earth would I care about that?"

"Because, well…we're not exactly talking Ethan Allen here."

Remembering his Atlanta decorator's horrified expression when he'd proudly shown her the Ethan Allen sofa he'd picked out all by himself for his condo's living room, Scott smiled. To Christina, Ethan Allen clearly had a different connotation than to dear Aileen, to whom Ethan Allen reeked of *bourgeois*. Poor woman never had recovered.

"I'm sure it's fine. But couldn't your mother have taken you?"

"Apparently not. And now I need you to leave so I can get dressed." She grimaced at the strange assortment of clothes piled on the bed, picking up the shiny, lurid purple…things. "Although *dressed* might be overstating it."

Chuckling, Scott left her to it. But he'd no sooner shut her door behind him than his phone buzzed—a text from Wendy: In OR waiting room. Dr here. Where r u?

On my way, he texted back.

Twenty minutes later, Scott stood on the hospital's rooftop deck, his phone clamped to his ear. He'd caught Dr. Rhodes as the man was about to leave for the very gala the Fortunes were supposed to be hosting. Scott succinctly relayed what Javier's surgeon had said about his case—that they'd operated to relieve the pressure, were keeping him in a medically induced coma until the swelling subsided—then released a sigh.

"They're not even being 'cautiously optimistic.'"

"Understandable, given the circumstances. Although obviously I can't comment, not being familiar with the case—"

"That's why I'm calling. To see if you'd consider flying out—on our dime, of course—to see Javier yourself."

"Damn, Scott…I'm sorry. With my schedule that would be very tricky. But you said San Antonio Memorial?"

"Yes."

"Liz Cuthbert's head of neurology there, as I recall. We did our residency together a million years ago. She's excellent, trust me. In fact, if I ever needed a neurologist, I'd want it to be Liz. I swear. Look…what I can do is give her a call, make sure she's aware of the case. And I'll be glad to consult by phone, if Liz thinks it's warranted. But your friend is in very good hands already. And their rehabilitation facilities are second to none."

"If you're sure…"

"Couldn't be more so. Can't promise miracles—I learned a long time ago that way lies madness—but I can promise you if any team could pull him through, it's that one. But, from the sounds of it, you all are damn lucky things weren't a lot worse. Please give my best to your parents, won't you?"

Marginally reassured, Scott slipped his phone back inside his pocket and returned downstairs to check on his parents. His mother was overjoyed to be reunited with her luggage, especially her carry-on with her jewelry.

"Jewelry can be replaced, Mom," Scott said, as she pawed through the various pieces with her good hand, her eyes alight.

"And if I'd bought it for myself, I'd completely agree with you. But your father gave me each and every one of these. And that can't be replaced. And yes, I know he probably had his PA pick out half the pieces—"

Try all of them. But whatever.

"—but in his case, it really is the thought that counts. Especially since I know he's never bought jewelry, personally or otherwise, for any other woman. Except for your sisters, of course," she added with a smile.

That much was true, at least, although his mother's conviction was a testament to her faith in her husband. That, or the services of a private investigator. Still, for all his father's faults—his workaholic tendencies, his emotional detachment—he'd never cheated on his wife. And not, Scott knew, for lack of opportunity, since he'd witnessed firsthand his father rebuff any number of all-too-eager, would-be successors to his mother. And with, as far as Scott could tell, not even a trace of regret.

Oh, yeah, his father had left broken hearts strewn all over Atlanta. But his mother's was not one of them.

As if on cue, John Michael appeared at the doorway to his wife's room, the only man on earth who could manage to still look dignified in a faded hospital gown and wrinkled cotton robe. "I asked the nurse to bring my meal in here so we could eat together," he said, and his mother beamed.

"What a good idea!" She giggled, her loose hair around her face making her look like a girl again. "I ordered the fish. How about you?"

"The same." With a heavy breath, he took the chair beside her bed, his mouth curving at the sight of the jewelry. "Got you that bracelet when Emily was born, as I recall."

"You did indeed," his mother said, her "told you" gaze sliding to Scott's.

Perhaps it wasn't as difficult as he'd thought to understand what bound them to each other. After all, there was a lot to be said for simply knowing the other person would never leave you.

Which he supposed began, he mused as he left his mother's room and started the long trek back downstairs where—he hoped—Christina was waiting, with finding someone you never wanted to leave.

Chapter Five

By the time Scott returned, Christina had had some time to think over a few things, not the least of which was to wonder what on earth had prompted her to apologize for where she lived. It was what it was, she was who she was, and since he was leaving the next day, anyway, what the heck difference did it make?

"Turn left at the light, then keep on to the end of the road."

Scott glanced over at her, his brow drawn. "How're you doing?"

"Just dandy." She glared at the lovely, knee-high contraption she was sporting, courtesy of the House of Frankenstein. Which hadn't seemed so bad while she was still in the hospital. Out here in the wild, however, especially when she factored in the crutches…

"If it's any consolation," Scott said, "I broke my foot my senior year of high school." A grin pushed at the corners of his mouth. "And please don't ask how. My brothers still won't let me live it down. But anyway, I had the boot, the crutches, the whole nine yards. In my case, for eight weeks." He sighed. "So much for that track season."

"You ran?"

"Not that year, I didn't. I did, however, make straight As. Since there wasn't a whole lot else I could do other than study. And play Nintendo. Although I have to admit…" The grin spread. "There were certain…advantages."

"Ah. As in, pretty girls falling all over themselves for the privilege of lugging your backpack around?"

"More than could be numbered."

Christina sputtered a laugh, only to feel her eyes sting. Because in her case there would be no entourage eager to fetch and carry and wait on her. Oh, her landlady would certainly help out, but Enid had her own life, and there was only so much she could do. All her old friends had either moved or married and had their hands full with husbands and houses and little kids…

The stinging spread to the back of her throat, forming a lump. How on earth was she going to manage, with no car, no job, this blankety-blank cast…?

When a renegade tear slid down her cheek, Christina dug in her purse—which one of the rescuers had amazingly found in the rubble nearby—for a tissue to blow her nose, hoping Scott wouldn't notice.

"Hey," he said, and she thought, *So much for that.*

"What?"

"It's going to be okay."

"Sure."

"I mean it—"

"You have no idea what I'm facing, Scott," she said, his equanimity suddenly irritating the very life out of her. "None. And since you don't, you have no right to tell me everything's going to be okay. You don't know that. *I* don't know that. So please—spare me the platitudes."

Silence stretched between them until he said, "I take it reality just hit?"

She snorted. "Like a ton of bricks. Sorry."

"No apology necessary. Nice to see you're human, after all. But…you don't think I'd understand what you're going through?"

"Not a whole lot, no."

"Because…?"

"Because that hospital bill you took care of without a blink? Would've taken me years to pay off—"

"Which is maybe why I paid it?"

"And I'm grateful, I really am. But it only points out how different we are. That you're so used to things coming easy for you there's no way you could even begin to comprehend what life is like for the rest of us peasants. Now you've done your good deed you can tuck yourself into your thousand-count Egyptian sheets at night with a clear conscience…what are you doing?"

Gravel sprayed as he yanked the car off to the side of the road by somebody's pasture. In the distance, by a stand of trees, a half-dozen fat and sassy horses grazed. The engine cut, Scott twisted to face her, his left hand gripping the steering wheel, the anger in his eyes boring straight through her.

"Hopefully setting you straight." His gaze darkened. "I work hard for my money, Christina. I've earned it. As has my whole family. And I'm not going to apologize for it, or them, or pretend this isn't who I am because it offends you." When she turned away, her face hot, he said, "I know you're scared, Christina—"

"I'm not—"

"Don't even give me that. Right now you're like a

wounded animal backed into a corner, lashing out at me not because I have money, but because you're afraid I'm somehow going to make things worse. Not that I blame you. You don't know me from Adam, for one thing. And, for another, no matter what I say you're going to think I'm patronizing you. Which irritates me no end, but I get it. *However,*" he said when her eyes cut back to his, "I didn't pay your bill, or offer you a lift, so I could check them off some hypothetical 'good deeds' list."

Christina broke free of that penetrating gaze to look out the windshield. "Then why—?"

"Because I *like* you, dammit. Is that so hard to believe?"

"Why?" she said again, more softly.

"I don't know, maybe because you're *likable?*" he said, adding, when her eyes bugged out of her head, "But the why is immaterial. The point is, there's no way I'm leaving you in the lurch. You're going to need help, honey. And I'm going to make sure you get it. Because that's how I roll."

After a brief but intense conscience-grappling session—although why she should feel guilty about accepting whatever assistance he could give, she had no idea—Christina blew out a long, shaky sigh. "You must think I'm a few sandwiches short of a picnic."

"No," Scott said with a sigh as he pulled back onto the highway. "I've dated crazy before. Trust me, you don't even come close. But I do wish you'd judge me by what I do. Not what I am. That you'd simply…give me a shot."

She could feel her heart beat throbbing at the base of her throat. "At…what?"

"Well, to begin with…how about the chance to prove I'm a human being and not a stereotype?"

"Oh, Lord…" Christina lifted one hand to her flaming face. "I deserved that, didn't I?"

"'Fraid so, petunia," he said with a light laugh, then glanced over. "So do we have a deal?"

"Sure," she said, since, at the moment, it didn't appear she had much choice. Although whether Scott was her guardian angel, or she'd just made a pact with the devil, remained to be seen.

She was an odd little duck, that was sure. His entire adult life Scott never been able to tell if women were interested in him or his bank account—a major reason why he'd never let himself fall in love, most likely. Christina, on the other hand, almost seemed afraid of his money. Or, at the very least, found it suspect.

Go figure.

"It's right up there—you can't miss it."

Gravel from the disintegrating blacktop crunched under the wheels as he pulled into the parking lot. "You live in a motel?" he said, regretting the question the instant it left his mouth.

"*Used* to be a motel," Christina said. Almost cheerfully, as though maybe that air-clearing a few miles back had done some good. One could hope. "Since, as you may have noticed, this is no longer a through road, about twenty years ago Enid—that's my landlady—and her husband Eddie converted it to apartments. After a fashion."

Scott's gaze swung to the murky, leprous hole in the ground in front of the units. "I take it the pool is no longer in service."

"Not since I've been here. I'm up at the far end, by the way. No extra charge for the second window."

"Good deal."

"I thought so."

He parked in front of her unit. The architecture was strictly midcentury Minimalist—varicosed stucco walls, plain brown numbered doors, slider windows, a flat roof. A five-foot overhang sheltered the cement slab "porch," dotted with a couple of banged-up molded plastic chairs, a kid's lower-rider tricycle, a cheap charcoal grill.

A scene that by rights should have been unrelentingly dismal. Except for the occasional wind chime or sparkly porch ornament, a glittery Christmas garland entwining one of the porch posts, a wreath of bright red poinsettias on one door. And, lining the entire edge of Christina's allotment of porch real estate, pot after pot of multicolored pansies, bravely shivering in the cool breeze.

"Home is what you make it, you know," she said, as if seeing the picture through his eyes.

"I couldn't agree more."

He got out to help her from the car, saw her bite her lip as she fitted the crutches under her arms. "Lean on your hands."

"That hurts, too."

"I know. But this will hurt less. Trust me."

"Say that enough times," she grumbled, hobbling to her door, "I might eventually believe you."

After several obviously frustrating moments trying to juggle her purse, her keys and the crutches, Scott took the keys to unlock her door—behind which he heard very excited whining and scratching.

"Should I be worried?" Scott asked as the lock tumbled.

"Only if you're in the way."

He pushed the door open, barely avoiding the four-legged torpedo that shot out, a bow-legged, stout-bodied, floppy-eared canine concoction whose sole purpose was to love, love, love. Laughing, Christina practically threw down the crutches to somehow lower herself to the porch, where she wrapped her arms around the wriggling mass of unbridled bliss, burying her face in his golden brown ruff.

Scott sternly told himself it was stupid to be jealous of a dog. Okay, maybe not jealous. Envious?

Still dumb.

"Hey, guy—gotta pee?" A question that apparently ratcheted up the excitement factor another level or two, before, with a joyful woof, the pooch bounded like a jackrabbit for the stand of trees a few feet away and did his thing.

"Tough little dude," Scott observed.

"Yup. Like a gymnast. Lots of power in a small package."

Gumbo sauntered back, grinning like he was hot stuff, the tail wagging the entire dog. Then he seemed to notice Scott, schlurping his tongue into his mouth and cocking his head, his furry forehead furrowed before he sidled back to Christina. Scott could have sworn the dog nodded in Scott's direction as if to say, *So who's the dude?*

Still on her rump on the porch, Christina lifted her eyes to Scott. "Sorry. I don't bring…visitors here very often—"

"Ohmigosh, you're back!"

Scott no sooner hauled Christina to her feet than a scrawny redhead in a flowered housecoat, a bright orange down vest and a pair of scuffed-up sneaker clogs grabbed Christina out of Scott's grasp and into her own. For a moment he feared for Christina's rib cage. The woman barely came up to Christina's chin and had arms like a plucked chicken, but that was one fierce hug. Then she let go, her painted claws clamped around Christina's elbows as she scrutinized her from head to broken foot. "Lord, child, where did you get those clothes?"

"My mother. 'Nuff said. Scott, this is my landlady, Enid Jackson. Enid, this is Scott Fortune. Scott and I…got trapped together in the same part of the airport. After the tornado."

From behind a pair of burgundy glasses that had been cutting-edge ten years ago, Enid's beady gray eyes latched on to his like a burr to a dog's underbelly.

"Fortune? As in the family that owns half the ranchland in these parts?"

"Distant cousins. But yes."

Arms crossed underneath where her bosom should have been, the old woman studied him for what seemed like an eternity, then gave a sharp nod. "Thank you for bringing my girl home. I would've come to get her myself, but my sight ain't what it used to be. In fact..." Her carefully drawn eyebrows plunged as her gaze swung to Christina. "I don't suppose you're gonna be doing much driving for the next little while."

"No," Christina said on a sigh. "And not only because of my foot. Ellie Mae...they told me she didn't make it."

When Enid softly groaned and again took Christina into her arms, Scott wondered if the storm had claimed another victim he wasn't aware of, until Enid said, "She was a good old car. I'll miss her."

"Yeah. Me, too. Now if you don't mind...I need to get inside and put my foot up."

Not waiting for an invitation, Scott simply gathered Christina's things from the car and carted them in behind her. Enid had gone ahead and was helping her settle onto the plain beige sofa at right angles to a slightly lopsided taupe recliner, the once-plush fabric worn shiny on the arms. The room looked pretty much as he'd expected, the few pieces of furniture dull and threadbare, cheap fake pine paneling smothering the walls, the appliances in the bare-bones kitchenette chipped and scarred and sorry.

You deserve so much better than this, he thought, appalled in spite of himself. And humbled, as he realized how much greater her struggle to leave even the tiniest scratch on the world, let alone a mark, was than his had ever been. No wonder she resented his life and its relative ease. Yes, he worked hard, not only to support his very comfortable lifestyle but also to overcome the trust fund baby stigma. For damn sure he wasn't a slacker. Still, Christina was right—he'd never, not once in his entire life, worried about money.

Or had to live like this.

And yet…the banged-up appliances gleamed, he noticed. Bright prints obliterated much of the tacky paneling. A cheerful patchwork quilt gently hugged the back of the bland sofa. On a stubby little table, a small fake Christmas tree proudly shimmered in a patch of late-afternoon sunlight pouring through the window. The *spotless* window. And against one wall, cinder block-and-board shelving bowed under the weight of hundreds of books.

What Christina lacked in means, he realized, she more than made up for in spirit. And that spirit, her spirit, permeated the small space with something the best decorator in the world couldn't supply, easing inside him as importunately as Gumbo—now wedged on the sofa beside his mistress—nudged at Christina's hand until, laughing, she scratched his head.

Questioning blue eyes lifted to his, a slight smile curving her lips. Behind her, Enid fussed over something in the kitchenette. "You don't have to stay, you know. And your family must be wondering what happened to you."

"I suppose I should check in on them. Especially since they're all leaving in the morning."

Her hand stilled in the dog's fur. "They? Aren't you going with them?"

"No. I—" He stopped, having no idea what to say. How to explain something he didn't yet fully understand himself. "Will you be all right for a while?"

"You're coming back?"

"Soon as I take care of a few things, yes." He met Enid's very astute gaze. "Can you keep an eye on her for a couple of hours?"

"You bet. Especially since I'm guessing our girl's about to pass out, anyway."

"Just go on and talk about me like I'm not here," Christina said, yawning and tugging the quilt off the sofa's back, snuggling underneath it with her dog.

He glanced back when he reached the door. She was already asleep, Gumbo's head protectively propped on her thigh, the dog's big brown eyes clearly saying *Mess with her and you're dead meat. Got it?*

Yeah. He got it.

John Michael glowered at Scott from the high-backed upholstered chair in his hospital room. "Don't be ridiculous. Of course you're coming back with us."

His arms folded across his chest, Scott stared his father down. "No, I'm not. Someone needs to stay to keep tabs on what's going on with Javier, for one thing—"

"You can keep tabs every bit as easily from Atlanta."

"This isn't a business deal, Dad. This is Wendy's brother-in-law. Family." Wendy, who at the staff's insistence had gone home to rest, had updated him on the phone shortly after Scott left Christina's. Javier had come through both the orthopedic and neurological procedures as well as could be expected, but now the wait-and-see part of things began. "The family's so stressed…if I can help in any way, I'd like to."

His father pushed out a heavy breath. "But your work—"

"Nothing Mike can't handle for a few days."

John Michael's heavy brows lifted. "So *now* you're sharing? And don't give me that look. You two have been like two dogs fighting over the same bone since you were babies."

"I didn't think you realized—"

"The competition between you?" His father barked out a short laugh. "Who do you think fostered that rivalry? And why wouldn't I? It made both of you work harder, didn't it?"

Not that Scott hadn't suspected as much for years. Still, hearing it voiced… "In other words, you sacrificed your own sons' relationship for the business."

"Oh, don't be so damn melodramatic. The family, the business…it's all the same thing." His father lifted his hands, the fingers tightly linked. "All *one* thing." His hands dropped back into his lap, then he sighed. "I suppose you're right, though. About staying around for Javier. For Wendy's sake. No need to upset her any more than she already is. Now what was the second thing?"

"The second thing?"

"You said *for one thing*—meaning Javier—from which I deduced there's another reason you want to stay. So what is it?"

He hadn't planned on telling his father about Christina—especially not before he had it sorted out in his own head—but there was nothing to be gained from not being honest. To a point.

"The young woman I was trapped with—Christina. Her foot's broken, meaning she's going to be laid up for some time. I don't feel…it's right to leave before I make sure she's taken care of."

His father frowned. "She doesn't have family? Friends?"

"Her support system is apparently pretty meager. Nor can she afford nursing care."

"And she knows you're a Fortune."

"Well, yes, obviously she does. Although she hasn't

asked for anything, I assure you," he said to his father's *Watch out* frown. "But the least we can do is make sure she's okay. And since I'm hanging around for Javier, anyway…"

"One week, Scott," his father said, jabbing his index finger in Scott's direction. "You make sure this…Christina has whatever she needs, then you get your butt back where it belongs. Is that clear?"

"Perfectly," Scott said, knowing, as he left his father's room, that he wasn't going to feel any differently in a week than he did right now…that there was something here he needed. Something he'd risk everything he'd ever known, ever been, to get.

He doubted his father would ever understand. But for the first time in his life, Scott thought as he climbed behind the steering wheel, right now he didn't much care.

At the purr of Scott's rental car pulling up in front of her apartment, Gumbo bounded off Christina's lap and boing-boinged across the floor to the front door to sniff and whine and wag until Scott let himself in. Two days, two years, whatever, it made no difference to a dog—they were now friends for life.

"Hey, guy—no, this isn't for you, so back off." Gumbo now in retreat—for the moment—Scott grinned over at Christina, holding his prize aloft, and her heart boing-boinged worse than the dog. Which was getting to be a habit. A very, very bad one.

"How're you feeling?"

"Better," she lied. The doctor had been dead-on about how sore she'd be. Her foot didn't even hurt that much anymore, but man, every muscle in her body ached. Since she didn't want to get too cozy with the big-gun pain meds, however, she'd been popping Tylenol like there was no tomorrow. Not that it helped much.

"Have you been moving, as the doctor suggested?"

She glared at Scott. "You bet. What's in the bag?"

"Dinner. From Red. Some new chicken dish Enrique came up with. You hungry?" he said, heading into the tiny kitchen for plates and flatware while holding a nonstop, one-sided conversation with the dog. This person who'd been waiting on her hand and foot since his family's return to Atlanta was definitely not the same uptight dude who'd flinched at the idea of drinking plain coffee…a metamorphosis she'd been observing with a combination of amusement and sheer terror.

Because let's be real here, boys and girls—she could like this new, improved Scott Fortune a whole lot. Yes, even more than she'd liked the old one. Not good. Especially since she figured he probably saw her as some sort of, well, charity project.

"Sure," she said, even though she rarely felt like eating much, what with her only exercise these days being getting up to pee every few hours or point the remote. Whoopee.

Humming, he carted in their food, setting hers on the TV tray that had become a permanent fixture beside the sofa, and the light from the lamp played across his handsome face, provoking all sorts of prickles of a sexual nature. Which only went to prove that God did indeed have a very strange sense of humor.

"I hate this," she muttered.

Scott frowned. "You haven't even tasted it yet."

"No, I mean *this*." She waved her hand toward her foot, stretched out in front of her underneath one of her long summer skirts, which were easier to deal with than jeans. "I'm not incapacitated, I can walk with the crutches—"

"After a fashion. And you also know if you don't keep the foot elevated it will take longer to heal."

"Are you always this irritatingly logical?"

"Yes. Are you always this argumentative?"

"Only around irritatingly logical people," she grumbled, hefting her fork to begin her nightly ordeal of picking at her food. Except when she finally put a bite into her mouth, she practically swooned. "Ohmigosh, this is good."

"Told ya," Scott said, his crisp, upscale khakis, deep blue dress shirt and la-di-da sweater—part of the haul overnighted from various online clothing companies to replace his lost luggage—so at odds with the poor old recliner it almost hurt to look at him. Them. "I called a medical supply company, by the way. Said they'd have a shower chair delivered in the next couple of days."

"I'll make sure I'm here, then," she said drily, only to then notice half her food was already gone. Wow.

"So," Scott said, looking all relaxed and whatnot in the chair. As opposed to Gumbo, who was about to quiver his fur right off at the prospect of something, anything, falling off Scott's plate and into his mouth. "You up for taking down the tree tonight?"

Christina's gaze swerved to her little tree, still valiantly twinkling away in the corner. "Or I could simply let it stay up until next year, save the trouble of doing it all over again."

"I did that one year. When I was, I don't know...eight or nine, maybe? We were all allowed to have a tree in our rooms, if we wanted. And that year I decided to decorate mine with action figures. GI Joes and He-Man stuff, mostly. Coolest tree ever," he said, chewing. "Couldn't bear to take it down. So I didn't."

"Ever?"

"Might still be there, for all I know," he said, and she laughed. Then she sighed.

"It is tempting, to leave it up. But if I do, what've I got to look forward to next year?"

Setting his plate on the floor—to Gumbo's unbridled joy—Scott propped his elbow on the arm of the chair to rest the side of his face in his hand. "You really see yourself in the same place next year? In your life, I mean?"

His question caught her up short. "I…don't know. I hadn't thought about it."

"Then maybe you should," he said softly, rising to take her plate, as well as his dog-slimed one, to the kitchen.

"No," she said to his back, making him turn. "No, you're right…of course I don't see myself in the same place."

His smile warmed her heart. And scared the heck out of her. Nobody ever paid this much attention to her, ever. Or cared two hoots about her plans. Her dreams. To be treated like a grown-up, and an intelligent one at that…

"Good girl," he said, then pointed to the tree, one eyebrow raised.

Christina nodded, sighing as Scott began to dismantle it, handling the cheap ornaments like they were precious heirlooms.

Just like he's handling you, she thought, stifling a sudden urge to throw something at the man.

Scott had meant what he'd said—to his father, about feeling a responsibility to help Christina; to Christina, about genuinely liking her. Nor could he deny the immediate *whoosh* of attraction, off-the-wall though that had been. However, if he were being honest, another thought had niggled, that those feelings would pass. That the mist of infatuation would clear and he'd see Christina as simply a sweet, very pretty young woman who could use a helping hand. Period.

Four days on, he was pretty sure he could put that worry to rest.

Especially since he'd seen Christina at her worst, during those four days—frustrated and cranky and given to periodic bouts of pure muleheadedness just for the heck of it, as far as he could tell. Once or twice she'd even snarled at him. But was he put off?

Nope.

And how could he be, when she'd also laugh at herself for being such a pain in the butt. Or compliment his cooking skills, such as they were, with a sparkle in her eyes that turned him inside out. Or ask him what courses he thought she should take to help her reach her goals. And with every laugh, every tease, every sparkle, the mist cleared a little more, leaving Scott even more convinced that while adrenaline and testosterone might have fueled that initial, kick-to-the-head reaction, neither accounted for what he was feeling now.

What the next step was, however, was anybody's guess.

He'd spent most of the day putting out metaphorical fires Mike couldn't, or didn't want to, handle back in Atlanta. Now he pulled up in front of Christina's apartment, making a mental note to research an outfit that could fix that pool. Enid's insurance would take care of the tornado damage, but he was guessing the pool had fallen victim to insufficient cash flow. That, he could handle…

He saw Christina's curtains twitch as he got out of the car, a bouquet of flowers in hand. A moment later the landlady came out onto the porch, silently shutting the door behind her and huddling inside a heavy cardigan against the night's chill. They'd only chatted a couple of times since Scott brought Christina home, but now the old woman's protective, suspicious expression, even in the jaundiced light from the caged bulb over the door, put him on alert.

"I'm just leaving, I think my hanging around was making her twitchy," Enid said with an eyeroll behind the glasses. "But she's already had supper, dog's been fed, too."

"Thank you—"

"So what's your deal with her, anyway?"

"Pardon?"

The old woman snagged his arm—with a far stronger grip than he'd expected—and tugged him out into the parking lot, where she crossed her arms over her bony chest and somehow managed to back him against his own car.

"Mr. Fortune, not that I'm not appreciative of everything you've done for Chrissie, but you need to know…that gal's been through the mill. Been screwed over too many times by too many people. That she's as sweet as she is, is nothing short of a damn miracle. So you feel sorry for her, or what?"

"As in, pity her? No. Do I think she deserves better than life's given her so far? Absolutely." He palmed the car's fender. "I take it you don't have a problem with that?"

"Depends."

Scott suppressed a grin. Barely. A lesser man—or a smarter one, perhaps—would be halfway to the hills by now. "Mrs. Jackson—I promise you I only want to help. And I can give her whatever she needs—"

"Oh, I imagine you can *buy* her plenty. But before you go bandying around the word *give,* you might want to think about what that really means."

Okay, that gave him pause. Because…did he? Know how to give in the way she meant it?

"Are you saying she's fragile?"

"Oh, hell, no. Gal's as tough as they come. She's had to be, you know? That don't mean she might not mistake your...kindness for something more. That she can't still be hurt. That she's not still hurting. And I'm not talking about her foot."

"I didn't think you were—"

"I love that little gal like she's my own, and that's the Lord's truth. More'n her own mama ever has, from everything I can tell. So the last thing I want is for some fancy man to come along and break her heart all over again. Do I make myself clear?"

"Perfectly. Are we done here?"

"No." Enid backed up, barely, her eyes pinched nearly closed. "I ain't never been rich, Mr. Fortune. But I cleaned houses for enough wealthy families over the years to come to a conclusion or two about 'em. Either they pretend the poor don't exist, or they're curious about us, like we're a different species. Christina don't need you being *fascinated* with her, that's all I'm saying."

Scott pulled in a deep, steadying breath through his nose. Even though her sentiments weren't far off from the very thoughts he'd been wrestling with, they still rankled. "Mrs. Jackson," he said quietly, "my mother drilled it into all our heads from the time we were babies that people are people, that who they are isn't defined by what they have. Or don't have. I'll admit, I am fascinated, because I've never known anyone like her. But when I say that, I'm talking about her character. Who she is. Not *what* she is. Do I make *my* point clear?"

Several seconds passed before a soft cackle fell from Enid's shapeless, wrinkled mouth. "I guess you do at that. Don't mean I'm still not keeping my eye on you."

And he thought the dog was bad. "Wouldn't have it any other way," he said with a little salute, then walked back to Christina's door, realizing he'd been gripping the flowers hard enough to practically bend the stems.

* * *

Over Gumbo's excited barking, Christina yelled, "Door's open, come on in! Dog! For crying out loud, hush!"

Scott's entrance sent Gumbo into his happy-happy-joy-joy dance, his long tail wagging so hard it was a wonder it stayed on.

"Sit," Scott commanded, and after some effort the poor animal managed to lower his wriggling butt so it hovered right above the carpet, eyes glued to Scott in rapturous adoration. To complete the look, one ear, then the other, slowly flopped out.

"That's as close as it gets," Christina said fondly. "Something about the way he's put together, he can't get his backside all the way to the ground."

Then she noticed Scott had turned his frown on her and a chill snaked through her whole body, and that was the sorry truth. Good Lord, he was big. Bigger than she remembered, frankly. Or maybe it was only that her apartment seemed smaller.

"Why're you looking at me like that?"

"Like what?" he said. Still frowning.

She sighed. "Like your little chat with Enid isn't sitting so well." The dog looked from Scott to her, figured nobody was paying attention to him—which would never do—so he sashayed over to the sofa and hopped up beside her. Wedging his sturdy little body between her hip and the cushioned back, he laid his head on her lap with a contented groan. "Those flowers for me or the dog?"

"You can share," he said, handing her the bouquet. "You heard us?"

"Your voices, yes. Not what y'all were saying." She buried her nose in the delicate lavender mums, the scent fresh and sweet, then lifted them to Scott again. "I don't even own a real vase, but you might find a jar under the sink that'll work. I take it she was doing her Rottweiler number on you?" she said as he crossed to the kitchen.

"I was thinking more along the lines of rabid Chihuahua, but yes."

"She means well," she said over the water's thrashing into a big olive jar. "And it is nice to have somebody on my side."

Scott returned with the flowers, which he set on the fabric-covered footlocker she used as a coffee table. Still standing, he pushed back his jacket, shoved his hands in his pockets. Frowned some more. "I'm on your side."

"I mean somebody who's gonna stick around."

Silence. Then: "She wanted to know what my intentions were. Toward you."

"Oh, for heaven's sake," Christina said, even as she thought, *Yeah, wouldn't mind knowing the answer to that one myself.* "She sure has the wrong end of the stick there, doesn't she? I mean, you've been real sweet and all, but—"

"But what I haven't been, is entirely honest."

"About?"

Chafing his palms together, Scott sank onto the edge of the old recliner, pushed out a short, dry laugh, then lifted his eyes to hers. "Okay…those hours we spent together in the airport…jarred something loose in my brain. *You* jarred something loose, and…I don't want to say too much, too soon—the last thing I want to do is scare you off—"

Like she had any place to go?

"—and anyway, at first I thought…well, never mind what I first thought, that's immaterial now. Because the thing is, the more time we spend together, my feelings—for you, I mean—they're becoming more…real."

Then he gave her That Look. Like the one the Jane Austen hero always gives the heroine when he finally comes to his senses.

Except that's always at the end *of the movie, you goober! Not the frickin' beginning!*

"Scott," she said when she finally found her voice. "You can't be serious. Besides the fact we met less than a week ago…I'm not even remotely your type!"

A half smile tilting his lips, he leaned back, his hands gripping the chair's arms. Nice, strong hands, she couldn't help but notice. Because she was observant like that. "Yeah, well…I've dated plenty of women who were supposedly 'my type' and have never felt…drawn to them the way I am to you."

Christina opened her mouth to argue, only to hear a little voice in her head *pssst* at her, reminding her there was no arguing with Scott Fortune. Men like that, once they made up their mind, that was it.

Except…what was it he'd made his mind up about, exactly? So he was "drawn" to her. Big whoop. Didn't mean anything would come of it. Especially since…

"May I remind you, in case it escaped your notice, that my home is here? And yours isn't?"

"Well aware of that—"

"And even if that weren't the case, I simply do not have the wherewithal right now to be in a relationship. Or even think about one. So if there's an ulterior motive behind your wanting to help out, you might want to rethink a thing or two."

He laced his hands high on his stomach, looking completely relaxed. And not the least bit perturbed. Except the steely look in his eyes sent another one of those shivers scooting up her spine.

"So Enid was right. That you've been screwed over?"

Christina's eyes narrowed. "What did she tell you?"

"Nothing more than that."

"Then let me fill in a blank or two. I was married before,

when I was very young. It ended badly. I've dated some since then, and those relationships all ended badly, too—"

"Which is why you haven't dated in two years?"

"Did kinda put me off, yeah," she said, wondering what else she'd said that night that he'd remember. And she might not. Ergh. "And I finally realized," she said, hoisting her little booty back on track, "I needed to stop trying to define myself by looking to other people. Especially the wrong people. Because until I figure out who I am, I have no earthly idea who I need. Or what I need."

He tented his fingers in front of his face. "And why do I get the feeling you're leaving out several huge chunks of the story?"

"Because it's kind of hard to break free of the past if you keep revisiting it."

"None of us can fully escape our pasts, Christina—like it or not, the past shapes who we are—"

"Not if we don't let it. The sores are healed over. For the most part, anyway. Please don't ask me to rip them open again."

They stared each other down for some moments before Scott said, "I don't give up easily."

"Then this should be interesting, because I don't give in easily. Not anymore. And I told you, my home is here."

Seconds ticked by, punctuated by another groan from Gumbo.

"You're absolutely sure of that?" Scott said at last.

"Yep. So, see?" She lifted her hands, palms up. "Pointless."

"Okay, then," Scott said, getting to his feet and heading to the door, "I'll…see you tomorrow."

Except, after he left Christina didn't feel all that relieved, truth be told.

And that made her very, very nervous.

Chapter Six

"Here," Wendy said, setting a towel-covered basket on the wrought-iron table in front of him, along with a knife and butter dish. "I made muffins."

Glancing up from his iPad, Scott smiled for his sister, her dark brown hair glowing in the morning sunlight flooding the whitewashed, glassed-in porch snuggled up against the back of her and Marcos's modest three-bedroom house in town, where he'd been bunking since the family's return to Atlanta. Apparently, the former leather-and-chrome "décor" had been centered around the big-screen TV in the living room, until she'd wrought her magic. Now Barebones Bachelor Pad was turning into a fun, funky mix of contemporary sleek and cozy cottage, as sassy and sophisticated as its new mistress.

"You spoil me," Scott said, setting down his coffee mug to pluck a still-warm pumpkin muffin from the basket. "And aren't you supposed to be off your feet?"

Air rushed from Wendy's lungs as she sat across from him, then dragged over another cushioned chair to prop up her feet, a pair of puffballs underneath her fuzzy slipper socks. It was pretty obvious she was about to go stark raving bonkers from boredom. And, Scott suspected, loneliness. After finally convincing Miguel it was okay for him to return to New York, Marcos was rarely around, between tending to his duties at Red and frequent trips to San Antonio with his father and Rafe to keep tabs on Javier. In which case, considering the shenanigans his sister *could* get up to, a baking binge was the least of their worries, her puffy ankles notwithstanding.

"Giving you breakfast is hardly spoiling you," she said. "Especially since this is the first morning I've caught you before you left again. I mean, I know you didn't hang around to keep *me* company, but still." She faked a pout, only to immediately grin. Then she grabbed her own muffin, yanking it apart like a starving urchin and slathering it with soft butter. "By rights, I should be mad at you."

Scott frowned. "For what?"

"Usurping my position as the family's black sheep."

"Nobody ever thought of you as a black sheep. A lost one, maybe," he said with a smile. "But not black."

Chewing, his sister waved one hand. "Whatever. But my point is, I was always the one voted most likely to do something crazy. Not you." She reached for the rest of her muffin. "You do know they all think you're nuts, right?"

Thinking, *Oh, just wait,* Scott leaned back in his chair, his gaze wandering outside and past their yard, to the vast, serene sky delicately veined with bare tree branches…as his thoughts wandered to that conversation with Christina, where she'd declared she'd never, ever leave Red Rock.

"They can think what they like. For the first time in my life, I feel as though things are finally making sense."

"Poor baby. You've really got it bad, don't you?" When Scott nodded, she laughed. "So you're telling me Christina is as down with…whatever this is as you are? After a week?"

"I didn't say that," he said, which got a snort from his sister. Scott glowered at her, then looked outside again. "As you said. It's only been a week. Right now I'm just in…the exploratory stage. Not anywhere near ready to sign on the dotted line."

Which was never going to happen as long as Christina kept him at arm's length, doling out bits and pieces of herself as though they were rationed. True, he might have given the impression that if she didn't want to talk about her past, that was her prerogative. And in theory he was fine with that. Except it bugged the life out of him, that she didn't trust him. Not entirely, at least. Understandable, he supposed, given the circumstances, but—

"May I say something?" When Scott faced his sister, a crease marred the otherwise smooth space between her brows. "I know you're used to making things go your way. Heck, we all are. Especially after hearing our entire lives how anything's possible if you work hard enough for it." A wry grin twisted her mouth. "Or throw enough money at it. But—and bear in mind I don't know Christina, so I could be talking through my hat—" The crease deepened. "This is a human being we're talking about. Not a business transaction. Have you considered how you're going to feel if she never…comes around?"

"What makes you think she won't?"

"What makes you so sure she will?"

Inexplicably annoyed, Scott got to his feet, grabbing his

leather jacket off the back of his chair and digging in the pocket for the keys to the SUV.

"And now I've chased you off," Wendy said, clearly amused.

"Brat," Scott muttered without heat, and she chuckled.

"By the way, have you talked to Blake since they left?"

Although still several years older than Wendy, his youngest brother and baby sister shared a special bond that had been cute as all get-out to witness when they were little. And he knew they talked nearly every day, even now. "No. Why?"

"He seems…I don't know. Different, somehow. I can't put my finger on it. So I was wondering if he'd said anything to you."

Scott shook his head. "No. Things were so crazy after the tornado I didn't really get a chance to talk to any of them. But…"

"What?"

"That experience…I doubt any of us are the same. Except for Mike," he said with a humorless laugh. "Nothing affects him. And I mean nothing. I swear, sometimes I think the man's an android."

Wendy laughed. "That would explain a lot. Oh…take the rest of the muffins to Christina, will you? Otherwise, I'll eat the whole batch. And that would be wrong."

He returned to get the basket, then met his sister's gaze, realizing with a rush how much he adored her. How much he'd like—

"Wanna meet her?"

A huge smile lit up Wendy's beautiful face. "Yes, please!" Then, on an "Oh!" she clapped her hands together. "She could help me pick out stuff for MaryAnne's nursery! Oh, don't give me that look—she's probably going as stir-crazy as I am, with her broken foot and all. And what woman doesn't like to help decorate? It'll be fun, I promise."

At the hope twinkling in his sister's eyes, he sighed. "I'll give her the message."

Leaning painfully on her crutches as Scott drove up, Christina stood on the porch watching Gumbo zigzag around the small plot of grass bordering the trees next to the complex.

"What are you doing outside?" Scott asked as he got out of the car. Completely at ease, like they'd never had that conversation. Brother.

She angled her head, squinting at him through the sun. Wondering when he was going to snap out of…whatever this was. "Drying my hair. Letting my dog do his business." Then, with a sigh, she looked back at Gumbo, sniffing in the weeds. Happy as a dumb clam. "Cleaning up after him is a bit tricky, though. Enid said she didn't mind if I let it go for a bit, it being winter and all, but I do."

Scott set the basket he was carrying—like he was Red Riding Hood or something—on the lopsided metal table by the front door, where Christina had dumped the scooper and stuff. Which he then grabbed. "I can do that—"

"Oh, no…I cannot let you clean up my dog's poop!"

"After mucking out a horse's stall? No contest."

And off he went to tend to a chore she guessed was not part of his usual routine, chatting away to the dog trotting alongside him, presumably to show him the ropes. Or whatever. Then Scott calmly disposed of the little package in the Dumpster at the end of the parking lot, looking ridiculously pleased with himself.

"Now that I'm completely mortified…" Christina mumbled as she thumped through the door. Scott washed his hands at the kitchen sink—thoroughly, she noticed—then disappeared back outside. For good, if he was smart.

But no. Because no sooner had she resumed her usual spot on the end of the sofa, her foot stretched out in front of her, than he and the dog returned with the basket. Which, no matter how he held it, made him look extremely silly.

"You really mucked out horse stalls?"

"I really did. I gather from your wet hair the chair finally arrived?"

"It did."

"So how was it?"

"The chair? Hard."

"I meant your shower."

"Awkward. But after a week of sponge baths? Glorious."

"Did your foot hurt? Without the cast, I mean?"

"A little. But I was real careful not to put any weight on it."

"Maybe you should have held off until I was here to help you."

Silence hummed between them.

"Wendy sent muffins," he said, carting the basket to the small kitchen table, then rattling around in her cupboards for plates and utensils and things. If not his dignity. "Pumpkin orange. Although she looks nearly as miserable as you do. She can't go in to work, Marcos is rarely around, and her doctor's told her to keep her feet up as much as possible until the baby comes. She's not taking it well."

The dog hopped back up beside her to stretch out on his back, paws in the air, head upside down in her lap. Like he was waiting for her to feed him grapes. "Tell her I feel her pain." Realizing Scott was watching her, she glanced up with a too-bright smile. "Bless her heart. Thank you," she said when Scott set a muffin and a glass of orange juice on the coffee table within her reach, then sat on the chair across from her. "Are we pretending everything's fine between us?"

"I wasn't aware things weren't."

"But you—"

"I know. And I apologize for spooking you. Eat your muffin. You won't regret it."

Realizing he'd given her an out, Christina picked up the muffin, pinched off a piece and popped it into her mouth, where it exploded into awesome. Except thinking about Wendy led to her asking how Javier was doing, and Scott's quiet, "No change," stirred up all the weird, unsettled feelings that had plagued her off and on for the past couple of days—even before that bizarre conversation—and killing her appetite.

When she set down the muffin, Scott reached over and touched her knee. She couldn't decide whether she wanted to smack his hand or grab it. "Hey. What's wrong—"

"I think about how scared everybody must be for him, and about that poor flight attendant..." Who he'd finally told her about a couple days before. "And here I sit, having the gall to feel sorry for myself because I'm laid up for a few weeks. It kinda puts things in perspective, doesn't it?"

He gave her a strange look. "I suppose it does."

Picking up the muffin again, she took a bite, fed a piece to the dog. "Still. It's driving me bats, that I have to let people wait on me. Do stuff I'm supposed to be doing for myself. It feels all...backwards." She sighed. "Not to mention dangerous."

"Dangerous?"

"Yeah. Because..."

"Because you don't like being waited on."

"No, I don't. I'm used to being the one doing the caring. Like with Enid. Or babysitting the neighbors' kids sometimes. That makes me feel good. This makes me feel… weird."

"And would you feel the same way if, say, it was Enid waiting on you? Or your mother?"

"Oh, honey—if it was my mother waiting on me I'd feel like I'd been warped to an alternate universe. This was the woman who'd leave the box of cereal and a cup of juice where I could reach it so she wouldn't have to get up to make me breakfast. When I was *three*."

"That's harsh."

"Whatever. It toughened me up."

"I don't think three-year-olds are supposed to be tough," he said gently, his eyes all sympathetic and whatnot, and feelings she never, ever indulged tried to do a number on her head. So she changed the subject.

"Do you have flashbacks? About what happened?"

That got another strange, pensive look, one that sent heat racing up her neck. *Oh, for pity's sake, it was just a kiss. Snap out of it!*

Never mind that was the first kiss she'd had in…a long time. Hence the hot neck. Among other things.

"No," he finally said. "Actually, it all feels pretty much like a dream."

Doesn't it just? she thought, then said, "It felt like that for me then, too," she said, shifting to get comfortable. Like that was even possible. "So I didn't realize it would come back to haunt me like this later. I think I was a lot more afraid than I realized." She smirked. "Or wanted to admit."

"You know what your problem is?"

Yeah. You.

"I'm borderline psychotic?"

"I'll take that into consideration. But I was thinking more along the lines that you need to get out of here."

"Now that's just mean."

"I'm serious." He got to his feet, a man with a plan. Eyes all lit up and everything. "Where would you like to go?"

"Anywhere but this house," she said, then shut her eyes and released a breath. "And there I go sounding bitchy again—"

"Honey, believe me. You've got many, many miles to go before you reach bitchy."

"Not as many miles as you might think," she muttered, then directed a baleful glance at her foot. "But this thing…"

"You can ride in the back of the SUV with your foot on the seat, how's that? And I'll play chauffeur—"

Terror streaked through her. That he was being too nice, that she'd get too attached, that he *would* snap out of it and/or leave…and then where would she be? "Scott, seriously, you don't have to do this—"

"Yes, I do. Now can you make it on your own or do you want me to carry you?"

She actually had to think about that for a second. Until reason returned, bless its little heart, and she said, "I'll walk. But can Gumbo come?"

Still on his back, the dog lifted his head to give Scott what Christina knew was the Starving Orphan face. "If he wants to, sure. So where do you want to go?"

"Not shoe shopping, obviously. But…how about the airport."

"Really?"

She nodded. "Gotta face the demons sometime, right? Besides, my car's still there. Or what's left of it. I need to say goodbye."

With Gumbo as his copilot, Scott navigated the meandering country highway as it sliced through miles of winter brown pasture, then Red Rock proper, before stretching out again on the other side of town and toward the airport.

Since his arrival, he'd driven this road maybe a couple dozen times at the outside, but it had already become as comfortably familiar as his ten-year-old leather jacket.

As had the chatty blonde in his back seat, he thought with a grin as she prattled on about how it felt like *months* since she'd been farther than her front porch.

"Oh, my…I knew I'd missed the open space, but I had no idea how *much* I missed it."

"I can understand that."

She paused. "I doubt it, Mr. City Boy."

He glanced at her in the rearview mirror, then refocused on the road while he was still able to tear his gaze away from her bemused grin. The impish gleam in those sky blue eyes. Ten points to him, for getting her out of that damn apartment. "It's true. Although I fought it tooth and nail that first week I was here. But now…" He paused. "Where other people might see nothing and nowhere, I see…possibilities. Freedom."

That apparently shut her up. If for only a second.

"We might make an honorary Texan out of you yet—oh, no," she said, twisting to look behind her.

"What?"

"There used to be the neatest old barn right in front of that stand of trees," she said on a sigh. "Judging from the chewed-up look of the land, I'm guessing the tornado got it. It hadn't been used in years, but it was like some sweet old man you get used to seeing every day." Another breath left her lungs. "That's so sad. That it's gone forever, never to be replaced."

The old barn, maybe not. But every couple of miles, it seemed, they passed a cleanup or building crew, like beavers in hard hats, setting things to rights. Because, by and large, human beings were an optimistic lot. Or at least Texans were, Scott thought with another smile.

When they passed the spa where Scott and his family had stayed, Christina said, "I always wondered what that place is like inside."

"Quite nice."

"You've been there?"

"Yes."

"Luck-y," she said lightly. A few minutes later the airport—or what was left of it—came into view, and Christina sucked in a breath. "I know I was there, but…holy moly."

They pulled into the parking lot, mostly cleared of debris but now filled with assorted construction vehicles. He helped Christina out of the car, leaving a woefully disappointed Gumbo inside. The still, clear air reverberated with the off-sync banging of hammers and nail guns, a drill's high-pitched squeal. The ear-splitting "pop" of a power riveter. Sounds of hope and optimism and determination. In the distance he spotted Tanner Redmond, who acknowledged Scott with a wave of his hand.

Then, beside him, he heard Christina's low moan.

She hobbled over to what apparently had once been her car, now a mangled hunk of metal. Leaning on one crutch, she let go of the other long enough to lovingly stroke a brutal dent in the left fender.

"I'm so sorry," Scott said behind her.

Christina sniffed. "She lived a long, happy life. At least she was happy once I rescued her from the idiot teenager who'd abused her. Poor gal already had more than 200,000 miles on her at that point and her shocks were shot. But I nursed her back to health and she served me well for going on four years." She laid a cheek on the roof. "What an awful way to go. I'm so sorry, Ellie Mae."

Scott came up and put an arm around her shoulders. "If it's any consolation, I don't think she suffered," he said, and she gave a short laugh, then clamped her quivering lips together.

"What do you want to do? With the car, I mean?"

"I...I honestly don't know. Have it towed somewhere, I suppose..." Then, on a soft, strangled cry, she turned and buried her face in his chest.

"Hey...hey..." Wrapping her in his arms, he said, "It's okay, really..."

"Oh, yeah?" she mumbled into his jacket. "I didn't have comprehensive insurance. Couldn't afford it. And didn't figure the insurance company would give me more than a buck fifty for her, anyway." Watery eyes lifted to his. "So right now I have no job, no car and no way to get a car to get to a job." She pulled away, angrily swatting at her cheek with the heel of one hand. "Or any way to drive if I did have a car. So my usually upbeat outlook is sorta struggling right now."

His hands on her shoulders, Scott bent to look into her eyes. "You have your dog."

She looked over at Gumbo, doing his sad-sack look at her from the car window. "Not sure I'd get much for him as a trade-in, though—"

"And you have me," he said, and her eyes swung sharply back to his.

"Oh, no," she said, hooking her crutches under her arms and doing her Monster Mash lurch back to the Escalade. "I let you pay my E.R. bill, and pick up my dog's poop, but you are not buying me a car, no sir."

Scott easily caught up to her, opening the car door and helping her get settled inside. Then he stood with one hand on the door, the other propped on the roof.

"Actually, that hadn't occurred to me. I'd only meant I'd take care of the car so you wouldn't have to. But thanks for giving me the idea—"

"And you might not want to provoke an already aggravated woman with crutches at her disposal."

"I'll take my chances. Look, Christina…if it's so important to you, you can pick out whatever you feel comfortable with, then pay me back in installments when you do get a job. But we're going to get you another car. But lunch first, dammit, because I'm hungry." Then he slammed the door shut and stalked around to the driver's side, slamming that one shut, too, after he got back behind the wheel.

Silence engulfed them as they drove back to town. Even knowing Christina as little as he did, something told him this was not a good thing.

She was still miffed, frankly, by the time Scott eased the SUV into a space between a Mercedes and something else big and fancy and shiny in Red's parking lot. But more at herself than at him, for a boatload of conflicting reasons. For not knowing how to handle whatever this was between them with at least a modicum of grace. For realizing how easily she could let herself get sucked into the fairy tale. For liking the man even though she knew it was dumb and foolish and wrong, because he was caught up in the fairy tale, too, wasn't he? Playing the Prince to her Cinderella.

Then again, maybe she should simply accept the blessing and shut the heck up. Seize the day—and the car—and be grateful. Enjoy the moment while it lasted.

Scott opened her door, offered his hand. Glowered when she didn't immediately take it.

"Christina—"

"Once again, I'm sorry I'm acting like…whatever I'm acting like. But…but your coming along, acting like some fairy godfather…it makes me feel like that tornado got inside my head somehow, making an awful mess in there. So you're just going to have to be patient with me until everything settles down." She angled her head to peer up at him. "Okay?"

"Okay," he said after a moment. "Although I'm not sure I like the 'fairy' part of that description." But she was too busy gawking at the beautiful hacienda-turned-restaurant to pay him any mind.

"I'm not exactly dressed for this place, you know. I was thinking more along the lines of a drive-through burger and fries."

He hauled her to her good foot, his hand landing at the small of her back to steady her as his gaze took a leisurely stroll over her fitted pink hoodie, her ankle-length, tiered denim skirt, like she was wearing one of those fringed-and-sequined numbers from *Dancing with the Stars.* Oh, boy. Her foot might be broken, but everything else was apparently very much ready to rhumba.

"You're dressed fine," he said, his voice sounding a little raspy. "And I'd rather poke sharp sticks in my eyes than eat that crap."

"Snob."

"Not at all. But I would like to live past fifty." He left the window cracked for Gumbo, then steered her and her crutches toward the door. "And I'd like you to live past fifty, too."

It was a throwaway retort, she was sure. Didn't mean anything. And yet, her eyes stung. Dammit. All this time she'd done fine on her own without some ding-dong muddying the waters. Then *this* ding-dong comes along, flinging both his money and his pheromones left and right, and there goes all her hard work right down the drain.

Finally, Scott got her inside. Precariously balanced on the crutches, Christina glanced around, willing her eyes to adjust to the darkened interior and feeling every bit the rube.

"Two?" the smartly dressed hostess asked.

"Yes. And my friend needs to keep her foot up as much as possible, so if we could have a booth, or a table with an extra chair…?"

"Not a problem. Follow me."

The hostess led them to a table for four beside an arched window looking into a central courtyard anchored by several Mexican fan trees and dotted with pine tables and chairs, the brightly colored umbrellas over them mostly closed. Even in the sun it was a little chilly to dine outside, Christina guessed, but dormant vines still gracefully tangled around arbors, scrambled up support posts underneath the overhanging, clay-tiled roof. And in the center, an exquisite Mexican-tiled fountain softly gurgled and splashed, the soothing music audible even through the closed window.

Scott helped her get her foot propped up on the chair opposite, then sat at right angles to her, the ambient light glancing off his dark hair, his sharply defined jaw, as he studied the menu.

Terrific.

"This is very nice," she said, forcing her eyes to her own menu. Trying not to gasp at the prices. *Seize the moment, seize the—*

"You've never been here?"

She shook her head, then looked around, grateful to see she wasn't the only person dressed…casually. Then she giggled, pressing her hand to her mouth. "I'm sorry," she whispered, "but I can't help it, I feel like I'm playing grown-up."

Scott did that unsettling raking-her-with-his-eyes thing again—although not in a creepy way, at least—then said with a half smile, "You are very much a grown-up, Christina. Get used to it."

"Aw…do I gotta?"

His mouth twitching, Scott lowered his eyes to the menu. "Yes." She gave an exaggerated sigh, and his mouth twitched harder. Then he said, "What's your favorite color? To wear, I mean?"

"Color? I don't know, I've never really thought about it. Blues and turquoises, I suppose. Like the colors in those tiles," she said, indicating the fountain. "Why?"

He simply smiled, then nodded to her—like, you know, a gentleman?—when the peasant-bloused waitress appeared to take their orders. Christina gave hers—some grilled shrimp dish that sounded amazing—then mused, as she listened to Scott give his, that it was a good thing she was done with men, since this dude was totally going to spoil her for anybody else.

A thought that didn't give her nearly as much satisfaction as she'd hoped.

Clearly, Scott thought, amused, as he watched tiny little Christina chow down her lunch like a linebacker, if he wanted her to open up, all he had to do was feed her.

Not that the conversation was personal to any real degree. At least on her end. She still avoided discussing her past, deftly sidestepping any questions that might lead to answers she clearly didn't want to give. Although instinct told him she simply wanted to avoid pain more than, say, jail time, a more guarded woman he'd never met. Which provoked as much admiration as annoyance.

About her private life, at least. Because about everything else—from politics to world affairs to their favorite movies—she had no qualms whatsoever about locking his gaze into hers as she leaned over her plate, her hands going a mile a minute to emphasize her point. There was little she wasn't interested in—or didn't have a fervently expressed opinion about—and the longer the meal went on, the more Scott became aroused, by her intelligence, her quick wit, the way her cheeks pinked when she got excited.

By that adorable little crease that kept playing peekaboo with her forehead. She was simply…amazing. And the most amazing thing about it was that she had no idea how amazing she was. She made him think, she made him laugh, she made him feel like doing a Gene Kelly number. With an umbrella. In the rain. And every minute he spent with her made him realize even more what an idiot he'd be to let her go.

That *this* was what all the fuss was about.

Now if he could just figure out how to overcome those pesky trust issues, he'd be set—

Not for the first time during the meal, his phone buzzed. Carefully drizzling honey into a sopapilla, Christina nodded toward it. "You can go ahead and get that, you know. Doesn't bother me in the least."

"It's rude."

"Not if it's okay with me. Scott…I know you're a busy man. As it is, I can't figure out how you're pulling this off. You've left your life to be here…that can't be easy."

No, I've found *my life,* he wanted to say. Except why ruin the good mood? So all he said was, "A lot easier than you might think." When she frowned, he added, "This is the first time I've…" He caught himself before he said, *been on a date,* figuring that would not go over well. "I've shared a meal with someone where my phone wasn't the third person at the table. Not only did my companions not appreciate it, I didn't enjoy it, either. Believe me, multitasking is highly overrated."

She gave him more of that steady gaze, then said, "You know, you sound tired. I don't mean physically—"

"No, I know what you mean. And you're right, I am.

For once in my life I'd like to focus on one thing and savor it, rather than three or four and not enjoy any of them. And right now," he said, grasping her free hand, "I'm here, having lunch with you, and enjoying the heck out of it. So can I have my moment, please?"

For several seconds her eyes held his, as sharp and discerning as an old woman's. "Sure," she said, at last, her smile relaxing more than it had yet, and his heart seized up so hard and fast he nearly flinched. Wendy was right, he had it bad.

Speaking of his sister…

"By the way," he said, releasing Christina's hand, "Wendy suggested you might like to come help her make decorating decisions about her nursery."

"Oh, Scott…" Her eyes lowered, she removed her napkin, painstakingly refolding it before tucking it underneath the rim of her plate. Then her mouth twisted into a funny little smile, the same one she'd given him when he'd first mentioned his sister. "What do I know about decorating?"

"Knowing Wendy, I imagine she used the term *help* very loosely. Basically, I think she's looking for a yes-man. Or in this case, woman. So will you do it? Might do both of you good. And I think…she could use a friend."

He'd stopped short of saying he thought *Christina* could use a friend, even if it was true. Because right now it was patently clear the woman sitting across from him needed to regain her footing, in more ways than one. And one of those, he surmised, was by feeling needed. Useful.

"Maybe in a few days," she finally said, the smile reappearing. "When I'm feeling more…myself."

"Good deal," he said, gesturing to the waitress for the check. "Now where's the best place to shop for a car around here?"

"San Antonio. But, Scott—I can't even drive yet—"

"Strike while the iron's hot, I always say." The credit card slip signed, he got to his feet. "And I'm in the mood to buy something. You might want to take advantage of that."

She gave him a look that could either have been indulgent or exasperated. Then she sighed, and there was no doubt at all what *that* meant.

"I'm sorry," he said, "I don't mean to push you—"

"Like you're not hardwired to do exactly that. And if I told you no, flat out, that I don't want you buying me a car, you'd probably do it anyway. Right?"

"Can I admit I'd at least be tempted?"

Her mouth pulled flat. Definitely exasperated. "What am I going to do with you?"

"Let me buy you a car?" he said, and she gave a weary laugh, those sweet eyes finally touching his.

"Will it really make you happy?"

He came around to help her stand, trying to figure out why the scent of her drugstore shampoo should wreak such havoc on his senses. Let alone his common sense. Because what would make him happy right now wasn't anything they could do in Red, that was for damn sure.

Nor was there any way he could tell her a few thousand dollars meant nothing to him and not come across like some ego-bloated braggart who assumed money could buy him any woman he wanted.

So all he said was, "Yes. It would make me very happy. Will that work for you?"

"I guess it'll have to, won't it?" she said, then started toward the door.

Somehow he thought victory was supposed to feel sweeter than this.

Chapter Seven

Christina sat on the porch in the warm afternoon sun, her leg propped up, staring at the pretty little VW Jetta. Silver. Three years old, barely twenty thousand miles on it. A week on and she still couldn't believe it was hers.

Which only added to the rapidly growing list of things she was having a hard time believing. Like Scott's still being here after two weeks. Not to mention her sorta getting used to letting him do stuff for her. Without feeling guilty about it, even. Or at least not as much.

Beside her, in an original-edition webbed lawn chair, Enid grunted. "I cannot believe you let the man buy you a car."

Which the older woman had only said a million times since she'd first seen it sitting in the parking lot. And with no less vexation in her voice now than the first time. Never mind that she'd told Christina yesterday that Scott had paid up her rent three months in advance. Or that he'd ferried

Enid to Walmart right after. Both on the sly, of course. Honestly, Christina never knew whether to hug or strangle the man. Or strangle herself. On the upside, at least there'd been no more silly talk about her past. Or those "real" feelings he'd mentioned a week ago. 'Cause for sure *somebody'd* be dead by now if there had been.

"Well, I did. And don't tell me you can't wait until I drive you to your hair appointment in it."

"It does look like a very nice car, I gotta admit. So where's Lover Boy today?"

"I don't know and don't call him that. He said he had some things to take care of. I didn't figure it was any of my business to ask what."

"He going back home soon?"

Her heart knocking in her chest, Christina looked over to where Gumbo was rustling around in the underbrush, looking for something to chase. Or pee on. "I suppose."

"You don't know?"

"Don't see how that's any of my business, either," she said, and Enid grunted. "By the way, did I tell you? I registered to take online classes for the next semester, so I don't have to worry about getting to campus. I also did some research and found this website that matches up tutors with kids who need help with basic skills. We can either work together in person or on Skype."

"What's that?"

"This cool computer hookup where you can see the person you're talking to. You know that jewelry commercial where the guy overseas is talking to his wife and son? That's Skype."

"Oh." Then her landlady shook her head. "I swear, things move too damn fast for me to keep up."

Christina laughed. "Don't feel bad. Even I feel as if technology changes every five minutes. Anyway, soon as the outfit that runs the program finishes up my background check to make sure I'm okay to work with kids, I'll have a job. And one that pays a lot better than waitressing at the airport ever did, that's for sure. And why are you looking at me like that?"

"Because you are one of the smartest gals I ever met, and that's a fact."

"Hardly—"

"And don't you go acting all modest on me. It's true. I mean, look at you—instead of wallowing in your troubles, you figure out how to solve your problems. You are something else, young lady—"

"Hey. I wallowed. I wallowed plenty."

"For, what? A week?" She blew a dismissive *pfhh* through her lips.

"And if Scott hadn't jumped in to help with the medical expenses, and the car—"

"Yeah, yeah, I know, but that's all the immediate stuff. What you did, that's taking care of the future. Did Lover Boy have anything to do with that?"

"Well, no, but—"

"Then just accept the damn compliment, will you?" Over Christina's chuckle, Enid added, "You know, I'm gonna miss you like nobody's business when you leave."

Christina's head snapped around. "Leave? No way. Red Rock's my home, Enid. Where I belong. Unless you got a crystal ball in your pocket that knows something I don't."

"No, but I've been around a lot longer than you, which means I'm real good at readin' people. You ain't even begun to reach your full potential, and…and you don't need to be letting some man derail you, neither, making you all starry-eyed and whatnot and then first thing you know you can't remember the last time you did something for yourself. You got things to do, missy, even if you don't know yet what those are…and now why are you laughing at me?"

"Because you're not telling me anything I don't already know. In case you forgot. You bet I've got things to do, but there's nothing saying I can't do them right here in Red Rock. Or close by, anyway. I'm not about to let a man mess with my head, believe me." She thought about the look in Scott's eyes that night, like he would've liked nothing more than to sweep her off to Atlanta to turn her into a proper Southern lady. A thought that made her shudder. "Or take me places I don't want to go." Then she said, "You don't like Scott, do you?"

"Ain't got nothing to do with liking the boy. I like him just fine. He's good folks, far as I can tell. But it ain't me he's courting, is it?"

"He's not *courting* me, either—"

"The hell he ain't. And a man like that, he can be hard to resist. Make a gal forget what she's about, what she's got to do. Nothin' against Scott. I just want you to be sure."

"Of what?"

"Of whatever you need to be sure about."

Christina looked away. "No worries. Promise."

"Well. Okay, then," her landlady said with a sharp shake of her head that did not so much as disturb a single hair on it. "Got a cleaning crew coming in a bit, you know Marlene and her kids moved out of number 5, right? Left the place in a right mess, too. Least she didn't stiff me for the last month's rent like so many of 'em do, but it's gonna cost me near that much to get the place back in decent shape…" She stopped, her lips pulled thin. "I love you, girl, you know that, right?"

Tears pricked at Christina's eyes. "I love you, too, Enid. But I'm okay. Promise."

Which she sternly told herself after Enid left and she

saw the Escalade turn into the parking lot, and her heart ka-thumped so hard in her chest it nearly made her burp. She hadn't been expecting him, even though he'd shown up every single day. Sometimes twice. But *expecting* him—expecting *anything*—would have been foolish, and she liked to think she'd outgrown foolish a long time ago.

Gumbo, of course, bounded over to the car before Scott had even cut the engine, all flapping ears and wagging everything. Because dogs had no pride. Or inhibitions. You love somebody, you let him know. Simple. To the point.

And when Scott finally disentangled himself from Gumbo's totally inappropriate PDA and lifted his eyes to Christina's, she thought—with a sharp pang—how much easier it would be to be a dog. To simply love because that's what you did, with no regard for the consequences. Or worry about potential heartbreak.

But she wasn't a dog. She was a human being whose brain and heart—and body, no point leaving that out of the equation—were at severe odds with each other right now. Because for all that she really was grateful he hadn't *said* anything more, she got the real strong feeling the issue had not, by any means, been laid to rest.

And right now? Watching Scott Fortune cross toward her like he owned the whole state, his eyes fixed on hers in the way of a man who clearly had hanky-panky on his mind?

It wasn't the fantasy scaring the bejeebers out of her.

It was the reality.

She was giving him the same look she always did, a fake aloofness she had no clue how to pull off with any degree of conviction.

Oh, he had no doubt her resistance was sincere, that there were real reasons behind the ambivalence haunting her eyes, her blatant avoidance of any prolonged physical contact. She was clearly leery, although whether of him or relationships in general, he still had no idea.

And over the past week, that had begun to worry him more and more. Not her wariness, but the very real danger that…she might be onto something. That the thrill of the challenge might be motivating his interest far more than he wanted to admit. After all, Christina was one smart cookie. And when *had* he last pursued any sort of relationship—business or pleasure—that didn't serve his self-interest in some way?

Did he even know how to have a relationship for its own sake? To be with someone simply because he wanted to be with her? Was his almost constant ache for Christina—the bad timing on that notwithstanding—simply because it'd been a while, or because he genuinely ached for *her?*

"What's up?" she asked, her obvious attempt to keep things light twisting his heart. The pansies nodded at him as he approached, the gentle breeze easing through his Oxford shirt, teasing strands of pale gold across Christina's cheeks. Her lightweight top was a field of softly blurred flowers, blues and lavenders and deep pinks, lazily strewn across her shoulders. Her breasts. Very feminine. Very her.

"Thought you might like to meet Wendy today," he said, suddenly realizing exactly how much he wanted to pulverize that wall keeping her locked inside herself…and then shield her from whatever had made her erect that wall to begin with.

At which moment he also realized exactly how groundless his earlier worries were. Oh, yeah, he was in it to win it, no question. But because he wanted *her,* not because he wanted to win.

"She said the decorator left a bunch of swatches," he continued, as though all hell wasn't breaking loose inside his head. "The two of you could have lunch together, I'll pick you up later."

Confusion flickered in her eyes. "You won't be there?"

"No, I've got…some business to attend to."

"Oh. Well, then…" A smile bloomed across her face. "Sure. Why not?"

"And bring the dog. Wendy wants to meet him, too."

When he opened the rear door, however, for her to climb into the back seat, she shook her head. "The swelling's all gone. I'd like to sit in front, if you don't mind?"

"Not at all."

Once again, getting out seemed to relax her. Her enthusiasm contagious, she told him all about her signing up for online classes, her potential job.

"So you like working with kids?"

She nodded, her gaze fixed out the windshield. "I love kids. What about you?"

"I think kids are the neatest things going. The way their minds work—slays me every time."

Her eyes cut briefly to his. "So…any plans to make a bunch of baby Fortunes?"

"Don't know about a bunch…but I suppose so. Although, to be honest, I hadn't really given it much thought until recently."

"Oh, yeah? What made you change your mind?"

"I never said I was opposed to the idea, it's just…" His fist tightened around the steering wheel. "Since getting married wasn't on my radar, neither was having kids. Then we came out here for Wendy's wedding, and she's pregnant and happy and…"

"And you got all broody."

"I suppose."

Several seconds ticked by before Christina said, "Betcha

there's a whole slew of gals in Atlanta who'd be thrilled to hear that."

Scott pushed out a dry laugh. "No doubt," he said, nosing into his sister's driveway beside a hedge of rangy, unclipped euonymus. "And here we are. It was Marcos's before they got married. As you can tell, yard work isn't exactly a top priority…no, wait, let me help you—"

"Nope, got it," Christina said, pushing open the door, grabbing her crutches from behind his seat and hauling her adorable little bottom out of the car the same moment Gumbo scrambled out behind her. When Scott reached her, she laughed. "Get me, huh?"

I'd love to, he thought as Wendy waddled outside, looking like a shiny red balloon in her stretchy top. Then Scott noticed his sister's way-too-high, rope-soled shoes…about the same time Christina did.

"Ohmigosh—those shoes are awesome!" she said, moving much more gracefully with the crutches than she had even a few days ago.

"Thanks!" Wendy said, awkwardly twisting around to show off the three-inch heel, then bending over—sort of—to pet Gumbo. "These are my favorites, I can't fit my fat feet into anything else these days! And aren't you the cutest thing going?" she said to the dog, who'd already propped his pudgy feet on her thighs to get some love. Then Wendy turned her smile on Christina. "Well, come on in, I've already got lunch on the table, Scott's told me so much about you—"

"I'll be back in a couple of hours," Scott called, but they were already inside.

Laughing softly to himself as he walked back around to the driver's side, he pulled out his cell phone and punched in the number already on speed dial. "I can meet you out there in ten minutes," he said, climbing in behind the wheel and backing out of the driveway.

He still hadn't decided if he'd lost his mind or finally found it. He did know that whichever that was, none of this was going to be easy. He knew what he wanted, was pretty sure he knew why, but from this point forward it was all uncharted territory.

But as he sped down the highway, his grin stretched his face so hard it hurt.

"You don't think the colors are too much?"

Grinning at the blinding array of tropical hues splayed out on the nursery's carpet, Christina shook her head. A few feet away Gumbo snoozed in a puddle of sunlight, ears akimbo. "I love them. Especially this for the drapes," she said, holding up the bold, contemporary floral print, orange and fuchsia and lemon-yellow flowers on a bright aqua background. Christina sat on the floor, her healing foot stretched out in front of her, while Wendy held court from the aqua-and-white glider already in place in the corner, her feet planted on a matching ottoman.

"The furniture and walls are all going to be white," Wendy said, "so I figured I could go a little crazy with the rest of it. And I've already hired an artist to come paint a border of the same flowers on the opposite wall." Then she laughed. "When I was little, my room was princess pink. Every square inch of it. It was like waking up every morning inside a glob of cotton candy."

Christina smiled, the image mercifully blotting out the memories. She seriously doubted if Wendy could even fathom what some of Christina's sleeping arrangements had been like. "Were your sisters' rooms pink, too?"

"Heavens, no. Emily's was all yellows and creams, and Jordana's was pale blue. Of course, they might have been pink at the start, but that didn't last long. Any more than it did with me," she said with another giggle. "I marched into my parents' room on my tenth birthday and announced I wanted a red room. Or else."

"Oh, dear. How did that go over?"

"Oh, I got my red room, all right. Except then I started having nightmares about vampires attacking me in my sleep. So I ended up with a nice, soft periwinkle."

"Sounds perfect." Christina skootched back to rest her back against the wall, itching—literally—to remove the cast. "And…your brothers? What were their rooms like?"

"Typical boy, I suppose, I never paid much attention. And I was still really small when Mike and Scott went off to college and Mom turned both of their rooms into guestrooms. Very Atlanta traditional, dark wood furniture, striped wallpaper, floral bedspreads." She made a face. "Tasteful but boring. Blake's, though—I remember his, since I spent so much time in it. Über high tech. A fish tank large enough to hold a shark. Okay, a small shark… hey. You okay?"

Jerking up her head, Christina nodded, not about to let on that listening to Wendy talk about the family had taken her back to those hours she'd spent trapped with Scott after the tornado. Despite their wealth, in many ways the Fortunes sounded like your average American family, some of the bonds between various members stronger than others. Still and all, what they had—and she didn't mean their money—was far more than she could've even imagined—

"I'm fine, I just wonder where Scott is." At Wendy's raised brows, she smiled. "You must be very ready for me to go home by now."

"Don't kid yourself. This is the most fun I've had in ages. I cannot wait until this little peanut is outside and I can walk more than three feet without getting winded. And drive. Nobody tells you when you're short that if you adjust the steering wheel so it doesn't stab you in the stomach, your feet won't reach the pedals!"

But the young woman's can't-hold-it-in happiness certainly tempered the moaning and groaning. Yes, more than a few vestiges of her privileged upbringing still clung to her—the baby girl's nursery was not being done on the cheap, nor were the silver bangles that softly clinked every time Wendy gestured with her left hand, Christina didn't imagine—but all the trappings couldn't hide the real sweetheart underneath. Wendy, too, was "good folks," as Enid liked to say.

Then Wendy said, "You mind if I ask you something?" and a faint prickle of alarm tracked up Christina's spine.

"Depends on what that is, I suppose."

Rubbing her belly, Wendy glanced out the window to the backyard beyond, then returned her gaze to Christina, a tiny wrinkle etched between her dark brows. "Did something…happen between you and my brother when y'all were trapped together after the tornado?"

Christina's face flamed. "What—what do you mean?"

"I'm not sure. That's why I'm asking. And I know the question sounds totally out of line…" She huffed out a sigh, then a little laugh. "I know it's not possible, but I swear sometimes it feels as if the baby's pushed everything inside me all the way up into my brain! But if you'd known Scott before…"

She wagged her head. "Everything he did, even when he dated, it all felt so…controlled. Calculated. I never once saw him do something on the spur of the moment. I mean, okay, so all my brothers and sisters live, eat and breathe that business. Just like Daddy. But I always got the feeling Scott was like that because he thought he had to be. Not because that's who he really was."

Christina picked up a fabric swatch again, smoothing it over her thigh. "And now you think something's changed?"

"Oh, I know something's changed. There's a light in his eyes I don't ever remember seeing before. Only thing is, I can't quite tell what's put it there."

Lifting her eyes—and running smack dab into Wendy's pointed look—Christina nervously laughed. "And you think it's me?"

A devilish grin spread across the young woman's cheeks. "Can't think of another reason why he's still here. Blake says Daddy's about to have five fits that Scott's not home yet."

And you're young and in love and running on pregnancy hormones, Christina thought, not unkindly. Because maybe only a few years separated them, but what Christina lacked in privilege and wealth she more than made up for in experience—a treasury that easily trumped the younger woman's a hundredfold.

"Even if that was true," she said carefully, "no way would I come between him and his father. Because I've been there before, and it wasn't pretty."

"Oooh..." Wendy's brows lifted. "I'm guessing there's a story behind that comment."

There was—a long, sorry one—but Christina had already said more than she should have. Through the open window she heard the SUV pull into the driveway. Praise be.

"Nothing worth resurrecting," she said lightly, hauling herself to her feet and grabbing her crutches at the same time Wendy got to hers and pulled Christina into a hug.

"Listen, I can be a good friend," she said, her expression earnest. "I also know how to keep my mouth shut. What I'm saying is...you need somebody to talk to, I'm your girl.

But I swear on my life not one word would get back to Scott if you don't want it to."

Oddly, Christina believed her. Or at least she believed Wendy's good intentions. But she'd been that route before, too. So all she did was hug her back and thank her for the offer, just in time to look up and catch Scott's bewildered expression from the nursery doorway.

"What was that all about?" Scott asked mildly after they were on the road again. Christina frowned over at him. "I heard you thank her for her offer."

"Oh." She faced front again. "To…give me some of her recipes."

"You are one lousy liar, you know that?"

She was quiet for a moment, then said, "Not to be rude or anything, but it was girl stuff, okay? No boys allowed. So…did you have a successful afternoon?"

The gentle, but firm, rebuke hit its mark. Although considering he wasn't ready to come clean to her yet, either, this time he could hardly fault the woman for playing her cards close to her chest.

"Not entirely, no. But there's always tomorrow." And yet, when she didn't say anything—in other words, didn't play the game the way he wanted it played—it mildly ticked him off. "Aren't you even remotely curious?"

"Not even remotely," she said. Staring *really* hard out the window.

That's my girl, he thought, grinning. "As I said. Lousy liar."

She scratched the side of her nose, then tightly folded her arms across her ribs. "Bein' curious and thinking you have the right to pry into somebody's private business are two different things. Especially when that business has nothing to do with you."

"What makes you think it doesn't?"

The car bumped over some debris in the road. "In that case, I *really* don't want to know."

Scott chuckled. "You are one strange bird, you know that?"

"Never said I wasn't…why are we turning off here?"

"Don't you recognize it?"

"Well, yeah, it's where the old barn used to be, but—"

"Then you probably know there's a pretty little stand of pines by a pond on the other side of the property. It's a beautiful day—I thought you might like to go sit by it for a bit."

She looked like a little girl being teased by somebody holding a favorite doll out of her reach. "Whoever owns the land might not take kindly to us trespassing, you know."

"The owner's in New Mexico. Has been for twenty years. I doubt she'd care."

"How do you know all this?"

"I make it my business to know these things. What is it they say about nature abhorring a vacuum? So does my brain."

"You do realize how scary that sounds?"

"Does it scare you?"

After a moment's apparent contemplation, she shook her head. "Not especially."

This time he didn't call her on the fib. Especially since, this time, he wasn't amused. Odd, how all his adult life he'd worked the intimidation factor, figuring if a little fear got him where he wanted to go, it was all well and good. Even in his personal life—the minute he felt a woman was getting too comfortable, felt his control of the relationship slipping, she was history. But it was different with Christina. *He* was different. The idea of her being afraid of him, even a little, made him sick to his stomach. Sure, he still wanted what he wanted, but what he wanted…

Was for her to want him, too. Every bit as badly as he did her.

On her terms. Not his.

He drove the SUV to the end of the dirt road, Gumbo bursting from the backseat the instant Scott opened the door to bound across the field like the jackrabbits he probably hoped to find. Then, an old blanket purloined from Marcos's car in hand, he helped Christina out. Her eyes grazed his for a moment, questioning, before she turned away. Shielding her eyes from the sun, she scanned the landscape, bright gold under a clear, cloudless sky. And let out a long, slow breath.

"Now this is what you call pure Texas," she said. "Standing here, with all this sky and sun…it's like being reborn."

He couldn't have said it better himself. Smiling, Scott let his gaze wander further west, over the sweet seven hundred or so acres nobody but he—and his Realtor—knew he had an eye on. And until it was a done deal nobody else was going to know he'd finally made the decision that would change everything.

"Come on, sit," he said, shaking out the blanket and smoothing it over a bed of needles underneath one of the pines. Christina sat, folding up one leg to hug her knee while Scott stretched out beside her on his side, propped up on one elbow. In the distance, Gumbo let out a happy bark, bounced into view as if to say *I'm okay, Mom, see?* then bounced off again.

"So you gonna tell me the real reason why you brought me here?"

"Just thought you'd like it. That's all."

"Apparently I'm not the only one who's a lousy liar."

Scott plucked at a pine needle that had blown onto the

blanket, twirling it in his fingers. "If I told you how much I'd like to kiss you right now," he said, "would you be a, flattered, b, annoyed or c, ambivalent?"

"What is this, one of those questions on OkCupid?"

He looked up at her. "You've been on a dating site?" To his immense delight, she blushed.

"Never you mind about that—"

"Answer the question."

"What's *annoying* is that I can't simply get up and stomp off right now."

He grinned. "Yeah. I know."

On a groan, she dropped her head onto her folded-up hands, then lifted it again, staring off into the distance. "Scott…you don't want to kiss *me*."

"I sure don't want to kiss Gumbo."

She laughed softly, then said, "No, I mean…you want to kiss who you think I am. Or who you think I could be. Take your pick."

"And you think *my* brain is scary?" He reached up to curl his fingers around her hand. "Honey, I—"

"Now, see?" she said, pulling her hand from his. "You can stop right there with your 'honeys' and 'sweethearts' and 'trust mes.' Because they're nothing more than words a man uses to make a woman think things she has no business thinking."

Scott felt his forehead pinch. "And what is it you're so sure you have no business thinking?"

"Not important," she said, even as Scott thought, *Says who?* "But…but your sister said she thinks everything that happened with the tornado and the aftermath, it all messed with your head, somehow. That you're acting different from what she's used to. No, wait, let me finish."

After a little rustling around she stretched out next to him, mirroring his position, eyes locked in his. Her hair had worked loose, tumbling in soft waves around her shoulder. "I'm not saying it didn't. In fact, I have no business saying otherwise, seeing as it messed with my head, too. Big-time. But if anything it made me see things more clearly. Made me more sure of what I wanted. What I needed. But you…"

Sighing, she rolled onto her back, her hands resting on her stomach. "From everything your sister tells me, it sounds like you've been focused so hard on your work all these years that you lost sight of *you* somewhere along the way."

She angled her head to look at him. "Then this crazy storm comes along and shakes you up. Throws everything out of whack. But the thing about storms is, eventually they end. And when they do, you look around and realize…everything's messed up. Not new. Not better. Just… messed up. Maybe I'm different from every other woman you've ever known, but that doesn't mean our getting stuck together was some kind of sign. All of this…it's a novelty to you, Scott. I'm a novelty. Or a project, I haven't quite decided which yet. So I meant what I said, about you not really wanting to kiss me. Because you're only seeing who you want to see. Not who I really am."

Scott looked at her for a long time, then said, "You could have just said 'no.'"

She blinked. "About what?"

"This," he said, then closed the few inches between them and lowered his mouth to hers.

Chapter Eight

There were, Christina knew, hot kisses and mediocre kisses and kisses so boring you found yourself contemplating what was on TV that night. But never, not even during that period of her life she thought about as little as possible, had she ever experienced a kiss like this.

Oh, my, yes, she thought, as Scott wrapped his hand around her neck, possessive and gentle and warm, angling their mouths to go deeper, *this* kiss was in a category all its own.

This kiss was Ferris wheels and warm summer breezes and spinning around and around with your arms held wide until you fell over, dizzy and laughing. Bubbles of delight scurried along her skin, through her blood, making things tingle and curl and sweetly ache and her brain feel like it'd exploded into a thousand sparkly bits underneath her skull.

Scott broke the kiss and eased away, his fingers toying with the hair at her temple, the lopsided grin on his face making her want to smack him. And/or kiss him all over again.

And she thought she'd been in trouble *before*.

"I never did answer your question, you know," she said, her heart whomping so hard against her sternum it almost hurt.

"I took a gamble," he said, still grinning. "And I think I can safely say that first kiss? Wasn't a fluke. Or terror-driven."

Apparently worn out from his exploits, Gumbo trotted up and wedged himself between them, exhilarated and panting. Scott let go of Christina to scratch the dog's head.

"The kiss was okay," she said, sitting up again. Frantically searching for her composure. If not her common sense.

"Like hell." Scott sat up as well, cupping her jaw to bring her face back around to his. Thinking he was gonna kiss her again—and not at all sure how she felt about that—Christina sucked in a breath. But all he did was stroke his thumb across her cheek, over and over, and stare into her eyes like he all but knew she was hiding something in there.

She looked away. "Don't."

Because she was. All kinds of things she didn't talk about, ever, because they hurt too much. Made her feel weak and vulnerable and dumb all over again. Or worse, would make him feel sorrier for her than she suspected he already did. And that was one card she refused to play.

He dropped his hand. "I have no intention of hurting you, Christina."

"I'm sure you don't. Doesn't mean you won't." She grabbed her crutches. "Can we leave now? My foot's beginning to give me fits."

Another lie. And he probably knew it. But she desperately needed to get back to reality, to what she knew. What she could control.

Nodding, Scott helped her up.

Neither said a single word the whole way back to her place. Until, when they turned into the complex's parking lot, Christina spotted her mother's bright red Ford Fiesta parked next to her new car. And, on her porch, the woman herself, all decked out in a too-low top, too-tight pants and too-big hair.

"Your mother?" Scott said beside her as he pulled up.

"None else. Although why she's here I couldn't tell you."

"To make sure you're okay?"

Christina reached around to grab her crutches from the back seat, briefly meeting Scott's eyes. "After two weeks? The saying 'day late and a dollar short' comes to mind."

She waited until he'd come around to help her out. Pride was one thing. Making herself look like a blamed fool was something else again. But before he offered her his hand, he leaned close enough to say, "You don't have to face this alone. Not if you don't want to."

Gumbo leapt out and waggled over to her mother, who jumped up with her hands in the air, screeching. "Call your dog, Christina—oh, for heaven's sake, get *down!*"

"I can handle my mother, Scott. And besides…"

"You want me to leave."

Once again, their eyes met. And, oh, dear God in heaven, did she want to believe what she saw in them. But how could she when she doubted he truly believed it, either? "I *need* you to leave. Red Rock, if at all possible."

For the first time, she saw something like doubt flicker in his eyes. "Do you really mean that?"

"Does it matter? Scott," she said quickly when he looked away, "I'm not deliberately trying to piss you off. I'm more grateful than I can say for everything you've done for me, but I have to be realistic. Why can't you understand that?"

Several strained seconds passed before Scott walked around to the driver's side, got in and drove off. If the universe had a shred of decency, that would be the last time she saw him.

Never mind that the thought of never experiencing another kiss like that made facing her mother sound delightful in comparison.

Speaking of whom…

"I wondered where you'd gotten off to," Sandra said, patting down her thighs where Gumbo had left dusty footprints.

At her door, Christina dug her keys out of her jeans' pocket. "Sorry. Were you waiting long?"

"Almost a half hour."

The door opened, Christina let her mother inside first, then stomped in after her and shut the door, immediately feeling like all the air had been sucked out of the room. "You should've called. If I'd known you were coming I would've made sure I was here."

"It wasn't planned. I had to go into San Antonio and thought I may as well drop in, since it was on the way. Especially since I had to use the toilet and you now how I hate public restrooms." Of course. And with that, Sandra vanished into Christina's bathroom, emerging a scant two minutes later, glancing around the apartment without really looking at Christina. "So I guess you're getting on okay?"

"Sure. Thanks for asking."

Her mother's lips pursed. "That the same young man who was at the hospital? The Fortune fella?"

"Scott. Yes. Would you like something to drink?"

"Sweet tea, if you have it. And I cannot believe you're going down this path again."

Ditching the crutches long enough to pull the tea pitcher out of the fridge, Christina felt her jaw clench. "I'm not going down any path, Mama. Scott's been very kind to me, is all." She poured her mother her tea, setting the tumbler on the tiny dining table.

"Kind enough to buy you that car?"

"Yes, if you must know."

"Oh, Christina…"

"It wasn't like I asked him. In fact, I told him not to. He insisted."

"Because he's trying to get into your pants, no doubt."

"No, because he's a kind, decent, generous man," she said, turning so her mother wouldn't see her blush. Not that she thought for a minute Scott's motives were solely…that. But she'd be a fool to believe the subject hadn't been hovering between them, especially after that kiss. What would frost her mother, though, was how little Christina would mind the prospect. Even knowing it would be—or would have been—strictly one of those for-the-moment things.

"And I can't believe you didn't learn your lesson the first time—"

"Mama! Stop. Now."

"I'm only saying—"

"I learned, okay?" Christina said, refusing to listen to her stinging eyes. Because while Enid's lectures stemmed, she knew, from genuine concern, her mother's hailed from that bottomless pit of self-interest that had motivated her every comment, her every action, for as long as Christina could remember. "Oh, boy, did I learn. So nothing's happening between Scott and me. And it's not going to. And you know, you've got some nerve coming here and butting into my personal life when you couldn't even be bothered to drive me home when I got out of the hospital."

"You don't get to talk to me like that," Sandra said,

pushing herself up from the table. "After everything I've done for you, raising you all alone—"

"*Done* for me? Are you serious? Here's a newsflash, Mama—*you* don't get to be a mother only when it's convenient. Or when it suits your purpose." On a roll now, Christina pointed to the door. "That man, who you're so all-fired convinced is only after one thing? He's paid more attention to me in the last two weeks than you have in the past five *years*. Frankly, if he did want to get in my pants? I'd let him, gladly. Because he's *earned* it, dammit!"

Her mother looked like her hair was going to catch fire. Which would only be an improvement. "You don't mean that."

Christina blew out a long, rough sigh. "Fine, even if he were sticking around, I'm not going to jump the man's bones. But everything else? Every single word."

"He's not staying?"

So much for making her point. "Of course not. His work, his whole life, is in Atlanta. So, see? The whole thing's moot."

Her mother looked at her for a long, hard moment. "I never realized how much you hated me."

"I don't hate you, Mama," Christina said, wearily. "But I don't understand you. Why you are the way you are. Why you've always treated me like I was an afterthought. That makes me sad, and more than a little angry, but it is what it is."

After another long look, her mother traipsed to the door and let herself out. Exhausted, Christina collapsed into the sofa, Gumbo immediately hopping up to smush up against her side and lay his head on her knee.

"Guess it's just you and me, boy," she said. "Like always."

Then, much to her disgust, she burst into tears.

* * *

On hearing Wendy's laugh from the living room when Scott walked into the house, Scott hesitated, not wanting to interrupt a private conversation. Until he realized she was talking to his youngest brother. He found her stretched out on the black leather couch with her phone pressed to her ear while playing remote roulette with her other hand.

"I'm fine, I promise…and speak of the devil." Angling the phone, she said, "Blake's asking if you know when you're coming home yet."

Sighing, Scott reached for the phone, carrying it into the kitchen so Wendy could watch her fashion-makeover show in peace, wiggling her bare, unpainted toes as she nibbled on a bowl of trail mix.

Scott slid onto a barstool at the counter dividing the kitchen from the small dining room, massaging the bridge of his nose. "Hey."

"Hey, yourself. You told Dad a week. It's been two. And from everything Wendy said, it sounds as though things are under control as far as Javier's concerned. As much as they can be, at least. You do remember you have a job here, right?"

Letting his hand drop to the laminate surface, Scott stared across the serviceable but woefully outdated room, listening to the benign hum of the white refrigerator. *A job.* Funny to think that he'd poured ten years' worth of time and energy into something that, when all was said and done, was just that: a job. Not a career or a calling, but…a job, his shares of the business as a family member notwithstanding.

No time like the present, he supposed, to come clean.

"I'm not coming back, Blake."

Stunned silence vibrated in his ear, followed by, "You can't be serious."

"I've never been more serious in my life. Mike can continue to handle whatever's on my desk—since most of it came from him, anyway—or it can be divvied up among the others. That guy who filled in for me last year when I was in Europe? He's ripe for promotion, anyway, hand some of it to him—"

"Whoa, dude—what have you been smoking? You can't simply…walk away."

"Watch me."

"Holy crap. Does Dad know?"

"Not yet. And not a word. I'll deal with him soon enough."

Blake snorted. "Not to worry. You can drop that little bombshell yourself. But…why?"

"Because when I was lying underneath half an airport's worth of rubble, it occurred to me life's too damn short to spend it doing something simply because it's what's expected of you. That I've worked my ass off for ten years pursuing somebody else's dream. Not going to do that anymore."

"I don't understand. You've always been so gung-ho about the business, working harder than any of us, except maybe Mike. Are you saying it was all a lie?"

"No," Scott said on a breath. "I wasn't faking it. Then again, I was also too busy to realize there were other options. Options that might actually make me smile when I get up in the morning."

Blake released a nervous laugh. "This is crazy, Scott."

"No guts, no glory." *Or peace,* he silently added.

"So…what's the plan?"

"You know me, never talk about a work in progress until it's a done deal."

"Ah. This…wouldn't have anything to do with that girl, would it? Christine?"

"Christina," Scott said softly. "And since I can only imagine what Wendy's already told you, there's not much point in denying it."

Blake let out a long, low whistle. "Ho-lee crap, Scott. You're in *love?*"

Scott abandoned the stool to pace in front of the dining table, one hand clamped around the back of his neck. There was that question again, demanding he quit sidestepping the issue and answer it, already, once and for all. Still, remnants of the old Scott, the cautious Scott, the man whose life had been predicated on obligation and a hyper work ethic that left little room for sentiment, kept him from giving his brother a straight answer.

He lowered his hand to hook it on his hip. "All I know is, I want Christina in my life in a way I've never even imagined wanting any woman before. And that if I let this opportunity slip through my fingers before I've explored every angle on how I could make it work, I'll regret it for the rest of my days. And I can't exactly explore those options in Atlanta." After several more beats passed, Scott asked, "You still there?"

"Yeah. I'm here. And you know what? You're right, we only get one shot at this. So if this is what you want, go for it. But, for all our sakes, don't wait much longer to tell the others."

"I won't. I promise."

He disconnected the call, then turned to find Wendy standing in her kitchen doorway, her eyebrows about to fly off her head.

"You're *staying?*"

"It would appear so."

"For *good?*"

"Sure hope so."

His baby sister gawked at him for several seconds, then, on a squeal of delight, waddled over to give him a huge hug.

After a rotten night's sleep, constantly interrupted by disturbing dreams involving Scott and her mother and being all tangled up in tornado debris that turned into a giant cobweb she couldn't break out of because her feet were encased in cement, Christina awoke with a start, scaring poor Gumbo half to death.

Then she remembered she had a checkup with the orthopedist that day and whimpered. Because how, exactly, was she supposed to pull that one off?

However, being an intrepid soul, she decided that since her broken foot actually felt more or less okay, and she drove with her other one, and here was this perfectly good car sitting right outside her front door, she'd drive her own dang self into San Antonio. What was the worst that could happen? The doctor would yell at her?

Except when, an hour later, Scott landed on her doorstep, she realized, no, *this* was the worst that could happen.

"Hey, boy," he said, squatting to roughhouse with the ecstatic dog, and Christina didn't know whether to scream or cry or laugh or what. "I didn't…I thought…after yesterday…" She stopped, grabbed a breath. And hopefully a coherent sentence. "Why are you here?"

"You have a doctor's appointment today, right?"

"Um, yeah. But I was going to drive myself there."

Scott looked up at her as if she'd said she'd just had breakfast with Elvis. "I don't think so." Then he rose, and before she could blink took her face in his hands and kissed her. Sweetly. Gently. But still like a man used to going after what he wanted. And getting it. And once again her spirit did that roller-coaster thing, soaring to what felt like the top of the world, only to drop right back down, leaving her dizzy and slightly woozy and unable to get her bearings.

"You don't play fair," she whispered, dropping her head to his chest.

"I never do." Then he tucked his fingers under her chin, lifting her face so their eyes met, and whispered, "Trust me."

Her eyes flooded. "Why would you even say that?"

"Because you need to know you can. Now let's get moving or you're going to be late."

Yeah, didn't take a brainiac to interpret that dream, did it?

"How was your visit with your mother?" Scott asked once they were on the road.

He would bring that up. "Short. And not exactly sweet."

"I'm sorry."

"So'm I." Then, because she was feeling ambushed and off balance and still light-headed from the kiss, she said, "She's convinced you're only interested in me for sex."

She could practically feel him flinch, followed by a short, startled laugh. "Excuse me?" When Christina shrugged, he tossed a frown her way. "Don't tell me you agree with her?"

"I don't know," she lied. "Are you?"

"No! Not to put too fine a point on it, but if that's what I was after, I would have hardly chosen a woman nursing a broken foot, now would I?"

"So…you don't have the hots for me?"

He got very quiet. "In case you missed it, I didn't exactly kiss you yesterday like I would have kissed my grandmother. But the implication that I—" He stopped, his jaw so tight she could've sharpened a knife on it. "I *care* about you. A great deal. But I know you're skittish, for reasons known only to you—"

"And what difference does it make, what those reasons are? Eventually, you'll go back home, and I'll fade into a vague memory—"

"Except I'm not."

"Not, what?"

"Going back."

Now it was her turn. "*Excuse* me?"

"You heard me." His eyes glanced off hers before he returned them to the road. "I've been scouting out ranch properties with a Realtor the past couple of days. And I think I've found the perfect place, right next to your field where the old barn was—"

"Wait, wait, wait…you're buying a ranch?"

"Yep."

"Here. In Red Rock."

"Since that's where you are, it seemed like a logical choice."

Silence stretched between them like the interminable country highway before Scott blew out a breath.

"And did that sound like stalker-speak as much to you as it did to me?" he asked.

"From anybody else it sure would."

He coughed into his hand, then said, "I meant what I said, about not giving up easily. Call me stubborn, or an idiot, but…I'd still like to see where this goes. Between us, I mean. And I can't do that from four states away. Besides, I always wanted to raise horses—remember my telling you how much I loved to ride when I was a kid?—but once I started working for my father I shoved that dream aside, thinking maybe after I retired…"

And on he went, like the world wasn't imploding around them. Or maybe his world wasn't, maybe his world really was finally landing right side up. Well, whoop-de-do for him—hers sure as heck wasn't. Her world had gone *kaplo-oey,* like a hot dog cooked too long in the microwave.

Because how could she deny that, given her druthers, part of her wanted to see where this was going, too. Even if that part—which would be that tiny remnant still clinging to the fantasy—was at odds with the much larger part that knew exactly where this was going: nowhere. That no matter how many detours they took along the way, or how pleasant those detours might be, they'd still end up at the same place, wouldn't they?

Christina turned her face to the passenger-side window so he wouldn't see how hard she was fighting tears. *Damn* the man—her only safety net had been that he'd go home someday. But if he was staying…

Kaplooey.

"Does knowing how well your foot's healing make it feel better?"

Hanging on to Christina's crutches in case she needed them at some point, Scott leaned against the far wall of the hospital elevator, giving her the space she so obviously needed. Talk about feeling like a first-class dolt—she'd barely looked at or talked to him since his announcement. And here he'd prided himself on being an expert at finessing the client, knowing exactly when to take the next step in negotiations.

"Yes, actually," she said, giving him a meager smile.

Except Christina wasn't a client. Or a convenient, willing distraction from his work. He'd do well to remember that. Apologizing wasn't something that came naturally to him—he was his father's son, after all—but even he knew he'd blundered, big-time, by springing his news on her before she was ready.

He waited until they'd gotten out to his car in the parking lot before saying, "I'm sorry—"

"You threw me a curveball, Scott," she said quietly, then finally looked at him. "I honestly thought..." Shaking her head, she looked away.

"What?"

Her eyes met his again. "That you were flirting. Okay, that's not fair, considering everything you've done for me, but..." She heaved a sigh. "I guess I figured you were simply amusing yourself. That there was no way you could be serious."

"Why is it so difficult to believe that I am?"

"Ohmigosh—where would you like me to start? Like I said before, we're so different. And the way we met...honestly, meeting on *The Bachelor* would be more normal—!"

He cupped her face, watching the words snag in her throat, silently cursing at all that ambivalence in her eyes. "And I've been on more 'normal' first dates than I can count, 95 percent of which I couldn't wait to be over so I could get back to work. So tell me one thing, and be honest—no qualifiers, no prevarication, just the truth. Do you have feelings for me, too?"

Their gazes tangled for what seemed like an eternity until she finally said, "Yes. But—"

"Then I don't give a damn how we met, I'm only glad we did. Because you woke me up. Made me take a good, long look at myself and realize I didn't like what I saw. Who I'd become. If nothing *ever* happens between us I'll always be grateful for that."

He released her to lean against the car, his arms crossed. "Yeah, I stuck around because of you. I never denied it. But I'm staying because to go back to what I was before, *who* I was before, would be a lie. And every day I'm here the clearer that becomes."

After another exchanged look, she said, "My leg's getting tired, I need to sit."

Scott stepped aside so she could get into the car—under her own steam—shutting the door after her then going around to his side. By the time he got in, she'd clearly regrouped. "So you're saying no matter what I do you're still buying that ranch?"

He could almost feel the relief radiating from her. He started the car, backed out of the space. Finally, got it through his thick head that if he had any hope whatsoever of this working he'd have to let her call at least some of the shots. "Yup."

Christina lifted her hand to gently scrape the edge of her thumbnail across her bottom teeth, a habit she indulged when she was nervous, he'd noticed. Then she dropped her hand and he ventured, "Would you like to see it?"

A pause. "I thought it wasn't yours yet."

"I can't get into the house, but I can drive onto the land. The owner's not there."

After a moment she nodded. "Yeah. Okay. Why not?"

Even though it nearly killed him, Scott managed not to grin *too* hard.

She could have lied. Kept her traitorous feelings to herself. Except for one thing they'd already established—she was a sucky liar. And for another, she mused as Scott took her by the hand and leisurely led her across a vast pasture, she couldn't hide her emotions from him if her life depended on it. No man had ever given her the freedom to be herself as he had…or threatened her peace of mind more.

Good news, meet bad news.

"How big did you say the spread was again?"

"Not huge." His elbows now propped on the split-rail fence overlooking a pond edged in live oaks, Scott looked content in the way of a man who could pretty much make anything happen he wanted. "By Texas standards, anyway. Seven hundred acres and change. Close to a thousand if I can wrangle that adjacent parcel."

Christina laughed in spite of herself, even though she couldn't imagine owning that much land. Or any land, for that matter. "What on earth are you going to do with a thousand acres?"

"Anything I want?" And his being as nonchalant about buying an entire ranch as she might have been buying, oh, a carton of milk, only proved they were from different worlds. Why he couldn't see that—or refused to—she did not know. "Raise some horses. And kids. Watch those kids learn to ride."

She started. "So…how many kids are we talking?"

"Dunno. Two? Six? Haven't decided."

"Six?"

"Why not?" He nodded toward the house, a two-story, dormer-windowed jewel with a wraparound porch, set on a tree-crowded berm a half mile or so from where they stood. Late-afternoon sunshine gilded the white clapboards, the simple but stately columns. "House has seven bedrooms. May as well fill them."

"Because it would be inefficient otherwise?"

He glanced over, his grin doing very, very bad things to her stomach. If this was his way of backing off, she was in serious trouble. "That would be my take on it. House is barely five years old and impeccably decorated, by the way. And everything stays, down to the towels in the bathroom cupboards."

"Really? How come?"

"Owner passed away about a year ago. The widow's moving to California to be with their daughter, wants to start completely over. So she's selling the house furnished." He made a face. "Although I could do without the heads."

"Heads? Oh. As in, deer and such."

"As in. Will they let me stay in Texas if I don't hunt?"

"That could be an issue," she said, and he gave an exaggerated sigh, making her laugh. Making her regret… so much. Then he pointed to the west. "There's state-of-the-art stables for twenty horses, right on the other side of the house. Training arenas. Pastures for days." He paused. "And a kennel."

"A kennel?"

"She raised champion beagles. It would be perfect for—"

"Don't say it."

"—your doggy hotel."

Her throat got all tight. "You're doing it again."

"Taking your needs into consideration? Guilty as charged."

"Speaking of dogs," she said, before her imagination ran away from her. "I need to get back to mine."

"Sure thing," Scott said lightly, offering her his arm to walk back over the uneven ground to the car. He plugged his iPod into the car stereo and chose his classical playlist for the ride back to her place, the soothing music filling the space where conversation should have been. When he pulled up in front of her apartment, however, he said, "I have to leave for a few days. Will you be okay?"

"Of course. But why—?"

"I can't very well dump this on my father over the phone."

Steady though his voice might have been, even she could hear the faint anxiety edging his words. "Scott…if this is the right decision, it'll all work out exactly the way it's supposed to."

His eyes tilted to hers, the barest of smiles curving his lips. "Exactly what I keep telling myself," he said quietly, and too late she realized what she'd said. A second later he leaned over and touched his lips to hers, then kissed her forehead. And oh, my, was it hard to get out of the car, to watch him drive off, feeling like her heart was gonna pop out of her chest. At which point she finally, hopelessly admitted that all that kicking and screaming she'd been doing to not fall for the guy?

Had been one big, fat waste of time.

Chapter Nine

"Like hell you're moving to Red Rock," John Michael said, his voice lethally soft. A voice Scott recognized all too well. And had more than steeled himself against.

"I'm not sixteen anymore, Dad," Scott said, every bit as softly, his hands shoved into his pants pockets as he stood in front of his father's massive, curved black glass desk at FortuneSouth's headquarters. Through the floor-to-ceiling windows behind his father the entire Atlanta skyline seemed to glower at Scott in disapproval. "This is what I need to do—"

"Become a *rancher?* Have you lost your mind?"

"No, Dad. I've finally found it."

To his right, leaning against a wall of mahogany bookcases, his brother Mike released an incredulous laugh. "You've dedicated your whole life to FortuneSouth. You can't simply walk away on a whim. For crying out loud, Scott—what about *loyalty?*"

Scott's eyes swung to his brother's. "Considering the amount of business I've brought in? The untold number of fires I've put out over the last ten years? Somehow I think I proved my loyalty some time ago."

His brother looked genuinely perplexed. "Then why—?"

"Because I finally woke up and realized this isn't me." He faced his father again. "And why would you want me in a position of authority if my heart's not in it anymore? That's only a lose-lose situation for everybody, don't you think?"

As Mike muttered something Scott was frankly grateful he couldn't hear, he and his father stared each other down. Then John Michael lowered himself into his leather chair again, rubbing his mouth for a moment until he let his hand fall to squint at Scott. "I know what this is. It's some kind of post-traumatic reaction, from the tornado—"

"No, it's not. Yes, what I went through made me reassess my life, but trust me, I'm thinking perfectly clearly. More clearly than I ever have in my life—"

"You can't quit," his father blustered. "I won't hear of it. To leave me, to leave us, in the lurch like this…that's not the way I raised you."

"Then consider this my thirty days' notice," Scott said mildly. "Whatever duties I can't immediately assign to someone else I'll continue to handle from Red Rock. If nothing else, I can promise you a smooth transition. I owe you at least that much."

"You owe me a helluva lot more than that."

"No, Dad. I don't. Especially since you've made it more than clear that Mike's the heir apparent. Which is fine by me," he said, facing his brother again. "I'm done competing with you, big brother." At his brother's snort, Scott frowned. "What?"

"Can't *deal* with the competition anymore is more like it. That's what this is all about, isn't it? You've finally caved."

Scott laughed. Not what his brother expected, judging from the slightly startled look on his face. "Not at all. I did realize, however, what a waste of energy it is, fighting for something I *don't even want.*"

He caught the exchanged glance between his brother and father, fought the surge of irritation that neither was taking him seriously. "Don't give your notice yet, Scott," John Michael said. "Go on back to Red Rock, take all the time you need—"

"Dad. You're not listening. I'm not going to change my mind. When have you ever known me to make an impetuous decision?"

"Never. Which is why I know this is an aberration. That given enough time you'll realize what a damn fool idea this is and come to your senses—"

Mike's laugh brought both their heads around. "I can't believe I didn't see this sooner… Dad, don't you get it? It's about that gal from the airport, isn't it?" he said to Scott. "The one you stayed behind to 'help'?"

His father's gaze rocketed to his. "Is that true, Scott?"

Until things were settled with Christina, Scott had intended to leave her out of the equation. Especially since he knew his parents hadn't yet fully reconciled themselves to Wendy's precipitous marriage, their approval of Marcos notwithstanding. But at least Wendy's relocation to Red Rock hadn't left a gaping hole in the company's infrastructure, even if it had in his mother's heart. Now, however, he realized he did owe his father something even more than that smooth transition—he owed him the whole truth. Or as much of it as Scott himself knew.

"Yes," he said, over Mike's triumphant, "I knew it!"

"A…woman?" his father said, his expression even more

gobsmacked than before. "You're chucking it all for a *woman?*"

"Not just *a* woman, Dad. The woman I want to spend the rest of my life with." *If she'll have me.*

"So let me get this straight…you met somebody in Red Rock barely two weeks ago and you're ready to give up everything you've ever known, everything you've achieved, for her?"

"That about sums it up."

"Then…what was all that about wanting to be a rancher?"

Suddenly, Scott wanted nothing more than for his father to *understand,* to feel the scorching heat from inside Scott's belly that had rendered him willing to incur not only his father's disapproval, but his wrath—the exact opposite of everything he'd ever thought he'd wanted. Feeling like a Jimmy Stewart character, Scott grabbed the back of the chair in front of John Michael's desk and yanked it out, then dropped into it, pitching toward his father to snag his gaze.

"What keeps you going, Dad? What makes you glad to be alive?"

John Michael looked slightly taken aback. "Pride," he shot back after a moment. "In this business. In family—"

"Exactly. Now tell me why."

"I don't have time for this—"

"Of course you do. Answer the question."

A beat or two passed before his father said, "Because they're mine."

Scott fought a smile. "Then don't you wish the same for your children? To be able to take pride in their *own* accomplishments? To be their own people the way you've been?" He paused. "To have families of their own they can be proud of?"

"Then marry some girl right here in Atlanta. You could have your pick—"

"I don't want 'some girl' from here. I want Christina."

"Why?"

"Aside from her being the most genuine woman I've ever met? Or that she's not impressed with my investment portfolio? Not to mention I get this, this incredible *rush* every time I hear her laugh, or see her smile…" He paused, caught a breath. "I want this woman in my life because she's smart and funny and brings out the best—or at least what I hope is the best—in me without even realizing she's doing it. And because I know if I let her go, especially without putting everything I have into trying to make things work between us, I'll spend the *rest* of my life comparing every woman I meet to her."

Taking no small pleasure in his father's even more flummoxed expression, Scott leaned back in the chair, his hands loosely folded over his abs. "You know, you can be pissed at me all you want, but you have no one to blame but yourself."

"Me?"

"You. Because not only do we all carry your genes, but nobody has ever set a better example of how to go after what you want—and getting it—than you." He let the smile bloom. "Mom's told us it took you three years to convince her to marry you."

To Scott's great delight, color flooded his father's face. Then John Michael stood, linking his hands behind his back as he turned to the window and the vista beyond. "But the ranching thing—"

"Dad—from the first time I rode I've *always* wanted to be around horses, to be able to walk outside my front door and see nothing but land and sky. But to please you, I did my best to convince myself that what I wanted didn't matter. Or that it could at least wait. So tell me—in my place, would you have done the same thing?"

His father turned, the window's aura behind him obliterating his expression. "And this woman…she's really worth the risk?"

A sweet, soul-deep calm such as he'd never known settled over him. "Yes."

John Michael faced the window again. "I need some time to process all this."

"Take all the time you want," Scott echoed, getting to his feet. "As long as you keep in mind that I'm not changing mine."

Mike followed him through his father's outer office and into the black granite-walled, tenth-floor lobby fronting the elevator bank. Scott punched the down button, then stepped back, his eyes cutting to his brother's frowning profile. "Okay. Spit it out."

A moment passed before, a tight smile curving Mike's mouth, he angled his head toward Scott. "I don't think you have any idea how worthy an opponent you've been. How much knowing you were breathing down my neck kept my ass in check all these years. Hard as this is for me to admit, I wouldn't be nearly the asset to FortuneSouth I am if it hadn't been for you."

His turn to be poleaxed, apparently. "Thank you—"

"I'm not done yet." Sucking in a deep breath, Mike glanced toward the elevator door as it silently slid open. As the brothers entered the stainless steel-and-cherrywood-trimmed car, Mike punched the first-floor button and leaned back. "But I can honestly say I never really *admired* you." One corner of his mouth tilted up, he looked at Scott again. "Until today. Nobody knows better than I do the guts it takes to stand up to Dad. So whatever you do,

I'm behind you. A hundred percent. Because damn, bro…" Mike extended his hand. "You *rock.*"

A moment passed before, laughing, Scott gripped his brother's hand. Now, he mused as he crossed through the glass atrium main lobby and through the middle of three massive revolving doors, the only obstacle left was winning over Christina.

Piece of cake, right?

With a loud, frustrated groan, Christina threw off her bedcovers and grabbed for the cast, strapping it on and clumping to the kitchenette to make herself some instant cocoa. From the end of the sofa, Gumbo heaved a great doggy sigh and slid to the floor, yawning as he plodded across the floor to sit catawhompus at her feet.

"I wasn't supposed to miss him, dammit!"

Gumbo wagged his head in slow motion, his big old ears flapping, followed by the *God, again?* eyeroll.

So she might have expressed the sentiment a time or six over the past couple of days. But if the turkey's plan had been to get her so used to having him around she'd feel downright lost when he wasn't, it was working.

Dammit.

The cocoa made, she clomped back to the living room and eased herself onto the sofa, the wind's melancholy moan outside doing nothing to boost her mood. Gumbo hopped up to lay his head on her lap, offering sympathy for about ten seconds before he passed out again.

Of course, she supposed there was always the possibility that, once back home, Scott would come to his senses and realize this whole thing with her and wanting to buy a whole *ranch,* for heaven's sake, had been about as real as Oz had been to Dorothy. Except she'd caught the look on his face when he'd shown her the property, like he'd seen heaven. So she was going to take that as a "no." Especially since Scott didn't strike her as the kind of man given to being fickle.

And every time he looked at her…oh, dear Lord, she got tingles thinking about it—

"No!" she said, loudly enough to wake the dog. Sensing her distress, Gumbo gave her a worried look and several slobbery kisses, doing his level best to make it better. On the table beside her, her phone buzzed—an incoming text. At two in the morning?

She snatched up her cell, getting all tingly again at the sight of Scott's picture, a stealth one she'd taken when they'd been at the ranch.

Pathetic, thy name is Christina.

Can't sleep. Missing u.

Christina stared at the message for the longest time. She didn't *have* to answer. Really. After all, it wasn't like he expected her to. Or anything.

U do realize, she typed, is middle of night?

Gumbo? That u?

See, it was stuff like that, that had her all balled up and confused and, okay, fine, wanting him so bad she could hardly see straight. The goofy stuff, the unexpected stuff. The stuff that made her laugh even as she rolled her eyes harder than the dog. Smirking, she texted back, Yeah. But, dang, is hard 2 txt w nose.

Seconds later the phone rang. With a mix of excitement and dread, she answered. "Hello—?"

"Oh. I was expecting Gumbo."

The grin popped out before she could catch it. "Oh, shoot, was he texting again? I really wish he wouldn't do that, I keep getting these random texts from some poodle named Snooki." So sue her, it was two-freaking-thirty in the morning.

"Ah," Scott said. "Too much eyeliner, enormous..." He paused. "Hair?"

"The very one, how'd you know?"

"I can smell the cheap perfume from here. Tell Gumbo he needs to watch out for those Jersey bitches—they'll eat him alive."

Christina burst out laughing. "That's *terrible*."

"But true. If he knows what's good for him, he'll stick with the local gals."

"Clearly your experience with Texas gals is limited."

"Also true," Scott said, the smile in his voice making her toes curl. "But a situation I look forward to remedying as soon as possible."

"Um...we're not talking about Gumbo's love life anymore, are we?"

"Nope."

Her face burning, she hauled herself to her feet and hobbled into the kitchen to rinse out her mug. "So...how'd it go with your dad?"

"You could at least try to be subtle."

"Subtle is for weenies. So?"

Scott sighed. "I said my piece, he fumed and ranted and refused to accept my resignation, but no blood was shed so I'm counting it a success. He's also convinced I'm out of my mind, of course, but then, so is everyone else."

"And that doesn't at least give you pause?"

"What everyone else thinks? Why should it? I'm done seeking other people's approval, Christina. And I cannot tell you how freeing that is. Which reminds me...my Realtor called, the owner accepted my offer, so we can go to closing next week."

Back in bed, she froze in the middle of tugging up the covers. "Oh. Wow. So...fast?"

"Great, huh? Anyway, I'm taking an extra day or two

here to tie up some loose ends, pack up my personal things from the condo, put the place on the market. But I have a surprise for you."

"O-oh?"

"You remember the resort we passed on the way home from the hospital? There's a gift certificate for you and a guest waiting at the front desk, for a full day of pampering."

"Scott…no. I mean, that's very sweet, but you've done so much for me already—"

"And I'm going to keep doing things for you, so deal. Get some sleep now, and I'll see you when I get back to Red Rock. Okay?"

"Okay," she said, heaving a great sigh as she set her phone on her nightstand. *Okay?* Not even remotely.

Which undoubtedly made her the most reluctant Cinderella in history.

"Frankly," Wendy said as she settled her enormous self into the chaise next to Christina's in the spa's luxurious sunroom, "I don't know whether to kiss you or my brother for thinking of this. I haven't been able to see my feet since November, let alone paint my toenails. So this is heaven."

At one with a chaise so comfortable Christina almost wouldn't have minded dying in it, she had to agree. Unlike Enid, who'd turned down Christina's invitation with an impassioned declaration that the very *idea* of people she didn't know from Eve touching her half-naked body was at the very least unseemly, if not downright repulsive. Not that Christina didn't have to fight the giggles while trying to select from the long list of scrub/wrap/massage options that sounded more like lunch than treatments. But once the skilled staff began their ministrations…ohmigosh, she was a goner within a minute flat.

Besides the massages—they even had special accommodations for Wendy's pregnant belly—they'd had facials and mani-pedis, although Christina had had to forgo the "pedi" part of that for obvious reasons. Now, wrapped in plush white robes, they lounged by the kidney-shaped indoor pool, shaded by a veritable forest of trees and shrubs happily thriving in the sunlight-flooded room. Lunch would follow, the magical day ending with Christina's first professional haircut in…years.

So maybe she could get used to this.

She settled back in the chair and closed her eyes, the gurgling of an unseen fountain mingling with Mozart or somebody in the background. "Marcos doesn't mind?"

Wendy had hinted that her husband had some issues with not being able to keep Wendy in the manner to which she was accustomed. Even though Wendy had assured him that having her own home and a husband who adored her far outweighed the frills she'd willingly given up.

"That he gets a very happy wife at the end of the day? Not a bit. So…I suppose you know Scott's found his ranch?"

So much for relaxed. Opening her eyes, Christina faced her new friend. "Yes. But tell me something, since you know him a lot better than I do—do you think he's making the right choice?"

"Why wouldn't he be?"

Christina looked down at her lap. "It seems so…fast."

Opening the neck of her robe a bit, Wendy sagged back in her chair and tossed Christina her trademark disarming smile. "It's the Fortune impulsive streak. Like our own personal fault lines, long overdue for some major shifting." The smile widened. "Except for me, who's been shifting constantly since I was born, much to my parents' dismay. I'm guessing Scott's has finally worked its way to the surface. You mark my words, though, the others will follow. And sooner rather than later, if my hunch is correct."

"I'm confused—so you do think Scott's being impulsive?"

"For once in his life, yes. But that's not a bad thing, considering that my siblings' usual modus operandi is to think everything to death before they make a decision, and then only if it's one guaranteed not to ruffle feathers. If you ask me, it's about time Scott—and everyone else—started thinking with their hearts. Doing what *feels* right instead of what they *think* is right."

"But what if that impulse *isn't* right? Because there's a lot to be said for thinking through something as important as changing your entire *life*."

"Oops." Scott's sister reached across the space dividing them and touched Christina's wrist. "This isn't about his buying the ranch, is it?"

"Oh, Wendy..." Her forehead pinched, Christina met Wendy's amused gaze. She wanted to believe in new beginnings, in taking chances, she really did. But for every thought that came, encouraging her forward, ten more rushed in to remind her of the risks. "What on earth does he see in me? We have virtually nothing in common—"

"Neither do Marcos and I. On the surface. And yet I've never felt this comfortable with anyone in my whole life. Christina...this may be a stretch, but I'm going to guess my brother sees what I see—besides the whole cute-as-all-get-out thing you've got going, I mean. That you're fun to be with and bighearted and *good* with a capital *G*. If you've got those basics down, the rest will follow."

"Meaning he sees me as a diamond in the rough."

"No, I meant that if those core values mesh, nothing else means squat." Wendy frowned. "Do you really think Scott sees you as someone he can mold into whatever image he wants you to be?"

"It had occurred to me."

"That's not Scott, Christina. And if that's what he'd wanted, believe me, there were *plenty* of women only too willing to turn themselves inside out to please him."

"And that's supposed to make me feel better?"

"Yes. It is. Because he didn't want any of them. He wants you. Exactly as you are."

"So you're saying I should cancel the hair appointment?"

Wendy laughed. "No way. We always have the right to re-create our *own* image." Then she sobered. "Look, it's not my place to tell you what to do, or what you should think. But I love my brother, and it's pretty clear he's very, very serious about you. If you feel the same way, then why not simply roll with it?"

With that, Wendy leaned back and closed her eyes as if it was all solved, leaving Christina to think, *Why not, indeed?*

Chapter Ten

With a jolt that sent a renewed thrill of anticipation through him, Scott's commercial flight touched down in San Antonio, on a clear, mild day that hinted of spring. Marcos met him at the airport, looking marginally more relaxed than the last time Scott had seen him. Then again, that could be sheer exhaustion.

"Hate to ask…but how are things going?" he asked as he shouldered his carry-on bag and fell in step with Marcos through the concourse.

"Javier's still hanging in there, the restaurant's still standing and your sister and I are still married," Wendy's husband said with a tired smile. "So I'm counting my blessings. But since we're already in the city, do you mind if we swing by the hospital?"

Scott checked his watch. "I'm closing on the ranch at four, so that's two hours yet. Plenty of time."

"Then it's a done deal?"

"All but the signing. And the check."

Grinning, Marcos clapped him lightly on the back. "I'm glad. And Wendy will be beside herself. She doesn't complain—too much—but I know she misses her family."

They arrived at the hospital twenty minutes later, running into Dr. Cuthbert, the neurologist Dr. Rhodes had praised so highly, as she emerged from Javier's room. The tall, graying brunette shook hands with Marcos before steering them back to the nurses' station.

"I just got off the phone with your father. But I'll tell you what I told him, that Javier's making enough progress to start bringing him out of the coma within a week or so. And no," she said, her expression kind, "we have no idea what to expect. How, exactly, the brain works remains very much a mystery, and every patient's experience is different. He may well be disoriented at first, or even angry that he can't remember what happened. This is going to require great patience on everyone's part."

Marcos nodded, then pushed out a breath. "And…his legs?"

"His orthopedist can explain everything in more detail, but from what we can tell the broken bones are healing very well. But there was a lot of muscle damage, and Javier will have been immobile for nearly a month." The doctor paused. "He may have to relearn how to walk."

When Marcos softly swore, Scott frowned at the doctor. "Dr. Rhodes said your rehab facility is good?"

"A lot better than good, Mr. Fortune. One of the best in the country. In fact…Leah?" She called out to a slender young woman in bright blue scrubs chugging past, her long auburn hair caught back in a ponytail. She turned, pale brows lifted in a makeup-free face. "I'd like to introduce you to Leah Roberts, the rehab nurse who'll most likely be assigned to Javier's case. Leah, this is Javier's brother, Marcos. And Marcos's brother-in-law, Scott Fortune."

"Oh!" Closing the space between them, Leah tucked her clipboard under her arm to shake Marcos's hand, then Scott's, her grip firm and confident. As was her smile. "I saw your brother earlier today," she said to Marcos. "Along with the rest of his team. We've been discussing various options for his rehabilitation once he's brought out of the coma."

"How long…?"

Leah clasped the clipboard to her chest. "That will depend on your brother," she said gently. "But he's got youth and health in his favor." Then her smile flashed into a full-out grin. "Not to mention an enormous support system, from what all the nurses up here tell me. That counts for a great deal." Her pager buzzed. "Shoot, I'm so sorry," she said, apology flooding her hazel eyes as she backed away to punch the elevator button. "I'm already late for my next appointment. But they've got your number on file, right? So I'm sure we'll be in touch."

The doctor made her excuses as well, leaving Scott and Marcos free to see Javier. Thanks to an MP3 player with speakers, classical guitar music greeted them when they entered—one of Javier's favorite musical genres, Scott already knew. Although the obligatory heart and blood pressure monitors were doing their thing, as well as the ever-present IV, for all intents and purposes Javier simply looked asleep, if thinner than Scott remembered.

"Hey, man," Marcos said softly, twining his fingers around his brother's and launching into a funny, upbeat monologue about something that had happened in the restaurant the other day. As heavily as his brother's condition must have been weighing on the younger man's heart, clearly he was determined not to let it show.

When Marcos said, "Scott Fortune's here, he wants to say hi," Scott stepped closer to the bed. Picking up on the obvious cue, Scott told Javier about his decision to move to Red Rock, the ranch that would soon be his, how much he was looking forward to being a real part of the community.

Once back on the road to Red Rock, Marcos glanced over Scott with a half smile. "Thanks. For talking to Javier like that."

"No problem."

"Not for you, maybe. For other people…they forget that just because he can't outwardly respond, it doesn't mean he's not aware. Nobody knows how much he's taking in, obviously, but Dr. Cuthbert told us how important it is to keep the atmosphere positive, to not talk negatively about him when we're in the room, or act like he's not even there. And that sensory stimulation helps—the music, touching, reading to him, even favorite smells. It all helps keep him connected. We hope, anyway."

"I'm sure it does."

They chatted about Scott's plans for the ranch for the rest of the ride, until they pulled into Marcos's driveway alongside Wendy's car. Having finally turned in the rental when he flew back to Atlanta, Scott followed his brother-in-law into his house long enough to dump his bag, give Wendy a hug and ask if he could borrow the prized vintage Mustang she'd had driven out to Texas.

"Keys are in my purse. I take it everything went okay with Dad?" she said, slowly following him back to the front door.

"As well as could be expected." The keys retrieved, he bent over to give her a quick kiss on the top of her head. "And I promise to tell you all about it later."

Her arms like chicken wings as she supported her lower back, Wendy grinned. "Don't hurry back on my account."

"Wasn't planning on it," he said, her laughter following him all the way out to her car.

He might have said, "Hi." Maybe even, "I'm back." Christina didn't remember. Or care, frankly.

Not that she'd planned on locking lips with the man the second she opened her door. Nor was she sure who had launched him/herself at whom. But now, ten, fifteen seconds into the kiss, all she knew was she could no more *not* have kissed him right then than she could have flown.

Although come to think of it, she was flying pretty darn high right now, wasn't she?

Their mouths still joined, she vaguely heard the slam of her front door as Scott kicked it shut, Gumbo's whine of concern, then her back was against the wall, her hands held over her head as Scott sweetly assaulted her mouth with more passion—and talent, it should be noted—than she'd ever experienced. And her entire body egged her on, as well as her heart, scurrying along behind and whispering, *Me, too, me, too, me, too.*

Or maybe her heart was in the lead, it was kinda hard to tell what with all the sighing and gasping and the idiot dog hopping around as if he wanted to get in on the act.

Finally Scott backed away and looked at her. And smiled. And her heart whispered, *Would I lie to you?*

Just like the serpent chatting with Eve, yep.

But Scott was fingering her hair and grinning like nobody's business, and thinking was kinda not her top priority, right at the moment. "I like it," he said, and she clicked in enough to remember she'd more or less given the stylist at the spa free rein.

Christina combed one hand through the shorter, highlighted layers feathering around her neck and shoulders, the weightless bangs which made her eyes look enormous, exactly as the stylist had promised. "Good thing, since you paid for it."

"But do *you* like it?"

"Me? I love it."

"Then that's all that matters." He kissed her again, light and breezy, then grabbed her hand, dangling a set of keys in front of her with the other.

House keys.

"It's yours?"

"Every square inch of it." Scott's hand found her waist, tugging her close. "How 'bout a tour?"

Anticipation sizzled in the pit of her stomach. And not only about seeing the house, she thought as the sizzle meandered to points north and south and pretty much everywhere in between. And you know what? Maybe it was time to give in to the sizzle. To simply enjoy the moment. Because for darn sure she didn't have a whole lot of moments like these.

Sorry, Mama, she thought, even though she wasn't.

"I suppose I could fit it into my schedule."

Scott kissed her nose. Then her lips. Then, briefly, her neck. Right under her earlobe. Yeah. There. "I hoped you might. C'mon, boy—"

"Um…how's about we leave the dog home this time?"

Scott's eyes swung to hers, dark and curious, like those of a man wondering if he'd heard right. "You sure?"

"Very," she said.

Even though she wasn't at all.

"Good Lord," Christina said when they finally wound up back in the spacious, slate-floored family room off the cook's paradise of a kitchen. "You need a GPS system just to find a bathroom!" Her brow furrowed, she glanced up at the enormous buck's head mounted over the stone fireplace, shuddered, then clomped to one of the two leather sofas facing each other and collapsed into it.

"So what do you think?" Scott grabbed a suede pillow off the other end to cushion her foot when she lifted it onto the square, also Texas-sized, inlaid coffee table between the sofas, then sat beside her, plunking his feet up on the table, too.

On what sounded like a weary laugh, she faced him, her newly lightened hair fanning over the caramel-colored leather behind her head. The woman looked better in jeans and a hooded sweatshirt than most women sporting a thousand bucks' worth of designer fashion. No lie.

"It's real pretty and all, but criminy, Scott—this room alone is twice the size of my whole apartment. I do realize you're used to living in places a bit bigger than that, but doesn't this feel a little…over the top? Even for you?"

His arms crossed over his chest, Scott contemplated his Italian loafers for several seconds. "For one person, you mean?" he said at last.

"Well, yeah. Unless you're plannin' on having the horses live in here with you."

Laughing, he unfolded his arms to slip one behind Christina's shoulders and pull her close. She didn't resist. "One thing you need to know about me—I never do, or buy, anything without considering its investment potential." Massaging her shoulder through the soft fabric, he laid his cheek on her head. "How much something will increase in value over the years."

"You mean…like if you wanted to sell it at some point down the road?"

"In some cases, yes. But not in this one."

She lifted her eyes. "I don't understa—"

He caught her mouth with his, a little "Yes!" sounding in his brain—and other places—when she immediately softened, opening to him, her tongue meeting his in a playful dance that he found exceptionally…encouraging. But when he broke the kiss, her eyes still searched his, rife with questions.

"This is an investment in my future," he said softly, stroking her cheek. "And I hope…an investment in ours."

"Ours. As in…you and me?"

"And Gumbo, if he's up for it."

"Don't make jokes, Scott, don't…" She pulled out of his arms, floundering about in an attempt to get up.

"I'm dead serious, Christina. I always have been. And if you don't believe me—" he fumbled a bit himself, pulling the ring box out of his shirt pocket "—believe this."

She gawked at the aqua velvet box in his hand as though it were about to blow up in her face, then turned the gawking on him. "You *are* insane."

And it probably was crazy, to make this kind of commitment, this soon. Even crazier to ask her for one. But his entire life he'd deferred to logic, to common sense and reason and doing things the "right" way and none of them had ever made him feel one-tenth of what he felt when he looked into Christina's eyes. So he flipped open the box, anyway, to reveal the ring, a modest emerald-cut sapphire flanked with diamond baguettes.

"You said you liked blue," he said.

"Oh, for pity's sake," she said, laughing a little, and he felt the anxiety unfist inside him.

Her smile faded, though, as she shook her head. "You'd really put your heart on the line like that for me?"

Scott glanced down at the ring, still in his hand. "I think I already have." When she hmmphed out another soft laugh, he said, "Look…if you're not ready to think of this as an engagement ring, then don't. I completely understand. But I couldn't think of another way to show you I'm not flirting, I'm not teasing…and for damn sure I don't see you as some sort of 'project.' I want to share this house, my life, with you. I *love* you," he said softly into her I-don't-believe-I'm-hearing-this eyes. "And I promise I'll wait as long as it takes to close the deal."

On a cross between a huff and a groan, Christina finally got to her feet and stiffly walked to the picture window overlooking the sweeping lawn and one of the ponds beyond. "Is that what I am to you? A deal?"

Yearning bled through her words, gave the lie to her defensive posture. Scott came up behind her to wrap her up in his arms. "The best damn deal I've ever run across," he whispered into her ear, feeling her rapid pulse compete with his. "And the only one I've ever truly cared whether I landed or not."

Gently, he twisted her around to face him, his fingers winnowing through her hair to cradle the back of her neck, their mouths so close he could feel her breath, coming in short, sweet bursts. "And if you can't trust your intuition, trust mine. Because it's never been wrong yet."

Never in her life had she wanted to believe so badly. To let herself fall into the promise in those warm brown eyes. *If this is a dream,* Christina thought, *I don't want to wake up. Ever.*

But nobody knew better than she did that wanting wasn't enough to change what was. And that trusting had gotten her into trouble before. In other words, eventually she'd wake up. And so would Scott, she wagered.

Only, when she did, she didn't want it to be one of those frustrating dreams that comes to a screeching halt right before the good stuff happens. And anyway, if she initiated it, she was in control, right?

So she stood on tiptoe to kiss him, deep and open-mouthed and with what she hoped was clear intent, melding her body with his until she felt his unmistakable response against her belly, dimly remembered sensation though that was.

His hands found their way to her shoulders, gently setting her apart as hope and caution tumbled in his eyes. "Just so we're clear…?"

Christina blew out a breath. "You want to talk deals? Here's mine. I want to make love to you so badly I can barely think straight." When his brows shot up, she added, "But it has to be on my terms. Meaning…no promises. And I know that's not fair to you—"

"Why don't you let me be the judge of that?" he said with a lopsided grin, slipping his hands around her waist and yanking her so close you couldn't've slipped a credit card between them. Then he kissed her again, all slow and sweet, at which point she realized that staying in control was a pipe dream. He swept her into his arms and carted her off upstairs into the master bedroom, all done up in shades of green, or maybe blues—she wasn't exactly focused on the décor at the moment—and set her on the bed.

"Don't look up," he said, and of course she did, to find a great horned animal of some sort looming over the bed. "Told you not to look," Scott said when she shrieked out a laugh, then lowered her eyes to discover he was nekkid.

She couldn't move. Or speak, barely. Although she did manage to get out, "I don't know how frisky I can be, with this foot."

And he said, "Not to worry, I can be frisky enough for the two of us."

Man wasn't just whistling Dixie. Whew.

Grinning, he started to undress her. Like he wasn't in any hurry, certain evidence to the contrary. She felt like… like a much-looked-forward-to present being carefully unwrapped, a thought that made her giggle and brought tears to her eyes at the same time. And when, after what felt like hours, there was nothing left between them but heated glances and dry-mouthed anticipation, he got down to serious business.

How is it I've lived without this? she idly wondered as Scott patiently—and, apparently, with no small delight—stoked fires she'd thought long gone cold, only to realize what she'd had before? No comparison. Still, she was in control, in charge, nothing was happening without her permission, her consent—

"Let go, sweetheart," Scott commanded, thrilling her, even as she thought, on a gasp, *Let go? Completely? Not on your life,* a moment before she arched and tensed and screamed—wasn't like anybody could hear her…and then—*then*!—he made her scream again.

"I didn't know I could do that," she got out when her breathing finally slowed and her brain cells came out from hiding.

"I did," Scott said, and then started up all over again with the kissing and the stroking and the feathery touches in—oh, sweet heaven!—exactly the right places until her eyes damn near crossed, and the phrase *putty in his hands* came to mind before he levered himself over her, capturing her gaze in his as if he could see right through to the other side. "How's the foot?"

She sputtered a laugh. "What foot?"

He reached for a condom—and where had that come from, pray?—but she shook her head, kicking the sadness to the curb. "Not necessary, I'm safe." Then she smiled. "You?"

He stroked her bangs off her forehead. "You trust me that much?"

And oh, dear Lord, did she. About this, anyway. "Yes. I do." Then before she could shift underneath him, lift her good leg, he did it for her, sliding inside her, his gaze still welded to hers as he took charge. Took over.

And there wasn't a damn thing she could do about it. Or, frankly, wanted to, at that moment, the surrender too sweet, too heady. Until she linked her hands at the back of his neck and snaked her good leg around him, to hold him still when he tried to move.

"Not yet," she whispered, her eyes closed. "I want to remember this forever."

Chuckling, Scott nuzzled her neck and every nerve ending she possessed sighed with bliss. Traitors. "Not sure about forever, but I can maybe give you thirty seconds."

"Deal," she said, opening her eyes to nearly choke on the desire and hope and trust she saw in his. Once again, the fire kindled, and she caught her lip between her teeth as the first wave rolled through.

And kept on going.

This is getting to be a habit, she thought as she floated back to earth in time to catch Scott's liftoff, and she twined her arms around him and held on tight.

As if he were actually hers.

Afterwards, he settled between her legs, his head on her chest where she could toy with his dark, rumpled hair as the regrets already began to show their smarmy little faces, taunting her for yielding the one thing she'd promised herself she wouldn't.

And she didn't mean her body.

At her sigh, Scott lifted himself up enough to meet her gaze again, his brow puckered as he knuckled away the single, lazy tear dribbling down her cheek. "Hmm. Not the reaction I was going for."

She frowned back at him. "You made love to me."

"Um…yeah. Kinda thought that was the point."

"No, I mean…" With a shaky laugh, she touched his cheek. "You made love to *me*. Put me first. Nobody…" Her eyes filling again, she shook her head.

Scott shifted to hold her close, tucking her head underneath his chin. "You're welcome," he said, and she burbled a laugh. Then he said, "Don't move"—as if she could—and got out of bed, grabbing a throw from a nearby chair to wrap around his waist before he left the room. A minute later he was back.

With the ring.

Seated on the edge of the mattress, he twisted the ring so the stones flashed in the afternoon sunlight. "You want forever?"

You have no idea, Christina thought sadly as she tugged the sheet up over her breasts. But how could she possibly trust what she knew absolutely nothing about? And yet she felt powerless to resist when Scott took her hand into his, slipped the ring on her finger. "It's a promise of my commitment. Not yours. But every time you look at this I want you to remember, as close as we just were?" He smiled. "It's only the beginning. Because I will always be here for you, honey. I swear."

Staring at the ring, she felt her face burn. She needed to come clean. Now. While there was still a chance of getting out of this without anyone getting hurt.

"Scott, I—"

"If you don't like it, you can pick something else out that suits you better."

"No, I love it, it's just—"

From somewhere on the floor, his phone rang.

"You should probably get that."

"That's what voice mail is for. You were saying?"

"Get it," she said, forcing a smile as she pushed him aside to get up. "I'm going to go take a quick shower, anyway," she said, gathering her clothes. "I'll be back in a jif."

Shaking, she closed the bathroom door behind her, crossing her arm over her breasts to watch the pretty little ring wink in the lights bordering the giant framed mirror. She could almost hear it chiding her, for being at the very least dishonest. For letting Scott believe he could make her into something she'd never be.

She stretched out her hand, her blurred vision softening the sparkle.

But not the ache in her heart.

By the time Scott dug his phone out of his pants pocket, he'd missed his father's call. John Michael's message was typically brusque. *"Call me."*

Talk about an afterglow killer.

Although truthfully, Scott thought as he ducked into another of the four upstairs bathrooms to take his own shower, there was nothing his father, or anyone else, could say or do to derail how good he felt right now. A feeling that went way beyond that relaxed state that came with sexual release. Because while Scott was no stranger to sex, this was the first time he could say he'd *made love.*

And man, was that an eye-opening experience, or what?

For Christina, too, he thought on a chuckle as the hot water pummeled his back, if all those startled gasps were any indication, the mind-blowing yin yang of her asserting, then yielding control. Never had a power struggle been so much fun.

Except…it was driving him nuts, that he had no idea

how to banish the uncertainty still fighting for purchase in her eyes. That had sent her scurrying away, clearly not wanting company in the shower. Judging from what they'd just shared, he highly doubted he was pressuring her into something she didn't want. Desperately, if his intuition was correct.

So why, he wondered as he headed back to the bedroom, a towel wrapped around his hips, did she still look so damn afraid to trust him?

Afraid of *him?*

His mood now soured, he returned his father's call, putting the phone on speaker mode as he buttoned his shirt.

"Hey, Dad—what's up?"

"Brad Stevens called, wondered why you haven't been in touch with him."

Scott pulled in a deep, silent breath through his nose. "Because I turned that account over to Mike. Which I explained to Brad when I spoke with him yesterday."

"But he likes *you*."

"And I'm flattered. Really. But he's not my client anymore. He's Mike's. By the way, you and Mom are going to love my new house. Seven bedrooms, everyone can stay here when they come out after Wendy's baby arrives. Christina says the hunting trophies have to go, though, they creep her out—"

"You already bought her a house?"

Slightly taken aback, Scott paused in the midst of buckling his belt. "I bought myself a house. Which, yes, I want Christina to share with me—"

"Dammit, Scott—I cannot believe you're chucking it all for some snack bar waitress!"

Never, not once, had his father ever struck any of them. But his words now stung with all the force of an actual blow. Then he frowned.

"Who told you she was a waitress?"

"It doesn't matter. Why? Isn't she?"

"No. I mean, she was, yes—as a means to put herself through school, for heaven's sake. Which for one thing is hardly a crime against humanity and for another doesn't even begin to define who she is. You're many things, Dad, but I've never known you to be a snob. Mom was your attorney's receptionist, for crying out loud—"

"The summer we met, yes. Between her junior and senior year at Smith. The woman's after your money, Scott—can't you see that?"

Furious, Scott snatched up his phone from the dresser and put it back on private…the precise moment he glanced into the mirror to see Christina behind him in the open doorway. The eyes met for barely a second before she wheeled on her casted foot and clomped away.

"I've got to go, Dad," Scott muttered as he went after her, pocketing his phone before his father could reply.

"Christina, stop!"

Since it wasn't like she could exactly run down the curved staircase, she halted at the top, one hand clutching the wooden bannister. "Please don't say that sounded worse than it was. And don't touch me!"

She sensed Scott take a step back. Sensed, too, that he was not a happy camper right now. "Yeah, that was pretty bad. I'm also sure it's a knee-jerk reaction, because I'm resigning, moving away. He's upset, but he'll get over it. Besides, it's what I think about you that matters, not what my father thinks—"

"He called me a gold digger!" she said, wheeling on him, the déjà vu making her dizzy. "Or as good as. How on earth could we possibly have a relationship when your father clearly hates me?"

"He doesn't even know you—"

"Didn't stop him from judging me, did it? And I told you not to touch me!" she said when he grabbed her shoulders and yanked her to his chest.

"Tough," Scott said into her hair. "Look, I'm none too pleased with him, either, at the moment. But please believe me—" He relaxed his hold to set her back, his gaze caressing hers. "Whatever you heard, it's highly uncharacteristic. When he does get to know you, he'll love you as much as I do—"

His phone buzzed. "See, that's probably Dad right now, calling back to apologize…oh." Frowning, he brought up the text message, then looked at Christina, all the color drained from his face.

"That was Wendy. She's in labor. And she can't get hold of Marcos."

Chapter Eleven

Twenty minutes later they pulled into Wendy's driveway, the worry tensing Scott's face twisting Christina inside out. There'd been no time to get her home first, which seemed to bother Scott a lot more than it did Christina, who'd switched into crisis mode the moment she'd heard.

"Wen?" he called out the instant they were through the door. "Where are you, sweetheart?"

"In our b-bedroom!"

Scott roared down the short hallway, Christina right behind him. Wendy was lying on her left side on top of the covers, her arm protectively curled around her bulging middle.

"There was some sort of supply crisis at the restaurant," she whispered. "M-Marcos had to make a quick trip up to New Braunfels, I wasn't doing this when he l-left! And I didn't call him right away because I thought it was gas or something at first—"

"Shh, shh, shh..." Scott sat on the edge of the bed, stroking her hair away from her tear-streaked face and making a lump rise in Christina's throat. "Did you call your doctor?"

"What d-do you think? S-she said to d-drink a couple g-glasses of water and lie on m-my left side to see if the c-contractions stopped. It's been more almost an hour and they h-haven't."

Scott stood. "What's her number? We can meet her at the hospital."

"It's on the refrigerator. But she said—"

"I don't give a damn what she said. I'm not about to take any chances with you. Or my niece. And I'll call Marcos while I'm at it. He can meet us there, too."

After Scott left in search of the number, Christina awkwardly lowered herself to her knees to fold her hand around the young woman's, willing herself to stay in the moment. To not give in to the fear. The memories. Wendy gave her a shaky sigh.

"I'm glad you're here."

Christina returned her smile. "Me, too. Did your water break?"

"N-no."

"Then this is probably just a very scary false alarm—"

"Ohmigosh!" Turning over Christina's left hand, Wendy's eyes flashed to hers. "What's this? Did Scott *propose?*"

Damn. With everything else going on, she'd forgotten about the ring. "It's...no. Not quite." Christina shoved her hair behind her ear and tried to remove her hand from Wendy's viselike grip. "It's more like...a promise ring."

Wendy angled Christina's hand to get a better look. If nothing else, at least it distracted Wendy from her own plight. "That must've been some promise."

You have no idea, Christina thought as Scott returned. "Okay, it would be quicker for me to get you there than to wait for the EMTs, so let's get cracking. Do you have a bag or something?"

"It's so early I hadn't p-packed one yet…oh!"

At her scrunched face—although more in fear than pain, Christina surmised—Scott scooped his sister into his arms, only to let out a curse. "Crap—I can't take you in the Mustang!"

"There's a minivan in your neighbor's driveway," Christina said, hustling out of the room as fast as the stupid cast would let her. "Maybe they'll let us borrow it!"

The pleasant, middle-aged woman who answered the door was more than happy to oblige, handing over the keys before her husband could even lever himself off the recliner behind her.

"Oh, my goodness, that sweet girl! You tell her Morton and me'll keep her in our prayers, you hear?"

"Got 'em!" she called to Scott seconds later, who swiftly carted Wendy across the yard, gently settling her into the van's middle seat. A minute later, they were off.

"Hurry," Wendy whispered behind them.

"You got it, honey," Scott said, gunning the poor minivan probably faster than it had ever gone before.

Scott dropped into the waiting room chair, exhausted but still tingling from the previous hour's excitement. Marcos had gotten there not five minutes after they did, the same time as Wendy's doctor. After her exam Wendy had been admitted and was being given medication to stop the labor. If it took, she could probably go back home tomorrow, although she'd be on strict bed rest for the rest of the pregnancy—no muffin baking!—which ought to make his always-on-the-go sister even more nuts.

If it didn't, he thought with an anxious spasm, Dr. Curtiss assured him they had an excellent neonatal unit, that MaryAnne would get the best care possible.

Returning from the ladies' room, Christina sat beside him, her makeup-free face pale in the ghastly artificial light. Scott reached for her hand, holding on tight in an attempt to pick up where they'd left off when Wendy's frantic text had come through.

Her eyes briefly cut to his before, blushing, she looked down to brush nonexistent lint off her lap. "They're going to be fine, Scott."

He frowned slightly, wondering if she'd deliberately misinterpreted the gesture. Then he exhaled. "Wendy was a preemie, too. Six weeks early. Scared us all half to death."

"I can imagine," Christina said after a moment. "Then again, she certainly didn't seem to suffer any ill effects from it, right?"

One side of his mouth tilted. "Physically, no. Although there's a reason she was spoiled to death."

"I don't think she's spoiled at all."

"You didn't know her back then. Whatever she wanted, she got. Or made everyone miserable until she did." He looked over; Christina's eyes were still lowered. "You did good back there. Keeping Wendy from losing it. Not to mention me."

Slipping her hand out of his, she sort of laughed. "Oh, yeah, I'm just a regular rock," she said, twisting the ring around and around on her finger, like Gumbo trying to make himself comfortable on his bed. "Long as it's somebody else's drama."

"Hey. You okay?" When she lifted bewildered eyes to his, he said, "We kind of left things…unfinished. Back at the house."

"Oh. Right." Her nostrils flared when she blew out a breath. "It's not that. Well, not entirely. It's…being here. It brings back memories."

"From after the tornado?"

"No. From—"

"She's asleep," Marcos said, coming up behind them and sinking into the chair catty-corner to Christina, the lingering concern in his eyes duking it out with the relief evident in his relaxed posture. "So far the meds seem to be working, she hasn't had a contraction for an hour. But she's already three centimeters dilated and 50 percent effaced, which the doctor said is unusual for a first-timer this early in pregnancy."

"So…what does that mean?" Scott asked.

"That they're going to keep her for a few days instead of sending her back home tomorrow. Just to be sure." Then he gave them a weary smile. "Thanks for everything, but you guys don't have to stick around."

"She's my sister, believe me I don't mind—"

"I know you don't," Marcos said, getting to his feet. "But hopefully she's going to stay asleep for a while now and keep that baby inside. So please. Go."

Scott stood as well, holding out a hand to help Christina up. "You call me, though, if anything changes?"

"You got it."

However, he waited until they were in the van and out of the hospital parking lot before he said, "So what were you saying before Marcos showed up? About being in the hospital bringing up memories?"

Her gaze fixed straight ahead, Christina forked her fingers through her bangs, then folded her hands in her lap, and for a moment Scott thought she was going to clam up again. Before he could call her on it, however, she said, very quietly, "Seven years ago, I was in that maternity wing. Only, that time, there was nothing anybody could do."

Scott's breath caught in his throat. "You lost a baby?"

"I wasn't as far along as Wendy. Only four months. But, yes."

"Damn, honey…being around Wendy—"

"And you can stop that right now. For one thing, you didn't know. And for another, it's not like I can avoid pregnant women for the rest of my life. Besides, I've always believed God puts us where He needs us to be. And that we don't always get a vote in the matter. This wasn't about me, it was about Wendy and MaryAnne."

"Well, now it *is* about you." Scott's hands tightened around the steering wheel. "Why didn't you tell me about the baby?"

"For what it's worth, I was going to earlier, only Wendy called and somehow that didn't seem like the right time for a stroll down memory lane."

"When has it ever been?"

He sensed her eyes cut to his profile, then back to the taillights a hundred feet in front of them. "You said it didn't matter."

"As to how I feel about you? No. But it's obviously coloring how you feel about me." He gave her a brief, hard look. "In which case, yeah. It matters. Because whether you want to admit it or not…it's holding you back."

"I know," she whispered, then sighed out a breathy laugh. "It's like…my head's that closet crammed to the gills with all that stuff you simply do not want to deal with. Which is kinda funny, when I think about it, considering how much I detest clutter of any kind…"

She did that raking her thumbnail across her bottom teeth thing for a moment…then, with a sigh, finally yanked open that closet door.

* * *

They'd been high school sweethearts from their sophomore year on, she said quietly, steadily, as Scott drove, focusing on the headlights piercing the darkness in front of them. Chris and Chris, joined at the hip, homecoming king and queen. The perfect couple who never had a single fight.

Even though he came from money and she didn't.

"Not that it made a lick of difference to us," Christina said as a sick knowing-where-this-was-going feeling shuddered through Scott. "Or so I'd convinced myself—but his folks weren't exactly thrilled. Especially since Christopher was their only child, and they had Big Plans for him. Which did not include little ol' me. So I guess we had that whole Romeo and Juliet thing going on. Although that story didn't end too well, either, did it?"

Scott hesitated, then said, "Since you're still here, I take it there was no poison involved?"

"Not the kind you drink, no. But thoughts can be a kind of poison, too. Even if it takes a long time to take effect. In any case, right after graduation we eloped, because it was rebellious and romantic and proved we were adults who could make our own decisions. Only then he brought me home—his home, I mean—as his wife and all hell broke loose."

"I take it his folks didn't come around?"

Her laugh sounded raw. "You might say. His father pointed at me like I was a stray dog who'd followed Chris home and said, 'You're old enough to marry that piece of white trash, then you're damn well old enough to pay your own bills.'"

"Crap," Scott said softly, realizing. "Then my father—"

"Yeah, that was definitely one of those déjà vu things. At the time, however, I was still caught up in the dream and determined to make it work. We were both working crappy jobs, but the plan was he'd go to college and get his degree, then I could get mine. Except…" She paused. "Except then I got pregnant. And Chris freaked. Told me no way could we deal with a baby right then, that I had to get…to get rid of it. And…I told him I would."

"Damn, honey…"

"Oh, I had no intention of going through with it. But I would've said almost anything to get him to stop yelling at me. To buy me some time. Lord, Scott, I was scared out of my gourd. Yeah, he'd begun to snap at me now and then, but I chalked it up to his being tired all the time. That night, though…it was pretty bad. But by that point, I *couldn't* give up. Couldn't let on I was in over my head, that my mother had been right all along—"

"About what?"

"That I had no business being with somebody like him. That he'd get tired of me eventually, realize he'd made a mistake. Same as my daddy had done, apparently. Because, you see, he'd come from money, too. So the last thing I wanted was to hear her *I told you so.* Not that I had clue one what I was going to do, but I guess I hoped once the shock wore off Chris would adjust to the idea. Because we were a *team,* right? As we had always been. Only…"

Crossing her arms, she snorted. "Here's what I didn't realize until much later—while I was all about the romance, apparently Chris's primary goal was to piss off his parents. So he married me." She shrugged. "Why it never occurred to him they'd cut him off, I do not know. But they did. And…I guess he felt pretty trapped."

Scott glanced at her. "By what? And please don't say 'me.'"

"By circumstances, then."

"Of his own making."

"True, but…we did have some good times, Scott. I swear. A lot of good times."

"As long as things were easy?"

Her shoulders bumped again. "As long as he got his way. Then again, maybe I was expecting too much of him—"

"Don't defend him, Christina. Or make excuses. He was your *husband,* for crying out loud."

Several beats passed before she said, "In theory, yes." A long breath hissed from her lungs. "In any case, suddenly I was four months gone, no closer to knowing what I was going to do than I had been when that little plus sign showed itself…right about the time Chris pulled his head out of his butt long enough to realize my body was changing. We had another fight. A big one. He grabbed his keys and stormed out of our second-floor apartment, yelling that that I'd broken my promise and that he should've listened to his parents, should've…" She shook her head, her hand fisting in her lap. "I ran after him. But my heel caught on one of the steps and I fell."

Even though he already knew the outcome, Scott felt his heart turn over. "And Chris?"

Christina tucked her hair behind her ear. "To give him some credit, when I screamed he turned back, looking scared out of his wits. He called 911, stayed with me the whole time. And even though I was devastated about the baby, I truly thought he'd had his come-to-Jesus moment, that we'd be fine.

"But we weren't. Not by a long shot. He refused to let me talk about my feelings, acting like it'd never happened…" She shook her head, then sighed. "Eventually I had to admit that our relationship had miscarried long before the baby. Especially since…since I realized I couldn't stay married to somebody I no longer respected. And I h-hated him for what he'd asked me to do."

Scott's jaw hurt from the effort to not say what he was really thinking, what he'd be sorely tempted to do if the little weasel ever crossed his path. Instead he said, "Why wouldn't you?" and she shrugged again.

"We got a no-fault divorce a few months later. At least, it was called no-fault."

"It sure wasn't yours."

"I didn't shoulder the entire blame, of course not. But..." They pulled up in front of her apartment, but she didn't seem in any hurry to get out of the car. Instead, she shifted enough to face him, her forehead pinched.

"My mother and I have issues aplenty, God knows, but in this case she was right. I *should* have known better. Heck, I've always prided myself on being a realist, even as a kid. But I was so, I don't know...flattered, I suppose, when Chris picked me. Out of all the girls in school. *Me.* He seemed so confident. So in charge. Like he could make anything he wanted to happen. And it wiped common sense clean out of my head. Because when the chips were down we were obviously looking at life through different lenses. And all the wanting in the world for things to be different wasn't going to change that."

Dread swamped him even before she started to twist the ring off her finger.

"Christina—"

"I can't accept this, Scott. No matter how much I want to, or how much I love you. And I do love you, you've gotta believe that. But that doesn't change the fact that you and I, we look at life through different lenses, too. We can't help it," she said when he started to protest, "it's just the way things are. So, here—"

"Honey...you're tired and shaken because of what happened with Wendy—"

"Dammit, Scott—listen to me! Even if I didn't believe,

with all my heart, that we're not suited for each other… you know that vision you had of filling all those bedrooms with little Fortunes?" She grabbed his hand and pressed the ring into his palm, closing his fingers around it so hard the stones cut into his flesh. "I can't make that happen for you. Because the miscarriage, somehow it messed me up inside and I can't have b-babies. That had been my only shot. And it was selfish of me to sleep with you, to let you put the ring on my finger, when I knew I could never help you realize that part of your dream—"

On a sob, she shouldered open the door and clumsily got out, leaving Scott feeling like the wind had been knocked out of him.

But only for a moment.

She was still blindly fumbling for her keys in her purse when Scott pulled her into his arms, holding on so tight she could barely breathe.

"Let me go, dammit!"

He released her immediately, only to clamp hold of her upper arms, fury thrashing in his eyes.

Christina lowered hers. "I'm sorry I made you mad—"

"Oh, I'm way past mad, honey. You say you love me, but you have so little faith in me that you couldn't share what's probably the most important thing about you—?"

"That I can't have kids?"

"No! That you're in pain! And why on earth do you think you have to lug that pain around all by yourself?"

"Because maybe it's no one's concern but mine."

"Well, you're wrong. Dead wrong." He let his hands drop to stuff them in his jacket pockets, but his jaw was still rigid. "Independence is all well and good, it's one of the things I admire about you. But if I've learned nothing else in business it's that nobody accomplishes squat by themselves—"

"And maybe I do! Maybe I'm the exception to your rule!"

"Nobody is the exception to that rule. Nobody. Did you even tell your mother about the baby?"

"Oh, God, no," she said on a bitter laugh.

"Why not?"

"Because she would've only said the same thing Chris did, that it was just as well I'd lost it…that I wasn't any more ready than she'd been to have a kid."

"You don't know that for sure—"

"Enough to know I wasn't up for taking that chance. Scott, you're still not getting it. You can argue your point until you're blue in the face, but you can't *make* this work anymore than I can. Because nothing you can say changes the simple truth that *I don't know how to do this!*"

"Do *what,* for God's sake?"

"Let myself be loved! Be part of a healthy relationship! Whatever you want to call it. Because nobody, and I mean *nobody,* has ever stuck around long enough for me to figure it out." Tears streamed down her cheeks; furious, she swatted them away. "Being alone…it's safe. And after what I went through, I'm all about being safe. Although heaven knows you came closer than anybody to breaking through those barriers. Criminy, you're the first man I've slept with since my divorce. What does that tell you?"

His trembling grin would be her undoing. "That I should be honored as hell?"

"Nice try. But how about…it's like part of me is broken and I don't know how to fix it—"

Scott grabbed her shoulders again, gently shaking her. "And maybe you don't have to fix it yourself, dammit!

That's what *you're* not getting! Or don't you believe my feelings for you are real?"

"Of course I do!" she said to his tortured gaze. "But… but I still can't wrap my head around how it would work between us in the long run, any more than it did between Chris and me—"

"Sorry, honey, but that dog don't hunt. It never did, at least not from my perspective. Sweetheart—you and Chris were *kids*. We're not. *I'm* not. And in an adult relationship, both partners—*partners*—work on that relationship together. Work out the *problems* together. Children…"

Closing his eyes, he let his head drop back, like he was asking for guidance, then looked at her again. "My heart breaks for you because you can't have them. For *you*. Not me. Because I know," he said, palming his chest, "I'd love a child we adopted every bit as much as I'd love one you gave birth to. I *love* you. And I've never said that to another woman. How's that for a confession?"

Her heart shattering, Christina touched that beautiful face. "I hear everything you're saying, I really do. But…I can't help it—this all still feels like something out of a storybook. And I don't dare trust it, no matter how much I want to. Especially since…"

Turning, she shakily got her key in the lock, not facing him again until the door was open and Gumbo rushed outside. The only creature, she realized, whose love she did trust. And how sorry was that?

"You know, I used to wonder, once the Prince married Cinderella? If he looked at her one day and realized…they really had nothing to talk about."

Scott looked at her for a long moment, then said quietly, "This isn't about trusting the fairy tale. Or even me. It's about trusting yourself. What *you* want. What you *deserve*. And it pisses me off to no end that for someone so determined not to let circumstances define her…that's exactly what you're doing."

Then he stalked back to the car and got in, slamming his door so hard it set off the Jetta's alarm.

Chapter Twelve

Scott was still in a slamming and banging mood when he got back to Wendy's, although he took care not to show his irritation when he returned the minivan's keys to the neighbors, giving them a brief rundown on what had happened. Minutes later he was on the couch, his phone in one hand, his head in the other as he waited for Blake to pick up. Although he agreed with Wendy that it was probably best not to tell their parents about her condition, at least for the moment, Blake would skin him alive if he discovered they'd deliberately kept him out of the loop.

And calling his brother would divert Scott's overwrought brain from dwelling on what was going on with Christina. Or would have, had not Blake's voice mail picked up the call instead of the man himself.

Annoyed, Scott left a curt message, then stood, ramming the phone into his pocket and heading back outside before he suffocated in the tiny house. Granted, part of him was inclined to cut his losses and walk away. Unfortunately, the stubborn part—which would be the part that grabbed a project by the throat, refusing to let go until he'd seen it through—wasn't onboard with that idea.

At. All.

Especially since the…resignation in her voice, which only intensified the deeper she got into the story, make him abso-freaking-lutely crazy. Maybe it wasn't up to him, he thought as he found himself walking toward Main Street, to fix her, to eradicate her pain…and maybe it was. Because what if God or whatever *had* put him in that part of the airport for a reason, and that reason was to save—for a lack of a better word—Christina?

Or for her to save him, which was a far more likely scenario.

Whichever it was, how could he turn his back on that?

Sure, he'd been momentarily blindsided by her bombshell that she couldn't have children. But, come on, he hadn't even considered having kids a month ago. So pretty stupid to allow it to derail him now—

His phone buzzed.

"Hey, guy," Blake said. "What's up?"

"Wendy's in the hospital," Scott said as he walked. "She went into early labor."

"Holy crap, Scott, is she okay?"

"Yeah, yeah, she's fine. They got it stopped, but they're keeping her for a few days to make sure it doesn't start up again. But the plan is to let her come home, as long as she stays in bed."

"For more than a *month?*"

"Three weeks, at least. If she goes into labor then, she'll be far enough along that the baby won't be considered premature."

"Wow. Who's going to take care of her?"

"Now that you mention it, I have no idea. Marcos's time is already splintered between the restaurant and seeing to Javier—"

"I'll do it. Come out there to help out, I mean."

Scott laughed. "You? Wait on the Princess?"

"She adores me. It'll be good, I promise. I'll simply work from there. Did you get the ranch?"

Instantly, visions flashed, of Christina gawking in astonishment at the huge kitchen…the late-afternoon light haloing her blond hair as she stood in front of the family room window…of her sweet cries as she shattered beneath him—

"Yeah. It's mine. Plenty of room if you'd rather stay there instead of Wendy's."

"And…Christina?" At Scott's dry laugh, Blake asked, "What's going on?"

"Damned if I know."

"Dude."

"Let me clarify that. She's told me plenty, enough to figure out there's a lot of past garbage cluttering up her head. Then, as if that's not bad enough…" He sighed. "She overheard Dad basically accuse of her being after my money."

"Ouch."

"Yeah. Even though that couldn't be further from the truth."

"You sure?"

"Positive. As positive as she is that I'm going to wake up one day and realize I've made a mistake."

After too long a pause, Blake said, "You sure you won't?"

"I'm not infatuated, if that's what you're asking. And no, this isn't about the thrill of the chase, either. And, sorry, obviously I didn't call to bitch about my love life."

"Good. Then we can talk about mine."

"Wasn't aware you had one."

"Har, har. But, as you said, that staring death in the face thing really does have a way of making a person reassess his life. Choices he's made, opportunities that slipped through his fingers."

"Such as…?"

"Brittany."

Scott's scalp prickled. "Blake…no—"

"Gorgeous gal like her…why is she still single? I'll tell you why—because we left things hanging. You remember that fundraiser we attended in the fall? How she and I 'just happened' to keep running into each other? Maybe the timing was off before, but now…it's fate, I tell you. And this time I intend to give fate a helping hand—"

"And there's nothing more pathetic than a man trying to win back his old college girlfriend. Give it up, guy. Let the past stay in the past—"

"No can do, bro. And I have you to thank for the inspiration. Now all I have to do is formulate a plan—"

Scott grimaced.

"—and you—don't you dare give up. You want this woman, you fight for her, you hear me? And I'll let you know tomorrow when I'm coming in."

Pocketing his phone, Scott ambled past the hodge-podge of architectural styles that made up the little residential street, frowning so hard his head hurt. Because while Blake was clearly off his rocker for wanting to resurrect a dead relationship, giving up on one that hadn't even gotten off the ground yet was something else entirely. But Christina was right, too, that this was one thing he couldn't *make* happen—

He stopped dead in his tracks as large chunks of their last conversation replayed in his brain, and with them, an idea. A crazy, long-shot idea that could seriously blow up in his face. But if he wanted to be Christina's prince, it would appear he had some dragon slaying to do.

He once more dug out his phone, scanned his Contacts, hit Send. She answered on the first ring, her already familiar cackle making him smile. "Yeah, figured I'd hear from you sooner or later..."

Scott had debated whether to call first or simply show up, finally deciding that, while the element of surprise often proved useful in business dealings, it could backfire in personal ones. Not the best way, perhaps, to establish a relationship with his potential mother-in-law. So he'd called.

Clearly nervous, Sandra invited Scott into the kitchen of the modest ranch house in the middle-class Houston suburb, where she offered him coffee and a slice of boxed Danish, both of which he refused.

"Your husband's at work, I presume?"

The woman's mouth tightened before she carefully closed the Danish box, then slid it toward the backsplash. "He's not here, no. Well. I suppose we may as well go and sit down..."

The living room was simply and inoffensively furnished, the only spot of color a bright orange, long-haired cat sprawled across the back of a gray-and-beige-striped sofa.

"Have a seat—"

"I'd rather stand, thank you," Scott said, pulling an old trick of his father's out of his arsenal and using his height to his advantage. Not to intimidate, exactly, but definitely to keep the upper hand in the proceedings.

Christina's mother briefly frowned, then shrugged, the gesture eerily reminiscent of her daughter's. In fact, beneath the trying-too-hard makeup, the defensiveness stiffening her shoulders—not that Scott could blame her for that, he supposed—he caught a glimpse of the same vulnerability as well.

Something else, God forgive him, that could possibly prove useful.

"Suit yourself," she said, sitting on the sofa. The cat immediately left his perch to settle on her lap. "I'm assuming Christina sent you?"

"No. She doesn't know I'm here."

"Then how'd—?"

"Doesn't matter. Mrs. Hastings—"

"Sandra, please," she said, apparently regaining her composure. "I haven't used that name in years."

"Fine. Sandra. Quite simply, I'm here because I love your daughter. Very much. And I want to marry her."

Despite an obvious attempt at keeping her expression blank, agitation bloomed in eyes more gray than blue. "And, what? You want my blessing?"

"Right now I'm more about getting answers. Because something's keeping her from saying yes."

The agitation yielded, barely, to a tight, yet almost triumphant smile. "How about...maybe she doesn't *want* to marry you? Nothing I can do about—"

"I don't think that's true." Scott shoved aside the front of his leather jacket to slip his hands into his pockets. "In fact, I know it's not. This isn't about what she does or doesn't want, but what she's believes she can't have—"

"And if, after all this time, everything I've been telling her has finally taken root? Then hallelujah. And frankly," Sandra said, gently pushing the cat off her lap to get to her feet, "I don't think you and I have anything more to discuss—"

"What's taken root," Scott said, blocking her way when

she sidestepped the coffee table on her way to the front door, "is fear. Fear that I have very good reason to believe you planted—"

"So what if I did? After everything that happened—"

"And what 'everything' would that be? Chris turning out to be a loser? Or her father walking out on *you?*" When Sandra's chin jerked up, Scott blew out a sigh. "Yeah, crap happens. People screw you over. So because of that she should never be happy again?"

She scooped the mewing cat off the coffee table, clutching him to her chest. "You rich men, you love to put ideas in girls' heads. Make them believe they're somebody they're not. Until you get bored with your little game and then…you leave. And you know what the worst part of it is? That you've shown 'em a world nicer than anything they've ever known, letting 'em play in it for a while, only to yank it away when you go. Do you have any idea what that's like, Mr. Fortune? To wake up and realize…it was all a dream?"

And there they were, the daughter's words echoed in the mother's. And, Scott could now see, the pain. Sandra's not wanting her daughter to suffer as she had—and she had clearly suffered, of that he had no doubt—was understandable. But he also suspected there was something else at work here. What, he wasn't sure. What he did know, however, was that the bogeyman was finally out of hiding.

Or at least showing his face.

"For whatever you and Christina have gone through," he said gently, "I'm truly sorry. I know you've both been hurt. But having money doesn't make me a bastard, Sandra. At least, I hope not. And I have never toyed with a woman's feelings in my life, or ever made a promise I wasn't absolutely sure I'd keep. So I'd hardly do that to someone who means everything to me. And make no mistake, your daughter has become the most important thing in my life."

Several seconds passed before Sandra stepped around him and continued to the front door, which she opened. Taking his cue, Scott joined her, where she laid one hand on his arm, the defiance mostly gone from her eyes.

"If I don't tell my daughter to be careful, who will? Because no matter what you think, I love her—"

"Then you might want to rethink how you show it."

Her hand popped off his arm as though she'd been stung. "You've got no right to say that to me."

"Your daughter's happiness is at stake, Sandra. If not her entire future. And I'll damn well say whatever it takes to make you realize that."

He started through the door, then turned, zipping up his jacket against the suddenly stiff breeze. "Nothing would thrill me more than to help Christina turn her dreams into reality. *Her* dreams, not mine. She'll also never want for anything. Not only for the moment, for the rest of her life. But far more than either of those, I can give her the one thing she's apparently had in pretty short supply, which is my pledge to love her as long as I live. Now I ask you… what mother wouldn't want that for her child?"

When she didn't answer, Scott let himself out of the house, praying more than he ever had in his life that his words had hit home.

Chapter Thirteen

It hadn't been the best couple of days she'd ever had, but Christina had always prided herself on being able to function, no matter what. Being productive instead of moping in front of *Judge Judy* and stuffing her face with Doritos. Or raw cookie dough. Which they now said could kill you, anyway. So she washed her hair and cleaned her house, tackled a few course assignments and tutored a couple of kids. Even took Gumbo for a slow, but steady, walk up to the 7-Eleven and back. Ogled the hunks who'd mysteriously appeared to get the pool up and running again. Like she didn't know who was behind that, even though Enid was playing coy.

She even took the Jetta for a spin. Of course she sobbed her lungs out when she got back, but still. It was something she needed to do.

Of course, if she'd thought all that activity was somehow going to keep her from thinking about Scott, and the hash she'd made of things, she was dead wrong.

It made no sense—she'd been perfectly okay before he'd blown into her life. Not only did she enjoy being alone, she cherished it. And she supposed she'd cherish it again, someday. When she was sixty, maybe. Or somebody invented a drug or machine or something that wiped out memories, so she'd stop thinking about that afternoon in his house.

Because she ached. Oh, dear Lord, she ached.

Sighing heavily, she finally gave up reading the excruciatingly boring text for her marketing class and got up from the kitchen table to go stand at her living room window, if for no other reason than to look at something besides the same four walls. It'd been cloudy and windy all afternoon, threatening rain and rendering the view even more dreary than usual. Unbidden, she thought of the views from Scott's ranch…the house…that bedroom…

"For pity's sake," she muttered, grinding her fingertips into her forehead like she could rub away the thoughts. "Cut it out!"

But still the memories jeered, sending tears streaming down her cheeks. She'd really, truly believed she'd loved Chris, that he'd loved her, had suffered mightily when it all fell apart between them. Compared with what she felt for Scott, however…

Like comparing "Chopsticks" to a Beethoven symphony.

Christina knew he thought she was Looney Tunes, that he didn't fully understand why she had to reject his offer. His love. But being in that house…it only proved what she'd been saying all along—that she wasn't enough for him. Heck, she wasn't even enough for the *house*. For herself, yes. Even for some other man, at least in theory. Because it would always be so…one-sided, wouldn't it? Scott had so much to offer her, but what did she have to offer him in return? And how soon would that be used up—?

"Oh, hell," she muttered, her thoughts scattering like roaches when she saw her mother's car pull up, wondering what truly terrible things she'd done in a past life to deserve this.

Christina watched helplessly as Sandra got out of the car, glared at the roiling clouds, then marched toward the front door, which Christina had opened by the time her mother hit the porch.

"Oh!" Sandra's hand flew to her chest. "You startled me!"

"Wasn't exactly expecting you, either."

"Is it…okay if I come in?"

"Um…of course." From where he lay beside the heating vent, Gumbo lifted his head, took in the situation, decided it wasn't worth his time or energy to investigate and flopped back down again.

"Can I get you anything?" Christina asked as her mother removed the same red wool three-quarter-length coat she'd had for years.

"No, I'm fine. And listen to you, acting like I'm a church lady paying a call." She looked…subdued, Christina thought. Less makeup, smaller hair. Like she'd lost some weight, judging from the way her hostess dress—a black sheath, adorned with a print scarf—hung on her frame. She carefully lowered herself to the edge of the sofa, her hands on her knees. "Your young man came to see me," she said, and Christina nearly fell over.

"Scott?"

"You got more than one?"

"No." Although she didn't exactly have that one, either. "Why?"

"I'm still not entirely sure, to tell you the truth. Although..." Sandra stretched out her fingers, then covered her left hand with her right. "He says he asked you to marry him."

"Not in so many words, but...he gave me a ring, yes. I didn't keep it."

Her mother frowned. "How come?"

"Because it didn't feel right. *I* didn't feel right."

"You're sure? I mean, it was entirely your decision?"

"Well, yes." Wondering what the heck was going on, Christina slowly sat on the ratty old recliner. "What's this all about?"

"He seems pretty convinced I had something to do with it. That I've...unduly influenced you. Or something."

"Oh. Well...you haven't exactly been encouraging—"

"Because I couldn't bear for you to go through again what you did with Chris." She reached up to fidget with the Hermes knockoff. "Like I did with your daddy when he left us high and dry, without hardly two quarters to rub together."

Color flooded her mother's pale cheeks as she leaned forward, becoming more and more agitated. "You and I, we're cut from the same cloth, you know? Attracted to the same kind of man. Only it never works out, does it? Not for me, and not for you. So I had to make sure you wouldn't make the same mistake, didn't I? To *protect* you, baby. That's all. That Scott Fortune...don't you believe all his pretty talk, Christina, you hear me? Because he can promise you the moon and stars and everything in between, but that doesn't mean he'll deliver. You know that, right? That we're both better off alone than having our hearts broken again by some rich SOB who thinks he can toss us away like old garbage—"

At that, Sandra burst into tears.

Tears Christina realized weren't for her.

"Ohmigod..." She looked at her mother as though seeing her for the first time. "This isn't about protecting me at all, is it? Which should come as no surprise since you never really have. This is about not wanting me to be happy because you never were!"

A tissue plucked from the box on the table beside the sofa, Sandra gaped at Christina. "What an awful thing to say!"

"But it's true!" Bolting to her feet, Christina clamped one hand to her mouth as one by one, the pieces fell into place. "Because it's always, always been about you!" When her mother pulled a face, Christina shook her head. "Was this supposed to be some sort of *pact* between us? That if you were miserable I was supposed to be, too?"

Her mother seemed to crumple in front of her. "Do you have *any* idea how I felt when you and Christopher started going together?" she whined. "That after everything that'd happened you took up with a *rich boy?*"

"And what did that have to do with you?"

Fresh tears leaked from her eyes. "I felt like I'd been betrayed!"

Christina wheeled around and crossed to the window, her arms tightly folded over her middle. "And you wonder why we don't get along."

After a long silence, her mother said, "No, I don't."

Frowning, Christina faced her again. "Come again?"

Her mother blew her nose again, then gave her head a little shake before lifting her gaze to Christina's. "Even then, I suppose I knew what I was thinking was wrong, even if I didn't know how to fix it. But the green-eyed monster had me by the throat so bad I couldn't think straight. And it only got worse, after you two got married. I was so lonely. And mad. At your daddy, at myself..." Her sigh was shaky. "And I was so busy wallowing in the mad and the hurt it never occurred to me there might be something past it."

"So, what? You cheered when my marriage fell apart?"

"No, of course not. I'm not that far gone. But…" She pressed her lips together. "But I guess I did feel vindicated, somehow."

"And you're still holding on to all this crazy, even though you're remarried?"

On a humorless laugh, Sandra stretched out what Christina realized with a start was her ringless left hand. "Harry left me," she whispered. "Two days after New Year's."

Christina bit her lip, feeling all those years of bitterness and frustration and anger dissolve in the face of her mother's obvious, and genuine, misery. The woman looked absolutely defeated.

"Oh, Mama…I'm so sorry." And she truly was. For so many reasons. "But why didn't you say something when you were here?"

"I was ashamed, okay? Didn't want to admit I'd messed up again."

Despite everything, sympathy tugged at Christina's heart. "It takes two to mess up, Mama."

But Sandra didn't appear to have heard her. "I was barely holding it together as it was, and then I saw you and Scott together that day, saw the way he looked at you, and that monster reared its ugly head all over again. I'm sorry, too, baby," she whispered. "More than I can say. If I think about it for more than five seconds, of course I want you to be happy. And much as it pains me to say this…I think Scott might be the one to do that for you. Because for sure I never saw in Chris's eyes, or your daddy's, what I saw in Scott's. B-but is it so wrong for me to be h-happy, too?"

And if she truly believed the Good Lord put people where He needed them to be…

Sighing, Christina sat beside her mother and took her hand. The woman grabbed on like she'd drown if she let go. Which Christina supposed wasn't that far from the truth. "Of course it isn't. But you need to talk to somebody. A professional, I mean. You've got some heavy-duty issues to work through."

"Like I can afford a therapist—"

"We'll work it out. I promise," she said. "Maybe we can find one of those two-for-one deals on Groupon or something."

Sandra pushed out a soft laugh. "You're probably right. But I have no idea where to even begin..."

"I'll take care of it." Not that she had any idea where to begin, either, but the prospect of venturing into hitherto-unexplored territory didn't hold nearly the terror for her that it obviously did for her mother.

Um, hello? Are you listening to yourself?

Christina sucked in a quick breath at the promise behind that revelation. She could practically feel her thoughts shifting, realigning themselves in her brain. Letting in the light. Holy cow—nobody had ever done for her what Scott had. Taken that kind of risk...for her. Put his butt on the line... *for her.*

But first things first. Like tending to the relationship in front of her, whether she wanted to or not. Except...she did, she supposed. After all, it wasn't like she could trade out this mother for a new one.

Besides, as tempting as it was to hold on to the bad feelings, not only had they not proved all that useful, when you got right down to it, but Christina knew it had also taken guts for her mother to show up here. Even if her original intent had been to cover her own patoot, the truth had worked its way to the surface anyway, hadn't it? So now maybe they could both work on healing.

"Mama? Do you suppose we could, I don't know. Start over?"

Sandra blew her nose. "You think that's even possible?"

"I have no idea. But I'm willing to try. If you are."

"Then…I think I'd like that. Very much."

"Okay, then." Her hands knotted on her knees, Christina shut her eyes, took a deep breath, then said, "I never told you why Chris and I broke up."

"I assumed it was because the two of you weren't suited."

"That's certainly part of it. But not all," she said over the rapidly rising lump in her throat. "I got pregnant."

"Pregnant? But…" When Christina's eyes flooded, her mother let out a soft moan. "Oh, honey…come here."

And she wrapped her arms around her daughter and stroked her hair as she cried, like it was the most natural thing in the world.

So they started talking. And kept talking, and sometimes crying, not only long into the night, but well into the next day—after Christina spent the rest of the night wide awake, praying her little heart out. So it was the middle of the afternoon, after Sandra finally headed back to Houston, before Christina brought up Scott's cell number into her phone, holding her breath for a moment before hitting Send.

"I need to talk to you," she said when he answered.

"Christina?"

"You were expecting Gumbo?"

After that soft, caressing, sending-shivers-up-her-back chuckle, he said, "I'm at the ranch. Out by the stables. Where are you?"

"On my way."

"I'll wait."

At the entrance to the long drive leading to the property, Christina pulled the Jetta onto the soft, weed-choked shoulder. Gumbo wriggled between the seats to nose her arm; she smiled down at that goofy face fixed so steadily on hers while the rest of his body shimmied. Then, looking back out the windshield, she sighed.

"Do I dare to do this?"

Still wagging, Gumbo cocked his head, the skin all pleated between his ears. Then he barked—it did take him a while to process information—and stretched his neck to give her forearm a slurpy kiss.

Admitting she was wrong meant chucking everything she'd believed about herself for more than five years…a burden she was only too glad to jettison. And small potatoes compared with what Scott had chucked for *her.* On another sigh, she started driving down the dirt road toward the house, rolling her eyes at the sight of the big-ass pickup parked in the driveway. It suited him, though, substantial but not flashy. Sort of a pewter color. Dignified. At least, as dignified as a truck the size of a small house could be.

She pulled up alongside it and got out, shielding her eyes from the sun as she and the dog walked—well, she walked, Gumbo bounced—around the house toward the stables. As she approached, a horse's whinny caught her attention. Her gaze veered to the right, to a magnificent black beast with a jagged white blaze, clearly entranced by whatever Scott was saying to him as he stroked the horse's neck. And oh, my, if he didn't look almost like a real horseman in his jeans and boots and black shirt underneath a denim jacket, and Christina's breath caught in her throat as she finally gave her heart its head, letting her love for this man flood her very being until it became so vast, so…*all,* it simply, finally, completely obliterated the fear.

Home, she thought, the single word as comforting as an angel's kiss—

"Gumbo, no!" she called when he made a beeline for the animal—dumb cluck probably thought the horse was a big dog. But when he reached the fence, he stood on his hind paws to brace his front ones on the middle rail, and the horse slowly lowered his head, making soft whuffing noises as he inspected this silly, stubby creature with the big ears and no sense whatsoever. Then he seemed to nod as if in approval before cantering across the paddock to the other side, tossing his shiny black mane.

"Took you long enough," Scott said softly, and she thought, *You ain't whistling Dixie, Bucko.*

Scott's chest constricted at how beautiful she was, the breeze messing with her hair, her long skirt gently molding to her thighs as she walked toward him.

"He's gorgeous," she said when she got close enough for Scott to hear her, to see the smile in her eyes a moment before he reached for her waist and pulled her in for a kiss. And she tugged him even closer and gave him everything she had. Everything he wanted. At least, as much as she could, he imagined, considering they were out in the open.

"So're you," Scott whispered, brushing her hair out of her eyes and making her blush.

"You don't seem all that surprised I'm here."

"You did call."

"No, I meant—"

"I know what you meant. And what I am, is damn happy."

She kissed him again, then pulled free to fold her arms across the top of the fence. But not as she might have before—nervously, in retreat. If anything she seemed completely at ease.

Content.

"When did you get him?" she said as the horse calmly plodded back over to check her out, too. Scott dug in his pocket for a piece of apple, which he handed to her. She held it out to the horse flat-palmed, giggling a little when his lips tickled.

"Yesterday. One of my cousins here told me about this couple who rescues abused horses and rehabilitates them."

When the horse softly nibbled her shoulder, Christina laughed and rubbed his velvety nose. "He's a rescue?"

"Yep. He'd lived the life of Riley before his original owner died. Kids sold him to some jerk who mistreated him. Animal control took him away about a year ago. Guy I bought him from said it took months to get Blackie to trust him—"

"Blackie?"

"Minute they told me his name, I knew he was mine." When she laughed, he mimicked her position. "I missed you."

"I could tell," she said, grinning. But focused on the horse. "How's Wendy?"

"You're stalling."

"You could say that. Well?"

The breeze shifted, cocooning him in her scent. He inhaled deeply, then said, "Coming home tomorrow. Blake's flying out to help take care of her before poor Marcos loses his mind. Between trying to keep on top of things at the restaurant and going back and forth to see Javier, he's already pretty fried. The last thing he needs is to worry about my sister, too."

Her cheek resting on her folded arms, she looked up at him. "And how is Javier?"

"They've started to bring him out of the coma. It's a

slow process, I gather. And once he's conscious…" He sighed. "We just don't know."

Nodding, Christina stepped away from the fence, holding out her hand. Scott took it, giving it a slight squeeze before leading her toward the house and up onto the porch, gilded in the late-afternoon sun. The white porch swing complained a little when they sat on it, laughing, but it held, and when Scott wrapped one arm around her shoulders and pulled her close, and when she leaned into him with a sigh, he knew what bliss was for the first time in his life.

Then Gumbo scrambled up the stairs to join them, his nails clicking against the floorboards as he trotted from chair to chair, sniffing, tail wagging the entire time, until he collapsed with a great sigh in a splotch of sunlight at their feet, and Scott chuckled.

Christina smiled up at him. "What?"

"Just thinking how crazy I am about that dumb little dog. Not quite as crazy as I am about his mistress, but close."

With a soft laugh, Christina lifted Scott's and her linked hands to kiss his, then held it against her cheek.

"This is promising," he said, and she released a breath.

"Had a surprise visit from my mother yesterday."

"Oh?"

"Don't you 'oh?' me. She said you'd been there."

"Busted."

"And how, exactly, did that come about?"

"I called Enid. Who was only too willing to help."

"I don't…oh. I guess I did give her my mother's contact info in case of an emergency."

"And she and I both agreed this definitely qualified."

Christina rolled her eyes. "I think she likes you. My mother, I mean. Don't think there's much question that Enid likes you."

"You *think* your mother likes me?"

"You have to read between the lines with Mama. And what I read was…whatever you said must've lit one heck-uva fire under her butt. Not that things started out all that great, but…we began a dialogue, as they say. And kept it up until things started to make sense. And I realized…"

Christina lifted her eyes to Scott. "That she'd infected me with *her* issues. Put voices in my head. Voices that kept playing the same loop, over and over and over. Except…those voices lied, making me think…" Leaving the thought unfinished, she pulled her mouth into a straight line. "Not that I don't have my own demons to face down. My father did abandon me. As did Chris, at least emotionally. He was also very controlling, even if I didn't understand it at the time. But you're not Chris. Or my father. And it was hid-eously unfair of me to tar you with their brushes."

"Thank you."

"No, thank you, for…not giving up." One side of her mouth lifted. "For sticking to the plan."

"Who said there was a plan?"

She snorted. "Scott Fortune, you are the most focused person I have ever met. I seriously doubt you've ever let anything *just happen* from the time you could walk."

"And that's where you're wrong. Because I couldn't have planned your happening if my life depended on it. You, this," he said, gesturing to the landscape in front of them, "was part of something else's plan, believe me. All I did was…listen."

"Point taken. But still, once you got on board with that…" She grinned up at him again. "You took steps, right? It's okay, sweetpea—that's just who you are. Anyway, I got myself off track. About those voices…"

She tucked her good leg up underneath her, leaning more into him. "There are good voices, the ones that lead you forward. Then there are bad ones, that hold you back. That keep you afraid. Only what I realized was, those bad voices, they don't have any power unless you give it to them. Which is what I was doing. And I'm not anymore."

"Huh," Scott said, and Christina reared back to look at him.

"That's it? *Huh?*"

"Oh, trust me, there's plenty more. When you're finished."

Her gaze softened. "I do, actually."

"Do, what?"

"Trust you. Trust…whatever it is between us makes me *want* to trust you. Even if it makes no sense on the surface."

"Logic is highly overrated."

She laughed and snuggled closer. "So I'm beginning to figure out. But I finally got it through my head that it's like you said, that letting the past dictate my decisions, my *life,* is not only stupid, but counterproductive. I mean, there I was, yammering to all and sundry about all these plans I had to move forward, to become more than everyone thought I could be…but only as long as I could keep my heart locked up all nice and tight where nobody could get to it. And how dumb is that?"

"I assume that's a rhetorical question—?"

"Because that's what my mother was doing. Giving the past control. But you—" She sat up again. "Ohmigod," she said, her earnestness about to crack his heart in two, "you're the best thing that's ever happened to me! I'd be an idiot to turn that down because I'm afraid it won't last."

Scott shifted to cup her chin, hook her gaze in his. "You're still afraid this won't last?"

"Okay, so maybe *afraid's* not the right word. But it's not as if I can undo a lifetime of conditioning in a couple of days." She stroked her knuckles across his beard-shadowed cheek, the sensation making his mouth go dry. And, in all likelihood, his pupils dilate. "I do love you, Scott. With all my heart. But that heart's kinda bruised and battered, you know? I really *don't* know how to be loved. So I need time. And patience."

Gratitude and joy practically making him dizzy, Scott tucked her into his side again. Time, patience…those, he could give her.

"I know, honey. I do. That you can't always make something happen, no matter how right it feels." He let his fingers lazily track up and down her arm. "Take Blackie, for instance. The guy I bought him from really emphasized that you can't will somebody—or something—to trust you, that it has to be earned. By proving, over and over, you can be trusted. For as long as it takes." He paused, then said, "I was pushing you into something you weren't ready for, and I apologize. Even the house…if it's too much for you, if you don't think you could be comfortable here, I'll sell it and we'll find something else."

"But…you love this place."

He set her apart, only to take her face in his hands and lock their gazes. "I love you a helluva lot more, sweetheart. A house can never be my life. But you already are."

Now *do you believe him?*

Christina got up and crossed to the porch steps, wrapping one arm around the nearby column, feeling its strength seep into her very being. And with it, the last of the lies—that she was somehow less than, she had little to offer—finally dissipated.

This could all be yours, the voice whispered, *if you've got the cojones to accept it.*

The faith to believe you deserve it.

"I suppose I could get used to the house. In time."

Chuckling, Scott came up behind her to slip his arms around her waist.

Deserve him.

Because not only had she never been "less than," she was, and always had been, more than enough. For anybody. But especially for this man.

In whose fingers the ring sparkled. Hopefully.

Christina laughed. "You are one persistent cuss, aren'tcha?"

"That, or an idiot." He turned her around, one hand resting gently on her hip, the ring still between them. "There's a catch, though."

She pulled a face. "Your father, right?"

"Hardly. I swear, that will be a nonissue as soon as he meets you. After all, you charmed me, right?"

"I suppose that's true," she said, smiling, planting her hands on his strong, solid chest. "So what's this catch?"

"That we don't get a wedding band to go with this until you're good and ready. When you're as sure as I am, that this is no fairy tale. *This*—" his lips brushed hers "—is as real as it gets."

"I know," she whispered, holding out her hand so he could slip the ring back on her finger, where it belonged. Then she let him pull her into the circle of his arms…where she belonged.

Forever.

* * * * *

“You know what’s wrong with you?

“You don’t know what you want. Love isn’t something you can form a stupid campaign around. You don’t ‘execute strategies’ to win someone—you watch them, you find out what they like, what makes them smile and then you try your damnedest to do the things that make them smile. You protect love, you nurture love, you don’t run a *campaign* for it.”

Katie closed her eyes, willing herself not to cry even though she could feel the angry tears starting to form. “You’re obtuse and blind and it’s my damn bad misfortune—pardon the pun—to be in love with you.”

Blake focused in on the only thing that was important to him. “You’re in—?”

“Yes!” she snapped. He might as well know. This way, maybe someday he’d realize just what he had allowed to slip away. “Love. L-O-V-E. Love. I’m in love with you. Or was,” she deliberately amended. “But I’m over you now. Oh, and by the way, I quit!”

Dear Reader,

I have been fortunate enough (no pun intended) to periodically revisit the Fortune family ever since I first wrote about one of them in F*orgotten Honeymoon*. This time it's a doubly nice experience for me because Wendy Fortune Mendoza was the heroine of my last book about the family. In this one, I get to watch her baby come into the world.

I also get to meet Wendy's best friend, Katie Wallace. Wendy and Katie have been friends since childhood—which is about the time that Katie fell in love with Wendy's brother, Blake. He has always been the center of her world, and with that in mind, Katie had gotten a business degree so that she could work with Blake at his father's company. So, when Blake asks his incredibly competent assistant to help him win back his ex—the one who got away—Katie is torn. She's never said no to Blake, but the request really makes her heart ache. Until Wendy comes up with a plan to make her brother fall in love with her best friend.

As ever, I thank you for reading, and from the bottom of my heart I wish you someone to love who loves you back.

Best,

Marie Ferrarella

FORTUNE'S VALENTINE BRIDE

BY

MARIE FERRARELLA

First published in Great Britain 2013
by Mills & Boon, an imprint of Harlequin (UK) Limited,
Eton House, 18-24 Paradise Road, Richmond, Surrey TW9 1SR

Special thanks and acknowledgement to Marie Ferrarella for her contribution to The Fortunes of Texas: Whirlwind Romance continuity.

ISBN: 978 0 263 90076 7
ebook ISBN: 978 1 472 00430 7

23-0113

Harlequin (UK) policy is to use papers that are natural, renewable and recyclable products and made from wood grown in sustainable forests. The logging and manufacturing processes conform to the legal environmental regulations of the country of origin.

Printed and bound in Spain
by Blackprint CPI, Barcelona

Marie Ferrarella, this *USA TODAY* bestselling and RITA® Award-winning author has written more than two hundred books for Mills & Boon, some under the name Marie Nicole. Her romances are beloved by fans worldwide. Visit her website, www.marieferrarella.com.

To
Helen with love,
despite the fact
that she has now moved
to a galaxy far, far
away

Chapter One

"Don't take this the wrong way, Blake," Wendy Mendoza said to her brother as she tried, and failed, to find a comfortable spot on her bed, "but with all this hovering about you're doing, I'm beginning to feel like a watched pot."

Blake Fortune dragged over the chair he'd brought into his younger sister's bedroom earlier and straddled it. "Isn't that actually a good thing?" he pointed out. "Watched pots aren't supposed to boil, or, in your case, give birth prematurely."

Which was, between the terbutaline injections to stop her contractions and the enforced bed rest, exactly what the doctor and she were trying to prevent.

But that didn't mean that she had to be happy about

this state of affairs, Blake knew. And the longer she lay there, inert, the more restless she grew.

"Isn't there something you could be doing?" she pressed, more accustomed to his teasing than his concern. "I mean, I really do appreciate you deciding to drop everything and come running back to Red Rock to hold my hand, but having everyone practically walking on eggshells around me is *really* making me feel very tense and nervous."

Which was, he knew, counterproductive to what they were all really trying to do—keep her pregnant until the baby was strong enough to survive on its own when she emerged.

"If this keeps up," Wendy warned, "I'm going to wind up giving birth to a neurotic baby who's going to go straight from the delivery room to some psychiatrist's couch."

Blake laughed, shaking his head. At least she hadn't lost her offbeat sense of humor. The whole family had gone through one hell of a trauma when that tornado had hit. And then on top of that, when Wendy had suddenly gone into premature labor, it had put a scare into all of them.

Thank God for modern medicine, he thought. Now she was back to her feisty self—except for not being able to get out of bed, he amended.

"Well, obviously the tornado had no effect on your imagination," he commented. But one look at her expression told him that she was being serious. She wanted him out of her bedroom. He supposed that if he were in her place, he might feel a bit crowded, too. "You've already kicked me out of your house to bunk with Scott at his place," he reminded her. "You want me to go altogether?"

Reaching out, Wendy caught her brother's hand and threaded her fingers through his. She loved all her siblings, but, as the baby of the family, Blake was the brother she was closest to. He was the second youngest. Together they were the bottom of the totem pole.

"No, I don't want you to go altogether," she told him with feeling, "but I don't want you putting your life on hold because of me, either." He'd been her constant companion for two days now. It was time he got back to his career, to his life. "With computers and teleconferencing, you could work anywhere. Why don't you set up a temporary office at Scott's and take care of business before Dad comes, breathing down your neck for dropping the ball, or whatever cliché he favors these days."

John Michael Fortune, who she felt certain did love his family in his own, private way, was ultimately responsible for the turn her life had taken. If her father hadn't insisted on sending her here, to Red Rock, Texas, in hopes of waking up her heretofore sleeping work ethic, she might have never discovered the two ultimate passions of her life: baking and Marcos—not necessarily in that order.

Her newfound passion for baking and creating desserts had come to light when she had gone to work at the restaurant that Marcos managed for his aunt and uncle, who were friends of her parents. At the time it was clear that Marcos felt he was being saddled with her and that he thought she was a spoiled little rich girl, totally incapable of doing anything right.

Marcos had been looking to fire her, while she in turn was looking for ways to prove herself. What neither one had been looking for was a life commitment, but they'd found it, in spades. Now she was married to Marcos and expecting his child any day.

A baby that had almost been born nearly a month ago, thanks to the tornado that had ripped through Red Rock just minutes before her family, who had flown out for her Christmas Eve wedding, were to take off for Atlanta.

It still left her breathless when she thought about it. One minute, she was saying her goodbyes, the next, they were being all but buried alive in debris as the tornado buzz sawed through the airport, collapsing it all around them.

The shock of it all, including having Marcos's badly injured brother, Javier, lapse into a coma, was too much for her. She found herself going into labor *way* before she was anywhere near her due date. Luckily, her doctor was able to temporarily curtail her contractions with injections. The hope was that she could hold on long enough for the baby's lungs to develop sufficiently to sustain the infant outside the womb.

Right now the process seemed as if it was taking forever. And having Blake constantly slanting wary glances in her direction really wasn't helping anything, especially not her frame of mind.

The problem was Blake could see her side of it. If the tables were turned, he wouldn't want people hovering around him, either, no matter how much he loved them. "I suppose you have a point."

Wendy smiled broadly, relieved that Blake wasn't offended by her strongly worded "suggestion." But then, this was Blake and, most of the time, they really did think alike.

"Of course I do."

Blake was already focusing on another project, one that had gone begging for his attention much too long. It was time to stop allowing it to take a backseat and get started on it in earnest.

"Actually, there has been something I've been meaning to do ever since we were practically buried alive in that airport," he confessed to her.

Wendy wasn't sure she was following him. "You were thinking of business at a time like that?" she asked incredulously. "God, Blake, you're more like Dad than I thought."

No, he highly doubted that any one of his father's offspring would ever be placed in the same category as their dad. The man ate and slept business and, while he expected the same of his children, none of them, Blake thought, would ever measure up to the old man's expectations. Blake sincerely doubted that anyone—besides a robot—could.

"Not business exactly," he explained. For the moment, he moved his chair in even closer to Wendy's bed, lowering his voice. This was something he wasn't ready to share with the immediate world—at least not yet. "When it looked like we actually might not make it, I promised myself that if we *did* survive, I'd stop putting my life on hold and do what I should have done years ago."

Intrigued, Wendy sat up a little straighter in her bed. She pushed another one of the pillows behind her, tucking it against her back. "Go on," she encouraged, curious where this was going.

"I promised myself that, if I survived, I was going to go after the woman who I allowed to slip away all those years ago." Smiling broadly at the plan that was, even now, evolving and taking on layers in his mind, Blake paused a second for dramatic effect, then shared the woman's name. "Brittany Everett."

"I changed my mind," Wendy told him. "*Don't* go on." She blew out a breath, sincerely disappointed with Blake's revelation. She'd hoped that the socialite Brittany Everett, would be a thing of the past in Blake's life. Actually, she'd secretly been hoping that when her brother's thoughts finally took a more serious turn toward things of a romantic nature, it would be images of Katie Wallace that ramped up his body temperature.

Everyone but Blake, apparently, knew that Brittany was just a spoiled Daddy's girl. In addition, she was someone who gave all "Southern belles" a bad name.

Trying her best not to look annoyed, Wendy slumped back on her pillows.

"What do you *see* in that woman?" she demanded in frustration. Before Blake could answer, she held up her hand. She was in no mood to hear any accolades for a woman she had never liked. "I mean, other than the obvious—that she could tip over if she turned around too fast." The woman under discussion had a pretty face, a large chest—and a completely empty head, not to mention no heart to speak of.

Wendy was pregnant and her hormones were undoubtedly all over the charts, Blake reasoned, so he let her last comment go and only said defensively, "You don't know Brittany."

Now, there he was wrong, Wendy thought. "Oh, but I do, Blake, I really do," she countered. Fixing him with an exasperated look, she insisted, "Blake, she's not good enough for you."

He laughed. When Wendy was very young, she'd been very possessive of him and jealous of any time he spent with anyone besides her. He supposed that there was still a tiny bit of that little girl left, even though she was now a married woman.

"You'd say that about anybody."

His protest made her think of Katie. Katie was extremely likable and had a great deal going for her. Katie's family lived practically next door to hers in Atlanta, and they had all grown up together. She was kind, pretty and smart—and not even the least bit self-serving.

Brittany, on the other hand, was convinced that the

world existed only for her own pleasure. Not only that, but it all revolved around her, as well.

Granted, Brittany and Blake had dated during his senior year, but from what Wendy had heard via the grapevine, she hadn't changed a bit.

"No," Wendy said firmly, "I wouldn't."

But Blake was convinced that he was right and that she was only acting like the overprotective little sister she'd once been. "Yeah, you would," he insisted. "But that's okay. My mind's made up. I'm going to launch a campaign—"

Were they still talking about the same thing? "A campaign?" Wendy questioned, looking at her brother uncertainly.

"Uh-huh. A business campaign." This was the very strategy he'd been missing, he told himself. He had to approach this goal of his by using his strengths and his skills if he hoped to ever win his "prize." "That's what I should have done in the first place, instead of just backing away," he told Wendy. The more he talked about it, the more convinced he became that this was the right approach. "If I'd gone after Brittany the way I usually go after a new client, I would have won her over a long time ago." He nodded at his sister's swollen belly. "And then little MaryAnne would have another doting aunt when she's born."

God forbid, Wendy thought, all but biting her tongue to keep from voicing her thoughts out loud.

"You know," Blake continued as his thoughts fell into place, "your idea about setting up an office in

Scott's house isn't half bad. If I want to approach this problem professionally—"

Wendy fought the desire to tell her brother that she'd been too hasty and had made a mistake. That she really needed him to hang around here and help her stave off the boredom.

But then, if this really was Blake's mind-set, she knew that he would continue talking about Brittany and how wonderful he thought she was. She also knew that she would come very close to strangling her beloved brother if he went on and on about Brittany and her so-called attributes. If nothing else, it would make her nauseous as hell.

Still, she had to find a way to at least *try* to throw a monkey wrench into this absurd "campaign" plan of his. Not that she actually thought that the heartless Brittany would wind up marrying her brother. She knew the woman well enough to know that Brittany was too accustomed to being fawned over by a host of men to ever give that up for just one man.

But if Blake went all out to win Brittany over, he would eventually have his heart cut out and handed to him—and not on a silver platter. Wendy was determined to do whatever it took to spare her brother that ultimate pain and humiliation.

But there was only so much she could physically do right now.

Wendy frowned, staring down at the bed that imprisoned her. Giving her word that she wouldn't get out of bed was the only way she had managed to bargain her discharge from a San Antonio hospital room. Her doctor had fully intended for her to remain in the hospital until such time as her baby was physically developed enough to be born. Complete bed rest was the only compromise available.

Which meant that she was going to need an ally to act in her place. More specifically, she needed the one woman who just might be able to get her brother to give up this ridiculous notion of asking Brittany Everett to become Mrs. Blake Fortune.

"If you're setting up your office," Wendy said, cutting in, "you might as well send for Katie and have her come join you."

Caught off guard by the suggestion, Blake stared at her. "Katie?" he echoed.

"Wallace," Wendy prompted needlessly. Katie was as much a part of her brother's life as anyone in the family. More, probably. "You know, your marketing assistant. Cute girl, twenty-four, stands about five foot five, has pretty brown hair and soft brown eyes—"

Blake snorted. "I know who Katie is." And then, as he replayed his sister's initial words in his head, he nodded. His frown faded. "You know, sending for Katie's not a half-bad idea, either."

Yes!

"Of course it's not a half-bad idea," Wendy informed him serenely, then couldn't help adding, "It's a completely wonderful idea.

"She can help you with your *work,*" she underscored pointedly, praying she could divert her brother's focus away from the girl he was mooning about and get him back on his usual track. Blake really was a very hard worker and a real asset to FortuneSouth Enterprises. This nonsense about Brittany was hopefully just that—nonsense. "Katie has wonderful organizational skills," Wendy reminded him.

Besides, Wendy added silently, if her brother interacted with Katie, maybe he'd forget about this stupid vow to win over Miss all wrong for him. Or at least feel too stupid saying it out loud in Katie's presence, which meant he wouldn't be putting whatever half-baked plan he was hatching into play.

Though they had never talked about it out loud, Wendy was certain that Katie had feelings for Blake. Maybe even loved him. It was all there, in her eyes.

Not that Blake ever looked, she thought, slanting a disparaging glance in his direction, which he seemed to miss totally.

"I'll get right on it," Blake was saying cheerfully. Rising from the chair, he stopped to brush a kiss against her cheek. "You're the best," he told Wendy with enthusiasm.

"Of course I am," she agreed, as he headed for the doorway.

"Katie, I need you."

Katie Wallace nearly dropped the receiver as Blake Fortune's voice echoed in her ear, uttering the words she had waited to hear for what felt like her entire life.

Words that she'd been fairly convinced she was *never* going to hear.

Katie, I need you. He'd said it. Blake had actually said it.

To her.

They weren't in the middle of an incredibly long meeting, or stuck in an all-night work marathon, the way they'd been all too frequently. They weren't even in the same room together. Blake was calling her from Red Rock, where he was on what she'd assumed was a vacation or some kind of family emergency.

Ever since the tornado had ripped through Red Rock she'd been watching the news reports religiously and reading everything she could get her hands on about the devastation that had befallen the idyllic Texas town where her childhood friend Wendy had taken up residence.

When the tornado had initially hit, a news bulletin had interrupted the program that was on TV. As she'd watched and listened, her whole world had ground to a halt. She'd wanted to attend Wendy's wedding, but because of circumstances, she'd had to remain in the office, manning her post, so to speak.

Her heart had all but stopped as she'd listened to the bulletin. She knew that Blake and Wendy, as well as the rest of their family, were all out there, stranded and in the tornado's path. The very thought unnerved her. She'd instantly started praying and searching for more information.

At one point, she had almost torn out of the office to

try to get the first flight out to Red Rock, but no flights were going out to Red Rock, not directly or with layovers. Moreover, as reports began to come in, apparently there no longer was an airport for the flights to land in. The tornado had taken care of that.

That first day, she'd stayed up over twenty-four hours, scouring the channels and the internet, searching for any shred of information. Looking for the names of those who hadn't made it—desperately praying she wouldn't see any she recognized.

Especially not the name of the man she had loved with all her heart since she was a little girl.

Not that Blake Fortune actually ever noticed her. Oh, he'd seen her, but never as what she wanted him to see. To him she was just his sister's friend, the annoying girl next door. Later on, he'd acknowledged her as a college graduate with a marketing degree and he'd been impressed enough with her skills to hire her. But he never saw her as what she was. A woman who could love him the way he desired to be loved.

Still, something was better than nothing, so, as a kid she'd settled for his teasing words, his pranks, pretending indignance and secretly loving the attention. *Anything,* she had long ago decided, that had Blake looking in her direction was fine with her.

After she grew up, of course, she'd wanted more. Couldn't help wanting more. She'd wanted him to look at her as something other than Katie Wallace, the little girl next door.

That was why she'd gone to college to get that marketing degree in the first place. This was the key to getting closer to him, if not in his private life, then in his professional one. She'd nurtured the hope that if she worked really hard and proved to be indispensable to him, Blake would eventually wake up one morning to realize that he had feelings for her beyond his role as her boss.

That had been her plan, but even so, right now she still was having trouble believing that she wasn't dreaming. Was Blake actually saying what she thought he was saying?

After all this time?

Her heart was hammering in her throat as she forced out the words, "Excuse me?" into the receiver, scarcely above a whisper. She cleared her voice and spoke up. "Could you repeat please that?" Then, in case he thought she was being coy instead of just shocked, she quickly explained, "There's interference in the line, I didn't really hear what you just said."

"I said I need you," Blake told her, raising his voice. "It looks as if I'm going to be here longer than I thought. At least a couple of weeks, maybe three. When can you get out here?"

Katie allowed herself to savor his words for exactly thirty seconds. Where were Dorothy's magic ruby-red slippers when you needed them? she thought. Because then all it would take was clicking her heels together three times and she would be there at his side. Just the way she desperately wanted to be.

She knew that this had to be about work and that

Blake needed her to get things done, but she viewed the phrase he'd uttered as her first step in the right direction. Someday, she promised herself, Blake was going to realize that he really did need her—and not just as his assistant.

"I can be on the first flight out there," she promised. Even as she spoke, she began searching the internet, pulling up the various airlines and looking at departure times. "I'll call you back the second I'm booked."

"That's my girl," he said. "I knew I could count on you."

That's my girl.

The three words echoed in her head over and over again as she all but flew back to her apartment and set a new world record for packing quickly.

That's my girl.

Definitely in the right direction, she thought happily.

Chapter Two

"You sure you don't mind me setting up an office in your house?" Blake asked his older brother Scott for a second time.

Ordinarily, he would have opted to use one of the offices in the building housing the Fortune Foundation in town. However, it was currently off-limits since it had sustained major structural damage during the tornado.

Scott had only recently decided to transplant himself from Atlanta to Red Rock and had just purchased a ranch and the house that stood on it. As of yet, he and Christina, the woman who had won his heart, were redecorating the rooms and several were still in limbo. Blake was temporarily claiming one for an office—as long as Scott had no objections.

"I mean, I'm already in your hair, bunking here

until Wendy's baby is strong enough to finally make us uncles." Blake thought for a moment, then decided to ask Scott, since he was now the Red Rock resident. "Maybe it'd be better if I rent a couple of rooms in town—"

Scott waved away what he anticipated was the rest of his brother's thought.

"After the tornado, whatever's available in Red Rock has most likely been commandeered for temporary living quarters for the folks who lost their homes, or whose homes are so damaged that they're not safe to stay in right now. Besides," Scott added as an afterthought, "turning part of my place into 'FortuneSouthWest' might just make points with the old man, though I doubt it."

Their father, as everyone knew, had very high standards, which at times, Scott couldn't help feeling, even God might have some trouble reaching. It didn't help matters that, in the aftermath of the tornado, Scott had decided not to go back to Atlanta but to make a life for himself here, with a woman he firmly believed was his soul mate. A woman he had only known for a little over a month. The senior Fortune, Scott felt certain, undoubtedly believed that he had lost his mind—instead of finally finding his soul.

"And you're sure I won't be in your way?" Blake probed.

This new, improved and far more relaxed Scott was going to take some getting used to, Blake thought. Up until a month and a half ago, Scott had been as big a workaholic as their father and oldest brother, Michael. But he was definitely of a mind that this change in his brother was for the better.

"Not unless you plan on lying in the front doorway like a human obstacle course," Scott answered. He grinned as he regarded his brother who, at twenty-seven, was five years younger than he was. "Might be kind of nice having you around for a while. Aside from that little buried-alive incident on New Year's Eve-eve—and, of course, Wendy's wedding—we don't get to see each other all that much anymore," he noted.

The observation amused Blake. "Said the workaholic," he interjected.

"Not anymore," Scott emphasized. "That tornado kind of made me reexamine my priorities." Almost dying did that to a man, Scott thought. He felt as if he'd been given a second chance for a reason—and he didn't intend to waste it by going back to "business as usual." "There's a lot more to life than finding different ways to continue building up a telecommunications empire."

His brother really was sincere, Blake thought. This wasn't just a passing phase. Scott was serious about putting his roots down in Red Rock because living here was so important to Christina, his future wife, and thus, important to him.

"Yeah, I know what you mean, about reexamining my priorities," Blake explained when Scott raised a quizzical eyebrow. "I told Wendy that I feel like my life's been on hold long enough and that it's time I did something about it."

"Anything you care to share with the class?" Scott asked, amused at the very serious expression on Blake's face.

"I'm going after the one who got away," Blake told him simply.

Scott nodded and smiled. He might have been a dedicated workaholic when they were all back in Atlanta, but that didn't mean that he had been wearing blinders 24/7. He was quite aware of how his young brother's assistant, Katie Wallace, looked at Blake when she thought no one was paying attention. At the time, he'd found it rather amusing. But now, finding himself on the other side of love, he understood how she must have felt—and continued to feel. But something wasn't making sense, he realized.

"I wasn't aware that she had exactly 'gotten away,'" Scott commented.

Blake supposed that Scott was either too busy to have noticed, or maybe he'd just forgotten. "Yeah, she did," he assured his brother.

Okay, maybe he'd missed a chapter or two of Blake's life, Scott thought. "So you're going after—"

"Brittany Everett, yes," Blake said, filling in the name for Scott.

For a second, all Scott did was stare at him. And then he murmured, "Oh," more to himself than to his brother.

"What do you mean, 'oh'?"

There was no point in talking about Katie if his brother's sights were set on a vapid prima donna like Brittany Everett. Like everyone else in the family, because of the circles they all moved in he was vaguely aware of the woman—and what he knew, he didn't find very compelling.

Scott shrugged, dismissing his slip. "Nothing, just surprised that you seem so determined to get together with her." For a moment, he thought back to his brother's college days. "Didn't Brittany dump you right after graduation?"

"No one dumped anyone," Blake insisted. "We just drifted apart."

"Right, after you caught her in a lip-lock with some other guy, if I remember correctly."

"I should have fought for her."

You should have cut her loose long before that, Scott thought. But Blake was a big boy now, able to make his own decisions. Besides, Scott had a feeling that the more he talked against Brittany—whose only attributes as far as he could see were strictly physical—the more, he was certain, Blake would dig in. They were alike that way, he and his brother.

So Scott dropped the matter, stepped back and hoped for the best. "If you say so. Look, I promised Christina I'd meet her for lunch, so I'd better get going. Good luck with whatever it is you're planning to do." *And I hope you come to your senses real soon.*

The reference to time had Blake looking at his own watch. "Hey, I'd better get going, too. I've got to drive over to San Antonio International Airport to pick up Katie," he said, joining his brother in the hallway. "She's flying in to help me with my strategy to win back Brittany."

Scott stared at him, utterly stunned. "She is?" he asked. This couldn't be right. "You actually told Katie that you were 'launching' this so-called campaign to get Brittany to become Mrs. Blake Fortune?"

"Well, not in so many words," Blake admitted. The next moment, he saw a very wide smile curving his brother's mouth. He was unaware of having said something funny. "What?"

"Nothing," Scott answered, waving his hand and struggling to keep the laughter under wraps. "Just, good luck with that." And then, he couldn't resist asking, "By the way, how many pallbearers would you like at your funeral?"

Maybe the tornado had shaken Scott up more than anyone realized, Blake thought. His brother wasn't making any sense. "What's that supposed to mean?"

But Scott continued grinning mysteriously. And then he patted him on the shoulder. "You'll figure it out, Blake," he assured him, just before he hurried off down the hallway and out of the house.

Blake shook his head as he followed slowly in his brother's path, heading for the car he'd left parked in the huge, circular driveway. He put the odd conversation with Scott out of his head.

Right now he had something more pressing to attend to.

The way he figured it, if the flight from Atlanta arrived on time, he was just going to make it to the airport by the skin of his teeth—barring the unforeseen. It was a footnote that he had gotten into the habit of adding ever since the tornado had turned his life and his family's lives entirely upside down, tossing them on their collective ears.

Katie had deliberately brought only carry-on luggage with her. She had no desire to spend the extra time required to wait for luggage.

So, in the interests of speed and efficiency, Katie had stuffed into a single piece of luggage everything she felt she would need that couldn't be purchased at some local shop between the airport and Red Rock. After engorging the suitcase to the point that it looked as if it would explode, she'd sat on the lid and fought with the zipper until she'd managed to bring the closure full circle.

She managed to secure the very last ticket for the next outgoing flight to San Antonio International Airport.

She didn't relax the entire flight, her mind busily embracing the key phrase Blake had used when he'd called her.

I need you.

Part of her still didn't believe she'd finally lived to see the day when everything she'd dreamed about for so long would actually start happening.

Don't start sending out the wedding invitations yet,

her mind warned. That was the part of her that was still waiting for the other shoe to drop.

She could warn herself all she wanted about not getting too excited—but she still was.

When the plane landed—reasonably on time for once, she noted, hoping that was a good omen—she was debating whether to just rent a car and drive to Red Rock or splurge and have a shuttle service do the driving for her.

The latter would prove to be the more expensive route, because of the distance that was involved, but she really wasn't too keen on driving by herself all that way. She was tired and the prospect of falling asleep behind the wheel was unnerving.

Maybe if she had a really strong container of coffee—

As it turned out, there was no need to debate the pros and cons of driving versus being driven, because, as she was weighing her options, she realized that she was being paged over the P.A. system.

Heading over to the customer service desk, she didn't actually see Blake, she saw his smile. But she knew that smile even at this distance. It belonged to Blake. Blake was here! And he was walking toward her.

Reviewing their phone conversation in her head, she couldn't recall him saying anything about picking her up at the airport. She knew where he was staying, thanks to the directions he'd texted to her on her phone. Scott Fortune had bought a ranch here and Blake was staying with him. Since, according to Blake, the company would be paying for her flight, she'd just assumed that she would wind up charging either the car rental or the shuttle service to FortuneSouth Enterprises. Never one to wantonly spend money, even if it was someone else's, she was just trying to make the best decision.

Was Blake this eager to see her that he had driven over himself?

The pounding of her heart went up another notch.

The exhaustion that had been slowly laying claim to her completely vanished as Katie picked up her pace, all but breaking into a run as the distance between them shortened noticeably. The heavy suitcase became nothing more than an unwieldy pull toy in her wake.

"You made it," Blake called out to her, obviously pleased at how quickly she'd managed to get here after he'd called her.

Katie beamed at him. "Nothing could have kept me away."

"Good," he pronounced with approval. "Then we can get right down to work as soon as you're ready. Here, let me take that for you," he offered, putting his hand over hers on the suitcase handle.

The brief contact still managed to steal her breath away, as it usually did. But what he'd just said pushed reality in, front and center.

"Work?" Her heart fell. Blake was still making noises like a workaholic. The hope that he would be just a little more laidback, a little more...*personal*... died a quick, bitter death.

Katie had a strange expression on her face. He took it

to mean that she was experiencing a little jet lag. Maybe she did need to rest awhile, although he'd known her to work tirelessly when the occasion called for it.

"Yes. Work," he repeated. "That's the reason I sent for you. It was Wendy's idea, really. She thought you could help me get my campaign underway."

"Your campaign," she repeated numbly. Was this why he "needed" her? To work on some marketing campaign? Here? She felt confused. Even so, she sensed her slim grasp on happiness slipping away as her heart constricted within her chest.

"Yes. My campaign," he asserted, then added the damning phrase: "To win back Brittany Everett." Not seeing her face all but fall, he laughed a little self-consciously. "I know it's not exactly what you're used to doing, but I thought that if I went about winning Brittany back the way we go about landing an account for FortuneSouth Enterprises, then I'm almost *guaranteed* to be successful."

So this was what shock felt like, Katie thought. Shock, mixed with acute disappointment. Her pounding heart now felt like utter lead in her chest.

"And Wendy suggested you send for *me* to help you procure this woman?" she asked in disbelief.

"Not procure," he corrected, bristling at the word she'd used. "That makes it sound sordid." He didn't want Katie starting out with the wrong idea about this. Otherwise, she'd be no help at all and, he had to admit, he had come to rely on her shrewd instincts pretty heavily these past two years. "Brittany and I had a connection in college."

"Yes, I remember," she answered grimly as they made their way down the escalator to the first floor.

There was deep regret in his voice as he concluded, "And then I didn't follow through. I want to win her back. I'll be taking her to the Valentine's Day fundraiser in Atlanta in a few weeks. That's when I intend to make my move."

Were they talking about the same woman? As she recalled, the woman was a little too Scarlett O'Hara for her taste.

"Kind of hard to get close to someone with that kind of a throng surrounding her," she recalled.

That, Blake thought, disturbed by Katie's comment, was an unwarranted, uncalled-for assessment. "It wasn't a throng," he protested.

"Okay, a swarm, then. Or maybe 'mob' might be a better word to use," she suggested crisply.

How could he? her mind cried. How *could* he think about getting together with a girl like that again? She'd never understood what had compelled him to get together with Brittany in the first place. Yes, she had what amounted to an almost-perfect body, but it was coupled with a completely imperfect personality for him.

They were outside the terminal now and approaching the valet's booth. Blake glanced in her direction as he gave the valet his ticket.

"I'm sensing a little hostility here," he noted.

"Just a little?" Katie muttered under her breath.

Blake cocked his head, bringing his ear a little closer to her. The noise level outside the terminal was even louder than it was inside, making it hard to maintain a conversation without resorting to shouting. And Katie hadn't shouted. Had he not seen her lips moving, he wouldn't have even been aware that she'd said anything at all.

"What did you just say?" he asked.

Katie was quick to shake her head. There was no point in arguing. "Nothing."

Besides, what did she expect? she silently upbraided herself. For the world to suddenly change? For Blake to suddenly wake up, come to his senses and see what was right in front of him? A woman who was willing to love him, flaws and all, for the rest of his life—for the rest of *her* life.

Leopards didn't change their spots and Katie couldn't believe that in the interim years a girl like Brittany Everett would become more compatible with Blake.

What was *wrong* with him? she silently fumed.

The next moment, she redirected the question toward herself. What the hell was wrong with *her?* Had Blake *ever* indicated that he had feelings for her that went beyond a boss appreciating his employee's work? Did he even indicate that he felt she went above and beyond the call of duty each and every time?

Well, that was her mistake, wasn't it? She did so in an effort not just to seem indispensable to him, but to have him suddenly look at her, *really* look at her and see her for the first time. See how good she was for him—not just for the company, but for *him*—and then maybe, just maybe, that could lead to something more.

The word *more* however had no meaning here—unless it was to indicate that she doubted if Blake could be *more* wrong in his choice of a future wife, which was where this whole stupid "campaign" was clearly going.

She couldn't do this, she thought. She couldn't go through with this. She couldn't be his master strategist, his Cyrano, to help him land a woman who would ultimately stomp all over the heart he was planning on serving to her on a silver platter.

Katie began to voice her protest, but then, before even a single word managed to come out, she changed her mind.

Blake was going to go through with this with her or without her and if she protested, he might just view it as being a case of sour grapes. But if she was there, at his side, helping him with this awful campaign, maybe it would finally hit him that she had all the virtues and assets that he, in his delusion, thought that Brittany possessed.

And, she added silently, if this all blew up on him, she'd be right there to help him pick up the pieces.

She'd be privy to every detail of his plan and with it all laid out for her, she would know how best to ruin his plans. And by ruining them, she would be able to ultimately save the man from embarrassment and making the mistake of a lifetime—if not the century.

And if, at the same time, she could get him to see that it was her all along who he should have been with, well, so much the better.

"Look, if I'm asking too much," Blake was saying, apparently having second thoughts about the wisdom of asking her to help, "then maybe you should—"

"It's not that you're asking too much," she said, cutting him off. "It's just that, well, I'm not sure if I'm exactly the right person for the job. This *is* a little different than the usual campaigns we work on."

"Of course you're the right person for the job. I mean, this is about what appeals to a woman. Brittany's a woman and so are you, right?"

She looked at him, a little stunned. "Is that a question?" she wanted to know. "I mean, really?"

"No, no, of course you're a woman. That's what I'm counting on."

He was either being exceedingly simpleminded—or insulting. She wasn't sure which bothered her more. "That all women are alike?"

He couldn't really explain why, but he had the feeling he was in over his head—and drowning. What was needed was a time-out so that he could gather his thoughts together and begin again.

Blake was more than certain that Katie was the right woman for the job. After all, someone as attractive as she was probably had guys making a play for her all the time. What sort of things made her reactions positively? That's what he needed to find out. He just had to find the right way to phrase this so she wouldn't think that, well, he was coming onto her. Because he wasn't. Even if, sometimes when she looked at him, he'd find something stirring deep inside of him. That was just a basic, *physical* thing, nothing more.

Taking a breather, Blake pulled himself back and refocused.

"Tell you what," he proposed. "Let's get you over to Wendy's. She's dying to see you."

At least someone was, Katie thought.

Chapter Three

"Oh my God, just look at you," Katie cried as she walked into Wendy's bedroom.

After everything she'd heard about Wendy going into premature labor, Katie had expected to find her friend pale and languishing in bed. Instead, Wendy looked just the way she always did: bright and animated, and very, very pretty.

Wendy's eyes crinkled the moment she heard the sound of Katie's voice. She shifted in bed, excited to finally see her old friend.

"I know, I know, I'm as big as a house," she lamented, only half kidding.

"I was going to say glowing," Katie corrected tactfully. Granted, Wendy looked a bit larger than she had the last time they'd seen one another, but nowhere near Wendy's self-deprecating description.

"But you *were* thinking that I looked as big as a house," Wendy prodded. There was no way anyone walking into the room could miss this "bump," which was currently the biggest thing about her.

Katie knew better than to argue. No one won arguments with Wendy. "Not a house," she insisted. "Maybe a little cottage." She held up her thumb and forefinger, keeping them about an inch apart.

With a laugh, Wendy held out her arms to her friend. Katie had always had a way of making her feel instantly better. Now was no exception. "Come here and give me a hug," she implored.

It was all the invitation that Katie needed. Bending over, she embraced Wendy, giving her a heartfelt squeeze and holding on tightly for a moment. She really was very happy to finally see her.

"God, I've missed you," she said fiercely, then, as she stepped back, she added in a lower, embarrassed voice, "I'm sorry I couldn't come to the wedding."

Wendy waved away the apology. "Being best friends means never having to say you're sorry," she said as if that was a given between them. And then she gave Blake an accusing look. "I know my slave-driving brother left you to hold down the fort."

"I take exception to the term *slave driver,*" Blake protested. "And what can I say?" he added with a careless shrug. "Katie happens to be very good at her job." And because she was, he had been able to fly to Red

Rock for an extended week to attend his baby sister's wedding along with the rest of his family.

"Oh, I don't know, maybe you could have said, 'Hey, Katie, since my sister's your very oldest, dearest friend, forget about the fort.'"

"It wasn't the fort that needed holding down," Katie told her. "We had a last minute problem with a customer demanding changes to a contract that was going out and someone in marketing was needed to handle it. I knew Blake didn't want to miss your wedding, so I volunteered to stay behind and deal with the client," Katie told her. "It was kind of my anonymous wedding present to you."

"And in a way, it turned out for the best," Blake pointed out. "If she'd come to the wedding, Katie would have been struck at the airport like the rest of us—and who knows? Maybe she would have even gotten hurt. The way I see it, maybe staying behind to deal with the client and smooth things out saved Katie's life."

Wendy rolled her eyes at his comment. "You're really reaching there, Blake."

Katie was nothing if not a born mediator and now was no exception. She sidelined any further discussion about something that couldn't be changed by redirecting the conversation to the present. "Speaking of the tornado, is Javier doing any better now?"

"He's finally conscious. It was touch and go for a while and I know Marcos was really worried that his brother might not come out of his coma." She pressed her lips together. "We still don't know how extensive the damage to his spine and legs really is. Right now, he can't move them, but the doctor said this could just be due to some swelling along his spinal cord. Once that goes down, he should be able to walk again." The key word here, she added silently, was *should*.

As if reading her unspoken thoughts, Katie said firmly, "Yes, he will." Like Wendy, she believed in positive thought, taking it a step further. Positive thoughts yielded positive energy.

Wendy beamed. Though far from a negative person herself, there was something exceedingly uplifting about the upbeat tone in her friend's voice. She caught Katie's hand in hers for a moment and just held on.

"God, but it's going to be good having you around," she said with feeling.

"Speaking of which," Katie said, looking at Blake, "you haven't told me where I'm going to be staying. I'd like to drop off my things—"

"At Scott's," Blake surmised, mentioning where he was currently staying. At the same time, Wendy was saying something entirely different.

"Why, here, with me of course." How could Blake even think she'd have her friend staying anywhere but with her? "Katie's going to be staying at my house," she said, reinforcing her initial words. "It'll make visiting so much easier."

He didn't get it. Sure, she and Katie were friends, but he was family. He and Wendy shared the same blood. This wasn't making any sense.

"She stays here but you just threw me out?" he protested.

"I didn't 'throw' you out," Wendy tactfully pointed out. "I 'moved' you out. There is a difference, and it's because you were hovering over me all the time. Besides—" she looked at Katie again, so thrilled that she had actually made it out here "—Katie and I have a lot of catching up to do."

Blake looked both hurt and insulted before he managed to hide it. "And you and I don't?" he asked.

"There's not all that much catching up to do, Blake," she said tactfully, and then reminded him, "You'd only been gone from here a little more than a week before you came back, remember?"

Still, he was family and Katie wasn't. "Not the point."

Wendy sat up a little straighter and caught his hand. "You *know* I appreciate you coming back out here again to keep me company, Blake, I just don't need to see you 24/7," she told him. She tried to sound as kind as she could, then quickly added, "And I won't be seeing Katie 24/7, either, because you're going to be working the poor girl to death most of the time." Switching gears, she looked at her friend and warned, "Don't let him work you to death, you hear? I don't care if he thinks he is your boss."

"I don't *think* I'm her boss," Blake pointed out. "I *am* her boss." What was that old saying? he tried to remember. Something about a prophet never being honored in his own town.

Caught in the middle, Katie thought it prudent to come to Blake's defense. "He's not a slave driver, Wendy. As far as bosses go, Blake's pretty good."

Blake inclined his head. "Thank you." And then he looked at his sister. "At least someone around here appreciates me."

Slanting a glance at Katie, Wendy smiled and shook her head, amused. *Obtuse,* that was the word for it, all right. "You, big brother, don't even know the half of it."

He had no idea what Wendy was referring to and chalked it up to the fact that pregnancy and the influx of all those extra hormones were making his little sister say some very strange things these days. Even more so than normally.

Maybe it was time to retreat for a little while. After all, it wasn't as if he didn't have things to do that would keep him busy.

"Yeah, well, I tell you what, I'll let you two catch up a little, the way you want, and I'll swing by Scott's place to check into a couple of things." He deliberately struck a courtly pose as he asked, "Will it be all right with you, your highness, if I come back here in, say two hours, and collect my marketing assistant?"

"That's entirely up to Katie," Wendy told him, raising her hands as if she had nothing to do with that sort of decision.

It took Katie a second to realize that the ball was now in her court and Blake was waiting for an answer from her. "Fine," she told him with feeling, coming to. "Two hours will be fine. Sooner if you'd like," she added as an afterthought.

"You heard the lady," Wendy said, taking charge again. For emphasis, she waved her brother away from the bed and toward the doorway. She was dying for some alone time with her friend. There were things she just had to find out. "Come back in two hours."

Blake almost reminded her that Katie had said "or sooner," then changed his mind. He wasn't about to argue with Wendy, not about anything if he could help it. Not in her present condition. Heaven only knew what might send her into premature labor again.

"Two hours it is," he agreed. And with that, he left the room.

"Wendy, I—" Katie began, only to be abruptly stopped by the mother-to-be before she had a chance to say anything more.

Wendy was holding her finger up to halt any further flow of words. At the same time she cocked her head, listening to something other than the sound of Katie's voice.

Her eyes shifted back to Katie. "Is he gone yet?" she wanted to know.

"Blake?"

Wendy seemed to indicate that she wanted her question answered before another word was said between them. Katie stepped into the hallway to make sure that the man who could raise her body temperature with just a single look in her direction was nowhere in the immediate vicinity.

"Yes," she said, reporting back, "he's gone." Curious, she crossed back to Wendy's bed and asked her, "Why?"

Because she planned to talk about her big brother and she didn't want him knowing that, Wendy thought. Out loud, though, she merely said, "I just don't want him eavesdropping on girl talk, that's all." She made a request. "You're going to be doing me a huge favor, making sure Blake keeps busy while he's here. Otherwise, he'll find some excuse to be over here night and day, watching me as if he expects me to suddenly explode or something," she complained. Being pregnant made her feel hugely vulnerable, not to mention grumpy. She just couldn't wait to be mistress of her own fate again.

"Sure thing," Katie readily agreed. That was what she'd initially thought was going to happen, anyway. It was just the car ride from the airport that had thrown a monkey wrench into everything. "I just wish that the campaign he wants me to help him with actually had something to do with work."

Wendy looked at her, momentarily speechless. Blake hadn't— He couldn't have— Her brother could *not* have laid out his half-baked plan before Katie. Not *seriously.*

Could he have?

"Don't tell me that Blake actually asked you to—" Wendy couldn't bring herself to finish the sentence, but the look on Katie's face made that unnecessary. Wendy covered her face with her hands. "Oh, God, not even

Blake could be that dense." But even as she said it, she mentally crossed her fingers.

The smile on Katie's lips was small and, when Wendy looked closer she saw that it was also rather sad.

"Oh, I wouldn't be putting any bets on that if I were you," Katie advised. "At least, not unless you're bent on losing."

Wendy just couldn't believe it. It was one thing to talk about the idea to her, but she would have thought that someone as savvy as Blake would have come to his senses shortly after he had hatched this stupid, half-baked plan of his.

Closing her eyes for a moment as she searched for strength, Wendy sighed. "Oh, God, Katie, he actually *asked* you to help him win over that dreadful woman?"

"Well, I don't know about dreadful," she allowed loyally, although for the life of her, she was beginning to wonder how she could harbor these feelings for a man who seemed to so easily disregard the fact that she had any feelings at all. "But he did say he wanted me to help him with his 'campaign' to win back Brittany Everett."

Wendy rolled her eyes in frustrated exasperation. "To win her back, my idiot brother would have had to *have* her in the first place."

"Wait, I'm confused," Katie protested. "Didn't he and Brittany go together just before they graduated college?"

She remembered how upset she'd been when she'd found out that Blake was seeing the beautiful young socialite. Katie had felt as if her entire world was crumbling right beneath her feet. It had taken her a while to get over it and get her mind back on her studies.

"Blake may have been 'going together,'" Wendy corrected. At least she remembered things clearly, even if Blake didn't. "Brittany apparently forgot. Besides, there's absolutely no comparison between the two of you. You *have* a heart. I think Brittany has a mirror where her heart is supposed to be. While my idiot brother was recruiting you for this impossibly ridiculous mission, did he happen to tell you how he and the Magnolia Queen came to 'break up'?" Wendy wanted to know.

Katie shook her head. "He didn't go into any details, no."

"Then allow me to fill you in," Wendy offered, warming up to her subject. "They were at a graduation party and became separated. At some point in the evening, he started looking for her. He walked around, searching the immediate party area, and found her making out with another guy."

Oh, poor Blake, was all Katie could think. "He found Brittany actually kissing some other guy?" she asked incredulously. How could she have even *looked* at another guy if she knew that Blake was committed to her?

Wendy shook her head, completely disgusted with her brother's choice in women. "Personally, I don't understand why Blake would even want to be in the same room with her, much less take her back."

Wendy was missing one very obvious point, Katie thought. “Maybe because Brittany’s pretty much drop-dead gorgeous.”

Wendy raised her chin. “So are you,” she insisted loyally.

It was Katie’s turn to roll her eyes. “Oh, come on, Wendy. I do own a mirror, you know. I know exactly what I look like.”

Wendy shook her head. Katie was missing the obvious. She’d been such a dedicated soul and hard worker for so long, she didn’t even remember how to use her feminine wiles, but that was all right. Wendy was devious enough for both of them.

“The only difference between you and that woman my brother *thinks* he wants is that she knows how to apply makeup to her best advantage.” Wendy’s eyes narrowed as she looked at Katie. “Nothing you can’t learn,” she told her emphatically.

Maybe, Katie thought, but not easily. And not quickly enough. “And while I’m busy learning how to make a silk purse out of a sow’s ear, Blake and Brittany will be exchanging wedding vows,” she concluded unhappily.

Wendy waved away the very notion. “Not in a million years, I guarantee it,” she promised with deadly certainty. She knew the Brittanys of the world. They took up space and looked attractive—as long as no one was looking closely. Because what they had was superficial. What Katie had ran deep. Clear down to the bone.

The next moment, Wendy lapsed into silence as she

paused, thinking the situation over—and seeing the potential that had been staring them in the face all along. It might just work.

"You know..." Her voice trailed off as an idea began to take serious shape. And then Wendy smiled. Broadly.

Katie was on her guard instantly. "Uh-oh, I know that look." It was Wendy's crafty expression.

The woman was up to something.

Katie held her breath as she asked, "What are you thinking?"

Wendy beamed at her. "Just that my beloved big brother might have just given us the perfect opportunity to make him see just how desirable a woman you really are."

"Right!" Katie laughed, shrugging off the compliment. But Wendy was obviously not kidding, she realized. "All right, I'm listening. Just how does my helping Blake put together his campaign strategy to bag the elusive Brittany-bird make him suddenly see how supposedly desirable I am?"

"Not supposedly," Wendy insisted. "You have to start thinking positively, Katie, or this is never going to work."

"I can *think* downright unshakably, that still doesn't mean that I—"

Wendy dropped her bombshell. "He'll have to practice on you."

Katie blinked. Had she missed something here? "Excuse me?"

"All these moves he's going to make on Brittany, he

has to practice on someone, polish them up on someone." To her it was a given. Rehearsals always helped attain the desired results. Wendy smiled at her. "That 'someone' is going to be you. Dinner—you, dancing—you, moonlight walks—you, seductive techniques—"

This time, it was Katie who halted the conversation, holding up not just a finger but a whole hand.

"I think I get it," she said, fighting a very real blush that was swiftly advancing up along her neck and splaying across her cheeks with the force of the evening high tide.

Wendy saw the blush and smiled with satisfaction. "Yes, I can see that you do. By the time we're finished—by the time *you're* finished," she amended with a smile, "my brother is going to forget that Brittany Everett ever existed."

Katie had her doubts about that, but she had to admit that she really liked the way it sounded. For now, she allowed herself to savor what to her was tantamount to an impossible dream. She figured it was the least she could do after Wendy had gone to all that trouble to come up with said plan.

Even if it wasn't going to work.

Chapter Four

"You know, if you were really concerned about me, you'd find a way to get me the hell out of here."

Javier Mendoza struggled to keep his voice from rising as he complained to his younger brother, Marcos. He'd finally been moved out of ICU into a single care unit, but the hospital walls were only so thick and his deep voice was the kind that carried.

There was a frustrated frown on his handsome face and he looked like a man who was just about to lose the last shred of what was left of his overtaxed patience.

Marcos sympathized with his brother. He knew how he'd feel in Javier's place, but there was just no way that his brother was leaving here, not yet.

"I *am* concerned about you, which is why I'm not going to help smuggle you out of here," Marcos informed him. There was an irrefutable note of finality in his voice that most people—except for his wife, Wendy—knew not to argue with.

But Javier wasn't listening to the sound of his brother's voice. He was too focused on his own exasperation. One minute, he was a virile, strong man in his very prime, the next, when he opened his eyes again, he'd lost a month of his life to a coma and had to train his body to do the very basic of life's functions. Things that most people took for granted—that *he* had taken for granted—were now challenges to him. His legs refused to obey him and that caused him no end of frustration—as well as scaring the hell out of him. The fear was something he wasn't about to admit to a living soul, not even Marcos.

Although he had a sneaking suspicion when he looked into Marcos's eyes that his brother already knew that. However, Marcos had wisely refrained from saying anything about it.

Marcos put a comforting hand on his brother's shoulder, which, he noted, was utterly stiff with tension.

"Look, Javier, you have to give these doctors a chance," Marcos urged. "They know what they're doing and they're a great deal more familiar with these kinds of...problems," he finally said, for lack of a better word, "than you are."

Javier's dark eyes narrowed angrily. "It's *my* body and nobody's more familiar with it, or how it's supposed to work, than I am," he insisted hotly. "Don't get all hypocritical on me," he warned. "They wanted to keep Wendy here and she put her foot down, so they gave in and you took her home—just like she wanted," his brother pointed out.

Marcos shook his head. "No, that was different," he countered.

"How's that different?" Javier demanded. He realized that his voice had risen again. Biting back his temper, he made a concentrated effort to lower his tone. "Because Wendy's your wife and I'm not?"

Marcos laughed shortly. "No offense, Javier, but you'd make a pretty ugly wife," he cracked, hoping to get some kind of smile out of his brother. He failed. "And it's different because we don't know how long Wendy would have to stay here before the baby is strong enough to be born. Wendy's four walls might have changed, but she still has to stay in bed day and night. She still can't get up the way she wants to." Javier had averted his face, but Marcos pressed on. "Now that the doctors have brought you out of that medically induced coma, they have a timetable for you."

"I'm not interested in *their* timetable," Javier snapped.

In his place, Marcos knew he'd feel the same way. But he wasn't in his brother's place and it was up to him to calm Javier down and make him be reasonable.

"Well, you should be," he said firmly. "Trust me, those doctors don't want to see your ugly face here any more than you want to be here. But this is the place where they can help you, where they can work with you."

"There's nothing to work with," Javier retorted coldly, staring down at the two stiff limbs beneath the blanket. The limbs that refused to move. "Look, if I've got to stay here, okay, I'll stay here. Doesn't really matter anyway. But I want you to tell everyone to stop coming."

"Why?" Marcos asked, stunned at this new curve his brother had just thrown him.

"Because I don't want them to see me like this, that's why," he said through gritted teeth.

Ordinarily, because Javier was his big brother and Marcos had grown up looking up to Javier, Marcos would have backed away and not pressed the subject. But this situation didn't come anywhere near close to fitting the description of being "ordinary."

"Like what?" he wanted to know.

"Like half a man," Javier shouted. "There, I said it. You happy now? Like half a man."

"This is just temporary," Marcos insisted.

"How do you *know* that?" Javier challenged. "You saw some written guarantee? How do you know that?" he shouted again.

"Because I do, that's why," Marcos shouted back, then caught himself and lowered his voice. "Once the swelling on your spinal cord goes down, you'll fully regain the use of your legs—and even if you didn't," he insisted, "who you are isn't trapped in any of your limbs. You're not you because of your legs or your arms or any other damn body part. You're Javier Mendoza because of what's inside of you. What's *here*," he said, jabbing his forefinger into the middle of Javier's chest. "You understand me? So stop your complaining and start focusing all that energy on getting better."

"You've got some mouth on you, you know that?" Javier retorted, but his voice was a little softer now. "Marriage do that to you?" It really wasn't a serious question, seeing as how, even though Wendy was expecting their first child at apparently any moment, Marcos and she had only been married for a little more than a month. A month that he had completely missed, Javier thought in rueful frustration.

"No, the tornado did," Marcos replied quite seriously. "Now, I mean it. Stop complaining and just be grateful that you're still alive and that you have the opportunity to mend. Not everyone was as lucky as you," he concluded more quietly, grimly recalling that several people he knew had lost their lives in the disaster.

Feeling just the slightest prick of guilt, Javier shrugged defensively as he stared out the window. "Easy for you to say."

"Easy?" Marcos echoed in disbelief. It felt as if he hadn't slept more than five hours in the past five weeks. "Ever since that tornado hit and they dug you out, I've been trying to find a way to split myself in two, being there for Wendy and here for you," he elaborated.

"I was in a coma," Javier pointed out. "There was no need—"

"There was a need," Marcos interrupted with conviction. "We all took turns reading to you. And there was music playing constantly. Wendy thought it might help. Just because you were in a coma didn't mean you couldn't hear," Marcos insisted. "And besides running back and forth between home and San Antonio, I still had to put in time at the restaurant," he reminded his brother, referring to Red, the restaurant that he managed for his aunt and uncle.

It was also the place where he had first met Wendy. Although he and the youngest member of the Atlanta Fortune family hadn't exactly hit it off at first—and that, he now had to admit, had been entirely his fault—the restaurant still held a very special place in his heart. He wouldn't have felt right about neglecting his duties there and having the other members of the staff pick up the slack for him, even if this was an unusual crisis.

Javier continued to stare out the window. "Well, you don't have to feel obligated to come back here and give me annoying pep talks."

Marcos moved around the bed and directly into Javier's line of vision, getting between him and the window. He looked at him for a long moment. "You really want me to leave and not come back?"

Javier opened his mouth, about to say yes. But in all honesty, it wouldn't have been the truth. And he wasn't angry at Marcos and his "pep talk," he was angry at the circumstances that had put him here. So he sighed and looked down at his motionless limbs.

"No," he mumbled. "I don't really want you to leave and not come back. It's just that—"

"You're so damn frustrated," Marcos filled in for his brother. He nodded. "Yeah, I know where you're coming from. It's hard being patient with things we have no control over. But the doctor said that the swelling *is* beginning to go down, so that means that you *are* getting better."

"Ha!" Javier jeered. So far, he didn't feel any different. "Not anywhere nearly as fast as I'd like."

Marcos laughed. He knew Javier. His brother would have wanted to be completely healed—yesterday. "I don't think that would be humanly possible, unless you had healing properties like Wolverine," he amended, thinking of the comic series he and his siblings used to read when they were children.

The mutant he was referring to was a favorite of *his* and Javier's. He'd never admitted that he had gravitated toward Wolverine *because* Javier liked the character as much as he did. Back then, he'd wanted to be exactly like his brother. Looking back now, he realized that what he'd had was a pronounced case of hero worship.

Childhood heroes shouldn't have to be talked out of making dumb mistakes, he thought, looking at Javier now. His brother should have better instincts than that.

"Just try to take it easy," Marcos advised. "Listen to the doctors and try to make gains during the physical therapy session—no matter how small," he urged. "Before you know it, this'll be behind you. I promise," he added, crossing his heart the way they used to as kids.

Javier looked totally unconvinced. He looked like a

man who was struggling to make peace with a life sentence. "Yeah, right."

"Unless you've found a way to make time stand still." The phrase, which he'd just plucked out of the air, made him smile. Wendy had done that for him, he realized. She'd made time stand still.

Not at first, of course. At first she'd made time sizzle because she'd been so maddeningly infuriating and he'd been saddled with her. He'd perceived her as a so-called poor little rich girl—slumming in the working world until she grew bored. Her parents had sent her off to Red Rock, and then to their friends, his uncle and aunt, in hopes that somewhere along the line their youngest born would develop a work ethic.

They'd had no idea that they were sending her out to meet her destiny.

And seal his.

Still frowning, but appearing just the slightest bit contrite now, Javier looked at him. "Yeah, I suppose you're right."

"Happens every once in a while," Marcos told him good-naturedly, with a laugh. He glanced at his watch. It was getting late and he was falling behind schedule. Again. "Look, I've got to get going." He put his hand on his brother's shoulder. "Promise me you're not going to do anything stupid."

"You mean like disguise myself as an orderly and sneak out of here?" Javier asked innocently. He saw Marcos's eyes grow wide. "Take it easy!" Javier laughed for the first time since before the tornado had hit. "I was only kidding. If I tried to sneak out as an orderly, I'd have to do it snaking my way out on my hands and knees, like a soldier trying to crawl through an open field under the enemy's radar. Remember? I'm the guy whose legs won't listen to him."

Marcos still wanted assurances. "So you'll be here when I come back tomorrow?"

Javier preferred to leave it open-ended. "Unless the doctors change their minds about sending me home."

Well, there was absolutely no way *that* was going to happen in the next twenty-four hours, Marcos thought, but for the sake of his brother's abysmally low spirits, he merely nodded and repeated, "Unless they change their minds, right. I'll see you tomorrow," he promised, crossing to the door.

"Tell Wendy I was asking after her," Javier called to his brother.

Marcos turned in the doorway and smiled as he looked back at Javier. "I will," he told his brother. "She'll like that."

His wife, family rebel though she'd once been, was exceedingly family oriented these days, especially now that they were beginning a family of their own.

Once he was out of his brother's room, Marcos quickly made his way down the hall to the bank of elevators. He was a man in need of a miracle, he thought. Preferably one that caused all traffic to either disappear or conveniently part for him, so that he could get back to Red Rock and the restaurant at something akin to a reasonable hour.

He supposed that made him an unrealistic dreamer.

"It's a thirty-day plan," Blake told Wendy proudly the next morning. She'd arrived a few minutes before and he had brought her into the makeshift office he had put together in Scott's house.

He was still having some difficulty in thinking of his brother as a rancher and not a forward-moving business dynamo. After all, he'd spent all those years watching Scott and Michael, his oldest brother, constantly competing with one another over absolutely everything they laid eyes on, each always betting against the other that he would be the winner.

How did someone go from that to a laid-back man of the earth? It didn't seem possible to him without involving stiff doses of tranquilizers.

Yet this was Scott's new life, one that he was happily embracing—and all because of a woman. The very woman he had been trapped with when the tornado had all but buried them alive in debris.

Well, if Scott could do an about-face and turn his life completely around, Blake thought, *he* certainly could launch a thirty-day campaign to win back the woman of his dreams. The woman he knew in his bones destiny had chosen for him, to remain at his side until death parted them—and maybe even beyond.

"Then you really were serious about wanting to go after Brittany and wear her down, like any of our marketing customers," Katie said as she sat down at her side of the desk. She'd really hoped that once he'd slept on it—*really* slept on it—Blake would realize how nonsensical that sounded and just move on. After all, it wasn't as if he didn't have any real work to do.

But obviously he didn't see it as nonsensical and he wasn't about to move on. Which in turn made it a problem she was going to have to deal with.

There were times when she fervently wished she didn't love the man as much as she did. But then, she might as well have wished that the sun wasn't going to rise the next morning. It really wasn't something that was going to happen anytime soon.

Or ever.

Blake caught the incredulous note in Katie's voice when she asked her question and, while he was convinced he was finally going about winning Brittany in the right way, he did value Katie's input. Over the past two years he had discovered that their onetime neighbor and his sister's childhood friend had an uncanny gift for putting things together and homing in on what needed fine-tuning.

He looked at her for a moment, trying to gauge what Katie had really meant. "You make it sound like I'm not playing with a full deck."

Katie shook her head. There was no way she was going to ever say something disparaging about him, especially to his face. There were times, when she looked around at other would-be applicants for her job, that she saw nothing but nubile, eager young women willing to do whatever it took to land a position. There was no way she could begin to compete against them on any level—other than demonstrating extreme competence. She was not about to do or say anything that would make Blake look for another assistant to take her place.

"Oh, no, the deck's full, all right—it's just a little different," she allowed, her voice trailing off as she frantically cast about for just the tiniest drop of the courage that she lacked.

His sister had insisted this morning that Katie go through with the idea that Wendy had come up with last night. She wanted Katie to strongly suggest that Blake try out each "step" of the plan on her first.

Katie sincerely doubted that he'd agree to that.

Here goes nothin'.

"You know," Katie began, feeling her way slowly around the words, trying her best to find the right ones, "since this plan of yours is such an unusual approach, maybe you should try it out first, you know, like a rehearsal or a dry run."

"Try it out?" Blake echoed. "I'm not sure I follow you."

Okay, she'd backtrack. "You want everything letter perfect, right?"

"Well, sure, that's the whole idea behind putting this down on paper and going over it," he told her, tapping what he had written on the eight-by-ten sheet of paper in the center of his desk.

"Having it down on paper doesn't give you a real feel

for it," she told him, wondering at the same time where these words were coming from.

Was she somehow managing to channel Wendy? Because that would seem to be the only answer. She knew that, even under fire, she wasn't capable of coming up with these words on her own, not when *she* had so very much at stake here.

Blake leaned back in his chair, crossing his arms before him as he studied her face closely. "And what would?"

"If you practice all this on someone else first," Katie said a tad too quickly. "If you took that person—that *other* person—to this play—" she tapped the name of the play that Blake had selected "—before you took Brittany." She could see he wasn't on board with this yet. Katie pitched harder. "That way, you could see if it—the play—was the kind that she enjoyed seeing. It would be just awful if the show turned out to be something that she'd feel uncomfortable about seeing. You never know, Brittany might think you had intentionally dragged her to see it for some reason." Katie pressed her lips together, not knowing if she was getting through to him. Only one way to find out. "Do you understand what I'm trying to say?"

He smiled broadly and she felt her heart do a backflip. Seeing that smile on his face always had the same results.

"Yes, I do. You want to make sure this is all perfect for Brittany. You want me to succeed as much as I want to succeed." He took hold of her shoulders and pulled her to him, giving her what amounted to a fierce bear hug. "You really are something else, you know that, Katie? You're absolutely one of a kind," he pronounced.

When he released her, Katie had to concentrate in order to make the room stop spinning and settle back down on its foundation.

"Okay," Blake, won over, declared, "we'll do it your way, Katie. We'll put every piece of this plan to the acid test. Together. And we'll start at the beginning and work our way down."

She tried to keep her excitement from surfacing in her voice. He was going to be taking her out and they were going to be doing things together. Fun things. Never mind that she was acting as a stand-in. She was going to be with Blake all this time. And maybe, just maybe, somewhere in all that time, he'd realize that she was the girl for him.

"That way," she said matter-of-factly, while cheering on the inside, "if something doesn't work, you can substitute something else in its place and she'll never know."

He nodded, pleased as the plan began to gel and come together in his head. "Like I said, you really are one of a kind, Katie Wallace."

Yes, I am, and you're just too damn thickheaded to realize that on your own, she thought, even as she kept her easygoing smile pasted on her lips. *But you will, Blake Fortune, God willing, before it's all too late, you will.*

Chapter Five

"Dancing?" Blake repeated.

His tone was less than happy as he looked at Katie uncertainly. In an attempt to snag a little of his father's attention, he'd forged his way into his father's business world at an early age. Some things, per force, had been sacrificed and certain rites of passage never even approached. Consequently, learning to dance was one of those things that just had never happened for him. If he was completely honest with himself, he'd never felt that he'd missed anything by neglecting this tiny portion of his social education.

He nodded now at the list on his desk. At the time he'd printed it, he'd thought it was a final copy of his campaign strategy. Apparently, he'd thought wrong.

"Dancing never made my list," he pointed out. What

with the play and other things, he felt that he had other ways to court the "Brittany Market" without having to resort to something that made him feel inadequate.

"I know," Katie replied simply. "But it should have."

She sounded pretty adamant, but Blake dug in his heels. He shrugged carelessly at the mere suggestion of being forced to move to a given beat. "It just seems so old-fashioned."

"Old-fashioned is good," Katie countered with conviction. The only way she was going to get through this, she thought, would be to focus on the concept that she was helping her friend reach his goal. If she allowed herself to dwell on her actual "motivation," then all bets were off. "Romance is old-fashioned, yet this is what you're really setting out to do, isn't it?" she pressed. "Romance Brittany? Sweep her off her feet?"

It was a rhetorical question and she hated the taste of every single word she was uttering. How she managed to talk and keep a forced smile on her lips, rather than hit him upside his head, was a credit to her strength of will.

"Yeah, but…" Blake's voice trailed off and he looked at her, one friend putting his trust in another. "You're sure about this?" he asked uneasily.

"I'm sure," she answered with conviction. "Take her dancing."

Blake took in a breath. "But I can't," he finally admitted.

Katie looked at him innocently over the desk that was between them. "Can't take her?"

He shook his head. He hated admitting to any shortcoming, even something as trivial as dancing. "Can't dance."

She knew that. Just as she made it a point to know everything else about him—except why in heaven's name a man as intelligent as Blake Fortune seemed to be so obsessed with winning back an airhead like Brittany Everett. Everything about the woman was so shallow—were these the qualities he *really* wanted in a wife? Did he really only want eye candy to hang off his arm?

Katie refused to believe that. She *knew* Blake, and the Blake Fortune she knew liked having intelligent conversations on a broad spectrum of subjects. Brittany Everett could conduct an in-depth analysis on why the color mauve brought out the hint of violet in her eyes. Moreover, she could go on for hours about which of the newest Paris fashions were the most flattering to her figure and her porcelain complexion.

But neither were subjects *she,* Katie, could stretch out for more than thirty seconds—if that long—nor did she have any desire to do so.

Brittany just *couldn't* be the kind of woman he was interested in.

And yet…

And yet here they were, laying out plans that rivaled the complexity of Allied maneuvers for the D-day invasion on Omaha Beach.

Make the most of this opportunity, remember? If you

teach him how to dance, he'll have to hold you in his arms in order to practice.

For a second, she could almost *swear* she heard Wendy's voice in her head, urging her on. She had to stop thinking about Brittany and just concentrate on the positive aspect here—she was spending a great deal of time with Blake, strategizing.

"No problem," she responded to his negative input with a wide smile. "I can dance and I'll be more than happy to teach you."

Blake continued to look at her with a doubtful expression. She obviously gave him too much credit, he thought. While he was a fairly decent athlete, he was convinced that he was in possession of two left feet when it came to being coordinated on the dance floor. There had been one attempt to teach him—he vaguely remembered one of his sisters trying to get him to master the tango when he was in middle school—and that had been quickly aborted.

"Why don't we put dancing on the bottom of the list?" he suggested. Picking up a pen, he was about to do just that.

But Katie pulled the paper away from him and shook her head. "No. It's always a good idea to tackle the hardest project first. Isn't that what you always say?" she reminded him.

Blake nodded, none too happy about having his words used against him. "Yes, but I didn't expect it to come back and bite me. You really do listen to everything I have to say, don't you?" he marveled, impressed despite the situation.

She hung on his every word, but that wasn't something she wanted him to be aware of. So instead, she used work as an excuse. "You're the boss."

That he could use to his advantage, he thought. "Well, if I'm the boss—"

"Except for here," she quickly interjected before he could get rolling. Then, because she could see how frustrated he looked, she pointed out the obvious. "You did tell me you wanted my help, right?"

Part of him was beginning to have second thoughts about the wisdom of his having approached Katie with Project Brittany. "Right," he muttered.

"Well," she concluded brightly, "this is how I'm helping."

"By making me feel like an idiot?" he challenged, because that was how he was going to feel, tripping over his own feet and pretending it was called dancing.

She wasn't even going to try to argue that point. Instead, she just forged ahead. "By making you see that you really can be light on your feet." She looked at him and said softly, but with certainty, "You can do anything you set your mind to." She could see that he was weakening. "When your father put you in charge of marketing, didn't you tell me that you overheard him saying that he thought maybe you were in over your head?"

"Yes, he did," he recalled. He also recalled how good it had felt to prove the old man wrong—not that his father would ever admit it, of course. But it was enough that his father now knew Blake could handle it.

"And didn't you tell me that you used his belief that you were going to fail to make you work twice as hard, just because you wanted to prove him wrong and show him that you *could* handle whatever he threw at you?"

"You listen to everything I tell you?" He'd already said it once, but now he was completely floored by the realization that there was someone who actually did take in what he was saying. Not once in a while, but apparently all the time. It made him feel good.

"Pretty much," Katie replied with a dismissive nod. It was time to get this portion of the program underway, she thought. A ripple of anticipation undulated through her. "Okay, we're going to begin your first lesson right now."

"Now? Here?" Blake looked around. "Don't we need more room or at least to roll up the rug before we get started?" he asked. The makeshift office he'd set up was good enough to use temporarily, but it wasn't exactly spacious. Not like his office back in Atlanta. If they practiced here, they'd be bumping into furniture constantly.

"Scott and Christina are going to be out all morning," she told him. She'd already thought to check with Christina regarding their schedule for the day. "We can use the family room. It lets out onto the veranda." And she imagined them dancing across both.

"And music," Blake quickly pointed out, raising another obstacle, one that he hoped provided more of a deterrent than the cramped quarters. He *really* didn't want to do this, even though he had to admit that she had a point. A lot of women did like to go dancing. "We need music, right?"

"Absolutely," she agreed.

He should have known that wouldn't be the end of it. Katie was opening her briefcase and taking out her iPod. She paused to hook it up to a deceptively small, metallic blue speaker.

Sensing he was watching her every move, she flashed Blake a triumphant smile. "Luckily, I came prepared. I have ballroom music on here," she told him, holding the small device aloft. "Tango, waltz, it's all here."

"You're kidding," he cried incredulously. It wasn't that he wasn't familiar with the capabilities of the gadget she had in her hand—he hadn't been living under a rock these last few years—it was just that he was surprised that her device contained something so tame, so classic as ballroom music.

Rather than refute him, Katie merely turned on the iPod, now hooked up to the single round speaker. One of Strauss's classical waltzes filled the air. He looked from the player to Katie. The woman was an endless source of surprises, he concluded.

"You always carry that around?" he wanted to know.

"My iPod? Yes. The speaker? No," she told him casually. "But I had a hunch you might need to at least brush up on some of your dance steps, so I put together a playlist on here for you," she confessed, holding up the iPod.

He'd been right to ask her help, he thought. The woman was exceedingly thorough and always seemed to manage to be ten steps ahead of him. He had a tendency to hang back if he felt uncomfortable about something and obviously, Katie had no qualms about kicking him in his complacency.

This was exactly what he needed.

Still, he didn't really like looking like a fool, even around an old friend who had never exhibited a judgmental moment in her life.

"Like I said," he murmured, "you really are one of a kind, Katie Wallace."

This time, Katie looked him squarely in the eye. "You're stalling."

He laughed. There was just no putting anything over on her. "I was hoping you wouldn't notice."

"I noticed," she informed him matter-of-factly. *I notice everything you do, everything you say. I notice everything about you.* "Let's go to the family room," she urged, leading the way. Blake had taken her on a quick tour of the house when she'd gotten here yesterday. She retained things like a human DVR, he couldn't help thinking.

Once she'd reached the family room, she quickly set up her iPod and hit the playlist she'd put together for him just last night.

"I thought we'd start out slow," she told him when

the waltz filled the air. "All right, I'm sure you know this part," she said, positioning herself.

When Blake did as she told him to, Katie could have sworn she felt a warm shiver skittering up her spine, despite the fact that she was wearing very sensible clothes rather than the backless evening dress she imagined Brittany would be wearing for such an occasion.

She'd temporarily forgotten this part, Katie realized. That he would actually be touching her if they were going to get this dancing lesson underway. Every single time he touched her, she had the same reaction: a warmth would spontaneously ignite within her, sending out beams of light all through her like a winter bonfire on the beach.

Focus, Katie, focus, she ordered sternly. She couldn't allow herself to dissolve into a puddle. She had to get through this, had to act as if she was seriously going through the motions of teaching him to dance.

So that he could "seduce" Brittany, an inner voice taunted her.

"That's right," she said, as his hand slid around her waist, her mouth momentarily growing very dry. "Now take my left hand in your right one."

Though he was considered suave and charming, when he was out of his element as he as with these lessons, Blake felt that he bore a distinct resemblance to a lumbering bear.

"Like this?"

She smiled her approval. "Like that. Can't really

mess that part up, seeing as how we both come with only one set of left and right hands," she teased.

He noticed that she seemed spunkier somehow and thought to himself that he rather liked this version of her. But then, he knew, there was nothing about Katie to dislike, at least he'd never encountered anything that had set him off.

"No, this part's easy," he contradicted, and then, in all fairness, he issued her a warning. "It's when I start stepping all over your feet that things are going to get rough."

"You are *not* going to step on my feet," Katie said firmly.

He raised one dark eyebrow as he regarded her. "You know something I don't?"

"Yes." She tilted her head up slightly, her eyes catching him. "I know that you're Blake Fortune and you can do absolutely anything you set your mind to," she told him, repeating the mantra she'd professed to believe earlier. Blake could be exceedingly stubborn when he wanted to be.

He sighed, prepared to give it his all—and hope that it was enough. "I wish I had as much faith in me as you seem to."

"No 'seem to' about it," she corrected with just the right touch of feeling. "I do." Well, now that he knew how to stand and what to do with his hands, it was time to let the games begin. She began to dance, but for the most part, Blake just stood there, his feet sealed in place. "All right," she urged, "now let the music talk to you."

He listened closer, but it was still the same. "There're no words," he protested.

"There don't have to be," she told him, then instructed, "*Feel* it." He looked at her a little blankly, so she elaborated. "Feel the rhythm, let it *seep* into your bones, into your system," she urged softly.

And then, strictly for his benefit, she began counting off the steps between repetitive movements.

At first, he was concentrating so hard, listening to her counting and trying to follow each of her movements, that he didn't realize just how close her body was to his.

And then it dawned on him that he could actually *feel* every movement she made. The motions echoed against his body, urging him to mimic what was happening. And then the warmth began to sink in. Really sink in.

He felt the warmth of her body against his—or was that his against hers? He wasn't sure who was causing what. All he knew was that the end result was he could feel the heat, both from without and from within.

He caught himself looking at her. *Really* looking at her. And then he stumbled, stepping on her foot and the moment, he knew, was broken. As perhaps, quite possibly, was her foot.

"Sorry," he apologized as she stopped dancing for a second and paused to try to feel her toes. "I tried to warn you," he said defensively, looking very chagrined beneath the bravado. "I told you I wasn't any good at this."

"You can't expect to be perfect the first time out," she told him. She took a deep breath, willing the radiating pain in her foot to scale back so that she could continue. The last thing she wanted to do was hobble in front of him. That would definitely sideline him for the duration and that was *not* the plan. "Actually," she went on warmly, "you're doing a lot better than I thought you would at this point."

"Really?" he asked incredulously. It was clear from his tone that he thought he was doing rather poorly.

She nodded. He looked like a kid who'd just built his first soapbox racer, she thought. A huge wave of affection washed over her as she regarded Blake.

"Really," she told him. She could feel him slowing down, could see by the look in his eye what he was about to do—or not do—next. "Now, don't stop dancing," she urged with feeling. "That's the secret, no matter what happens on the floor—unless the iceberg hits, just keep on dancing until the song's over."

"Iceberg?" he questioned. And then, belatedly, he recognized the reference. "Oh. Right."

Her eyes were smiling at him as she said, "Right."

Maybe it was the music, or her encouragement. Or the fact that he felt as if he was finally getting the hang of this dancing thing, but Blake could feel a level of enthusiasm building within him. Enthusiasm and something more. Something…stirring for lack of a better word.

He supposed that it was just the simple fact that he was moving around an imaginary dance floor with a soft and supple body less than a half breath away from his. If he wasn't careful, things might begin happening that he didn't want happening. After all, he wasn't exactly made of stone and as for Katie, well, he'd be the first to admit—although not to her *or* to Wendy—that she was damn attractive. If he wasn't so consumed with winning back Brittany…

But he *was* consumed, he reminded himself. And Katie was just here to help him with that campaign. She'd probably be upset if she knew what he was thinking right now, he told himself.

With more effort than he thought it would take, Blake bank down thinking altogether and just focused on dancing, nothing more.

By the end of their first full "work" day, Katie felt rather triumphant. During the course of that time, she had taught Blake the fundamentals of several dances.

For the last one, when he looked at her mystified after she'd verbally run through the steps his feet were supposed to be taking, she'd placed his hands on her hips and then deliberately exaggerated their movement in time to the music. His eyes widened and as he continued looking at her, she could feel her own heart melting. Was he surprised that she'd become so brazen, or was there something else going through his mind? For the life of her, she couldn't tell.

Initially, her objective for doing what she just had

was to help Blake absorb the rhythm so that he could begin to at least try to master this dance of lovers. However, she had a nervous feeling that she was the one getting trapped within her own web.

She just wasn't good at this, wasn't good at pretending she was some sort of a seductress. She was just a woman in love with a man who had held her heart captive ever since they'd been kids.

Blake knew Katie was just trying to help, but there was definitely something happening here besides his attempt to learn the steps of a dance that really had no place in his life. With his hands on her hips like this, he could feel their seductive sway and it was telegraphing itself throughout his entire body.

For just a split second, thoughts of sweeping Brittany off her feet slipped far into the background—so far that they were all but invisible. In the foreground was this new, troubling reaction he was having to his sister's best friend, to his marketing assistant—to a woman he had known almost as long as he had known himself.

This wasn't right. And yet, it was oddly tantalizing. He knew he should move his hands, mumble something about "getting it," and return to safer territory. But he let them keep dancing and let himself—just for this moment—continue the unexpected journey he suddenly found himself on.

How could he not hear her heart beating? Katie wondered. It was almost deafening. Feeling his palms spread out over her hips as she continued to move them in what could only be blatantly described as an open invitation was having one hell of a profound effect on her. She could feel every inch of her body reacting. Despite the throbbing music, time had suddenly and literally stood still for her.

Stood still while she found herself about an inch away from him. An inch away from his warm breath swirling along her throat and her face. An inch away from his mouth as he inclined his head ever so closer to her. Whether he was going to say something or had no idea that he'd reduced the space between them to nothingness, she wasn't sure, but she knew that being so close to him like this and not doing anything about it was become harder and harder for her.

Her heart was hammering so hard she was having trouble catching her breath. All she wanted to do was kiss him. Just touch her lips to his and taste them.

Just once.

But she knew she couldn't. She couldn't make the first move and if he chose not to make it, then there was no way she was going to allow herself to become embarrassed by taking the lead when he clearly wouldn't want her to.

Damn it, why aren't you kissing me? Can't you feel this? Can't you feel the electricity?

She struggled to regain control over herself. *You can do this, Katie. If you pass out at his feet, you're going to have to hand in your resignation, you know that. So get a grip!*

As Katie fought to center herself, she realized that she was also gripping Blake's shoulders for all she was worth. When he drew back his head to look into her eyes, she could see that he knew something was wrong.

Or, at the very least, that something was different.

Chapter Six

He forgot to measure.

The old adage, "Measure twice, cut once," the mantra of tailors, construction workers and exceedingly careful people who strove to avoid errors, had also been Blake's rule of thumb to a great extent. Because he worked for his father and knew that any mistakes he might inadvertently make would be greatly magnified in John Michael's eyes, Blake wound up applying the rule to every facet of his life. Which only seemed appropriate since most of his life of late was spent in the office.

But this time around he forgot to measure. He forgot to allow caution to guide him and had, for all intents and purposes, thrown that very caution to the proverbial winds and had gone, instead, with basic gut instincts.

One second he and Katie were trapped in a moment, mystified by the electricity crackling between them as seductive music played in the background, and the next, well, the next he'd brought his mouth down on hers and was kissing her.

Kissing Katie, not Brittany's stand-in, as he'd been regarding Katie all afternoon while they'd danced. Or rather, while she danced. As for him, he'd just shuffled and moved his feet, trying not to trip or pitch forward and embarrass himself. But during that entire—and at times rather awkward—time, he'd regarded Katie as just a placeholder for the woman he really wanted to hold in his arms. The woman he really wanted to sweep off her feet.

Brittany.

But the woman he caught himself kissing wasn't Brittany's stand-in. He had been drawn to Katie, was kissing Katie because he couldn't rescue himself from the swirling curiosity, a need, that had suddenly risen up, urging him on.

And the worst of it was, kissing Katie satisfied nothing. It certainly didn't put his curiosity to rest. Instead, it just seemed to feed some insatiable craving within him. An all-consuming craving he shouldn't have felt for so many reasons that it would have taken him the better part of an hour just to list them.

Any second now, Blake told himself. Any second now he would step back and end this. Step back from Katie and into what this was all supposed to be about—

a detailed campaign to win back the woman of his dreams.

But since he was already kissing Katie, he gave himself permission to continue this small aberration a few seconds longer.

After all, what were a few seconds in the ultimate scheme of things? They were so insignificantly minuscule, they didn't even register.

They didn't even—

They didn't—

Pulling Katie even closer to him, so close that he was in danger of merging with her very essence, Blake lost the train of his thought and then just gave up trying to think altogether.

Oh God.

Oh God, oh God, oh God.

It had finally happened, Katie realized in a panic. She had finally cracked under the pressure of her own desire and was now hallucinating. She *had* to be hallucinating because this just couldn't be happening.

Oh, she'd *wished* it to happen, and ordinarily, wishing didn't make something so. But somehow, this time around, she'd cracked and fallen headfirst down the rabbit hole where dreams became reality.

Except, that just *did not* happen. Not in her orderly world.

And yet, here she was, kissing Blake, losing herself in Blake. And dreams had become a reality.

Her body felt as if it was on fire as she rose up on

her toes, absorbing every inch of heat emanating from his rock-hard torso. What thoughts she had were rolling about in her head like so many scattered marbles, turning here and there with no rhyme or reason to their movements.

If this *was* a hallucination, she would be more than happily willing to continue existing in this Mad Hatter world. There was nothing in her own, even-paced world worth going back for.

Nothing at all.

Except maybe for Wendy, a tiny voice from somewhere on the perimeter of her consciousness whispered. Wendy, who needed her. Who needed a friend to hold her hand while she dealt with the complications of her first pregnancy.

With a superhuman effort, something she'd never even suspected she possessed, Katie drew on all her strength to move her head back a fraction of an inch. Just enough to create a tiny bit of space between them. A tiny space that had all the characteristics of a huge, cold chasm.

The first words out of Blake's mouth made the temperature of that chasm even colder.

"I'm sorry."

She could feel her heart pulling into itself in her chest. Standing outside of herself, she heard this disembodied voice—hers?—ask, "For?" The single word came out as an all but inaudible whisper.

He read her lips more than heard her voice. Feeling incredibly alive and yet incredibly confused at the same time, Blake tried to give substance to his apology. Because what he'd done was take advantage of both Katie and the situation.

That just wasn't like him.

Was it? he wondered uncomfortably.

"For kissing you," he said out loud.

Stung by his apology, Katie did her best to appear unaffected and pretended to just shrug off the entire incident, which would be forever and indelibly burned into her soul from this moment forward.

"It's not like you branded me with a poker," she told him flippantly.

Except that in reality, that was exactly what had just happened. His kiss, the kiss that she had dreamt about for half her lifetime, had turned out to be a hundredfold better than anything she could have remotely imagined. Time had stood still while the earth moved and, as incongruent as that might have sounded to anyone, that was the only way she could even begin to explain what had just happened to her.

The last thing she wanted was to have him marring this for her with a stupid apology that was heavy with his regret. Maybe he was sorry about what had just happened between them, but she wasn't.

"Besides," she continued with studied nonchalance, "it happens. Don't give it another thought."

But I will, Blake realized. *That's just the problem. I will.*

Needing some distance, however minor, between them, she went over to the side table where she'd set up her iPod and the speaker, and shut them both down. As she deliberately kept her back to him, Katie did her best to sound chipper and completely in control—even though her knees still felt watery.

"I think that was enough of a dance lesson for one day."

"Yeah. Yes," he amended, then echoed, "Enough," much the way someone else might have cried, "Uncle!" Though he wouldn't have admitted it to anyone, he was still not quite able to focus on anything. His brain felt incredibly fuzzy. Feeling adrift, he grasped onto the one thing that had been established: their routine. "Um, why don't I drive you back to Wendy's place?"

Turning around to face him, Katie glanced at her watch. It was only a few minutes after three in the afternoon. Way before the end of an actual workday. He really was eager to get rid of her, wasn't he? she thought with a bitter pang.

"I could stay and do some actual work," she volunteered. "Something that I would get paid for during a normal day," she clarified.

There was no way he could get his mind on work, not immediately. Not after what had just happened. Why did he feel as if he'd just fallen out of a twenty-foot tree, while she was acting as if nothing had happened? Hadn't she been on the other end of that kiss?

Maybe he underestimated Katie's experience level, he mused.

"No, I think you earned the rest of the afternoon off," he insisted.

Definitely eager to get rid of her, Katie thought again. And then more thoughts—questions—began to assail her. Had the kiss been that bad? Or that good? She suddenly caught herself wondering. Because heaven knew that kiss had just knocked the foundations of her world out from under her.

Maybe, just maybe, he'd experienced a slight setback in his plans, as well. Why else would he send her away in the middle of the day?

The more she thought about it, the more it heartened her. Finally, after all this time, a toehold.

"All right." She gathered together the iPod and its accompanying speaker, depositing them both back into her briefcase. "If you don't mind driving me back, I'll be ready in a couple of minutes."

Finally looking at him again, she felt another shiver dancing up and down her spine. God, but the man was just too damn handsome for her own good.

"You might want to stay and have dinner with Wendy once we get there," she suggested.

"Won't that be hovering?" he asked, thinking of what Wendy had accused him of doing. That was still a very sore point with him.

Her mouth curved in a grin. "No, I'm pretty sure that's just called dinner." And then she grew a little more serious as she crossed back to him. "Wendy's very grateful that you rearranged your life so that you could be here for her while she's going through this trial-by-baby ordeal."

He checked his pockets for keys to both Scott's place

and the rental he was driving. Right now, he wasn't all that certain about anything, but thankfully, the keys were in his left pocket. Taking them out, Blake led the way out of the house.

"She looked pretty annoyed with me the last time I saw her," he remembered.

Actually, Katie knew that Wendy had been downright angry because Blake was so consumed with the idea of going after Brittany, but Katie tactfully smoothed that over. "That's because she's worried about you."

"Worried?" he repeated incredulously. "Why would she be worried about me?"

Wendy was right, she thought. Men could be so thick sometimes.

"She doesn't want to see you hurt and she thinks that Brittany will rip your heart out and use it for a coaster." She paused for a moment, weighing the wisdom of saying the next part. She decided to plunge in. "The way she did the last time."

"No, she didn't," Blake protested, instantly coming to the absent woman's defense. "We broke up because of a misunderstanding."

Katie looked at him innocently as she asked, "You misunderstood why she was lip-locked with another man when you'd brought her to the party as your date?"

He was far from happy that had gotten out. Annoyed, he asked, "Has Wendy been talking to you?"

Katie pressed her lips together. She recognized her misstep the second she'd made it.

Holding up her hands in surrender, she gingerly backed away from the topic. Men, Wendy had told her, didn't like having their faults and mistakes pointed out to them. Even the big ones. *Especially* the big ones. Having grown up without any siblings and not really having any sort of a dating life to speak of, her experience when it came to the games people played with one another was severely limited. She believed in honesty, but obviously not everyone always saw it as the best policy.

"Sorry," she apologized. "Not my business." She lowered her hands. "Maybe I just got my details wrong." She had almost said "facts" instead, but that too would have wound up bruising Blake's ego.

He was too good for the likes of Brittany, but she couldn't say that, either. All she could do was hope that Wendy's plan for her to distract Blake while supposedly teaching him how to win Brittany would ultimately work.

And if it didn't, if she did too good a job and actually helped him with this pursuit, well, at least she was going to have a wonderful time as the understudy.

It wasn't much, but then, she'd never really asked for very much, she thought as she got into the passenger side of Blake's car.

Glancing in her direction, Blake waited for her to buckle up, then took off.

There wasn't much conversation to speak of.

The moment Wendy saw her brother and Katie walking into her bedroom, she knew something had changed. She could see it in their body language. It was there, in the expression on her friend's face and definitely there in the rather shaken look in her brother's eyes.

Something had happened and she knew she wasn't going to be able to find out what until she could get Katie alone to question her.

And that, apparently, wasn't going to happen until after they had dinner. Blake, once he started talking to her, gave every indication that he was more than willing to stay until long after the cows came home.

She couldn't chase him off without really alienating him. Frustrated, Wendy struggled to find some kind of compromising middle ground. It was everything she could do not to burst while holding her questions in check.

So, the three of them had dinner in the room that now held her a prisoner day and night. Because of her condition, Marcos had hired a housekeeper, a pleasant-faced older woman named Juanita, and the woman had served them a dinner that had come straight from the kitchen of Red, the restaurant that Marcos managed. Marcos himself was there now, which meant there were only the three of them for dinner.

Less than halfway through the meal, Wendy began to give the performance of her life, murmuring about how fatigued she'd felt all day, but, as sometimes happened because she was "stuck in bed," she'd been unable to really sleep.

"But now, after having this meal that my loving husband sent over from the restaurant," she said, pausing to stifle yet *another* yawn, "I think I'll probably be able to drop off like a brick." Her eyes shifted toward her brother. "If I fall asleep midsentence, you'll forgive me, right, Blake?"

"Better yet," Blake told his sister, shifting out of the way as the housekeeper collected the last of the dishes and cleared them away. "I'll get out of your hair and let you go to sleep." Leaning over the bed, he kissed Wendy on the cheek. "You get some rest and I'll see you in the morning when I swing by to pick up Br—eh, Katie." He looked at the woman who had unexpectedly set off such a chain reaction within him this afternoon. He was still trying to sort out just exactly what had happened and what it all ultimately meant. For now, he nodded at her as if everything was still the same as it had been just this morning. "I'll see you tomorrow, Katie."

Katie returned the nod, debating whether or not to walk him out, then deciding it was best if she didn't. The drive here from Scott and Christina's ranch had been a little awkward and forced. Both of them were careful to tiptoe around the elephant that was stuffed into the car with them. They both needed a little break to regroup, she thought.

Maybe by tomorrow, things would get back to normal—whatever that was now.

"Right, tomorrow." Even as she said it, she could feel her lips tingling ever so slightly from the memory of this afternoon.

As both the housekeeper and Blake walked out of the room, she turned to look at Wendy. Giving her a quick, preoccupied smile, she told her best friend, "I'll see you tomorrow."

Turning to leave, Katie was surprised to hear her exceptionally sleepy friend declare in a firm, emphatic and no-nonsense voice, "You get back here, missy. You're not going *anywhere* until you tell me absolutely everything."

Turning around, she stared at Wendy. Three minutes ago, the woman had been all but wilting. "What happened to being so tired you were afraid you were going to fall asleep midsentence?"

Wendy laughed, clearly surprised that Katie hadn't seen through the act. "And you believed me?" she asked, amused. "I said that for Blake's benefit. I mean, I can't ask you questions about what's going on with him sitting right there, so I wanted him to leave. But I knew that if I asked him to, he's so sensitive, his feelings would really be hurt." She sighed, shaking her head. "Blake still brings up the fact that I said he was hovering every chance he gets." She shifted her attention back to Katie, whom she had expected to see through her little act immediately. "God, Katie, aren't you paying attention?"

Second-guessing was just not the way she usually operated. "I thought I was, but I guess that I obviously wasn't." Katie shrugged. "Sorry."

Wendy waved away the apology as she shifted closer to the edge of her king-size bed. She wasn't interested in apologies, she was interested in why both her friend and her brother had looked off center when they'd walked into her room.

"Okay," she declared, then ordered, "give."

Katie stared at Wendy, confused. "Give?" she repeated.

"Yes." Suppressing an exasperated sigh, Wendy carefully enunciated her request. "Give me the details. Tell me what happened." When that didn't prompt an immediate outpouring of information, Wendy elaborated. "You and Blake both walked in with really weird expressions on your faces, like you'd both been standing on a mountaintop, watching a sunrise when you clearly were expecting to see was a sunset. *What happened between the two of you?*" she repeated, this time in a far more firm, demanding voice. "Spill it. *All* of it."

Her eyes all but pinned Katie in place, where she was going to remain until she told her what she wanted to hear.

"I took your advice," Katie began slowly. "I started to teach Blake ballroom dancing."

Wendy winced a little at the image that conjured up. "Blake has two left feet."

"So he said. Actually," Katie admitted, "given what I thought was going to happen, he wasn't all that bad."

Wendy was still waiting impatiently for something that would explain the dazed expressions she'd seen.

"Okay, well, it wasn't his feet that put that stunned expression on your face," Wendy concluded. Her eyes narrowed. Her hormones had her emotions all over the map and patience was in very short supply. "Are you going to make me beg?" she wanted to know.

"Of course not," Katie protested.

"Then tell me!" Wendy ordered, surrendering the last shred of her quickly failing patience.

Part of Katie felt almost silly saying this at her age. The other part felt almost as if she was betraying Blake by telling tales out of school. It took her a moment to calm herself.

Then, taking a deep breath, Katie said, "He kissed me."

Wendy's eyes almost fell out of her head. And then, the next minute, she was grinning so hard her face looked as if it ran the very real danger of splitting completely in two.

Chapter Seven

It took Wendy a second to collect herself. Her excitement over what was clearly a significant break-through for Katie and Blake was having an unexpected—and unsettling—side effect. She felt twinges, *strong* twinges that were reminiscent of what she'd experienced when she'd suddenly gone into premature labor.

Taking a breath in slowly, Wendy grasped the blanket on either side of her and offered up a silent prayer as she waited for the sensation to pass. Less than two minutes later—it felt like a lifetime and a half—it finally passed. But by then, she was perspiring and feeling somewhat light-headed. It took concentration on her part to keep the large room from spinning around wildly.

The next moment, she saw Katie peering at her face uncertainly. "Wendy, are you all right?"

Katie's voice seemed to echo in her head as she heard her best friend ask the question.

Wendy took another second before she answered. She didn't want to alarm Katie by sounding out of breath when all she was doing was lying here.

"I'm fine, Katie, just really excited about that kiss," Wendy lied. Wanting to get the focus back where it belonged, she pressed for some kind of details. "All right, Blake kissed you. Then what?"

Katie wasn't sure just what it was that her friend wanted to hear. "I kissed him back."

The contractions, now gone, took a backseat to impatience. "And?"

"And it was wonderful," Katie confessed wistfully. Her words were accompanied by a heartfelt sigh.

Wendy knew Katie too well to think her friend was trying to be coy or draw things out. Katie obviously didn't understand what she was asking her. So Wendy verbally sketched an outline and waited for her to fill it in. "And what happened after he kissed you and you kissed him back?"

The rise and fall of Katie's slender shoulders was guileless. "We came here."

Wendy enunciated each word through gritted teeth. "And nothing in between?"

"Well, yes," Katie conceded. It was a given, since she hadn't rented a car here, but nonetheless she added, "Blake drove."

Wendy pressed her lips together, suppressing a guttural sound of pure frustration. Pinning Katie with a look, she knew very well that her best friend wasn't teasing her—she was dead serious in her recitation. Clearly there were some things missing from Katie's education, despite her graduation from a top university with honors.

There was no delicate way to ask, so she didn't bother trying. Instead, Wendy bluntly asked, "Katie, do you know how to flirt?"

A defensive look crept into Katie's normally warm brown eyes. "Flirting wasn't a prerequisite for my degree."

Well, that answered that, Wendy thought. She'd thought that perhaps, because it had been a while since she and Katie had seen one another and people did change—she was living proof of that, transitioning from a party girl to a doting homebody—that Katie had developed some feminine wiles. Obviously she hadn't, but that was okay. That was what Katie had her for. "So the answer's no." Wendy shook her head and struggled to suppress a sigh. "Settle in, Katie," she instructed, pointing to the edge of her bed. "You and I have work to do."

Katie's radar went up. Wendy was going to try to change her and, while that kind of a breezy, flirtatious manner suited Wendy to a *T,* it just wasn't her, Katie thought. Wendy could effortlessly have men eating out of her hand—before she'd met Marcos, she'd *had* men eating out of her hand.

But flirting to Katie meant leading someone on just to satisfy her own ego—if she actually had one—and she didn't see the point of that. Still, she didn't want to sound ungrateful.

"Wendy," she began a little hesitantly, "it's not that I don't appreciate what you're trying to do for me, but—"

Wendy was very good about reading between the lines and knew where her friend was heading with this. However, the sad fact of life was that nice girls did finish last more times than not, and a little something extra to help tip the scales never hurt. She knew just what to say to make Katie come around.

"You'd rather he wound up with that spoiled Southern belle?"

Katie shook her head. Brittany would just use Blake all over again. They both knew that.

"No," she said with feeling.

Wendy had expected nothing else. With a smart nod of her head she declared, "All right then, case closed. You're learning how to flirt."

It was obvious Katie had no choice in the matter—there was no known record of *anyone* ever winning an argument with Wendy, at least not directly—so Katie surrendered. She settled in and listened to what her friend had to say. She had no intention of putting anything she was about to be told to any active use, but listening to Wendy was a great deal easier than arguing with her and refuting anything she had to say. So, in essence, Katie silently chose to take the high road.

Mercifully, Wendy was brief and succinct. The

lesson involved mastering alternating looks of adoration and out-and-out sexy expressions. There was also mention of a sexy walk, complete with a gentle, come-hither swaying of the hips, but since Wendy was bedridden, the instructions were all verbal rather than visual.

And just when Katie thought Wendy had exhausted her subject, her friend suddenly pounced on the topic of clothing.

Pressing her lips together, Wendy looked reprovingly at what Katie was wearing. "Does everything you packed look like that?"

Caught off guard, Katie looked down at what she had on. It was a navy blue skirt with a matching jacket, beneath which she had on a light pink blouse. It was crisp, subdued and professional. Katie saw nothing wrong with it.

"What's wrong with what I'm wearing?" she wanted to know.

Wendy didn't want to hurt her feelings, but there was a great deal at stake here—for all three of them. If Blake hooked up with Brittany, Katie would be heartbroken and Wendy herself would be in danger of being sent away for justifiable homicide. Brittany had *always* rubbed her the wrong way.

And then, of course, down the line Blake would be dumped and his ego would take a beating, never mind his heart. As far as she was concerned, it was crucial that Katie win this battle for her brother's affections.

"Nothing," Wendy agreed, "if you're bucking for Marketing Assistant of the Year. But if you want to be noticed as a woman, you need something softer and maybe just a tiny bit slinkier."

"I came to work, Wendy," Katie pointed out, "not to slink."

Wendy's eyes met hers. "Yes, but the 'office' is a room in my brother Scott's ranch."

Katie had no idea where Wendy was going with that line. "What does that have to do with anything?" she wanted to know.

"Blake improvised," Wendy pointed out. When the light apparently didn't dawn for Katie, she added, "You do the same." She could see she still wasn't getting through. Or, if she was, then Katie was resisting what she was being told. Wendy pointed toward the double doors on the other side of the room. "Open my closet, please," she instructed.

She didn't want Wendy's clothes. She liked her own just fine. "Wendy, I—"

"Don't argue with a pregnant woman." Wendy pointed toward the closet again, this time more regally, like a queen commanding her servant. "Open my closet," she repeated more firmly. "You and I wear the same size, or did before I became as big as a house," Wendy observed ruefully. She wanted this baby desperately. Loved this baby desperately. But she absolutely *hated* being pregnant. "Pick out something more feminine."

"Why?" she asked warily.

"Just do it," Wendy ordered wearily. "If I can't get you to flirt—and don't bother denying it," she interjected quickly, "I can tell by the look in your eyes that you're not going to do a thing I just tried to teach you to do—I can at least get you to stop hiding how pretty you actually are."

Now that just wasn't true, Katie thought. Where did Wendy get these ideas? "I'm not hiding anything," Katie protested.

Wendy didn't want to waste time waltzing around words. "All right, not setting your features off to their best advantage. Better?"

This was all useless, Katie thought. If Blake didn't want *her* as herself, then maybe there was no point in pursing this any further. She couldn't maintain a facade indefinitely, even if it meant having Blake in her life instead of his daydreaming about the likes of Brittany.

"Wendy—"

Knuckles digging into the mattress on either side of her, Wendy drew herself up in her bed.

"Do I have to get up and find clothes for you?" Wendy wanted to know. "Because I will." To illustrate her point, she threw back the covers from her bed and began to swing out her legs.

"Stop!" Katie cried. Hurrying over to Wendy, she pushed the covers back over Wendy's legs.

Wendy suppressed her triumphant smile. Instead, she calmly ordered, "All right, then you go and select some decent clothes. Just remember, if you win over Blake, you'll be doing me a favor. Because if Blake gets that woman to go out with him, and—God forbid—marry him, I'm going to have to kill her and then my baby is going to grow up with a jailbird for a mother."

Katie couldn't hold back her laughter. "When did you get so melodramatic?"

That was simple enough to answer. "When you started being so stubborn."

Katie relented. "Point taken. Okay, I'll pick out something."

That wasn't enough to convince Wendy. She wanted more of a commitment. "And wear it?"

With a sigh, Katie nodded and gave her word. "And wear it." Like a soldier on a forced march, she opened the closet doors and disappeared into its depths.

Only then did Wendy begin to relax. Katie never lied. "That's my girl."

"Maybe I should just wear a bikini to work tomorrow," Katie said sarcastically, her voice drifting out from inside the closet.

"Wrong season," Wendy pointed out matter-of-factly. "It's too cold for that. Otherwise, that would be a good solution."

Katie peered out to see if Wendy was serious. Her expression made it impossible to tell.

"Pick five outfits and bring them out," Wendy instructed. "So I can rank them."

Katie rolled her eyes. Wendy, apparently, was in full battle mode and dead serious. There would be no negotiating, no arguing with her. Resigned, Katie went back into the closet to find her battle armor.

* * *

"Have I seen you in that before?" Blake asked Katie the following morning. Picking her up for another day of strategizing amid a smattering of actual work, he'd been in the middle of talking as he led the way back to his car when he'd abruptly stopped and really looked at her. If the expression on his face was any indication, he was scrutinizing every inch of her.

"No," Katie answered quietly. Tossing her purse on the passenger floor, she got into the vehicle.

"Oh." He slid in behind the steering wheel. "Reason I asked is that it looks familiar."

She was wearing a long-sleeved, turtle-necked turquoise dress that lovingly adhered to her curves—and ran out of material about four inches above her knees. Like most of Wendy's clothes, it was an outfit that was intended to make a man sit up and take notice.

It was on the tip of her tongue to own up to that, but then she'd be forced to explain why she was wearing his sister's clothes. She didn't believe in lying and, anyway, she wasn't good at it. But telling him the real reason she was wearing this and had in her closet other bright, sexy outfits that his sister had made her borrow, well, that was just too embarrassing for words. To spare both of them, she went with a creative, evasive version of the truth.

"No," she said innocently, avoiding his eyes, "I've never worn this before."

Blake nodded absently, taking the information in. "It

looks nice on you," he commented and then dropped the subject.

Katie smiled to herself. *Score one for Wendy,* she thought. Not that she was going to tell her friend that, at least, not immediately. Wendy was in desperate need of something to occupy her mind and her time. If she thought that her order—it really couldn't be thought of as a suggestion at this point—had borne fruit, there was no telling what her friend might come up with next. Katie *knew* that Wendy was rooting for a torrid romance to ignite between her and Blake, but that just wasn't going to happen. Nobody looking at her, no matter *what* she was wearing, was going to associate the word *torrid* with her name, and she wasn't about to try to recreate herself in some femme fatale role. Blake would probably laugh so hard, he'd wind up injuring himself. Not something she wanted to contemplate.

"So listen," he began, looking, in her opinion, exceedingly uncomfortable. "About yesterday—"

She waited, but his voice had trailed off and he wasn't trying to fill in the void.

"Yes?" she finally asked.

He cleared his throat, intently watching the road. "That was a good idea you had, about dancing. I think that might really impress Brittany."

"That's our main goal," she said brightly, doing her best to keep the note of sarcasm out of her voice. She wasn't quite successful.

"So," he repeated, "I was wondering if you'd mind practicing with me some more—I promise not to let anything get out of hand again." He took a breath, but continued staring straight ahead at the road. "I didn't mean to offend you."

Why in God's name would he think she'd be offended? What was she in his eyes, some Victorian spinster, given to vapors?

"You didn't," she assured him. Then, in case he was going to continue apologizing—something she really didn't want to hear again—she told him, "I've forgotten about it already."

"Oh." He slanted a quick glance at her, then went back to staring at the emptiness ahead of him. "I guess we're okay then."

"Absolutely." *Just because you're behaving like an idiot, I won't hold it against you,* Katie silently promised.

Blake made an honest, concentrated effort to focus on the steps and techniques Katie was trying to teach him and not on the fact that holding her in his arms caused him to experience a very strong reaction to the woman. Her supple body was at times temptingly brushing against his, at other times pressed so closely to him that the thought of following the dance steps fled completely from his mind.

Those were the times when he would lose his train of thought entirely. His mind a near blank, he would forget to count steps in his head and then stumble, embarrassing himself despite her assurances that this was normal and he was doing fine.

After he stepped on her feet a third time during a rumba, Blake stopped moving altogether and called a halt to the practice. The session, with a few breaks, had gone on for three hours. Enough was enough.

"This just isn't working," he complained.

Unshed tears of pain stung Katie's eyes. This last assault on her feet had almost had her crying out in pain, but she managed to hold it back.

"I tell you what," she suggested with as much cheerfulness as she could muster, "why don't you stick to slow dances for now? You have those mastered—and it doesn't require all that much movement," she pointed out.

He knew what Katie was really saying. "Or stepping on feet."

Katie grinned, her eyes crinkling. "There's that, too."

He supposed he was just frustrated and tired, but there was a small part of him that was wondering why he had never noticed the way her eyes sparkled when she smiled.

Trying to block the thought—and the accompanying sensation that seemed to be shimmying through his system like a random electrical current striking without warning, he asked, "Okay, what's next on the agenda?"

Me, Blake, me. I'm next on the agenda. Or I should be. Brittany's never going to care about you the way that I do.

But there was no point in thinking what she couldn't

say out loud, so instead she said, "Next, you're going to write a love letter."

He blinked, staring at her and certain that he couldn't have heard her right. "I'm going to write a what?"

"A love letter," she told him brightly.

Okay, so it wasn't his hearing that was going. It was her mind. "You're kidding, right?"

"No, I'm not kidding." She saw a look that bordered ever so slightly on disgust. Another man who doesn't really like putting his feelings down on paper, she thought. Too bad. "Hey, you're the one who asked me to help you."

Blake had his doubts about the effectiveness of her latest suggestion. "Do women still like things like that?"

"Very much," she told him honestly. *If you wrote "I love you" on the back of a Band-Aid wrapper, I'd keep it forever.*

"But I don't know how to write poetry," he was protesting.

"Who said anything about poetry?" she wanted to know. "A love letter doesn't have to be flowery or rhyme," she assured him. "It just has to be honest. Tell her how you feel."

"I like her. No," he amended, knowing Katie was waiting for more. "I love her."

She kept her smile pasted on her face as she said, "Good start. Now, what else?"

"What else?" he repeated. "There has to be more?

What else is there?" he asked, looking as if he was at a complete loss.

Nothing, if you're dealing with a narcissistic Daddy's girl like Brittany. But, for the sake of form, she knew she had to at least go through the motions of helping him, even if her heart was wishing that she would be the one on the receiving end of this yet-to-be-written composition.

"Okay, give me a few minutes," she suggested, sitting down at his desk and kicking off her shoes. "Let me see what I can come up with."

He looked relieved to have her take over. "You're the best, Katie, you know that?"

"I've heard rumors to that effect," she quipped.

Ten minutes later, she looked up from the sheet she was writing on and said, "Okay, this is just a rough draft, but I think this is what you need to tell her." Even as she began to read the love letter out loud, she could feel her own anger begin to rise and fester. In no way did Brittany deserve to receive this.

"Dear Brittany,

I've loved you for a very long time. Whenever I'm not around you, it's as if the sun has left the sky. The only time it comes out again is if I catch a glimpse of you. The sound of your laughter fills my heart with happiness. Whatever went wrong between us the last time is in the past and I would welcome the opportunity to show you how much

I've grown as a person. I know that I am now capable of loving you the way you deserve to be loved."

Finished, she forced herself to raise her eyes to his face. "Like I said, it's just a rough draft right now, but that's the general idea. What do you think?"

Lost in the words she'd just been reading to him, it took Blake a moment to extricate himself. Because just for a moment there, watching Katie's lips as she read, he'd felt a glimmer of something. Something stirring. But then he roused himself and it was gone.

"What do I think?" he echoed. "I think if I send that to her, she's absolutely going to become putty in my hands," he happily responded, all but adding a joyous war whoop to his words. "You're right, that *is* good. Like I said, you're just the best, Katie. Send this to Brittany right away," he instructed.

She hadn't meant to be *that* successful. To be completely honest, she wasn't striving for simplicity, she'd been trying for just this side of nauseating. Obviously, from Blake's enthusiasm, she'd stopped just short of her goal.

Chapter Eight

"You look like I feel," Wendy commented when Katie popped her head in later that evening.

Her workday was over and Katie just wanted to make sure that Wendy was all right before she went on to her bedroom and pulled her covers over her head. If she was lucky, she thought dejectedly, she'd suffocate during the night and this nightmare, otherwise known as Project Brittany, would just be a thing of the past.

"Talk to me," Wendy requested with a note of urgency in her voice.

No way was Katie going to unload on Wendy, especially not if she was interpreting Wendy's demeanor correctly and her friend wasn't feeling well. She wasn't *that* selfish, Katie thought.

Katie flashed a comforting smile at her. "If you're

not feeling well, you should rest," Katie told her, then promised, "We'll talk in the morning."

"No, please, talk now," Wendy urged, putting her hand out as if to grasp Katie's—which wasn't exactly possible, given that she was still standing in the bedroom doorway, all the way across the room. "I need some distraction. Juanita just left for the night and Marcos has to stay late because there's a last-minute party booked at Red."

Wendy, ordinarily so full of energy, had to be going out of her mind with boredom, just lying here, day in, day out, Katie thought sympathetically. But there was something in her friend's voice that had her thinking there was another reason for Wendy's need to be distracted that she wasn't telling her.

"Why do you need to be distracted more than usual?" Katie wanted to know.

But Wendy shook her head. She didn't want to talk, didn't want to think.

"No, you first," Wendy insisted. "Why do you look as if you just found out your best friend was sent off to the farm in the country?" she asked, using the tried-and-true euphemism of parents explaining to their children why a beloved pet could no longer be found roaming around the house.

Katie crossed to the window to the right of Wendy's bed and stared out at the darkness. "You know that Project Brittany that your brother's trying to get off the ground?"

"Yes?"

"Well, I think it's about to take flight." *And I've got no one to blame but myself.*

Wendy filled in the blanks. "No," she protested. "You were supposed to turn the tables on Blake and make him fall in love with you."

Katie leaned her hands on the windowsill. "That was the plan," she agreed and then she sighed. "Unfortunately, I've succeeded *too* well. Blake's sure that he's going to have Brittany eating out of his hand."

"Oh, damn."

Katie smiled sadly at what she assumed was sympathy in her friend's voice. "Yeah, that about sums up the way I feel," she admitted.

"Oh damn, oh damn, *oh damn!*"

Wendy was almost taking this worse than she was, Katie thought. She felt guilty. Wendy had her own set of problems right now.

"It's okay, you don't have to take it that badly. It's not the end of the world, I guess." She turned from the window to face her friend. "Wendy, I— Oh, God, Wendy, what's wrong?" Katie cried, startled as she took a good look at her best friend.

Wendy's forehead was drenched in sweat and she had all but wadded up her entire blanket beneath her hands. It was as if she was searching for something to anchor her body to the bed, to keep her from spinning out into a world constructed out of an all-consuming, fiery pain.

"Ba-bee," Wendy managed to gasp out between gritted teeth, every inch of her body completely rigid. "The baby's coming!" she screamed.

A cold chill washed over Katie, bringing fear with it. She had to get Wendy to the hospital, but San Antonio Memorial was a good twenty miles away. Wendy didn't look as if she was going to be able to last long enough to get there.

"Hang on, I'm going to get you to the hospital," Katie promised.

She didn't have a car, but she knew that Wendy's was parked in the garage, dormant during her forced encampment. Marcos occasionally used it, just to keep the engine functioning properly, but for the most part, it remained in the garage—which meant that she could drive Wendy to the hospital without any delay.

"C'mon, honey, we're going to get you up," Katie told her.

But as she reached for her, Wendy grabbed her wrist and held it in what could only be termed a vise grip, squeezing it as hard as the contraction was apparently squeezing her.

There was desperation in Wendy's voice when she cried, "No time."

Ordinarily, Katie would have said that Wendy was being dramatic again, but there was something about the look in her eyes that made Katie believe her. She really didn't want to take a chance on being wrong. If that baby was coming, it was better that it come here than in the backseat of a car.

With effort, Katie extricated her wrist from Wendy's death grip. "Okay, we'll stay here." She picked up the cordless receiver from its cradle on the nightstand. "I'll call nine-one-one. They'll send an ambulance—and someone who knows what they're doing."

But Wendy shook her head emphatically. "No… time… Baby…*now!*" she panted, her eyes as huge as saucers.

Because she didn't know what else to do, Katie called anyway.

The maddeningly calm woman on the other end of the line asked the nature of the emergency and then wanted details. As coherently as possible, given that her heart was now lodged in her throat, Katie rattled off the problem and Wendy's address. She ended with a request for an ambulance. NOW.

"And a doctor," she added almost as an afterthought. "I need a doctor on the line," she cried just as Wendy scrunched up her face again.

"I'm afraid we don't have a doctor here," the dispatcher told her.

"Call…my…doctor," Wendy gasped, curling up into a ball and rocking back and forth, "…press three… speed…dial."

Katie immediately disconnected her call and then followed Wendy's instruction, praying that the dispatcher she'd talked to would come through with that ambulance she'd requested.

The doctor wasn't in, but given the hour, that was to be expected. Katie prayed she could track him down in time.

"The doctor is making his rounds at the hospital," the woman at the answering service informed her routinely. "Dr. Nickelson will be back in his office tomorrow morning at—"

Grasping the receiver with both hands, Katie said in a barely controlled, desperate voice, "Now, you listen to me. Tomorrow morning's too late. This baby is coming *now* and it's just Wendy and me here. You patch me through to Dr. Nickelson this minute. I need him to talk me through the delivery or God only knows what's going to happen. Do you understand me?" she demanded.

"I understand," the woman replied, suddenly sounding very human and sympathetic. "Hold on, I'm going to patch you through. Don't hang up."

"Not on your life," Katie said, but she was talking to a temporarily dead phone. Wendy cried out in pain. She squeezed Wendy's shoulder, feeling incredibly helpless. Praying that the answering service could get ahold of the doctor. "Hang on, Wendy, I'm getting help."

Five seconds later, the line came back to life and a deep baritone said, "This is Dr. Nickelson," into her ear. Before she could begin to give the physician a summary of what was going on, Wendy screamed again. That took care of any necessary introduction. "How far along is she?" Dr. Nickelson asked.

"Passed the goal line," Katie answered, as she looked at Wendy's contorted face.

Because he needed something concrete, Dr. Nickelson restated his question. "How far is she dilated?"

Oh God. "Sorry," Katie murmured to Wendy as she threw back the covers with one hand and then pulled up her friend's nightgown.

"Just…get…it…out!" Wendy pleaded, tears she wasn't even away of streaming down her face.

Katie's heart was hammering so hard, she could barely draw a breath. "I can see the head." Crowning, that was called crowning, she suddenly remembered. "She's crowning."

"Put the phone on speaker," the doctor told her, his voice calm, soothing. "You're going to need two hands. Is Wendy lying down in bed?"

What did that have to do with anything? she thought impatiently. "Yes," Katie all but snapped.

"Good. You need to get her propped up against the headboard so she has something to lean against as she pushes."

As quickly and gently as possible, Katie pulled Wendy up in bed so that her shoulders were up against the headboard.

"Done," she called out.

"Good," the deep voice pronounced again. "Now position yourself on the receiving end," he instructed as if this was an everyday occurence. "On the count of three, I want you to have her bear down and push as hard as she can. One—two—"

"THREE!" Wendy shrieked, then bore down for all she was worth, desperately trying to expel the baby and the pain at the same time. All she managed to expel was a gutteral sound that didn't sound quite human.

"Now stop," the disembodied voice on the speakerphone ordered.

"I…can't…do…this!" Wendy sobbed.

"Yes, you can and you will," Katie fired back in a no-nonsense voice, sensing that if she gave Wendy sympathy, her friend would really fall apart. She prayed that she wasn't in over her head. Over *both* their heads, she amended.

Blake took out the key that Wendy had given him and inserted it into the lock. He'd already swung by once this evening, but that was to drop Katie off. For once, he hadn't gone in and it was guilt that had brought him back. After all, his initial reason for being out here in the first place was because Wendy was a prisoner in her own bedroom until the baby made his or her appearance in the world. To allow himself to get so caught up in his pursuit of Brittany that he forgot to spend a little time with Wendy was just plain wrong.

Granted Katie was here with her, but it was Wendy he was really here to see, he told himself.

He stopped dead a second after he closed the front door. And then, just like that, he heard a baby cry. He ran up the stairs and heard Katie's voice coming from the bedroom. He burst in and was amazed—and surprisingly, nearly overcome with emotion—at the sight before him.

"It's here!" Katie announced, feeling her own body shaking as she held this brand-new tiny damp life between her hands. "You have a girl, Wendy," she nearly sobbed. "You have a girl." Her own head spinning badly and it took effort for her to concentrate. There was still a lot more she had to do, but for the life of her, Katie couldn't think of what that was.

At that moment the doorbell rang. "It must be the paramedics."

Blake turned to her and said, "You've done more than enough tonight. I'll go downstairs and let them in. You stay here." As he crossed to the doorway, he paused for a moment and looked at her over his shoulder. "You were magnificent," he told her in a voice filled with admiration.

His warm smile embedded itself under her skin even before he left the room.

Chapter Nine

When she looked back on all this later, Katie hadn't really intended to go to the hospital with Wendy and the baby, especially not in the back of the ambulance. Now that the baby had been safely delivered, she just wanted to get out of the paramedics' way and let them see to Wendy and her tiny girl. After all, the EMTs were the professionals and would take good care of both of them.

But one look at her best friend's eyes was all it had taken. It told Katie that Wendy, despite her bravado, was still shaken, still in need of reassurance. Still in need of a familiar face to be there with her.

So, at the last minute, she suddenly heard herself calling out, "Wait up. I'm going with her."

The paramedic inside the back of the ambulance

looked a little dubious for a second, then nodded. “Okay, come on,” he said as he extended his hand to her.

Grasping it, she got on and then perched on the tiny bit of space beside Wendy’s gurney. She had no idea how she was going to get back to Red Rock and the house, but that didn’t matter right now. All that mattered was that her best friend still needed her—at least until Marcos could be reached so that he could come down to the hospital to be with his wife.

“She’s so tiny,” Wendy murmured, exhaustion and a mother’s concern evident in every syllable. “Do you think she’ll be all right?”

“She’s a survivor,” Katie assured her. “And look who her mother is. Of course she’ll be all right.”

Wendy looked up at her. “Thank you.”

“Just telling you the truth,” Katie replied, shrugging off the thanks.

“No, I mean for everything. For being there and bringing the baby into the world.”

Katie smiled warmly. “She brought herself into the world. I was just the cheering section,” she said, looking at the very tiny bundle for the moment sleeping against Wendy’s breast.

Kissing the top of her baby’s head, Wendy looked back at Katie. There was wonder and disbelief mingled in her eyes.

“I’m a mother, Katie,” she said in hushed awe.

Katie smiled. “I know. I was there.”

When the ambulance finally arrived at San Antonio Memorial’s E.R. entrance, a team of nurses and a doctor were waiting for them. Mother and baby were whisked off to the recovery area, where they were separated and taken in different directions. Since the newest member of the Mendoza/Fortune family was on the rather small side, the physician on duty felt it best to place the infant in an incubator, at least to begin with. Wendy looked stricken when the baby was taken from her arms, but she knew it was for the best.

Just like that, Katie found herself standing alone outside the recovery room doors, relegated to the hallway. Having nowhere else to be, unfamiliar with the hospital layout and too tired to go exploring at this hour, she resigned herself to remaining where she was until such time as Wendy was taken up to a room on the maternity floor.

With a sigh, Katie leaned against the wall and closed her eyes. She hadn't realized just how very tired and drained she was until this very minute. She wondered if anyone would say anything if she just stretched out on the floor, out of the way. Things were relatively quiet and at a lull right now. Her mind began to drift, floating to different levels as sleep began to creep in around her, taking more and more of her away.

Someone placed a hand on her shoulder. "Is she inside there?"

Katie's eyes flew open. At the same time, she stifled a surprised gasp. The hand on her shoulder belonged to Blake. She hadn't expected him to come. He hadn't said anything about following her to the hospital. "What are you doing here?" she asked him.

Blake was by turns surprised and then amused by her question. "She's my sister, remember? And besides, I thought you might like a ride home—unless you've already made other plans," he qualified.

But Katie shook her head. "No, no plans," she admitted. "After what just happened, I'm afraid I haven't thought that far ahead."

Blake looked genuinely stunned. "Wow, Katie Wallace without a plan. This really is a red-letter day, isn't it?"

She took a deep breath, doing what she could to pull herself together.

"You might say that." There was something she needed to ask him—oh, right. Marcos. She turned to Blake and asked, "Did you call Marcos?"

He nodded. "The minute you took off in the ambulance with Wendy and the baby. He's on his way. I offered to pick him up, but he said he wasn't about to wait. I think he started running to the car the second he heard my voice." The bemused smile on his lips was mixed with concern as Blake shook his head. "I sure hope the roads are clear tonight. This would be a hell of a bad time for him to get into an accident."

Maybe it was because she was punchy, but the wording he'd just used amused her. "And exactly when is a good time?"

Blake stared at her, confused. He was beginning to feel that confusion was a somewhat regular occurrence around Katie these days. She said things that scrambled his brain lately—especially since he'd kissed her.

"What?"

"To get into an accident. You said now's a bad time for him to get into an accident and I'm asking if there's a good time to get into one?" she asked innocuously.

Definitely out to scramble his brain, he decided. "Point taken."

When he continued just standing in the hallway with her, saying nothing further, she felt compelled to ask, "Shouldn't you be calling your family?"

To be honest, Blake had felt so blown away by having taken an active part in the miracle of birth, calling everyone had completely slipped his mind. Trust Katie to remember, he thought. The woman really was very good at details.

"What would I do without you?" he asked, shaking his head as he took out his cell phone.

"Start keeping track of your own calendar, comes to mind," she quipped. Although it was exceedingly tempting, she refused to allow herself to take to heart too much of what he had just said. He hadn't meant anything by it. Probably didn't even know he'd said it, she thought, ruefully.

"You do it better," he told her seriously. Moving away from Katie for the sake of privacy, he pressed the first programmed number on his cell.

Instead of making five separate calls, Blake decided to just call his sister, Emily.

"Hello?" a sleepy voice said after the fourth ring.

He'd forgotten about the time difference. "Emily, it's

Blake. I'm sorry, I didn't mean to wake you. This damn time difference tripped me up," he apologized.

Hearing her brother's voice, the woman on the other end of the line became instantly alert. "What's wrong? Why are you calling?"

"Just thought you might want to know that you're officially an aunt now. Wendy had her baby about an hour ago." This uncle business was going to take some getting used to.

"Tell me everything. What does she weigh? How big is she?" Emily asked, eager for details.

He couldn't elaborate on any of that, he realized ruefully. "That's all I know right now. Wendy had the baby at home. Katie delivered it."

Emily was immediately concerned. "Oh my God—is Wendy all right?"

"Wendy's fine," he assured her. "She and the baby are at the hospital now. I'll call when I know more—but until then, could you do me a favor? Could you call Mom and Dad and the others and tell them?"

"Sure, no problem," Emily marveled, her voice growing soft. "I can't wait to see her. Give Wendy a hug for me and tell her I'll be there as soon as I can." And with that, Emily terminated the call so that she could call everyone else in the family and alert them to this latest development: the Fortunes of Atlanta had a granddaughter.

Blake closed his phone and put it away. He felt his energy dissipating and decided he needed an infusion of coffee—decent if possible, but at least black if the former was too much to ask for.

As it turned out, he had to settle for vending-machine coffee, which by definition was mediocre. He brought back two cups, one black and one so light it looked more like white-chocolate milk than coffee.

Katie was exactly where he'd left her, holding up the wall with her back and appearing as if she was about to drift off to sleep that way.

"Sugar and a ton of cream, right?" he asked as he handed her the appropriate paper cup.

That was enough to banish her fatigue, at least for the time being. "You remembered," she said in surprise.

To her recollection, Blake had never gotten her coffee. If anything, it had been the other way around, not that she minded. She had never felt it necessary to define herself by what she did or didn't do. Besides, if she was willing to groom Blake so that he would be more appealing to Brittany, bringing an occasional cup of coffee to the man was no big deal.

Having him bring coffee to her, however, was a big deal. At least in her book.

"I pay attention," Blake protested, then amended, "Sometimes," when Katie gave him a penetrating, knowing look.

Her smile was warm and grateful. "Thank you." She peeled off the plastic lid and then took a long, appreciative sip. "I really need this," she told him as she felt the warm liquid wind its way through her sleepy system. "I'm dead on my feet."

His eyes casually swept over her. For a wilting flower, she looked damn good. Maybe too good, he judged a split second before he banked down his thoughts. It was just the exhaustion taking over, he told himself, taking him to places he didn't intend to go.

"Could have fooled me," he commented. And then, changing the subject, he looked up and down the hallway. No one was coming. "Any word from Marcos?"

The question had no sooner left his lips than Marcos turned a corner and came barreling down the hallway, looking like a man who had run rather than driven the twenty miles to the hospital from the Red Rock restaurant he managed.

"Where is she?" he cried, latching onto his brother-in-law's arm. "Where's Wendy?"

"Catch your breath, Marcos," Katie told him. "Wendy's still in recovery."

Alarmed, his system on overload, Marcos cried, "Why? What's she doing there?"

"Recovering," Katie answered simply. "It was a big ordeal, Marcos," she elaborated, then couldn't help adding, "for all concerned. Her doctor wants to be perfectly sure she's all right before he sends Wendy to her room."

The fact that Katie had mentioned only his wife suddenly registered. "And the baby?" he asked suddenly. "Where's MaryAnne?"

"She's in an incubator. She's fine," Katie told him

quickly when his worried expression only deepened, all but pinching his handsome features. "She's just a little small right now, but the doctor said that was to be expected, remember?" Katie placed her hand on Marcos's shoulder. "She looks perfect," Katie assured him. "Trust me."

She wasn't prepared for what happened next. One moment, she was talking to Wendy's distraught husband, trying to reassure him, the next moment Marcos was suddenly enveloping her in what could only be described as a bear hug.

Caught off guard, Katie could only stand there, stunned and motionless for a moment, her arms pinned to her sides.

"Marcos?" she asked uncertainly. "Are *you* all right?"

"Blake told me everything you did, delivering the baby and keeping Wendy calm. I don't know if she would have made it without you. Thank you," he cried, squeezing her hard again. "Thank you!"

The more he thanked her, the harder he squeezed, until she couldn't draw any air in. "No need to thank me," she all but squeaked. The next moment, he released her and it was hard not to just go limp, but she managed to hold herself together. She gulped in a lungful of air. "I'm just glad I was there and could help. It's a pretty humbling experience," she confessed.

If either Marcos or Blake were going to say anything, she never got the chance to hear it because, just then, the double doors leading into the recovery room swung open. A nurse came out, guiding the foot of a gurney while an orderly pushed it out of the room and toward the service elevator.

Marcos instinctively moved out of the way before he realized that his wife was the patient on the gurney. When he did, his face lit up like a Fourth of July sparkler.

"Wendy," he cried, taking her hand in his and walking quickly beside the moving gurney. "I'm sorry I wasn't there. If I'd had the slightest idea that you were going to—"

"I'm not sorry," Wendy said truthfully, cutting into his apology. She saw no reason for it. "I wasn't exactly at my best."

"You were having our baby." Marcos's eyes were filled with love as he looked at his wife. "I can't think of a time when you could have looked more beautiful to me," he told her honestly.

Following behind the gurney, Katie deliberately fell back and then stopped walking altogether. Wendy and her husband needed some time alone together.

"Now, there's a marriage that's going to last forever," she murmured in admiration and envy.

"Think so?" Blake asked.

She hadn't realized she'd said the words out loud, or that Blake was so close to her. She flushed, embarrassed, but there was no pretending she'd meant something else—or that she wasn't just a tiny bit envious.

"Yes, I do," she said with conviction. "Marcos knows exactly what to say to make her feel beautiful, even when she knows, deep down, that appearance-wise, she's had better days."

He nodded, as if her words made perfect sense. This really *was* a red-letter day, she couldn't help thinking. Either that, or she'd fallen asleep against the recovery room wall and this was all a dream.

"Are you ready to go home," Blake asked, "or do you want to go upstairs to her room?"

Despite the coffee, she was having trouble battling exhaustion, which had returned stronger than ever and seemed only a half step or so away from flattening her. "Oh, so ready," she confessed.

Blake nodded with a smile, ready to turn in himself. "Home it is."

Katie fell asleep almost the moment he pulled out of the space in the hospital parking lot. She was still asleep when they reached the house, some twenty-five miles later. Pulling up the hand brake and turning off the engine, Blake looked at his sleeping passenger. He debated waking her, then thought better of it.

Instead, he got out of the vehicle and went to the front door. He unlocked it with the key that Wendy had given him. Then, leaving the door open, he returned to his car and opened the passenger-side door.

Her face looked softer when she was asleep, he thought. More at ease. He wasn't certain just how long he stood there, looking at her, letting his thoughts drift, before he snapped back to attention. He was grateful there was no one around to witness it.

Taking a breath, he very gently eased Katie out of the car and into his arms. She hardly weighed anything, he thought as he turned toward the house. Like a bridegroom with his new bride, he carried Katie across the threshold and then proceeded to carry her up the stairs.

She made a slight, dreamy noise just as he came to the landing and that in turn woke her up. A contented sigh escaped her before she opened her eyes.

As her surroundings penetrated, her eyes widened proportionately. By then she was inside her room. The next moment, she felt herself being lowered to her bed. She looked up uncertainly at the man who had brought her here.

"Blake?"

Anticipating her question, Blake explained, "You fell asleep. I didn't have the heart to wake you, and leaving you sleeping in the car didn't seem like a good option, either."

"So you carried me into the house?" she marveled. Who did that these days? That was straight out of some period piece—and she loved it!

Blake shrugged dismissively. "Seemed like the right thing to do at the time."

"I'm sorry," she apologized, feeling a tad self-conscious. "You should have woken me up."

He laughed softly. "Where's the chivalry in that?" he wanted to know.

"I don't know about chivalry, but at least your back wouldn't hurt." If he'd hurt it because of her, she'd never forgive herself....

"My back's fine. You don't even weigh as much as a sack of flour," he told her.

"I've had more flattering comparisons," she told him with a self-deprecating laugh.

"I'm sure you have," he agreed. "But none more sincere," he guaranteed. When she began to get up, he said, "Stay in bed, Katie."

"Is that an order?" she asked whimsically. *Or an invitation?* she added both silently and wistfully.

"It is if you need it to be," he told her. "Do you?" And then he smiled to himself. He was talking to an unconscious woman. Katie had fallen asleep again. Had to have been a hell of a day for her, he thought. He knew it had been for him.

Funny, he would have sworn that he knew Katie's limitations, having grown up with her. And yet, she had surprised him today, both with the way she had taken charge when his sister had gone into labor, and with her resilience and determination to be there for Wendy until Marcos arrived. And then, even though she looked utterly wiped out, she was the one who'd recalled that his family needed to be notified when he clearly should have been the one to remember.

Which just told him that, no matter how well you thought you knew someone, there were still surprises in the offing.

He paused long enough to lightly drape the end of her comforter over Katie and brush back the hair that had fallen into her face.

She looked peaceful, he thought. God only knew she'd earned it.

He'd let her sleep in tomorrow, he decided. There was no need to get started at the crack of dawn. Nine o'clock or so would be early enough. He had a feeling that tomorrow would be, in large measure, taken up by visits to Wendy and MaryAnne.

That was okay, he thought with affection. There was no hurry to get on with Project Brittany. As far as he was concerned they were already ahead of schedule. Besides, even if they weren't, Brittany wasn't going anywhere. The Valentine's Day fundraiser where he intended to make his move was more than a week away. Brittany had already agreed to go with him. Not because of any resurging affection on her part—she had a very practical reason for attending it with him.

He wasn't about to fool himself. She was in need of an escort and he had been in the right place at the right time. She wouldn't miss the annual event for the world. A great many people would be attending and she liked—no, loved—making an entrance, he thought.

As a matter of fact, she never missed an opportunity to be seen and fawned over. She was like an exquisite work of art and exquisite works of art, needed an audience to be properly viewed and admired, he thought. It was probably one of the first lessons that Brittany had ever learned. That, and that turning heads was extremely good for the ego.

And God knew that Brittany had no problem in that department, he mused. Her ego was alive and thriving.

Unlike Katie, he caught himself thinking.

Glancing at her one last time, Blake shut the light and eased her bedroom door closed. He deliberately ignored the odd, unsettled feeling in the pit of his stomach, the one that seemed to hint that the girl he'd grown up next to had turned in to the kind of woman he could grow old with.

Chapter Ten

The dream was so vivid, so moving, Katie felt it with every fiber of her being. Her body heated as the seconds ticked by, bringing with them more and more pieces to fill her mind.

But even while it was unfolding, she knew it *had* to be a dream. Because Blake was paying attention to *her.* Right in the middle of writing a love letter to Brittany—a sizzling, *hot* love letter, Blake had used her name rather than Brittany's. When she'd pointed out his mistake, he'd looked into her eyes and told her that for the first time in his life, he wasn't making a mistake. That his initial belief that he was in love with Brittany had been the real mistake.

And then he'd taken her into his arms and, suddenly they were dancing—and then they weren't. Because he was kissing her. Caressing her. Making love to her with every breath he took.

Katie couldn't remember when she'd been happier.

And then daylight had crept into her consciousness, nudging her awake, banishing sleep. She screwed her eyes up tight, reluctant to leave this make-believe place her mind had created for her.

But it was no use.

The dream broke up into wisps of vapor and then was gone.

With a sigh, she gave up and got out of bed. A quick shower had her almost feeling human. She had made her way down the stairs and reached the kitchen when the silence finally penetrated. She was alone in the house. Marcos, she realized, must have remained in the hospital with Wendy. Which was where Katie wanted to be.

The problem was how to get there.

Her first impulse was to call the man who had been her mode of transportation ever since she'd arrived in Red Rock. But her call to Blake's cell phone went straight to voice mail. Katie was in no mood to leave a message that Blake would listen to God only knew when.

She terminated the call abruptly, muttering a few choice words under her breath.

Frustrated and antsy, Katie impulsively went into the garage to see if there were any vehicles available. Marcos's sedan was gone, just as she knew it would be, but Wendy's car—the one Wendy had offered to let her drive on more than one occasion since she'd arrived here—was still there.

A peek inside told her the vehicle was all gassed up and ready to go.

She'd initially turned Wendy's offer down because she didn't like being responsible for someone else's car. They were called *accidents* for a reason—but this fell under the heading of an emergency, or at least something close to it, she reasoned.

The debate in her head went on for all of two minutes before it tilted toward yes. She retraced her steps back to the kitchen. As she recalled, Wendy kept her car keys hanging on a peg next to the bay window over the sink.

They were still there.

Ten minutes later Katie found herself hitting the open road. She was on her way to San Antonio and the hospital, thanks to the GPS device perched on the dashboard.

She left Wendy's vehicle in the hospital's guest parking lot, silently counting the number of cars in her row, and hurried into the hospital.

Her first order of business, Katie decided happily as she got into the elevator car, was to look in on the tiny human being she'd helped bring into the world last night. The infant wasn't even a day old yet, Katie thought with a wide grin as she got off on the maternity floor.

She'd never known anyone that young before.

Turning a corner, Katie stopped and hesitated for

a moment. She debated quietly slipping away until Marcos was finished visiting with his daughter. He was looking at the infant through the glass.

The tiny girl looked even smaller in the incubator, Katie decided.

The deeply concerned look on Marcos's face made Katie's mind up for her. She not only stayed but came forward and made herself known to him.

"She's doing fine, Marcos," Katie assured him, even as she placed a comforting hand on the man's shoulder.

Lost in thought as he stared at his daughter, Marcos jumped, startled, and swung around to see who was talking to him.

When he saw that it was Katie, he relaxed. "Oh, it's you."

Katie took a step back, not wanting to crowd him. "I'm sorry, I didn't mean to catch you off guard like that."

He waved away her apology. "I should be the one who's saying he's sorry. I was preoccupied," he explained. "I didn't even hear you come up."

His preoccupation brought her full circle, back to the concerned look she'd seen on his face. "You don't have to worry. The doctor told me she was very healthy," Katie said, in case he didn't recall her having said that to him last night.

Marcos nodded, a weary smile half curving his mouth. "I know. It's not her I'm worried about."

Katie jumped to the only conclusion she could. If he wasn't worried about the baby, that could only mean one thing. “Did something happen to Wendy—?” Even as she asked, she half turned, ready to dash down the hall to Wendy’s room.

He was quick to shoot down her mistake. “No, Wendy, thanks to you, is doing just great.” And for that she had his undying gratitude. “I’m just worried about Javier,” he confessed. Backtracking, Marcos explained, “I spent the night here, in Wendy’s room—one of the orderlies brought a cot in for me,” he told her. “This morning I went to look in on Javier, to give him the good news about the baby being born. He congratulated me and said to give his love to Wendy, but I could see that he was still having a really hard time dealing with his injuries. He’d always been so damn healthy, he doesn’t know how to handle this.”

Filled with frustrated energy and no release, Marcos fought the urge to start pacing. That wouldn’t do any good. The only thing that might help would be to knocking some sense into Javier’s head—literally.

“I know he thinks he’s never going to walk again and in his mind, that makes him half a man. It’s insane to think that way, but to be honest,” he told Katie, dropping his voice, “if I were in Javier’s place, I don’t know if I’d be thinking any differently.”

Katie took Marcos’s hand, as if to somehow physically transfer her own feelings to him. “He *is* going to walk again, Marcos. He really has to believe that,” she insisted. And then she looked at him for a long moment. “You have to *make* him believe that. A positive attitude is really important in this kind of a case. And besides,” she said, never wavering, "miracles happen every day, so why not for Javier?"

Marcos searched her eyes and realized that his wife's friend wasn't just saying something to make him feel better. "You honestly believe that, don't you?"

Katie nodded with conviction. "From the bottom of my heart."

Right now, he was willing to cling to anything, as long as it helped Javier get back on his feet. "I suppose, maybe miracles do happen," Marcos said, his tone just a wee bit guarded. "If you hadn't been there for Wendy and the baby last night, I might have lost them both."

She didn't like to dwell on that. Negatives were things she preferred to banish from her thoughts. "Instead, they're happy and healthy," she said cheerfully. "If you'd like me to, I could go and talk to Javier, make him see that there's every reason in the world to believe that he's going to get better. All it takes is patience and time—" she offered.

Touched, Marcos kissed her cheek. "No, you've already done more than enough for the Mendoza family," he told her, emotion brimming in his voice. "Dealing with my brother is my job. Tell you what. Why don't you head on to Wendy's room? I know she's dying to see you. You should go now, before everyone else gets here and it gets too noisy and too crowded."

"Crowded?" she repeated, a little confused.

He nodded. "Last I heard, they were all getting ready to fly back out here. Together." He liked Wendy's family, but if he were honest, he preferred them in small doses. This did not promise to be a small dose. "It's going to be standing room only around her bed."

"By everyone, you mean her brothers and sisters, right?" she asked cautiously. She knew what Wendy's father was like and it had been difficult tearing the man away from his desk long enough to attend the wedding.

"And her parents," Marcos added.

Katie made no attempt to hide her surprise. "You're kidding. Her father's coming?"

She would have expected Wendy's mother to want to come, but the woman rarely did anything on her own and her husband was all but married to his job. In her opinion, the foundation was his real wife and Wendy's mother was more like the mistress he had on the side.

Marcos laughed shortly, glad he wasn't the only one who felt that way.

"Surprised me, too. John Michael Fortune leaving his office twice in the space of a little over a month—I expected the Second Coming to happen before that. Just goes to show you, you really can never tell the kind of power a newborn baby has," he said with a laugh.

Marcos looked a lot better now than he had when she had first seen him in the hallway, Katie thought, a sense of satisfaction sweeping through her. Her work here was done.

"Then I'd better go see Wendy quickly," she agreed, starting to leave.

Marcos nodded, turning back to the nursery window. "Tell her I'll be along after I finish visiting with my daughter."

"I'll tell her."

That really was one lucky little girl. Marcos was going to make a great father, Katie thought.

She smiled to herself as she went down the hallway, reading off the room numbers until she came to Wendy's. She knocked on the closed door. But rather than stand on ceremony, waiting for a verbal invitation to come in, Katie pushed open the door and went in. After last night, she and Wendy had crossed a new threshold. The intensity of their relationship had deepened by several remarkable layers.

Wendy looked really pleased to see her. Blake, who was also in the room, was the one who was surprised.

"I thought after last night, you'd be sleeping in, recharging your batteries, that kind of thing," he told her.

The dream still very fresh in her mind, her pulse launched into double time at the very sight of Blake. Katie fervently hoped that a flush hadn't crept into her face, giving her away.

She did her best to focus on the present—and reality—not a wishful dream that hadn't a chance in hell of coming true.

"I don't need much sleep," Katie informed him almost stiffly. After all, he'd been through the same thing she had and now here he was, bright-eyed and bushy-tailed. Why did he think she would be anything less than that? Did he think of her as some fragile cream puff? "I helped Wendy deliver a baby, I didn't carve out the Grand Canyon with a soup spoon," she pointed out crisply.

Blake shrugged. Men were supposed to be heartier than women, but he knew better than to say that out loud. Besides, it was apparent that Katie was every bit as hearty as he was.

And then something occurred to him.

"Hold it. Since I pick you up every day and I'm here, just how did you get to the hospital?" Katie was extremely levelheaded and practically frugality personified. He couldn't see her calling a taxi to bring her here. So then, how had she gotten here? There was no public transportation that would have brought her from Red Rock.

"Magic," she retorted, remaining mysterious for exactly half a second before she confessed to Wendy. "I borrowed your car. You did tell me I could use it," she reminded her friend, mentally crossing her fingers and hoping that it was still all right.

Wendy put her hand on top of Katie's and smiled warmly. "After what you did last night, everything I have is yours," she said with feeling.

Relieved, Katie laughed. "Marcos might have a different opinion about that. Borrowing your car to come see you is all the payment I want," she told Wendy.

"Well, I'll leave you two alone to talk," Blake told his sister. "I'm going to go take another look at my niece and then head back to Red Rock."

"But you'll be back later this evening?" Wendy asked hopefully.

Blake knew exactly what his sister was really asking. "You mean when the Fortune family descends en masse? Sure, I'll be here. Wouldn't miss seeing the expression on the old man's face when he looks at his granddaughter for the first time." Although, he thought, his father would have undoubtedly been happier if the first grandchild had been a boy, born to one of his sons. "He's probably bringing a tiny little desk and chair for her so she can get started working for the company by the time she learns how to sit up." He lapsed into a deep voice, doing a fair imitation of their father. "'No time like the present, Wendy. You're never too young to start on the right path.'"

"Your father's not as bad as all that," Katie protested, coming to the man's defense. When her own late father had faced ruin, it was the senior Fortune who had found a position for him in his own company. She would always be grateful to him for allowing her father the chance to restore his dignity and his pride.

"Oh, yes, he is," Wendy and Blake told her in unison.

Not wanting to argue with her friends, Katie relented. It still didn't change the truth, in her eyes. She knew that John Michael had a great deal of difficulty in expressing his feelings, but in that he was not unlike a lot of other men, especially those in his generation. The bottom line was that he was coming, and that meant a great deal.

With a shrug, Katie retreated, saying, "Can't argue with both of you."

The look Blake gave her sent a shiver up her spine that she had a great deal of difficulty in masking. "Sure you can," he quipped as he went out the door. "And probably will."

Wendy pushed a button and the top portion of her mattress pivoted forward, allowing her to almost sit up. "So," she asked eagerly the second Blake had closed the door behind him, "how's it going?"

For a split second, Katie had let her mind stray back to her dream. She shook herself free when she heard Wendy's voice and looked at her friend. "What?"

Wendy rolled her eyes. "This so-called Project Brittany of his."

Katie was surprised that Wendy even wanted to talk about that, given the little miracle lying in the incubator down the hall. But her friend was looking at her eagerly, obviously waiting for some sort of a progress report.

She shrugged. "I was going to show him how to cook today, but I'm not sure if that's still on, given the circumstances." She looked at Wendy pointedly.

"Circumstances?" Wendy echoed.

How could Wendy even ask? "You, the baby—ring a bell?" Katie asked, her eyes meeting Wendy's. How could she even *think* of anything else? If she'd just had a baby…but then, that was never going to happen to her. She was probably just going to be "fun Aunt Katie" and wind up dying alone, while eating her dinner standing over her kitchen sink.

She didn't expect Wendy to become indignant and raise her voice. "Don't you dare stop because of me. I want you there, shoulder to shoulder with Blake until my empty-headed brother realizes that you are three times the woman that Brittany will *ever* be."

Katie shook her head. Maybe this was just a futile battle and she was fooling herself that she could get Blake to see the light.

"I don't know about that, Wendy," she confessed honestly. "Brittany's a socialite, she moves in your circle."

Wendy instantly came to her defense. "And you are a real person who doesn't *need* a circle. Now, please," she entreated, "if you're not going to do this for yourself, do it for Blake."

Katie frowned. Had the delivery wiped out Wendy's short-term memory? "Blake wants Brittany, remember?" she said with a note of dejection.

"No, my brother only *thinks* he wants Brittany," Wendy corrected. "And if by some horrible prank of nature, he managed to temporarily—and I stress the word *temporarily*—get her, what he'd wind up getting is cotton candy."

"Cotton candy?" Katie repeated. Just what was that supposed to mean?

Wendy nodded her head. "No substance, just air and sugar. And she'll break his heart on top of that," Wendy predicted. "She did it once, she'll do it again. That's one leopard who is *not* changing her shallow spots." She moved closer to Katie, taking her hand and saying earnestly, "Trust me, my brother needs a good woman in his life—and as far as I can see, there's only one good woman in this mix and it's you, Katie." She sighed, suddenly feeling exhausted. Leaning back on her pillows, Wendy released Katie's hand. "So go, get back to Scott's and get back to work. Save my stupid brother from himself and the stupidest mistake he could ever possibly make." Her eyes narrowed. "Kill her if you have to. You have my permission."

The atmosphere had been deadly serious—until the last two sentences. The tension dissipated and Katie laughed, shaking her head.

"Don't be shy, Wendy," she said in a coaxing tone. "Tell me what you really think."

"Go!" Wendy repeated, a slight grin on her lips as she pointed toward the door.

Katie saluted as if she were a dutiful little soldier. "Okay."

"And don't forget to call me and tell me how it's going," Wendy added, raising her voice as she called after her departing friend.

"Will do," Katie promised, just as the door closed behind her. "Provided there's something worth reporting," she added under her breath.

Blake looked up in surprise from the desk where he was making notes to himself. He hadn't heard her knock—she probably hadn't, he decided—but he had sensed rather than heard her the second she'd entered the makeshift office. It was, he thought, as if he'd somehow gotten attuned to Katie.

But then, why not? They'd worked together for over two years now, hadn't they? You got used to a person's habits and the scent they wore after two years, he reasoned. Provided, of course, that they wore a scent, he added wryly.

Out loud, to cover his surprise, he said, "I didn't expect to see you here today."

Katie put her purse down. "Why not? It's another 'work' day, right? Since you're here, you obviously didn't take it off," she pointed out. *You're that eager to win the wrong girl,* she added silently while maintaining a smile on her lips.

Blake nodded at the paper on his desk. "I thought I'd polish up that love letter you wrote for me. You know, add my own touches to it." He looked at her with just a little bit of hesitation. Or was he being thoughtful of her feelings? She caught herself wondering before dismissing the thought as merely wishful thinking. "You don't mind, do you?"

She shrugged. "It's your love letter." God, had that sounded as awkward to him as it did to her?

To her surprise, he pushed the letter aside. "I can work on that later. So, you have anything new in mind?" he asked her, sounding every bit like an eager student.

Oh, God, this man is so wasted on Brittany, she thought in despair. "I thought today I'd teach you how to cook."

"Cook?" he repeated, then frowned. Deeply. "Is that really necessary? I mean, isn't the saying, 'The way to a man's heart is through his stomach,' pretty clear that it's the woman who does the cooking? Not that I think that Brittany could boil an egg," he confessed.

She'd probably set the house on fire if she tried, Katie thought. "That saying was popular when women were regarded as second-class citizens. Times have changed," she reminded him. "Now, if you don't think you're up to it…" She let her voice trail off.

Nothing got him more motivated than a challenge. "Bring it," he said.

Katie nodded her head with a smile. *I fully intend to, Blake. I fully intend to.*

Chapter Eleven

"No, no, you *stir* the flour slowly into the consommé, you don't beat it as if you're some outraged supermodel, out for revenge," Katie protested.

On her way over to Scott Fortune's house, she had stopped at the store to pick up a few ingredients for the proposed cooking lesson. She'd decided to get Blake started by having him prepare beef Stroganoff, thinking it was a relatively easy recipe.

Apparently she'd thought wrong.

One second, she'd turned away for *one* second to retrieve the mushrooms from the refrigerator and when she'd turned back again, it was to see Blake all but attacking the pot, which now contained the carefully diced-up beef, the consommé and supposedly the evenly distributed quarter cup of flour.

"But it's all lumpy," Blake complained in frustration. He was unsuccessfully trying to change the consistency of the flour—which was beginning to look like dumplings at this stage—by hitting each small lump with the flat of his spatula. "It's not supposed to be lumpy, right?"

She suppressed the desire to laugh and solemnly said, "Right."

That could have been avoided if he'd poured the flour in slowly, stirring as he went, the way she'd told him to. But he had obviously just upended the measuring cup and tossed all four ounces in at once. Still, there was no point in mentioning that to him now. Now was the time for damage control.

"You *stir* like this," Katie told him, covering his hand with her own and moving the large spatula rhythmically inside the pot. "Get the feel of it?" she asked.

He turned his head, looking back over his shoulder at her. She was directly behind him, less than a hair's breadth away.

As close as the next heartbeat, he realized. "Yeah, I feel it," he murmured.

His breath seemed to graze her skin. Or was that just the steam coming up from the Stroganoff? The spatula in the pot wasn't the only thing being stirred, Katie couldn't help thinking. Belatedly, she released his hand and drew her own away.

Getting her heartbeat regulated took another minute or so longer.

She forced her mind back on the task at hand and looked down into the pot.

"See, the lumps are disappearing already." She raised her eyes to his, a pleased smile on her lips. "We'll make a chef out of you yet," she promised. *Now* was the time for corrections, she decided. "And next time, make sure you pour the flour in *slowly*. It won't form lumps that way."

"Next time," he muttered, wondering to himself if there really had to be a next time. This winning Brittany back campaign seemed like a great deal more trouble than he'd first anticipated. Oh, he didn't mind the wining and the dining—if dining meant eating out—and he could even take in stride the dancing and writing love letters. But this cooking business—well, he wasn't all that sure he really wanted to go that route.

He knew without having to ask that his father had never had to cook anything for his mother to win her over, or to get her to marry him. But then, his mother was far more easygoing than Brittany. And although even now she was a very pretty woman and must have been even more so when she had first caught his father's eye, he knew for a fact that his mother had never been drop-dead gorgeous like Brittany.

Blake resigned himself. Winning a special woman required going the extra mile—or more—and this was definitely that extra mile.

Standing beside him, her hair inadvertently brushing against his bare arm—he'd rolled up his sleeves when they had started this—Katie looked into the pot. She nodded, pleased.

"Looks like it's really coming along," she told him, referring to the consistency that they had finally achieved.

Why her praise really pleased him he wouldn't have been able to explain to anyone, not even himself. But it did. "Thanks."

She indicated the package on the counter she'd just taken out for him. "Now chop up the mushrooms and stir those in, too."

"Do I add them in slowly, too?" he asked, putting down the spatula and ripping open the package.

She grinned. "Doesn't matter. All they do is just shrink as they cook—and also add taste," she said, anticipating his next question, which would undoubtedly be why he was adding mushrooms if it didn't matter how they went in.

"Oh. Okay." Presented with a chopping board and the eight-ounce box of whole mushrooms, Blake went to work. Chopping was clearly his favorite part of cooking, she observed.

He glanced in her direction. "You have this all in your head, don't you? Recipes," he clarified in case she didn't know what he was referring to.

"There's not all that much to remember," she told him with a careless shrug, throwing out the empty paper box and plastic wrap.

She was selling herself short, he thought. Looking back, he realized that it wasn't the first time she'd done so, either. She had a habit of doing that. Modesty, he supposed. Something that Brittany wouldn't have known anything about, he mused.

"Still," he acknowledged, "that's pretty impressive."

It was all in how you looked at things, Katie thought. "You retain sales figures. Same thing."

In more ways than one, he thought. Or didn't she realize that? "You do, too," he pointed out.

Something akin to a tiny starburst nestled into her chest. Blake had actually noticed her proficiency with sales figures. *Score one for the underdog.* Katie silently congratulated herself on the tiny gain she'd just made. Smiling, she absently gathered up the mushrooms he had just chopped and deposited them into the pot, making sure to distribute them evenly.

"I thought I was supposed to do everything by myself." The initial object, when she'd told him about it earlier, was for him to make the meal from start to finish with only a little verbal guidance from her, but nothing more.

"I won't tell if you don't," Katie said. "Deal?" And then, as if to seal it, she winked.

He had no idea why—maybe it was the heat in the kitchen, or his preoccupation that it all turn out right—but there was something about that wink that seemed to burrow straight into his gut like a whirling dervish. His stomach tighten so hard in response that for a second, he wasn't sure he could catch his breath.

What the hell was going on here?

Had to be the heat, he decided with conviction.

Couldn't have had anything to do with the woman he had known all of his life, he silently argued. That would be just plain ridiculous.

"Deal," he muttered. He grabbed a large spoon and dipped it into the Stroganoff. "Wait," he said as she turned away. "You might as well try it." Pulling the spoon out again, he held it out to her.

Because there was steam rising from it, she blew on the spoon's contents, and again he felt his stomach tightening, this time yet another notch.

What the hell had gotten into him? He was acting like a simpering teenager—something he wasn't even when he *had* been a teenager.

Get a grip, damn it, Blake ordered himself.

The second Katie tasted the fruits of Blake's labor, her eyes instantly began to water. But it wasn't her eyes that were the problem. It was her mouth, which felt as if it was on fire. So much so that it was a full minute before she could successfully use her tongue. Even so, she was somewhat surprised that it hadn't burned off.

"What else did you put in here?" she wanted to know, her voice exceedingly raspy.

"Why? What's wrong?" he wanted to know, instantly concerned. When she didn't answer him immediately, Blake reviewed the list of ingredients, ending with, "and pepper."

"What kind of pepper?" she asked, the fire in her throat finally subsiding after she'd downed half a glass of water.

He looked at her blankly. "Pepper pepper," he said.

"I don't know. There're kinds?" When she nodded, he picked up the small container he'd used and held it up. "I put a tablespoon of this in."

She looked at the label. Now it made sense. "The recipe calls for a dash of pepper," she told him. "*Not* a tablespoon and it was supposed to be *white* pepper, not cayenne pepper."

"What the hell is a dash?" he demanded, irritated with his mistake.

"A lot less than a tablespoon," she told him.

He frowned. "White pepper?" he repeated.

"Yes."

This all sounded Greek to him. "There's a difference?"

Katie took another long drink of water. She was beginning to feel human again. "There's a difference."

His frown deepened as he looked at the pot of gently simmering Stroganoff. "So you're saying it's ruined?"

Not if she could help it, she thought. "No, it's not ruined," she answered.

"But you were just spitting fire," he said.

She opened up another can of consommé—she'd bought backup quantities of everything. "We'll just have to add more consommé and more flour to dilute it."

Hopefully, she added silently as she proceeded to do exactly that, moving a great deal faster and with more confidence than he had just displayed. Once she had stirred everything in and restored the balance, she told him, "Unless you've burned something down to a charcoal bit, you can usually salvage it in some manner." There, that was a good color, she congratulated herself. "You just have to be creative."

"*You're* the creative one," he told her, then confessed with a shrug, "It's not my thing."

"It'll come to you," she promised as she went on stirring the revitalized Stroganoff. "No one knows this stuff when they first start out. Remember, you were the one who came up with the marketing strategy to land the Fontaine account when it looked pretty hopeless," she reminded him, doing her best to restore Blake's confidence.

She hated to see him down, even if having him bounce back meant she was sending him directly into Brittany's finely manicured clutches.

"That was a Hail Mary play," he recalled honestly.

"So is salvaging Stroganoff—except that people's jobs aren't hanging in the balance like they were with the Fontaine account. Yours was the far more creative save," she pointed out.

When he grinned, she knew she'd done her job.

He watched her move around the kitchen and he couldn't help noting the way she handled everything with such assurance. He was never going to be that confident and he knew it. Maybe this was all just a waste of their time.

When she turned around to face him again, he asked, "Do I really have to learn how to cook?"

She could hear the resistance in his voice. "Think of it as a last resort," she promised. And then she smiled.

"You'll no doubt dazzle her with that footwork you've been working on. But if that fails, knowing how to whip up a good meal isn't really such a bad backup plan." She paused to take a taste of the now-salvaged Stroganoff. *Thank God.* "Here, you try," she coaxed, holding up the ladle that she'd filled for him.

Anticipating disaster, Blake took a very tiny, tentative taste, hardly touching his lips to the contents of the ladle. When they didn't fall off, he took another, decent-size sample this time. Surprise spread through him faster than the food.

"Hey," he cried, pleased, "not bad."

"No, not bad at all," she agreed, putting the ladle down on the spoon rest. "See? I told you. You really *can* cook."

There was a big leap between what he could do and what she had accomplished and he was smart enough to see the difference. "No, I can throw ingredients together. *You* can cook," he pointed out.

She wasn't about to stand here and argue with him, especially since, for the time being, he was right. "Let's just call it a joint project," she proposed. "And now, since this is ready," she indicated the pot, "why don't we have lunch?"

Eating something that he had actually prepared—or at least had had a hand in preparing—was rather a novel concept for him and the idea intrigued him. "Sure, why not? And after that, I'm going to be heading back to the hospital. I promised Wendy," he reminded Katie.

Since there was nothing pressing for her to attend to,

she welcomed the idea of going back to see her friend. "Mind if I hitch a ride with you?"

His eyes met hers just before he helped himself to a generous portion of their joint effort. "Don't mind at all."

The way he said it warmed up her insides far more than the Stroganoff.

"Why can't we go in?"

John Michael Fortune's deep voice boomed up and down the corridor as he directed the annoyed question at the very young, very inexperienced-looking nurse standing beside his wife. Still a very handsome man at sixty-two, his six-foot-four, athletic frame made him seem even more imposing than he already was. The deep frown on his aristocratic face didn't help, either. Grown men were known to cower before the expression that was presently on his face. Virginia, his wife of thirty-six years, merely looked passed it and waited for the storm to blow over. It always did.

The young nurse took her cue from her.

"I did *not* drop everything and fly out all this way just to stand outside my daughter's hospital door," he declared, glaring at the closed door. "I came here to *see* her."

"And you will, Mr. Fortune," the nurse was quick to assure him. "Just as soon as the doctor is through examining her. It really shouldn't be much longer," she added nervously.

Accustomed to getting his way, John Michael was

about to push his way past the little bit of a thing standing in front of him. Her words made him abruptly stop dead in his tracks.

"Examining her?" he echoed. "Well, why didn't you say so?" he demanded, more flustered than angry this time. "Damn it, girl, I almost walked in on my own daughter and embarrassed us both."

Relief flooded over the young woman's pale features. "But you didn't, and I did—say so, sir," she quickly tacked on when her patient's father looked at her quizzically.

Just then, the door behind her opened and with an even greater look of relief than a moment ago, the nurse stepped off to the side. She didn't have to be told that if she so much as hesitated even for a slight second, she ran the very real risk of getting trampled on by a man who allowed nothing to get in his way.

Nodding curtly at the physician who emerged, John Michael muttered, "It's about time," under his breath but loud enough for anyone within ten feet of him to hear. There was no doubt that the departing doctor heard.

The head of the Fortune clan, followed by the rest of the family that had flown out with him, strode into the room and crossed directly over to his daughter's hospital bed.

"You look pale," he observed.

"Must be the lighting in here," Wendy countered, then, because she had never been afraid to speak her mind, she admonished her father and said, "I heard you all the way in here, Dad. *With* the door closed."

If she was trying to make him express regret, she should have known better and just saved her breath.

"Good. I wanted you to know we were out there," he told his youngest child in his no-nonsense voice. And then he paused to look at her more closely. She really did look pale. "How are you feeling?"

Her mouth curved. "Much better, Dad," she replied. "Hi, Mom," she said as Virginia, the complete epitome of Southern gentility, leaned over and brushed a soft kiss against her cheek. Straightening, Virginia paused to push Wendy's hair away from her face in an old, familiar gesture that went all the way back to when she was a little girl whose bangs were always falling into her eyes.

John Michael, oblivious to the fact that his other children all had questions for Wendy, nodded as he leaned in closer. His very manner reduced the room down to only the two of them.

"No aftereffects? Everything okay?" he pressed in a slightly gentler tone that still, for all intents and purposes, sounded businesslike.

"Yes, Dad, everything's okay. Honest," she underscored when he raised his eyebrows as if he intended to grill her, the way he had when he'd caught her sneaking into the house after two in the morning. She'd just turned eighteen at the time.

"And the baby?" he wanted to know.

"Yes, how is she?" Virginia asked, adding her soft voice to the chorus.

"She's fine, too. Just a little small, so they're going to keep MaryAnne here in the hospital for a little while, make sure everything's going well." She said it so matter-of-factly, no one would guess that the thought of leaving her little girl behind when she went home tomorrow was all but killing her.

"So you really did have a girl, huh," John Michael said. He gave the impression that he'd thought perhaps the amniocentesis had been wrong.

Wendy did her best to hide her amusement. "Yes, Dad, she's a girl."

"And her name is MaryAnne."

She could hear her father's disappointment. "Don't worry, Dad. She's not going to be an only child. If the next one's a boy, maybe we'll name it after you."

Her father nodded, brightening at the possibility and trying not to show it. "You could do worse."

Virginia Fortune smiled at her daughter. "I think MaryAnne's a lovely name. I know I like it."

"Her name could be 'mud,' for all it matters," her sister Emily said with feeling.

The rest of the family all turned to look at her. Ever since the tornado had wreaked such havoc for all of them, Emily had been acting a little off center, but no one wanted to mention it, hoping that it would pass. They were all coping with the event in their own way and were cutting one another slack.

Still, this was something that Virginia felt needed to

be commented on. “Emily, that’s just an awful name,” her mother cried, appalled.

“What matters,” Emily continued as if nothing was said, “is that she’s healthy.”

“I agree with Em,” Michael chimed in.

John Michael shrugged his broad, thin shoulders. “Well, apparently we don’t have a say in the name,” he commented, still reflecting on the fact that his first grandchild would not bear any part of the family name.

Wendy braced herself to offer a defense of her choice, “Dad—”

But her father held his hands up to stop her protest before it was launched. “Hey, I said it wasn’t a bad name,” he reminded her.

Just then, the door to her room opened again and she immediately looked in that direction, hoping for reinforcements or a diversion. Her father had a way of belaboring a point if it suited him.

When she saw Blake and Katie walking in, the relief she felt was overwhelming. “You came back.”

Blake crossed to her bed and positioned himself beside her—and across from his father. “Said we would,” he told her.

Katie noted that he’d said “we,” when this morning, he had promised that only he would return. Was this progress? Or just the effects of too much cayenne pepper? she wondered wryly.

Either way, she savored it for a moment, telling herself that at least she had that.

Chapter Twelve

Within a few minutes, as they surrounded her bed, the sound of Wendy's family's voices began to grow and swell, until they were all but deafening. They were each vying for her attention.

Virginia attempted, rather unsuccessfully, to keep the volume down. After a few more minutes had passed and the decibel level continued to climb, it was inevitable that the noise would attract someone's attention. And it did.

Ten minutes into their visit, a tall, heavyset and seasoned nurse with the bearing of a drill sergeant stuck her head into the overcrowded single care unit and did a quick assessment of the situation.

Walking in, she announced, "There're way too many people in this room. I'm afraid you're going to have to take turns visiting with the new mama." Her tone left no leeway for argument.

Nonetheless, Wendy's father drew himself up to his full and rather intimidating height, then scowled down at her. She looked to be approximately ten inches shorter. "Young woman, do you know who I am?"

Meeting his steely gaze, she looked completely unfazed. "One of the people who's going to be waiting outside for his turn at the new mother's bedside," the nurse replied matter-of-factly.

The steely glare narrowed into slits. "I'm John Michael Fortune," he informed her coldly, "and I recently made a sizable donation to this hospital because they took such good care of my daughter when she went into premature labor."

"Did you, now?" For a split second, it looked as if the nurse was going to relent and back away, but then she merely nodded. "All right, then you get to be one of the ones who gets first crack at visiting, but I still need half of you to wait outside."

Ever the peacemaker, Katie quickly moved to the front of the group and said to them, "Why don't I show all of you the way to the nursery so you can meet the cutest baby you'll ever hope to see," she suggested, looking from one of Wendy's siblings to another.

Emily spoke up first, crossing to Katie. She hooked her arms through Katie's, as if to seal the deal. "I'd love to see the baby."

She said it with such feeling that, along with her earlier comment, Blake caught himself wondering if something was going on with his sister. He started to leave with the others.

But Wendy wanted him to run interference for her with their father. Ordinarily, she was more than up to it, but the delivery had literally and figuratively taken a great deal out of her and she needed an ally on her side—just in case.

"You just got here," Wendy protested, her eyes pinning Blake in place for a second.

He smiled at her. "I'll be back soon," he promised. "Besides, I don't want to monopolize you. The others haven't had a chance to talk to you yet—and we wouldn't want to upset your nurse now, would we?" he asked, smiling just a little too brightly at the woman waiting by the doorway. Their eyes met as he passed her on his way out.

The woman's expression never changed. "Not if you know what's good for you," she replied in a low, even voice.

Blake wisely kept to himself the laugh that bubbled up in response.

He caught up to Emily a couple of steps outside the room and fell into step beside her as Katie led the small cluster of Atlanta Fortunes down the hallway to the nursery. It occurred to Blake, out of the blue, that he would probably be lost without Katie. She seemed to anticipate whatever needed doing before anything was said and had a knack of heading off problems before they actually became problems. The woman was worth her weight in gold.

And right now, she'd cleared the playing field for him so that he could talk to Emily alone.

"Something wrong?" he asked Emily in a hushed, lowered voice.

He noticed that she stiffened ever so slightly. "Why do you ask?"

He didn't beat around the bush. "Because you don't sound quite like the cheerful Emily I know. You're okay, right?" He peered at her face and saw nothing to enlighten him. "No ill aftereffects from that little dustup with the tornado the other month?" he pressed.

"Is this you, being the concerned brother?" Emily asked, amused.

"Something like that," he conceded, then asked, "What's up?"

She sighed as they turned a corner. How did she phrase this without sounding strange? For a second, she pressed her lips together, debating just shrugging it off. But this was Blake and although they'd had their share of teasing—not to mention fights—they were close and she had never lied to him, at least not deliberately. Now didn't seem like a good time to start.

She began slowly, like a child dipping a toe into the icy ocean tide. "The tornado got me thinking."

"A lot of that going around," Blake assured his sister. After all, if it hadn't been for the tornado, he wouldn't have realized that he had let the opportunity of his lifetime slip through his fingers without doing anything about it. "So, this thinking you did, where did it lead you?" he asked.

God, she never thought she would be saying this. Or *feeling* this. And yet, here she was, filled with this insatiable longing that was ripping her apart.

Emily took a breath and dove in. "I realized I wanted a baby." She looked at him. He didn't look surprised—or even amused. She decided that he couldn't really be getting the full import of what she was telling him. Suddenly, it became important to her that he understand. "Badly. I want a baby badly—like that's all I've been able to think of."

Emily was older than he was. As far as he knew, there was no steady man in her life and maybe she was hearing her biological clock ticking—maybe the tornado had even set it off. He could sympathize with that.

"Stop thinking and do something about it," he counseled.

She blinked. She hadn't known what to expect from him as a reaction, but this certainly threw her.

"What?"

"*Do* something about it," he repeated. "Get a plan. Something with teeth, like a campaign strategy." He thought for a moment, then threw out various choices for her. "You could adopt, hire a surrogate, or go aggressively after the man of your dreams with the goal of starting a family. Those are just three options. But whatever route you decide is best for you, *go and do it*. Sitting and sighing and wishing isn't going to get you anywhere. It certainly isn't going to help you get a baby."

Stunned, Emily looked at him. And then she smiled.

"You know, for a younger brother, you didn't turn out half bad."

Blake held his hands up, as if to fend off her words. "Please, you'll make my head swell."

When she laughed, she sounded like her old self again. He knew then that she was going to be all right. And that he had succeeded in getting through to his sister. He had a very strong feeling that she was going to take his advice.

He watched her at the nursery window as she looked, not just at her new niece, but at all the other babies as well. There was love in Emily's eyes. Love and wistfulness. Emily wasn't just talking, she really wanted a baby.

Wow.

Quite unintentionally, his eyes met Katie's as she glanced toward him over her shoulder. There was the woman who was going to help him attain his own goal, Blake thought with growing affection. It was getting to the point that he honestly didn't know what he would ever do without her.

At times the thought struck him that he didn't know how he could have gotten so lucky. It was as if Katie could almost read his mind, knowing what he needed before he even did. There weren't many working relationships like that—or even regular relationships for that matter, he thought. She was, quite possibly, the total package. Smart, competent and beautiful to boot.

Was it his imagination, or had she gotten, well, *more* beautiful of late? Or was that just a result of their spending so much more time together? He wasn't sure. All he knew was that the past few days he'd become more…aware of her than usual. He caught himself looking at her as if he'd never seen her before.

Had to be the close proximity, he decided. They'd all but been in each other's pockets of late.

The next moment, his thoughts took off in another direction. He had to find a way to thank her for all the extra time she'd put in on this unorthodox project of his. It was only right. After all, there was nothing in her contract that said she had to help him find a way to capture his future wife's heart. That was going above and beyond.

One in a million, that was Katie Wallace, he thought. Smiling at her, he nodded absently.

It was hard for her not to lose her train of thought when he looked at her like that. But she couldn't just begin babbling, at least not when his older brothers and sisters were around her like this. They'd think she was crazy—which she was, she silently acknowledged. Crazy in love with Blake.

And once he's with Brittany, you'll just be certifiably crazy, nothing more, she told herself with sick resignation. *Face it, that day is coming, and soon. You can't keep burying your head in the sand like this forever.*

She pushed the thought aside. Later—she'd deal with the inevitable later. Right now, she had Blake's siblings to contend with.

"I can't tell you how good it is to be back in my own bed again," Wendy said with yet another deep, contented sigh. It was two days later and Marcos and Katie had brought her home after she'd been discharged. There was only one thing to mar her happiness. "Everything would be perfect if I could have brought the baby home with me, too."

"She'll be here soon enough," Katie told her reassuringly. She sat on the edge of Wendy's huge bed, the way she used to when they were younger and sharing secrets they were sure no one else knew. "If I were you, I'd get all the rest and sleep I could now, because there won't be any once MaryAnne is here—since you turned down your father's offer to hire a nurse to help you," she reminded her friend.

Wendy shook her head. "I want to be a hands-on mother," she said with determination, "not an occasional one."

"Still, it wouldn't be a bad idea to have someone here just part-time," Katie advised. "Just until you get the hang of the routine. No one would think any less of you," she promised, knowing how Wendy's mind worked. "This is your first time as the mother of a newborn and every little thing's going to seem like a crisis to you until you get used to the routine—and, more importantly, to the aberrations."

"How do you know so much?" Wendy asked with a mystified laugh.

Katie shrugged. She supposed that she did come off a little like a know-it-all. "I just read a lot, that's all."

Wendy inclined her head, leaning closer to Katie. "Okay, I'll keep my options open. To be honest, Marcos said something along the same lines," she admitted. "But I want to try to do this on my own first."

Katie gave her friend an alternate choice. "You know, I could hang around, pitch in for a while if you like. I don't have anything pressing to do anymore."

"What about Project Brittany?" Wendy asked. "Has Blake finally come to his senses and decided to scrap that?"

Katie did her best to look as if the thought of Blake cozying up to Brittany didn't tear her apart the way that it did.

"Well, the fundraiser that he wants to take Brittany to is this coming weekend and he feels that he's fairly well prepared to get his campaign underway." Each word she uttered felt like a sharp pin pricking her heart. "So there's no more plotting a course of action for him," she told Wendy. And then she sighed. "As a matter of fact, he wants to show me his gratitude by taking me out to dinner tomorrow night."

"Tomorrow night?" Wendy repeated, her eyes widening as she said the words slowly.

"Yes, tomorrow night." Katie stared at her friend's expression. "Why do you look like that?"

It was Wendy's turn to stare—in disbelief. "Katie, don't you know what tomorrow is?"

Since she had gotten here, it felt as if the days just fed into one another, especially after all the drama that had occurred with the way Wendy's baby had been born. She thought for a minute, then said hesitantly, "Thursday?"

"It's Valentine's Day. Blake wants to take you out on *Valentine's Day,*" Wendy emphasized.

Wendy was right, Katie realized. Tomorrow *was* Valentine's Day. But she had her doubts that Blake had been aware of that when he'd made the offer. "I'm sure that he doesn't realize that."

Wendy drew herself up as best she could, given that she was still in bed. "We'll *make* him realize it."

"We?" And just how was Wendy going to hope to accomplish that when Katie was the one who would be going out with Blake?

Wendy's smile was wide and dazzling in its confidence. "We," she affirmed. "Go to my closet," she instructed. It was impossible to miss her enthusiasm. "I have just the dress for you to wear."

Fifteen minutes later, Wendy was shifting impatiently in her bed. "Well, come out," she coaxed, raising her voice to carry through the bathroom door. "I want to see what it looks like on you."

In her opinion, Katie was taking an inordinate amount of time putting on the sexy black dress that she had selected for her.

Reluctantly, Katie finally opened the door and came out, moving very hesitantly.

"Where's the rest of it?" Katie wanted to know.

The slinky, black dress was clinging to her every curve. It only came down to her thighs and, although it had long, narrow sleeves that ended at her wrists and hinted at modesty, all hints vanished when she turned around. The dress was completely backless.

"There's just enough to make it interesting," Wendy told her. "Damn, but you look gorgeous!" she cried with no little pride. "And I've got just the shoes to go with that. A great pair of strappy high heels," she elaborated, then cocked her head as she studied Katie's reflection in the wardrobe mirror Katie was facing. "I'm going to have to fix your hair for you," Wendy said. It wasn't an offer, it was a given. One that made her grin in anticipation. "One look at you and that brother of mine is going to say, 'Brittany who?'"

Not from the way he talked about her, Katie thought. Although she hated raining on Wendy's parade, she didn't want to give her best friend false hope, either. "I really, really doubt that."

"I don't," Wendy countered cheerfully and with the confidence of a person who was seldom wrong. "Now, remember, when you enter the restaurant, walk as if every man in the room is looking at you."

"If I think that, I'm not going to be able to take a single step," she protested.

"Yes, you are," Wendy told her firmly, "because you know that every one of those men looking at you is living in the moment—and envying my big brother like hell." There was pure joy in Wendy's eyes. "This is going to be magnificent!" she prophesied gleefully, clasping her hands together in anticipation.

Katie tried her best to smile and ignore the full squadron of butterflies that had suddenly shown up as she began to earnestly think about tomorrow evening and all the different possible ways that she could embarrass herself.

Blake had chosen Red for his dinner with Katie, because he was familiar with it and because Marcos was the manager, so he knew the food was always excellent.

What he obviously *wasn't* familiar with, he thought ruefully, was the ordinary calendar. He'd been so busy with the campaign and with learning all the different things that Katie had come up with to help him win Brittany's heart, he'd somehow remained totally oblivious to the fact that today was Valentine's Day.

How could he have been this blind? He hadn't even sent Brittany a card. If his plan had only gone a little faster, he would have taken her out on the big day instead of having dinner with Katie. Well, there was nothing he could do about it now, he thought with resignation.

He was definitely going to have to pick up something to give to Brittany as a gift at the fundraiser. A belated Valentine's Day present, he thought wryly. He knew without being told that women didn't like being forgotten on this all-important day. But there was still Saturday. He managed to convince himself that it would be more surprising that way. Brittany definitely wouldn't be expecting a Valentine's Day gift three days after the actual day had gone by.

Maybe a pair of diamond earrings would do the trick.

No, diamond earrings would be too common a present for someone like Brittany. No doubt she probably owned at least half a dozen pairs.

He'd ask Katie, he decided.

Katie had had her fingers on the pulse of this thing right from the beginning—she'd know what kind of a gift to suggest to him. No point in his racking his brain about it now.

Katie, he couldn't help thinking with more than a trace of admiration, seemed to be up on just about everything. Lucky thing she had decided to come work for him when she graduated rather than pick some other, possibly more lucrative firm. Otherwise, who knew if he could even begin to pull this off? Her suggestions had been invaluable.

Because of her, he was more than confident that he was going to be successful. This time next week, Brittany and he would be back together and very possibly on their way to planning a wedding.

Blake glanced at his watch. Katie should have been here by now.

Where was she?

It wasn't like her to be late. She was usually early. He had offered to pick her up, as usual, but Wendy had insisted that he go on to the restaurant, pick out a table and wait for Katie there. She'd told him that Marcos would bring Katie with him when he returned from his break. Since she'd come home from the hospital, he looked at every break as an opportunity to drive home and look in on her.

Had to be nice, Blake mused, to be in love that way.

He wanted what Wendy and Marcos had. What Scott and Christina had.

He wanted a woman to love who loved him back.

He wanted Brittany.

Growing a tad impatient, Blake scanned the dining area, looking to see if Katie had arrived yet. But the only woman he saw walking in was a really hot-looking young woman who appeared, at least from where he was sitting, as if she was loaded for bear. She was certainly turning heads as she moved through the room.

Some guy was really going to have his socks knocked off tonight, Blake mused as he continued scanning the immediate area.

Okay, so *where* was Katie?

Most of the tables were full. The entire dining area was filled with couples.

And him, alone, he thought, darkly.

Maybe he should just postpone this, take Katie out to dinner some other time when there was more light available, he thought philosophically.

Tonight the tastefully decorated restaurant seemed fairly dim, due to the fact that a tall, white candle burned brightly in the center of each table. Including his.

Blake rose to his feet. He was going to go find Marcos and leave a message with him for Katie. Maybe Katie hadn't even come with Marcos, but if that was the case, wouldn't Marcos have come to tell him that? Of course, maybe they were stuck in traffic.

Preoccupied, Blake pushed in his chair.

Maybe—

"Hi, Blake, you're not leaving, are you? Am I that late?"

Recognizing her voice, Blake turned to answer Katie and the words dried up on his tongue, along with his ability to draw a sufficient breath. The sexy woman he'd noticed walking into the dining area just a couple of seconds ago had just walked up to his table—and him.

She was Katie.

Chapter Thirteen

"Katie?" Blake heard himself asking uncertainly. "Is that you?"

"Of course it's me," she said, sliding easily into the chair opposite his. "I am the only one you asked to meet you here tonight, right?" And then she looked up at him and saw the strange expression on his face. As if he was still trying to place her. "Why are you looking at me like that? Do I have a smudge on my face or a leaf in my hair?" she asked.

As she spoke, she shrugged off the shawl she had wrapped around her shoulders. The weather outside, blessedly, was unseasonably warm right now, but she was still a bit chilly in this dress that Wendy had insisted in no uncertain terms that she wear. Marcos had let her off right at the door, but that was still enough time for the evening breeze to find her and weave itself around her naked back.

She had to admit that the look in Blake's eyes did go a long way in heating her up again.

Katie leaned forward over the table. "Blake?" she prodded when he remained silent.

An uneasiness began to spread through her. Oh, who was she kidding? She was playing dress-up in fancy clothes that no more fit her personality than a leopard-skin bikini. He probably looked that way because he was trying not to laugh. She felt a blush creeping up her neck.

"*Say* something," she begged, unable to endure the silence much longer.

Blake leaned back in his chair as if he had been punched in the gut and was only now able to react. "Wow."

That wasn't the something she was expecting to hear. "Excuse me?"

"Wow," Blake repeated, unable to tear his eyes away from her. Half words were flashing in and out of his head like Fourth of July fireworks. "You look—wow," was all he could manage.

The silver tongue he had developed over the years was nothing more than a lead weight in his mouth right now as words continued to completely elude him. All he could think was that she was absolutely gorgeous.

How could he have missed that?

He'd seen her practically every day for the past two years, had known her since she was a gangly kid, playing dress-up with Wendy and staging sleepovers. When had all this happened?

He felt like Rip van Winkle, waking up to a whole brand-new world.

"Thank you," Katie murmured uncertainly. Still feeling self-conscious and not knowing what to do with her hands, when she saw a goblet of wine next to her plate, she gratefully reached for it.

Blake momentarily came to. "Oh, I told the waiter it was all right to pour the wine," he said, and then gave a small, self-deprecating laugh. "I don't even know if you drink wine," he admitted. By the time he finished his sentence, she had already raised the goblet to her lips and drank deeply, emptying half the contents. "I guess you do." He smiled to himself and then raised his goblet. "To surprises," he said just before he sampled his own wine.

Feeling oddly loose and at ease now, Katie asked, "Did you order dinner, too?"

"No," he answered quickly, then explained, "I didn't order anything else because I wasn't sure what you'd like to eat."

He usually had far less trouble talking, he upbraided himself. Even with strangers. Why was he tripping on his tongue now, with Katie of all people? She was just like another sister to him. He realized that he was watching the way her chest moved as she breathed—well, maybe not *quite* like a sister, he amended.

"Marcos tells me that everything on the menu is excellent," he added awkwardly.

"So I hear," she replied just before she took another long sip of wine from her glass.

She found, to her delight, that her nerves were no longer jumping around quite so much and that an easy, happy calm had begun to descend over her. This was much better, she thought.

Opening the menu, she scanned the two sides, then turned a page. While she was deciding, the waiter, on his way to another table with a full bottle of wine, paused over her goblet, a silent query in his manner.

Ordinarily, she didn't drink at all, but what the heck? she thought, stifling an unexpected giggle that rose to her lips. This was Valentine's Day, wasn't it? And most likely, her first and last dinner with Blake before he became part of the duo of Blake and Brittany, or, more likely, Brittany and Blake. Either way, he was going to be forbidden fruit to her.

"Yes, please," she said in response to the waiter's silent question, moving her goblet closer to him. The waiter filled her goblet, then automatically did the same with Blake's.

It was then that Blake realized he must have emptied his own goblet without even being aware of it. He was apparently *that* mesmerized by this new version of Katie—or had she just been downplaying what she looked like all these years?

He really didn't know.

He was staring and that was rude, he scolded himself.

Forcing himself to relax, he said, "You know, I really

want to thank you for putting up with all this." Katie raised her eyes to his, a surprised expression on her face. That made two of them, he thought. He hadn't realized he was going to phrase his thanks just that way until the words were out of his mouth. He needed to rephrase that.

"I mean..." His voice trailed off as he searched for the right words.

The search came up empty. His mind was just not functioning tonight, he realized in no small frustration. It wasn't functioning, he knew, because completely alien thoughts kept insisting on getting in the way. Alien thoughts such as wondering if that one time he'd kissed Katie and she had brought his world to its knees had been a fluke.

There was, of course, only one way to find out, but he wasn't all that sure she would welcome being kissed by him again. After all, she had just spent all this time helping him with his campaign to land the woman of his dreams. Having him kiss her might make her angry....

He blinked, looking hard at Katie. *Was* Brittany really the woman of his dreams, or was he just caught up in this whole thing because he felt she was an opportunity he'd lost? Was it the whole "you want what you can't have" syndrome, or—?

Or what? he demanded the next moment, his thoughts growing progressively fuzzier and utterly unfocused. What *was* focused was all centered around Katie.

Why hadn't he noticed that her eyes were like warm chocolate before? He had a weakness for warm chocolate. And cream. Her skin reminded him of cream.

Did it taste like cream?

What the hell was going on with him?

Why was he looking at her like that? Katie wondered. As though he wanted to be with her, when this dinner was supposedly to thank her for the big help she'd been to him these past few weeks? Right, she was helping the man she loved win the heart of another woman—a woman who was never going to care about Blake the way that she could. The way she *did.*

Katie opened her mouth to say just that, but then stopped.

What did it matter?

Blake loved Brittany. He *wanted* Brittany and he was going to go *after* Brittany no matter what she said or did. Hell, she could stand on top of this table and proclaim her feelings for Blake at the top of her lungs and it would make no difference—except maybe to get him to run out of the restaurant as fast as he could.

She might as well just enjoy this meal—when had she ordered it? she wondered, looking at her plate. And when had she almost finished it?

She couldn't remember.

Couldn't remember finishing her glass of wine, either, she realized. Was it just one, or had she had a second? She tried to think and remember—and then decided that it wasn't worth the effort. And it didn't matter, she told herself again. She wasn't driving.

Smiling to herself, content with the moment, Katie played with the stem of her goblet, moving it back and forth between her fingertips. She was simply enjoying the warm, rosy feeling that was spreading through her.

With effort, she tried to concentrate on what Blake was saying. It wouldn't do to have him think that she was ignoring him.

"Excuse me?" she said, hoping he'd repeat what he'd just said, because somehow his words had all vanished without registering.

How was that possible?

"I said I'm worried about Jordana," he repeated. He'd had occasion to talk to Jordana at the hospital when she came to see the baby and he came away with the feeling that something was definitely wrong with his older sister. "I tried talking to her at the hospital, but she seemed preoccupied—and a little off," he admitted. There didn't seem to be a better way to phrase that.

Katie nodded, then thought that maybe he wanted her to say something in response. She grasped at the first thing she could remember and hoped it made sense. Hoped that *she* made sense. Because right now, her brain felt like a bowl of cold spaghetti.

"Maybe it's because of the tornado." She paused, then thought that maybe that didn't make sense all by itself, so she continued. "Maybe coming so close to death made her take another look at her life."

There, that sounded better, Katie congratulated herself.

Blake rolled her words over in his head, then nodded. "Maybe."

Her mouth curved. Yea! She'd said the right thing. And then another thought danced through her head. Maybe if she said, "Kiss me," he would. The thought had just popped into her head out of nowhere, but when it did, she liked it. Liked it a lot.

She drew her shoulders back, about to make the suggestion when he cut her off.

"Well, I'd better take you home," he said out of the blue.

Surprised, she felt disoriented for a second. They had been eating just a minute ago. Why did he want to leave? Was it something she'd said? She tried to think—and couldn't.

"Oh. Okay," she murmured, trying to pull her shawl from the back of the chair. She was unsuccessful. It was stuck.

Rising to his feet, Blake moved behind her to help her with her shawl. It was then that he got a really good look at her back—as well as the lack of material at that portion of the dress. He felt his stomach do a few involuntary flips, then tighten really, really hard.

The effects of the wine he'd had at dinner had long since dissipated, but this made him think that perhaps they weren't completely gone after all. Either that or he was getting intoxicated in a whole new way that he never had before.

With the bill taken care of, despite his brother-in-law's protests—how could this be a "thank you for all you've done" dinner for Katie if Marcos was the one who paid for it?—Blake took her arm and gently guided Katie through the maze of tables and to the front door.

Pushing the heavy mahogany door open, they walked out and were immediately met by an evening breeze that was far chillier than it had been earlier.

As if instinctively, Katie huddled against him, which in turn caused all sorts of havoc in the pit of his stomach again—as well as parts beyond.

That was when he realized that the effects from the wine really had completely dissipated, but the effects from Katie were definitely intensifying. There was no getting away from it. She was a beautiful woman and he was attracted to her.

But he couldn't act on that attraction, or even explore it. It wouldn't be fair to her, or Brittany. Right?

It was an argument that had no winning side, he realized.

Instead, Blake focused on getting Katie back to Wendy's house and himself back to Scott's. The first part of that was easy enough.

But then, that was where things began to suddenly stall.

At the front door, Katie turned and looked up at him with wide, innocent eyes just before she turned the key in the lock.

"Why don't you come in for a little while?" she suggested.

He was debating the pros and cons of that when he suddenly found himself being playfully pulled across the threshold and into the semidark house.

Marcos, he knew, was still at the restaurant. That meant that his sister was home by herself.

"Maybe I can look in on Wendy," he agreed, even as he was doing his best not to think how damn sexy Katie looked in that black dress.

The winter-white shawl had managed to dip down, exposing her nude back. More than anything, he wanted to run his hand along her skin….

And that perfume she was wearing—had she worn it all along, or was this something new? Whatever it was, it was causing him to be exceedingly aware of every move she made.

It occurred to him that he had been relatively oblivious to the woman who, for the past two hours, had been occupying center stage in his thoughts. In his world.

He walked up the stairs like a man caught up in a dream.

He promised himself that once he started talking to Wendy, whatever it was that was wrong with him would pass. But when he came up to Wendy's door, he found that it was closed. That meant that his sister was either asleep, or almost asleep. Either way, he was not about to disturb her.

What he needed to do, he silently told himself, was to get a grip and to man up.

Turning away from his sister's door, he wound up brushing up against Katie, who was standing directly behind him—much too close for his comfort. It was time to take a stand.

What Blake fully intended to do when he took hold

of Katie's shoulders was to gently move her back and then aside so that he could go back downstairs and leave. He'd had absolutely no intention of drawing Katie to him so that she was even closer than before.

And he certainly hadn't thought he was going to lower his head so that his lips could touch hers.

And absolutely under *no* circumstances did he have any intention of kissing her.

But she was and they did and he was.

Moreover, he couldn't stop, even when deep down inside of him, he knew that stopping was the right thing to do.

Without knowing quite how, he swept Katie away from Wendy's bedroom door and somehow wound up moving down the hallway to the guest bedroom that she was currently occupying.

His lips never left hers during that whole time.

And all he was really aware of was that the more he kissed Katie, the more he not just *wanted* to kiss her but *needed* to kiss her. And the more he desperately desired her.

If this continued—

No, it *couldn't* continue.

With effort, Blake pulled his head back, breaking the connection between them. He saw the bewildered look in her eyes and felt that it clearly mirrored what he was feeling inside at the moment. Not that he could afford to share that with her.

"Katie," he whispered, "we have to stop—"

She wanted to shout: *No, we don't,* but she settled on a single word: "Why?"

The simple question completely threw him for a second.

Why?

Well, God knew *he* certainly didn't want to stop. It was for her sake, not his own, that he had pulled away. Couldn't she see that?

"Because if we don't," he told her truthfully, choosing his words slowly, "I'm going to wind up making love to you."

She searched his face, still unable to see why he would stop cold like that, just when her body temperature had reached the boiling point.

"And you don't want to?" she guessed, her eyes intently on his.

"Don't want to?" he echoed incredulously. How could she possibly think that? He was struggling to make the supreme sacrifice and she thought he was just passing the time of day here? Was she just pretending to return his kisses with fervor? Didn't she know what was going on inside of him? "It's the only thing I *do* want right now." he swore.

Katie smiled at that. Smiled in such a way that he could literally *feel* her smile right down to his very toes. Moreover, it jarred him as if he'd just stood in the path of a kicking mule.

The next moment, he heard her murmur, "Well, then?" just before she sealed her lips to his. Just before she sealed his fate.

The matter was no longer in his hands. He was on board a runaway train, clinging to the side of it for all he was worth, as heat, passion and desire roared through his veins, clamoring for tribute.

For fulfillment.

Even as every fiber of his being seemed to all but shout out for her.

The door to Katie's bedroom stood open, a silent invitation to them.

It didn't go unheeded.

They all but tumbled across the threshold and into her room. Blake was only vaguely aware of closing the door with his elbow. It was the only part of his body that wasn't consumed with showing Katie just how very much he desired her. Even as she filled every inch of his senses, of his soul, he craved even more.

The slinky, come-hither dress she had on fell to the floor after only a couple of tugs, leaving her clad in a black lacy thong and her strappy high heels, bathed in the heat of his desire.

One pull and the thong was no more. With her arms wrapped around his neck, Katie stepped out of the shoes. Only his desire remained steadfast, clinging to her skin like the hazy moisture from a sauna.

Yes, oh yes, her mind cried over and over again as she eagerly pulled at his clothing, tugging first his open jacket, then his shirt off his shoulders until they were both on the floor in a heap.

She fumbled with the belt at his trim, hard waist, then with surer fingers coaxed away the fabric from his thighs until those garments, too, joined the rest of his clothing on the floor.

His desire for her was clearly evident and every fiber in her being silently cheered as her anticipation mounted.

His lips were hot on her skin, kissing her everywhere, making the fog in her spinning brain widen until it completely swallowed her up as she felt the thrust of his tongue along the most sensitive part of her.

For her, there was nothing and no one, only Blake. Only this feeling that he had created within her, this feeling that was now exploding inside of her over and over again.

She frantically wanted to race to a climax, but at the same time, she wanted to hold it back, hold it back and savor this because even in her revelry, even with the wine coloring everything, there was a small part of her that thought, that *knew,* that something this wondrous might never happen again.

With all her heart, she wanted to freeze time, or, at the very least, make it progress in slow motion. So she reined herself in, lavishing kisses along his neck and chest the same way he had done to her. Reveling in the fact that his breathing had grown as labored as hers.

The sound filled her head even as demands and desires pounded all through her.

And then he was over her, pressing her into the bed, his weight hovering over her like the promise of rainbows in the rain. Her breath caught in her throat as he entered her, the movement as gentle as his first kiss had begun. And then, as with the kiss, the intensity grew, taking on width and breadth as the rhythm between them increased, growing in scope until that was all there was.

And then there was more.

Chapter Fourteen

Her body still throbbing, Katie seriously began to doubt that she would ever be able to breathe normally again. But eventually, she finally managed to drag just enough air into her lungs to dispel the need to gasp and pant. Her chest ceased heaving.

As did his.

Her head was resting against his chest now and she felt the beat of Blake's heart beneath her cheek. The steady rhythm was infinitely comforting and she felt that if she could remain like this forever, she'd never want for anything else.

She had discovered bliss and this was it.

But it was inevitable that this was finite. Blake shifted and she had to move, even if it was ever so slightly. The end of the interlude was drawing close.

But just as a sadness began to unfurl within her, Katie felt his arm close around her and, just as when they'd first walked out of the restaurant an eternity ago, she curled into his arm, huddling into his warmth. Drawing her contentment from that.

She felt Blake draw in a deep breath and then he said her name as if it was a precursor to something she wasn't going to like.

"Katie—"

Warranted or not, survival instincts immediately kicked in. A very real fear took hold that he was going to say something that would negate what had just happened, or, at the very least, leech some of the starlight away from it. She didn't want to risk losing that, not just yet.

So when he said her name, Katie raised her head and placed her fingertips against his lips, momentarily silencing him.

"Shh," she begged. "Don't say anything. Not a word," she instructed softly just before she laid her head back down on his chest.

Closing her eyes, Katie allowed her mind to peacefully drift off and soon, the rest of her did, too. Before she realized it, she was asleep.

She slept, while Blake, enveloped in the darkness—they had never turned on light in the bedroom—dwelled on what had just transpired.

Dwelled on what he had done.

What had possessed him? he silently demanded. Where was his control? His common sense? Why hadn't he just walked her to the door and left her there? Why had he felt so compelled to test the waters of this brand-new environment he'd suddenly found himself in?

He looked down at the sleeping woman curled up against him and felt—heaven help him—fresh stirrings.

For Katie.

Suddenly, the simple had become so very complicated. And it was all his own fault.

The darker it grew outside the bedroom window, the darker his thoughts became.

Moving her shoulders, Katie stretched her body like a contented feline waking from a long, decadent nap. She realized that there was a smile on her face, a wide, guileless, happy smile even before she opened her eyes. Her smile had nothing to do with any dream and everything to do with what had happened before she had surrendered to sleep.

She stretched again and this time realized that even though she was really extending her body to its limits, she wasn't coming in contact with anything other than sheets and part of a comforter.

She reached for Blake as she opened her eyes and discovered that she was reaching for someone who wasn't there.

"Blake?" she murmured.

When there was no reply, she said his name louder and turned her head in the direction of the bathroom. But there was no sound of running water, no sound of movement of any kind. The door to the bathroom stood wide open and she could see from where she was that there was no one inside the small room.

An uneasiness whispered along the perimeter of her throbbing head.

The wine, she remembered. She'd had too much wine.

Sitting up, Katie quickly scanned the bedroom. He wasn't there. And neither, she realized when she glanced down at the floor right before the bed, were Blake's clothes.

Had he quietly slipped out of bed, not wanting to wake her, gotten dressed and gone down for breakfast?

Katie realized that as she formed the question, it was accompanied by a prayer. Because if Blake hadn't gone down for breakfast, and he wasn't here, that meant that he'd left.

Left.

Left without even saying goodbye.

She didn't like the sound of that. A chill came over her heart as she suddenly remembered that he had a ticket for a flight out of San Antonio. A flight to Atlanta. She knew this because, as his assistant, she was the one who had made the reservation for him.

Katie moved as quickly as a woman whose head bordered on exploding could and threw on the first clothes she got her hands on. For the moment forgetting about such niceties as brushing her teeth or combing her hair, and ignoring the fact that she was barefoot, she ran out into the hall and all but crashed into the housekeeper.

Juanita Ruiz, a heavyset, motherly looking woman, was carrying a breakfast tray before her and stopped short just before Wendy's door. Quick thinking had her moving the tray out of range and saving her employer's breakfast.

"Are you all right, Katie?" the woman asked, concerned.

Katie didn't bother answering the question. She needed one of her own answered.

"Is Wendy's brother in the kitchen?" she asked the woman, wishing with all her heart she didn't sound so needy. But now wasn't the time to worry about appearances, there was something far more important on her mind than the way she came across to Wendy's housekeeper.

Since Wendy had several brothers, the housekeeper needed to know which one she was referring to. Given that it was the youngest Mr. Fortune who came to pick up Katie every day, she honed in on him.

"Are you asking about Blake?" Juanita asked. "No, he has not come yet this morning." The housekeeper was accustomed to admitting Wendy's brother around eight-thirty every morning, when he came to pick Katie up to take her to Scott's house. "Perhaps he is running just a little late," she suggested.

"Or maybe he's just running," Katie said under her breath.

"Katie? Is that you standing out there in the hall?" Wendy called out as the housekeeper came in with her tray. "Come talk to me," she coaxed, beckoning for

Katie to come into the room. She sounded even more restless than she had before she'd given birth. "The doctor said I needed to stay in bed for a few more days and if I go beyond the bathroom, Juanita tells on me," she said, nodding at the housekeeper.

Wendy was pretending to pout, but there was affection in her voice as she mentioned the older woman. About to say something else, Wendy's smile faded a little as she looked at Katie. Her friend appeared a bit disheveled as well as perturbed. Not to mentioned rather annoyed.

Wendy's antennae immediately went up. Something was definitely going on.

"My God, who died?" she asked, only half joking. When Katie didn't immediately answer, Wendy's eyes widened. "No one did, did they?" she asked nervously. She quickly reviewed a tally in her head. Her parents and family hadn't flown back yet, but as far as she knew, they were leaving this morning. Her husband was driving them all to San Antonio. "I just saw Marcos this morning before he left, but—"

"No *one* died," Katie assured her, putting emphasis on the second word.

"Okay," she replied cautiously. "But what did die?" Wendy wanted to know.

Katie stared off into space, waiting for the housekeeper to set down the tray and leave. When the woman finally did, closing the door behind her, Katie merely sighed. Silently, she called herself an idiot and seven kinds of a fool, but that didn't help anything or change anything, she thought darkly.

Blake was still racing into the arms of that woman. And she had helped to pave the way.

Oh, well, she tried to console herself, at least she'd had one good night out of it.

"Talk to me," Wendy urged and, from the sound of the exasperation in her voice, it wasn't the first time she'd said it. Katie hadn't even heard her say anything. "Didn't he take you out to dinner?" Wendy wanted to know.

"Yes, we had dinner," Katie replied. *And I volunteered to be dessert.*

"And?" Wendy pressed impatiently.

"He brought me home. Here," she clarified. in case Wendy thought she was referring to Scott's place, where Blake had been staying.

Nodding, she said again, "And?"

This time, the sigh was even deeper, coming from the very bottom of her soul. "And we made love."

Thrilled, Wendy clapped her hands together and all but cheered. "Wonderful!"

"Not so wonderful," Katie countered with a shake of her head.

Wendy's face fell as she obviously tried to fill in the blanks. "He's a bad lover?" There was an ocean of sympathy in her voice.

"Oh, no," Katie was quick to correct Wendy's wrong impression. "He's an utterly magnificent lover with incredible stamina. We made love twice and each time, he exceeded anything I could have ever imagined." *And it's going to be so wasted on Brittany,* she thought with a huge pang of regret.

Wendy didn't understand. "If he was so great, then why do you look like a kid who just found out that not only is there no Santa Claus, but she's going to be on the receiving end of coal for the rest of her life?"

"Because Santa Claus is on his way to Atlanta this morning for his 'big' date with Brittany at the fund-raiser tomorrow," Katie bit off. And that, he'd said more than once these past few weeks, was going to be the beginning of his life from here on in.

Wendy looked utterly horrified. "No, he's not," she cried.

"Yes," Katie answered wearily, "he is." And then, as much as it pained her, she gave Wendy the information to back up what she was saying. "I do all of Blake's bookings for his trips. I made this reservation for him and, since he's not here this morning, having ducked out sometime in the middle of the night," she couldn't help adding bitterly, "it's safe to assume that he is even now on his way to San Antonio so that he can catch his flight to Atlanta." Katie could feel angry tears forming in the corners of her eyes and she blinked hard to scatter them. "He's gone."

Wendy asked pointedly, "The real question here is, what are you going to do?"

Katie raised her eyes to Wendy's. "Do?" she echoed quizzically. *Do about what?*

"Yes. *Do,*" she emphasized. "According to you, the

two of you had a really great time last night. And then, apparently, my brother just took off early this morning without saying or writing a single word to you. That's just not like him," Wendy insisted, shaking her head. "God knows that man doesn't always connect the dots, but I've never known him to act like a Neanderthal jerk, either." Scooting to the edge of her bed, she gave Katie her theory. "My guess is that maybe being with you like that last night really shook him up. He saw you in a completely different light—"

"Yeah, he saw me naked," Katie said cynically.

"So, again," Wendy continued as if she hadn't been interrupted, "my question to you is, what are you going to do about it?"

Katie sank down on the bed, feeling frustrated, hurt and confused, not to mention angry. What made things particularly difficult was that she was feeling all these emotions at the same time.

Her shoulders rose and fell in an impotent shrug. "What can I do?"

"How about fighting for him?" Wendy challenged. The look in her eyes dared Katie to not just give up like this.

Having to "fight" for Blake was just another way of saying she was lowering herself, Katie thought. Lines had to be drawn somewhere.

"Look," she began patiently, "if Blake doesn't want me—"

Wendy cut her off. "I really doubt if that's the case."

She saw the disbelief in Katie's eyes and she persisted. "More than likely, my brother's really scared."

"Scared," Katie repeated sarcastically. Her tone of voice told Wendy that she thought that was just a big crock.

But Wendy wasn't about to let Katie just cast that—and her chances of real happiness—aside. From where Wendy sat, it sounded like a very plausible explanation. Sometimes the thought of finding real love—committing to that love—was a scary proposition. Besides, she knew a thing or two about how the male mind worked. Katie had been the girl next door, but she hadn't actually grown up with three brothers the way Wendy had. That kind of hands-on experience inevitably taught a person things.

"Yes, scared," Wendy insisted as she emphasized the word. "My brother's been telling himself all this time that he's in love with Brittany, and then the lid blew off his world when he saw you last night all decked out and sexy." Wendy warmed up to her subject. "And, just like that, the two of you wind up making love. A guy who's in love with one woman doesn't make love to another woman with wild abandonment," she concluded knowingly.

Rather than challenge Wendy's choice of words—the woman had seen *too* many romantic comedies, she merely stated, "It happens all the time."

Wendy remained firm. "Not to Blake. He's the faithful type. Go after your man, Katie," she urged her best friend. "Make him realize that he wants *you, belongs* with you. Face it, Katie, if you go after him, what have you got to lose?"

"My dignity comes to mind," Katie answered tersely.

Wendy shook her head, dismissing the excuse. "Seems to me that dignity would provide you with cold comfort if you're all by yourself, thinking about what might have been if you'd only had the courage to act. . . ." She let her voice trail off, watching to see Katie's reaction. She knew that Katie hated the thought of coming off like a coward.

And she was right.

"Okay," Katie finally cried, exasperated. "I'll go! But if this winds up blowing up in my face, I am going to come back and haunt you every day for the rest of my natural life—and then I'll come back as a ghost and continue to haunt you for all eternity."

Wendy smiled at her serenely. "I'm not worried. Now, go, get a flight out," she said, shooing her away with her hands as if Katie were a sparrow feeding on birdseed on the windowsill. "I'll have Juanita drive you to the airport when you're ready. Stop my brother from making a really stupid mistake." She leaned forward and took hold of Katie's hand. She squeezed it affectionately. "You're the best thing that ever happened to him and it's about time he admitted it and stopped running."

Katie *really* had her doubts about Wendy's take on the situation. But she knew that she really *wished* that her friend was right.

"Whatever you say," Katie answered as she extricated herself and then walked out of the room.

She was walking faster by the time she reached her own bedroom.

As it turned out, because of a severe storm and the threat of a possible tornado in the Atlanta area, Katie couldn't get a flight out until the middle of the next day. By then, after spending the night at the airport, she'd had enough time to work herself up to the point that she was very close to having steam coming out of her ears.

The upshot of it was that she was no longer hurt, she was just plain angry. Angry at Blake for leaving her the way he had, without a word, as if she was some woman he'd encountered at a party and gone on to have casual sex with. There was definitely *nothing* casual about the sex they'd had—because, from her perspective, it hadn't been sex, it had been lovemaking.

She wouldn't have felt what she had, the earth wouldn't have moved the way it had, if she hadn't invested her emotions in it. And, she was certain, though he hadn't said a word, that Blake had felt the same way. They had even made love one more time in the middle of the night. She woken up to his stroking her arm. When she'd turned her head and seen the look in his eyes—not a look a man had when he'd had just casual sex with a person he didn't intend to see again—she'd been so moved that, well, one thing had led to another and then another and they'd made love again.

If he loved Brittany the way he claimed, that wouldn't have happened, she silently insisted as she sat rigidly in her seat, waiting for the Atlanta-bound plane to land so that she could get this speech off her chest and onto her lips.

Then, after he heard her out, if he still wanted to remain with Brittany, well, there wasn't anything she could do about that. If he was that mentally impaired, then he and Brittany deserved each other and she didn't want him anyway.

But even if that *did* come to pass, at least she would have gotten a chance to tell him what she thought of him for being so thoughtlessly self-centered—and for throwing away something precious and real that they could have had between them.

Not that she would have allowed Blake to get away with that, Katie thought as she braced herself for a landing. She would have confronted him as he tried to make his exit. She would have put him on the spot, even though she really wouldn't have known what to say.

At least this way, she told herself, she'd had time to get her thoughts in order. She only hoped that once she saw him, she wouldn't become so angry all over again that she just wound up sputtering at him like some old engine that had run out of gas.

Oh, God, was she fooling herself about him? Or was Wendy right? Had Blake beaten a hasty retreat in the middle of the night because what had happened between them had scared him?

If that was true, God knew he wasn't the only one.

The intensity of what had gone on between them that night had scared her, too.

But what scared her even more was the thought of living the rest of her life *without* him.

With all her heart, she prayed that it was really the same way for him.

Chapter Fifteen

This was a mistake.

He'd made a huge mistake, Blake thought, not for the first time in the past two days.

The uneasy thought that he was running *from* something rather than *to* something had hit him a couple of minutes before he'd presented his boarding pass to the attendant at the airport. Because it was around that time that it had finally hit him that the scenarios he was replaying in his head were all about the night he'd spent with Katie, and *not* the possible future he was going toward by flying back to Atlanta.

By flying back to Brittany.

It was Katie's face he saw when he closed his eyes, Katie's skin he felt beneath his fingertips when he had allowed his mind to drift off for a moment as he'd stared out the window at the cloud formations on the horizon.

Yes, his pulse raced when he thought of Brittany, raced like the pulse of an adolescent involved with his first crush.

But the emotions that filled him when his thoughts turned to Katie belonged not to a boy, or to a hormonal teenager, but to a man, with a man's desires. And a man's needs.

Was it just a case of not knowing what he wanted? he'd challenged himself. Was he doomed just to want what he didn't have, or *couldn't* have at the moment?

Here he was, sitting at a table with Brittany at the fundraiser, just as he had been fantasizing about for the past three weeks, and the only thing he could think about was Katie.

Would he be sitting and pining after Brittany if he were sitting here with Katie?

No, he realized, he wouldn't.

Because he hadn't.

When he had been with Katie that night, made love with Katie that night, there wasn't so much as a single molecule in his body that longed for Brittany. He'd wanted to be just where he was—with Katie. Making love with Katie.

And he'd known it, he told himself. Known it because, even as he landed in Atlanta, he'd called his father to let him know that he'd decided not to attend the fundraiser.

His father had *not* been happy.

"You will attend." No request, just a command. The way it had always been. "You're representing the family at the fundraiser. If you don't attend with Brittany, there'll be all sorts of talk about it by morning. I won't have it."

He'd wanted to say he didn't care. That people would always gossip because they had no lives of their own to occupy themselves with, but Blake knew how much his father despised gossips and rumors, wanting to always be above both. The man worked hard and he was exceedingly image-conscious.

"It's not like I'm asking you to marry her," his father went on to say. "Although—" he paused to speculate "—a merger between the two families might not be such a bad idea."

This was where Blake had drawn a line. He'd had to. "My marriage isn't going to be a merger, Dad," he'd said in no uncertain terms.

"Suit yourself," his father had responded, controlling his annoyance. "But you *are* attending the fundraiser."

To refuse would have been to fuel a huge argument he'd wanted no part of, so Blake had agreed.

Which was how he came to be sitting here, at the fundraiser, with a woman who was garnering all sorts of appreciative looks from men who obviously envied him his close proximity to her. He knew that a good many of those men would have given their eyeteeth to be in his position. As ever, Brittany was enchantingly beautiful—and he had absolutely nothing to say to her. Not a single word.

He had outgrown the Brittany he remembered. And, quite honestly, she was coming up lacking in every way when he compared her to Katie. She didn't have the deep commitments that Katie had—to her this fund-raiser wasn't so much about collecting money for the proposed new pediatric wing that the hospital wanted to build as it was about being seen—and admired—by the right people. She certainly didn't have the broad spectrum of interests that Katie had. Her interests all seemed to center around fashions—specifically, which ones were the most becoming on her.

She'd been expounding on the subject for what felt like an eternity now.

What could he have been thinking, wanting to win this woman? he upbraided himself. It would be like winning a gag gift, he thought, shaking his head.

Feeling trapped and counting the minutes until he could leave, Blake nodded his head periodically as Brittany droned on. Absently, he looked around the ballroom, searching for a familiar face that could afford him at least a temporary excuse to leave the table for a few minutes of respite. He really needed to clear his head of Brittany's endless chatter.

As he scanned the area, his eyes washed over a sea of faces, some very vaguely familiar, but most not.

Blake froze as his eyes widened.

Oh, God, now his mind was playing tricks on him. He actually thought that he saw Katie in the room. But that was impossible. This was a black tie, invitation only affair. She wouldn't have been able to get in.

Damn it, that *was* Katie, he realized. He'd know that determined expression on her face anywhere. It was hers exclusively. He stopped wondering *how* she'd gotten in and began wondering *why* she'd gotten in.

Was something wrong?

He sat up at attention as he watched her cut across the floor. She was heading for his table like a bullet—and right behind her, huffing and puffing as he attempted to catch up, was the heavyset man who had been standing at the entrance to the reserved ballroom, checking everyone's invitation.

Darting around the corpulent man as he tried once again—unsuccessfully—to grab her, Katie arrived at his and Brittany's table.

"So you *are* here," she declared angrily. A part of her had prayed that she wouldn't find him here. That at the last moment, he had realized how vapid Brittany was and had bowed out of the fundraiser, sending in a silent pledge in his place.

So much for the power of prayer, Katie thought cynically.

Still huffing, the gatekeeper began apologizing. "I'm so sorry, Mr. Fortune—"

Blake waved away the man's words. "That's all right, she's my assistant."

The man slanted an annoyed look at Katie. "Well, as long as you know her..." the chagrinned gatekeeper murmured. Bowing, he was grateful to just disappear and put this behind him.

Blake's attention was already focused on Katie. "What are you do—?"

Blake got no further than that. Katie swung around and gave it to him with both barrels. She was going to say her piece if they were the last words she ever uttered.

"You have one hell of a nerve, you know that?" Out of the corner of her eye, she could see that people were looking their way. She didn't care. He had this coming to him. "Standing there and acting as if you're happy to see me when the dust is still settling from the way you rushed away from Wendy's house in the middle of the night. You didn't even have the decency to wait until I was up and look me in the eye!"

Everything she was saying was true. He knew that if he couldn't make her understand, he was going to lose her. "Katie, I—"

Brittany rose to her feet, all but knocking over her chair. "*This* is Katie?" Brittany cried in disbelief. Critical eyes looked Katie up and down as if she were nothing more than a mannequin in a boutique. "*This* is why you've been acting like a damn fool to me all evening?" she demanded incredulously.

"I thought you were ready to get serious, instead, you've been preoccupied all night. You haven't paid attention to a word I've said. My *brother* pays more attention to me than you did tonight. And now I understand why—well, I don't understand," Brittany corrected haughtily, a contemptuous look on her face as she regarded Katie, "but I see why." Tossing her hair over her shoulder, she planted impatient hands on her small hips. "Why didn't you just come out and *tell* me you were in love with someone else, instead of making me endure this evening?"

Katie's mouth dropped open and she stared at Blake as if she'd never seen him before.

Unbelievable!

"You're in love with someone else besides Brittany?" she cried. How could she have *ever* been in love with this man? "What are you trying to do, start a harem? You think just because your last name is Fortune you can just go around, collecting whatever woman catches your fancy? Who the *hell* do you think you are?"

Bombarded from all sides by her rhetoric, Blake didn't know where to begin, but he knew he had to start somewhere. "No, I—"

Again, she wouldn't allow him to get further. Jabbing her forefinger in his chest, Katie continued to blast him.

"You know what's wrong with you? You don't know what you want. Love isn't something you can form a stupid campaign around. You don't execute 'strategies' to win someone, you watch them, you find out what they like, what makes them smile, and then you try your damnedest to do the things that *make* them smile. You protect love, you nurture love, you don't run a *campaign* for it."

She closed her eyes, willing herself not to cry, even though she could feel the angry tears starting to form.

"You're obtuse and blind and it's my damn bad misfortune—pardon the pun—to be in love with you."

He focused in on the only thing that was important to him. "You're in—?"

"Yes!" she snapped. He might as well know. This way, maybe someday he'd realize just what it was that he had allowed to slip away. "Love. L-O-V-E. Love. I'm in love with you. Or was," she deliberately amended. What she felt for Blake wasn't in the past tense, but she was determined to get it to be. There was no point in loving a man who spread himself so thin and couldn't even recognize what had been right in front of him all along. "But I'm over you now. Oh, and by the way, I quit!" she shouted at Blake.

He stared at her, stunned, trying to pull everything together into a large, coherent whole. "But you can't quit now—"

Her eyes narrowed. "Oh, no? Just watch me!"

With that, Katie quickly spun on her heel and ran from the ballroom as fast as Cinderella had when she heard the clock in the tower chiming midnight.

It took him half a second to come to. When he did, Blake rounded the table and took off after her.

Behind him, he heard Brittany call his name, demanding that he come back. He didn't bother turning around. He had no doubts that Brittany would find someone else to squire her around before the hour was up.

As for him, he had to make Katie listen to reason.

For a woman in high heels, he thought, Katie could

really move. Determined to catch her before she got to the parking lot, he poured it on and finally managed to get within reaching distance of her, just outside the main ballroom.

Grabbing her arm, Blake spun her around to face him. Then, before she could begin to upbraid him all over again, he kissed her.

Long and hard.

Both breathless to begin with, they only became more so as the seconds ticked away and the kiss deepened in width and breadth.

When his lips finally left hers, Katie was dazed, lost in the heat and the passion of the moment. Wishing with all her heart that things could be just that simple. But then, as the last few minutes and what she'd heard from Brittany came flooding back to her, her indignation spiked. Her automatic reaction was to haul off and slap him across the face. Her fingers stung, but it was a small price to pay.

And then, in case he didn't already know why she'd hit him, Katie *told* him.

"That's for kissing me when you're in love with someone else," she shouted, struggling in vain to get out of his grasp.

Blake continued holding on to her, his grip tightening. He was determined to make her listen to him. She had to know the truth.

"The only person I'm in love with is you," he shouted back at her.

Because they were attracting attention again and

she didn't want to be the object of anyone's pity, Katie forced herself to lower her voice.

"What about the other woman you've been seeing?" she accused.

"There *is* no other woman," Blake insisted. "Think," he implored when her face remained impassive. "The only woman I've been seeing night and day for the past few weeks is you. And you're wrong about my not knowing what I want. I *do* know what I want," he told her, his eyes caressing the soft, inviting contours of her face. "And it's you," he concluded in a whisper.

Right, like she really believed that. Just how gullible did he think she was?

"You want me," she said sarcastically. "And that's why you ran off yesterday morning and that's why you're here now, worshipping at Brittany's feet."

Okay, there he had her, Blake thought, beginning his rebuttal here. "Did Brittany *sound* as if she thought I was worshipping her?" he wanted to know. They both knew that the woman looked as if she'd wanted his head—or perhaps some other viable part of his body—on the chopping block.

"Well, no," Katie was forced to admit.

He looked at her for a long moment, debating the next thing he had to say. But, if he was going to get her back, he knew there *was* no debate. He was going to have to sacrifice his pride. There was no other way.

"And as for your first point," he began after taking a long breath, "much as it pains me to say this, I left you before you woke up because I felt all turned around.

Everything I thought I wanted, I didn't anymore. And what I didn't think I wanted, I did."

He was trying to confuse her, she thought. "I don't understand."

Blake laughed shortly. That was exactly how he'd felt when he'd found himself unable to fight the strong attraction he'd felt for her the other evening. And even more so that night, after they'd made love and she lay sleeping in his arms.

"Welcome to the club. I needed to sort things out. To decide what I did want and what I didn't. By the time I got to Atlanta, I knew what I didn't want. I didn't want to reconnect with Brittany."

Oh, God, if she could only believe him. But the evidence all pointed otherwise. "And yet," she pointed out, "here you are."

"I'm here because you might have noticed that my father is very big on obligations and I'm the one who's supposed to be representing the family at this particular affair." Never mind that he'd initially lobbied for it. Once it was agreed upon, there was no getting out of it, short of a funeral. His.

"Since I was supposed to be Brittany's escort," he continued, "I went through with the charade, but that was all it was, a charade," Blake insisted. "I sat there, counting the minutes until I could leave. And then you came and sprang me," he concluded with a smile.

Her resistance was beginning to break down and she was starting to believe him. Maybe because she wanted to so badly.

"And caused a scene."

He shrugged indifferently. "It'll give them something to talk about," he said, referring to the people attending the fundraiser.

But these were people he knew, people he interacted with socially. Now that she was regaining her composure, she didn't want him feeling awkward around these people. "Do you care?" she wanted to know.

"The only thing I care about is hearing your answer when I show you this—" he took out a black velvet ring box from his pocket "—and ask you a question." He took a breath. *Here goes everything,* he thought. "Will you marry me?"

She couldn't help it, she'd been hurt so much, that naturally her suspicions were aroused again. "If you don't want to have anything to do with Brittany, what are you doing with an engagement ring in your pocket?" she asked.

"It *isn't* for her," he replied, his eyes on Katie's. "I was bringing the ring back to give to you." He held it out to her a second time. "It belonged to my great-great-grandmother. Family legend has it that she was a spitfire, too," he told her with a grin, then grew serious when she didn't immediately accept the ring. "We can reset it if you like."

"Don't you dare. It's beautiful just as it is." She looked at him for a long moment, as if trying to decide whether or not this was ultimately a joke. "You're serious?"

"Never more serious in my life," he swore. "I'm

sorry I was too thickheaded to see what was right in front of me. I know I didn't deserve to have you sticking by me the way you did, especially when I came up with that hare-brained scheme."

He couldn't even bring himself to say the name. What the hell had he been thinking, expecting her to help him win over Brittany? Another woman would have pushed him off a cliff—and he would have deserved it.

"You mean Project Brittany?" Katie asked innocently.

Blake winced. The mere sound of that was painful to him now. "The only project I want to undertake from here on in is to make you happy for the rest of your life."

Katie struck a poker face. "I haven't said yes yet," she pointed out.

He was all too aware of that. "I know and I don't blame you if you don't, but—"

With a sigh, she rolled her eyes and then placed her fingertips to his lips to still them. "Will you *please* stop talking? That's what's wrong with you marketing geniuses, you never stop talking," she marveled. Removing her fingertips, she immediately replaced them with her lips and kissed him—even longer and harder than he had kissed her.

"Does that mean yes?" he whispered against her lips, wanting to hear her say the single, magical word.

Her eyes danced as she asked, "What do you think?"

Katie could have sworn that she tasted his smile as he lowered his mouth back to hers.

* * * * *

Special Offers

Every month we put together collections and longer reads written by your favourite authors.

Here are some of next month's highlights—and don't miss our fabulous discount online!

On sale 18th January

On sale 1st February

On sale 1st February

Find out more at
www.millsandboon.co.uk/specialreleases

Visit us Online

0213/ST/MB399